Sappers and Miners
The Flood beneath the Sea

by

George Manville Fenn

Sappers and Miners
The Flood beneath the Sea
by George Manville Fenn

ISBN: 978-93-67148-32-7

Published by

DOUBLE 9 BOOKS
2/13-B, Ansari Road
Daryaganj, New Delhi – 110002
info@double9books.com
www.double9books.com
Tel. 011-40042856

ABOUT THE AUTHOR

George Manville Fenn was a very productive author of novels, a writer, an editor, and an educator from England. He was born on January 3, 1831, in Pimlico, London. He mostly learned on his own; he taught himself Italian, French, and German. During the years 1851-1854, he went to Battersea Training College for Teachers and then became the head of a state school in Alford, Lincolnshire. In the early 1850s, Fenn started to write short stories and pieces for newspapers and magazines. The Old Forest Ranger, his first book, came out in 1856. Afterward, he wrote more than 100 books, many of them for teenagers and young adults. He was one of the most famous writers of his time, and his books were well-liked and read by many people. I also worked as a reporter and writer for Fenn. Among the newspapers and magazines, he worked for was The Boy's Own Paper, which he ran from 1866 to 1874. He worked hard to make children's books better and was a strong supporter of education and reading. The Englishman Fenn passed away on August 26, 1909, in Isleworth.

CONTENTS

Chapter One
Bass for Breakfast

"Have some more bass, Gwyn?"

"Please, father."

"You should not speak with your mouth full, my dear," said Mrs Pendarve, quietly.

"No, mother; but I didn't like to keep father waiting."

"And between the two stools you came to the ground, eh?" said Colonel Pendarve, smiling. "Never mind; hold your plate. Lucky for us, my dear, that we have only one boy. This fellow eats enough for three."

"Well, but, father, we were down by the boat at daybreak, and the sea air makes one so hungry."

"Say ravenous or wolfish, my boy. But go on. It certainly is a delicious fish, and Dolly has cooked it to a turn. They were rising fairly, then?"

"Yes, father; we rowed right out to the race, off the point, and for ever so long we didn't see a fish and sat there with our rods ready."

Gwyn talked away, but with his mouth rather full of fried bass and freshly-baked bread all the same.

"And of course it was of no use to try till a shoal began to feed."

"Not a bit, father,—and Joe said we might as well come back; but when the sun rose they were breaking all round us, and for half-an-hour we kept hooking them at nearly every throw. Come and see the rest of my catch; they're such beauties, as bright as salmon."

"That's right, but don't let any of them be wasted. Keep what you want, mamma, dear, and give the others away. What did you use—a big fly?"

"No, father, those tiny spoon-baits. They come at them with a rush. Then they left off biting all at once, and—some more coffee, please, mother—and we rowed back home, and met Captain Hardock on the pier."

"Ah, did you?"

"Yes, father; and we gave him two pairs of fine ones, and he said they looked as bright as newly-run tin."

"Humph! Yes, that man thinks of nothing else but tin."

"And he began about it again this morning, father," said Gwyn, eagerly.

"Indeed!" said Colonel Pendarve; and Gwyn's mother looked up inquiringly from behind the silver coffee-urn.

"Yes, father," said Gwyn, helping himself to more fresh, yellow Cornish butter and honey. "He said what a pity it was that you did not adventure over the old Ydoll mine and make yourself a rich man, instead of letting it lie wasting on your estate."

"My estate!" said the Colonel, smiling at his wife—"a few score acres of moorland and rock on the Cornish coast!"

"But he says, father, he is sure that the old mine is very rich."

"And that I am very poor, Gwyn, and that it would be nice for me to make a place for a mining captain out of work."

"But you will not attempt anything of the kind, my dear," said Mrs Pendarve, anxiously.

"I don't think, so, my dear. We have no money to spare for speculating, and I don't think an old Indian cavalry officer on half-pay is quite the man to attempt such a thing."

"But old Hardock said you were, father, and that you and Major Jollivet ought to form a little company of your own, and that he knows he could make the mine pay wonderfully."

"Yes," said the Colonel, drily, "that's exactly what he would say, but I don't think much of his judgment. I should be bad enough, but Jollivet, with his wound breaking out when he is not down with touches of his old jungle fever, would be ten times worse. All the same, though, I have no doubt that the old mine is rich."

"But Arthur, my dear," protested Mrs Pendarve, "think of how much money has been—"

"Thrown down mines, my dear?" said the Colonel, smiling. "Yes I do, and I don't think our peaceful retired life is going to be disturbed by anything a mining adventurer may say."

"But it would be interesting, father," said Gwyn.

"Very, my boy," said his father, smiling. "It would give you and Joe Jollivet—"

"Old Joe Jolly-wet," said Gwyn to himself.

"A fine opportunity for trying to break your necks—"

"Oh, my dear!" cried Mrs Pendarve.

"Getting drowned in some unfathomable hole full of water."

"Arthur!" protested Mrs Pendarve.

"Losing yourself in some of the mazy recesses of the ancient workings."

"Really, my dear!" began Mrs Pendarve; but the Colonel went on—

"Or getting crushed to death by some fall of the mine roofing that has been tottering ready to fall perhaps for hundreds of years."

"Pray don't talk like that, my dear," said Mrs Pendarve, piteously.

"He doesn't mean it, mother," said Gwyn, laughing. "Father's only saying it to frighten me. But really, father, do you think the mine is so very old?"

"I have no doubt of it, my boy. It is certainly as old as the Roman occupation, and I should not be surprised if it proved to be as early as the time when the Phoenicians traded here for tin."

"But I thought it was only stream tin that they got. I read it somewhere."

"No doubt, my boy, they searched the surface for tin; but suppose you had been a sturdy fellow from Tyre or Sidon, instead of a tiresome, idle, mischievous young nuisance of an English boy—"

"Not quite so bad as that, am I, mother?" said Gwyn, laughing.

"That you are not, my dear," said Mrs Pendarve, "though I must own that you do worry me a great deal sometimes by being so daring with your boating, climbing and swimming."

"Oh, but I do take care—I do, really," said Gwyn, reaching out to lay his hand upon his mother's arm.

"Yes, just as much as any other thoughtless, reckless young dog would," grumbled the Colonel. "I'm always expecting to have one of the fishermen or miners come here with a head or an arm or a leg, and say he picked it up somewhere, and does it belong to my son?"

"Really, Arthur, you are too bad," began Mrs Pendarve.

"He's only teasing you, ma, dear," cried Gwyn, laughing. "But I say, father, what were you going to say about my being a Tyre and Sidonian?"

"Eh? Oh! That if you found tin in some gully on the surface, wouldn't you dig down to find it where it was richer?"

"Can't dig through granite," said Gwyn.

"Well, chip out the stone, and by degrees form a deep mine."

"Yes, I suppose I should, father."

"Of course it's impossible to prove how old the mine is, but it is in all probability very ancient."

"But it's only a deep hole, is it, father?"

"I cannot say. I never heard of its being explored; but there it is."

"I've explored it sometimes by sending a big stone down, so as to hear it rumble and echo."

"Yes, and I daresay hundreds of mischievous boys before you have done the same."

"Why was it called the Ydoll mine, father?"

"I cannot say, Gwyn. Some old Celtic name, or a corruption. It has always been called so, as far as I could trace when I bought the land; and there it is, and there let it remain in peace."

"If you please, my dear," said Mrs Pendarve. "Will you have some more coffee and bread and butter, Gwyn?"

The boy shook his head, for there are limits even to a seaside appetite.

"Wonderful!" said the Colonel.

"What is, my dear?" said Mrs Pendarve.

"Gwyn has had enough for once. Oh, and, by the way, I have had quite enough of that dog. If ever I find him scratching and tearing my garden about again, I'll pepper him with shot."

The boy smiled and looked at his mother.

"Oh, you may laugh, sir, at your foolish, indulgent father. I don't know what I could have been about to let you keep him. What do you want with a great collie?"

"He's such a companion, father; and see how clever he is after rabbits!"

"Matter of opinion," said the Colonel. "I don't suppose the rabbits think so. Well, mind this: I will not have him tearing about among my young fruit trees."

Chapter Two
A Deep Investigation

Breakfast ended, Gwyn went straight off to the yard with half a fish and some bread; but before he came in sight, there was the rattle of a chain, a burst of barking, and a handsome collie dog, with long silky ears and a magnificent frill of thick hair about his neck, stood upon hind-legs at the full extent of the chain, and tried hard to strangle himself with his collar.

Then there was a burst of frantic yelps and whines, a kind of dance was performed as the boy approached with the dog's breakfast, and then there was peace over the devouring of the bread, which was eaten in bits thrown at him from a couple of yards away, and caught without fail.

After this performance the fish was placed in a pan; and as the dog bent down to eat, Gwyn pulled his ears, thumped his back, sat astride it and talked to the animal.

"You're going to be shot at if you go into the garden again, Grip; so look out, old chap. Do you hear?"

The dog was too busy over the fish, but wagged his tail.

"I'm to keep you chained up more, but we'll have some games over the moor yet—rabbits!"

The fish was forgotten, and the dog threw up his head and barked.

"There, go on with your breakfast, stupid! I'm off."

"How-ow!" whined the dog, dismally, and he kept it up, straining at his chain till the boy was out of sight, when the animal stood with an ear cocked up and his head on one side, listening intently till the steps died out, before resuming his breakfast of fish.

Gwyn was off back to the house, where he fetched his basket from the larder and carried it into the hall.

"Here, father—mother—come and have a look!" he cried; and upon their joining him, he began to spread out his catch, so as to have an exhibition of the silvery bass—the brilliant, salmon-shaped fish whose sharp back fins proved to a certainty that they were a kind of sea perch.

They were duly examined and praised: and when they had been divided into presents for their neighbours in the little Cornish fishing port, the Colonel, who had, after long and arduous service in the East, hung up his sword to take to spade and trowel, went off to see to his nectarines, peaches, pears, grapes and figs in his well-walled garden facing the south, and running down to the rocky shores of the safe inlet of Ydoll Brea, his son Gwyn following to help—so it was called.

The boy, a sturdy, frank-looking lad, helped his father a great deal in the garden, but not after the ordinary working fashion. That fell to the lot of Ebenezer Gelch, a one-eyed Cornishman, who was strangely imbued with the belief that he was the finest gardener in the West of England, and held up his head very high in consequence. Gwyn helped his father, as he did that morning, by following him out into the sunny slope, and keeping close behind.

The Colonel stopped before a carefully-trained tree, where the great pears hung down from a trellis erected against the hot granite rock, and stood admiring them.

"Nearly ripe, father?" asked Gwyn.

"No, my boy, not nearly," said the Colonel, softly raising one in his hand. "They may hang more than a month yet. We shall beat the Jersey folk this year."

"Yes, father," said Gwyn, and he followed to where the Colonel stopped before a peach tree, and stooped to pick up a downy red-cheeked fellow which had fallen during the night.

"Not fully grown, Gwyn, but it's a very fine one," said the Colonel.

"Yes father—a beauty. Shall I take it in?"

"No, not good enough. Eat it, my boy."

Gwyn did not need any further telling, and the peach disappeared, the stone being sent flying into the sea.

A little farther on, a golden tawny Jefferson plum was taken from a tree, for the wasps had carved a little hole in the side, and this was handed to the boy and eaten. A nectarine which had begun to shrink came next; and from the hottest corner of the garden a good-tempered looking fig, which seemed to have opened a laughing mouth as if full, and rejoicing in its ripeness. After this a rosy apple or two and several Bon Chrétien pears, richly yellow, were picked up and transferred to the boy's pocket, and the garden was made tidy once more, evidently to the owner's satisfaction. Certainly to that of his son, who was most diligent in disposing of the fruit in this way.

Then the Colonel sauntered into the little sloping vinery where the purple and amber grapes were hanging, and Gwyn thrust in his head; but as there were no berries to be eaten, and it was very hot, he drew back and went up the slope toward the wall at the top, carefully peeling one of the pears with a fishy pocket-knife.

He was in the act of throwing a long curl of peel over the wall when a sun-browned face appeared as if on purpose to receive it, and started back. Then there was a scrambling noise from the other side, as the face disappeared very suddenly, and Gwyn burst out laughing.

"Hurt yourself?" he cried.

There was the sound of scrambling, and the face re-appeared.

"What did you do that for?" cried the owner.

"To get rid of the peel, stupid."

"Well, you might have chucked a pear instead."

"All right—catch."

A pear was thrown, dexterously caught, and the newcomer immediately took a magnificent bite out of it.

"Oh! beauty!" he cried; and then, as he began to munch, he glanced down at the pit he had excavated with his keen teeth right to the core. "Er! Yah!" he cried, spitting out the piece. "Why, it's all maggoty!" and he threw the pear back with excellent aim; but it was deftly caught, and returned in a way that would have won praise at cricket. Joe's aim was excellent, too; but when a boy is supporting himself by resting his elbows on the coping of a high stone-wall, he is in no position for fielding either a pear or a ball. So the pear struck him full on the front of the straw hat he wore, and down he went with a rush, while Gwyn ran to the front of the wall, climbed up quickly, and looked over into the lane, laughing boisterously.

"Got it that time, Joey," he cried.

"All right, I'll serve you out for it. Give us another pear."

The request was attended to, the fruit being hurled down, but it was cleverly caught.

"Why this is maggoty, too."

"Well, I didn't put the maggots there; cut the bad out. The dropped ones are all like that."

"Go and pick me a fresh one, then."

"Not ripe, and father does not like me to pick them. That's a beauty."

"Humph—'tain't bad. But I say, come on."

"What are you going to do?"

"Do?—why, didn't you say we'd go and have a good look at the old mine?"

"Oh, ah; so I did. I forgot."

"Come on, then. Old Hardock made my mouth water talking about it as he did this morning."

"But we should want a rope, shouldn't we?"

"Yes. Let's get Jem Trevor to lend us one out of his boat."

"All right. I'll come round."

"Why not jump down?"

Gwyn gave a sharp look up and down the lane, but no one was in sight, and he lightly threw his legs over, and dropped down beside his companion.

"Don't want any of the boys to see that there's a way over here," he said, "or we shall be having thieves. I say, Joe, father's been talking about the old mine at breakfast."

"Then you told him what Captain Hardock said. I told my father, too."

"What did he say?"

Joe Jollivet laughed.

"Well, what are you grinning at? Why don't you speak?"

"Because you're such a peppery chap, and I don't want a row."

"Who's going to make a row? What did the Major say?"

"Sha'n't tell you."

"Who wants you to? It was something disrespectful of my father, and he has no business to. My father's his superior officer."

"That he isn't. Your father was cavalry, and my father foot."

"And that makes it worse," said Gwyn, hotly. "Cavalry's higher than infantry, and a major isn't so high as a colonel.—What did he say?"

"Oh, never mind. Come on."

"I know what he said; and it's just like the Major. Just because his wounds come out bad sometimes, he thinks he has a right to say what he likes. I believe he said my father was a fool."

"That he didn't," cried Joe, sharply; "he said he'd be a fool, if he put any money in a mine."

"There, I knew it, and it's regularly insulting," cried Gwyn, with his face flushing and eyes sparkling. "I shall just go and tell Major Jollivet that my father—"

"Oh, I say, what a chap you are!" cried Joe, wrinkling up his rather plump face. "You're never happy without you're making a row about something. Why don't you punch my head?"

"I would for two pins."

"There, that's more like you. What have I done? I didn't say it."

"No, but your father did, and it's all the same."

"Oh! is it? I don't see that. I couldn't help it."

"Yes, you could. It all came of your chattering. See if I go fishing with you again!"

"Go it!"

"I mean to; and I shall walk straight up to Cam Maen, and tell the Major what I think of him. I won't have my father called a fool by a jolly old foot-soldier, and so I'll tell him."

"Yes, do," said Joe. "He's got a touch of fever this morning, and can't help himself; so now's your chance. But if you do go and worry him, you've got to have it out with me afterwards, and so I tell you."

"Oh, have I? You want me to give you another good licking?"

"I don't care if you do. I won't stand still and have my father bullied by old Ydoll, Gwyn."

Gwyn turned upon him fiercely, but the sight of his companion's face calmed his anger on the instant.

"It's all right, Joe," he said; "I like to hear anyone sticking up for his father or his mother."

"I haven't got a mother to stick up for; but my father's ill and weak, and if you—"

"Don't I keep on telling you I'm not going, you stupid old Jolly-wet-'un. Come on. Didn't we two say, after the last fight, when we shook hands, that we would never fight again?"

"Yes; then why do you begin it?"

"Who's beginning it? Get out, and let's go and have a look at the mine. Let's stick to what we said: fight any of the fisher-lads, and help one another. Now, then, let's go on to the old mine, and see if we can get down. Pst! here's Hardock."

For at the corner of the stone-walled lane, whose left side skirted the Colonel's property, which extended for half-a-mile along by the sea, the estate having been bought a bargain for the simple reason that its many acres grew scarcely anything but furze, heather and rag-wort, the rest being bare, storm-weathered granite, they came suddenly upon a dry-looking brown-faced man with a coil of rope worn across his chest like an Alpine guide.

He was seated on the low wall dotted with pink stone-crop and golden and grey lichens, chewing something, the brown stain at the corner of his lips suggesting that the something was tobacco; and he turned his head slowly toward them, and spoke in a harsh grating voice, as they came up.

"Going to the old mine?" he said. "I thought you would, after what I told you this morning. I'll go with you."

"Did you bring that rope on purpose?" said Gwyn, quickly.

"O' course, my son. You couldn't look at the gashly place without."

Gwyn glanced at Joe, and the latter laughed, while the mining captain displayed his brown teeth.

"Right, aren't it?" he said. "Didn't tell the Colonel what I said, I s'pose?"

"Yes, I did," cried Gwyn; "and he as good as said it was all nonsense."

"Maybe it be, and maybe it ban't," said the man, quietly. "You two come along with me and have a look. I've brought a hammer with me, too; and I say, let's chip off a bit or two of the stuff, and see what it's like. If it's good, your father may like to work it. If it's poor, we sha'n't be no worse off than we was before, shall we?"

"No, of course not," said Gwyn, "what do you say, Joe—shall we go?"

"Of course," was the reply; and they trudged on together for about a hundred yards, and then climbed over the loose stone-wall, and then up a rugged slope dotted with gigantic fragments of granite. A stone's throw or so on their left was the edge of the uneven cliff, which went down sheer to the sea; and all about them the great masses towered up, and their path lay anywhere in and out among tall rocks wreathed with bramble and made difficult with gorse.

But they were used to such scrambles, and, the mining captain leading, they struggled on with the gulls floating overhead, starting a cormorant from his perch, and sending a couple of red-legged choughs dashing over the rough edge to seek refuge among the rocks on the face of the cliff.

It was a glorious morning, the sea of a rich bright blue, and here and there silvery patches told where some shoal of fish was playing at the surface or demolishing fry.

There was not a house to be seen, and the place was wild and chaotic in the extreme, but no one alluded to its ruggedness, all being intent upon the object of their quest, which they soon after came upon in the upper part of a deep gully, on one side of which there was a rough quadrangular wall of piled-up stones, looking like the foundations of a hut which had fallen to ruin; and here they paused.

"Now, look here," said the man; "that place don't look anything; but your father, young Pendarve, has got a fortune in it, and I want to see what it's like. So what do you say to going down with my hammer and bringing up a few chips?"

"Why don't you go?" said Gwyn.

"'Cause you two couldn't pull me up again. It's a job for a boy."

"Then let's send down Joe Jollivet. He isn't worth much if we lose him."

"Oh, I say," began the boy in dismay; but he read the twinkle in his companion's eye, and laughed.

"I wouldn't mind going down. Is the rope strong?"

"Strong?" said the mining captain. "Think I should have brought it if it warn't? Hold a schooner."

"Shall I go down, Gwyn?"

The lad addressed did not answer for a few moments, but stood leaning over the rocky wall, gazing down into a square pit cut through the stone, the wall having been placed there for protection in case four or two-legged creatures passed that way.

"But look here," said Joe; "would it be safe?"

"Safe, lad? Do you think I'd let you go if it warn't? How could I face all your fathers and mothers after?"

"But are you sure you could hold me if I went," said Joe, who began to look anxious.

"Feel here," said the man, rolling up his sleeves. "There's muscle! There's bone! That's something like a man's arm, aren't it? Hold you? Half-a-dozen on you. Man either."

Joe drew a deep sigh.

"I'll go," he said.

"No, you won't," cried Gwyn, fiercely. "It's my father's place, and I ought to go."

"But I wouldn't mind, Ydoll," said Joe, excitedly.

"I know that, but I'll go first, and you help Sam Hardock."

"Ay, you help me, my lad. I know'd he'd have the pluck to go down."

"You're sure of the rope, Sam?"

"Sure? There, don't you go down if you're afraid."

"Who feels afraid?" cried Gwyn, hotly. "There, how's it to be? Throw the rope down and slide?"

"No, no," growled the man.

"Loop and sit in it?"

"Nay; I'm too fearful over you, my lad. But do you mean it?"

"Mean it? Yes, of course," said the boy, flushing.

"Then, here you have it. I just make a knot like this about your chesty, so as it don't grow tight and can't slip. That's your sort. How's that?"

'The next moment he was being lowered.'

As he spoke, he quickly fastened the end of the rope about the boy's breast, tested the knot and then lifted Gwyn by it.

"Now, if you stick the hammer in your waistband, and have hold of the rope above your head with one hand to ease the strain, you'll go down like a cork, only keep yourself clear of the side."

"Mind and don't turn and roast, Ydoll," cried Joe; "but you'd better let me go."

"Next time. Ready?" said Gwyn.

"Ay."

"Then over I go."

As if fearing to hesitate, the boy got over the low wall and stood on the narrow edge of the old, crumbling, fern-hung shaft, and the next moment he was being lowered down, Joe turning a little faint from excitement as the upturned face disappeared, and he watched the rope glide through the man's bony hands.

"How far are you going to let him down?" he said, anxiously.

"Far as he likes, my lad. Till he comes to paying ore. You see that the rings o' rope run clear, and keep it right for me to run out. He's tidy heavy for such a little 'un, though."

Joe seized the coil, and made the rope run free, keeping spasmodically a tight hold of it the while, in case the man should let it slip.

And so some sixty feet were allowed to run out, with Gwyn keeping on cheerily shouting, "All right!" from time to time.

It was instantaneous.

Suddenly the mining captain started back and blundered against Joe, completely knocking him over. A wild shriek arose from the old shaft, sounding hollow, awful and strange, and the rope, which had either parted or come undone from the boy's chest, was swinging slackly to and fro in the great black pit.

Chapter Three
At Agony Point

Plosh!

There is no combination of letters that will more clearly express the horrible, echoing, hollow sound which, after what seemed to be a long interval, but which was almost momentary, rose out of the ancient shaft, followed by strange and sickening splashings and a faint, panting noise.

Then all was still; and Joe and the mining captain, who had been absolutely paralysed for the time being, stood gazing wildly in each other's face.

That, too, was almost momentary, and, with a despairing cry, Joe Jollivet dashed at the low wall and began to climb over it, dislodging one of the stones, which fell inward, and then plunged down into the pit just as Hardock seized the boy by the waist to drag him back.

"What are you going to do?" roared the man, and the splash and roar of the fallen stone also came rushing out of the mouth.

"Do?" cried Joe, hysterically; "try and save him."

"But you can't do it that way, boy," panted the man, whose voice sounded as if he had been running till he was breathless.

"I must—I must!" cried Joe, struggling to get free. "Oh, Gwyn, Gwyn, Gwyn!"

"Hold still, will you?" bawled Hardock. "Chucking yourself down won't save him."

"Then let me down by the rope."

"Nay; it's parted once, and you'd be drowned too."

"I don't care! I don't care!" cried Joe, wildly. "I must go down to him. Let go, will you?" and he struggled fiercely to get free.

But the man's strength was double his, and he tore the boy from the wall, threw him down on his back, and placed a foot on his breast to hold him as he rapidly ran out the rest of the rope, till only about a yard remained, and then he released him.

"Now, you keep quiet," he growled. "You're mad—that's what you are!"

Joe rose to his feet, awed by the man's manner, and grasping now the fact that he was about to take the only steps that seemed available to save his companion.

For Hardock hurried to the other side of the opening, where the wall had been built close to the edge, and there was no space between, so that he could, in leaning over the wall, gaze straight down the shaft.

And then he began jerking the rope; and as he did so they could faintly hear indications of its touching the water far below.

"D'yer hear, there?" he shouted. "Lay holt o' the rope. Can't you see it?"

As he spoke, he jerked the stout line and sent a wave along it, making it splash in the water far below; but the faint, whispering and smacking sounds were all the answer, and Joe burst out with a piteous cry,—

"He's drowned! he's drowned! Or he's holding on somewhere waiting for me to go down and save him. Pull up the rope, quick! No; fasten it, and I'll slide down."

"Nay, nay; you keep quiet," growled the man, whose face was now of a sickly pallor. "How'm I to hear what he says, if you keep on making that row?"

"What—he says?" faltered Joe. "Then you can hear him shout?"

"You be quiet. Ahoy! Below there! Ketch holt o' the rope. None o' your games to frighten us. I know. Now, then, ketch holt and make it fast round yer."

Joe stood there with his face ghastly, and his eyes starting, as, with his hands behind his ears, he strained to catch the faintest sound which came up as through a great whispering tube; but all he could hear was the splashing of the rope, and a deep low musical dripping sound of falling water.

"D'yer hear there!" roared Hardock, now savagely. "It arn't right of yer, youngster. Shout something to let's know where yer are."

"He's dead—he's dead!" wailed Joe. "Let me go down and try and get him out."

"Will you be quiet!" roared the man, fiercely. "D'yer want to stop me when I'm trying to save him?"

"No, no, I want to help."

"Then be quiet. You only muddles me, and stops me from thinking what's best to do. Below there! Pendarve, ahoy! Ketch holt o' the rope, I tell yer!"

But he called in vain—there was no reply; and though he agitated the rope again and again, there was no other sound.

"There, now, let me go down. I must—I will go down, Sam."

"There's a good two hundred feet on it, and it's gone right down into the water," growled the man thoughtfully. "It's him playing tricks with us, arn't it?"

"Playing tricks! Who's mad now?" cried Joe. "Will you pull up that rope?"

For answer the man jerked it again and again, then pulled up a few fathoms, and let them drop again with a splash.

"Now, then, do you hear that?" he cried. "If yer don't ketch holt we'll haul it all up, and leave yer."

"Oh, Sam, Sam, Sam," cried Joe, "let me go down. Do you hear me? If you don't, I'll jump."

"Will you be quiet?" roared the man, fiercely. "You just stay where you are, or I'll tie yer neck and heels with the rope. Think I want to go back and say there's two on yer drownded. Stop where yer are."

"But we can't stand without doing something. Oh, Gwyn, Gwyn! How can I go and tell Mrs Pendarve what's happened?"

"And how can I?" cried the man, angrily. "What d'yer both mean, coming tempting on me to let yer down. What's the Colonel going to say to me?"

"Then you do think he's drowned?" cried Joe, piteously.

"Who's to help thinking he is?" said the man, gruffly, and he wiped the thick perspiration from his brow. "They all did say it was a onlucky mine, but I wouldn't believe 'em."

"Gwyn! Gwyn! Gwyn!" shouted Joe, as he leaned over the wall and gazed down, but there were only hollow reverberations in reply.

"It's no good, my lad," said Hardock, bitterly. "Who'd ha' thought of that rope failing as it did? Good sound rope as it be."

"But you are not going to give up, and do nothing?" cried Joe, frantically.

"What is us to do then?" said the man, with a groan. "Let me down, I tell you."

"Nay; it would be too bad, I won't do that."

"Then go down yourself."

"How? Can you hold me, and haul me up? That's madder still. He's gone, my lad, he's gone; and we can't do nothing to help him."

"Run, run for help. I'll stay here and hold the rope. He may be insensible and catch hold of it yet."

"Ay, he may," said the man, meaningly; "but folk don't do that sort o' thing, my lad. Nay; it's o' no use to struggle over it. He's a dead and goner, and you and me's got to face it."

"Face it!" groaned Joe, letting his head go down on the top of the wall. "Face it! How can I ever face Mrs Pendarve again?"

"Ah! and how can I face the Colonel, his father. I can't do it, my lad, Ydoll Churchtown's been a happy enough home for me, and I've allus made a living in it, but it's all over now. I must be off at once."

"To get help?" cried Joe, raising his ghastly face from where it rested upon the weathered stone, and looking more ghastly now from the blood which had started from a slight cut on his brow.

"Nay; I've done all I could do here for young Gwyn—all as a man can do. I've got to take care o' myself now, and be off somewheres, for the Colonel'll put it all on to me."

"Go! Run away!" cried Joe. "Oh, you wouldn't be such a coward! Here, quick! try again.—Gwyn, old chap! The rope—the rope. Oh, do try and catch hold," he shouted down the pit.

But there was no reply; and wild now with frantic horror, the boy seized the rope and began to climb over the wall. "Ah! none o' that!" roared Hardock, grasping his arms; and now there was a desperate struggle which could only have the one result—the mastery of the boy. For at last Hardock lifted him from the ground and threw him on his back amongst the heath, and held him down.

"It's no good to fight, young 'un," he said breathlessly. "You're strong, but my muscles is hardest. I don't say nought again' you, though yer did hit me right in the mouth with your fist. I like it, for it shows your pluck, and that you'd do anything to try and save your mate. Lie still. It's of no use, yer know. I could hold down a couple of yer. There, steady. Can't yer see I should be letting yer go to your death, too, my lad, and have to hear what the Major said as well as the Colonel. Not as I should, for I should be off; and then it would mean prison, and they'd say I murdered you both, for there wouldn't be no witness on my trial, but the rope, and mebbe they'd give me that for my share, and hang me. There, will yer be quiet if I let yer sit up?"

"Yes, yes," said the boy, with a groan of despair.

"And yer see as I can't do nothing more, and you can't neither."

"I—I don't know, Sam," groaned the boy, as he lay weak and panting on his back in the purple-blossomed heath. "No, no, I can't see it. I must do something to try and save him."

"But yer can't, lad," said the man, bitterly. "There arn't nothing to be done. It's a gashly business; but it wouldn't make no better of it if I let you chuck yourself away, too. There, now you're getting sensible."

Joe lay with his eyes closed in the hot sunshine, glad of the darkness to shut out the horror of the scene around him; for the bright blue sky, with the soft-winged grey gulls floating round and round above their heads, and the far-spreading silver and sapphire sea, were dominated by the mouth of the horrible pit, from which with strained senses he kept on expecting to hear the faint cries of his companion for help.

But all was very still, save the soft, low hum of the bees busily probing the heath bells for honey in the beautiful, wild stretch of granite moorland, and the black darkness was for the unhappy boy alone.

For the knowledge was forced upon him that he could do no more. He felt that after the first minute Gwyn's position must have been hopeless, and he lay there perfectly still now in his despair, when Hardock rose slowly, and began to haul in the line, hand over hand, coiling it in rings the while, which rings lay there in the hot sunshine, dry enough till quite a hundred-and-fifty feet had been drawn on, and then it came up dripping wet fully fifty feet more, the mining captain drawing it tightly through his hands to get rid of the moisture.

"Bad job—bad job!" he groaned, "parted close to the end—close to the end—close to the end—well, I'll be hanged!"

He began in a low, muttering way, quite to himself, and ended with a loud ejaculation which made Joe sit up suddenly and stare.

"What is it?" he cried wildly. "Hear him?"

"Hear him? No, my lad, nor we aren't likely to. But look at that."

He held out the wet end of the rope, showing how it was neatly bound with copper-wire to keep it from fraying out and unlaying.

"Well," said Joe, "what is it?"

"Can't yer see, boy?"

"The rope's end? Yes."

"Can't yer see it aren't broke?"

"Yes, of course. Why, it did not part, Sam!" cried Joe, excitedly.

"Nay; it did not part."

"Then it came untied," cried Joe, frantically. "Oh, Sam!"

Chapter Four
Joe hears a Cry

"Here, what's the good o' your shouting at me like that, my lad? Think things aren't bad enough for me without that?" cried the man, in an ill-used tone.

"You did not tie it properly."

"Yes, I did, lad, so don't go saying such a word as that. I made that rope fast round him quite proper."

"No, or it wouldn't have come untied. And you boasted as you did! Why, you've murdered him. Oh, Sam, Sam, Sam!"

"Will you be quiet?" cried the man, who was trembling visibly. "Don't you turn again' me. You were in the business, too. You helped, my lad; and if I murdered him, you were as bad as me."

"It's too cruel—too cruel!" groaned Joe.

"And you turning again' me like that!" cried Hardock. "You shouldn't run back from your mate in a job, my lad," said the man, excitedly. "I tied him up in the reg'lar, proper knot, and you calls me a murderer. Just what his father would say to me if I give him a chance. It's a shame!"

"We trusted you, both of us, because you were a man, and we thought you knew what was right!"

"And so I did know what was right, and did what was right; that there rope wouldn't have never come undone if he hadn't touched it. He must have got fiddling it about and undone it hissen. It warn't no doing o' mine!"

"Shame! Oh, you miserable coward!" cried Joe, starting to his feet now in his indignant anger.

"Mizzable coward! Oh, come, I like that!" cried Hardock. "Who's a coward?"

"Why, you are; and you feel your guilt. Look at you shivering, and white as you are."

"Well, aren't it enough to make any man shiver and look white, knowing as that poor lad's lying dead at the bottom of that big hole?"

Joe groaned, and took hold of the rope's end.

"How could he have undone the knot, swinging as he was in the air? You know well enough it was not properly tied."

"But it was!" cried Hardock, indignantly. "I tied it carefully mysen, just as I should have done if I'd been going down."

"Don't use that knot again, then," said Joe, bitterly. "I wish—oh! how I wish you had let me go down instead."

"What?" cried the man. "Why, you'd ha' been drowned i'stead o' he."

"I wish I had been. It would have been better than having to go to the Colonel to tell him—I can't do it!" cried the boy, passionately. "I can't do it!"

"Then come along o' me, my lad."

"Where?"

"I d'know. Somewheres where they don't know about it. We can't stay here and face it. It's too horrid. You can't face the Colonel and his lady. Ah! they're quite right; the mine is an unlucky one, and I wish I'd never spoke about it; but it seemed a pity for such a good working to go to waste. But they all say it's unlucky, and full o' all kinds o' wicked, strange critters, ghosts and goblins, and gashly things that live underground to keep people from getting the treasure. I used to laugh to myself and say it was all tomfoolery, and old women's tales; but it's true enough, as I know now, to my sorrow."

"How do you know?" cried Joe, angrily.

"By him going. It warn't he as undid the rope—it was one o' they critters, as a lesson to us not to 'tempt to go down. I see it all clear enough now."

"Bah!" cried Joe, fiercely, "such idiotic nonsense! Let me tie the rope round myself, and I'll go down and try and find him. I don't believe in all that talk about the mine being haunted. I've heard it before."

"Course you have, my lad. But let you go down? Nay, that I won't. Poor young Gwyn Pendarve's drownded, same as lots of poor fellows as went out healthy and strong in their fishing-boats have been drownded, and never come back no more. It's very horrid, but it's very true. He aren't the first by a long chalk, and he won't be the last by a many. It's done, and it can't be undone. But it's a sad job."

"Let me go down, Sam," pleaded Joe, humbly now.

"Nay, I'm too much of a mizzable coward, my lad. I don't want to leave you and lose you."

"But you wouldn't," cried the boy. "I should tie the knot too tight."

"I don't know as yer could tie a better knot than I could, Master Joe Jollivet. And even if yer could, yer wouldn't be able to make my hands feel strong enough to hold yer."

"I'm not afraid of that; and he must be brought out."

"I don't know, my lad, I don't know. If he is to be, it'll want a lot o' men with long ropes, and lanterns to courage 'em up; but it strikes me that when they know what's happened, yer won't find a man in Ydoll Cove as will risk going down. They all know about the horrors in the mine, and they won't venter. I didn't believe it, but I do now. There, the rope's coiled up, and I may as well go."

"To get help? Yes, go at once," cried Joe, excitedly; "I'll stay."

"Nay, yer won't, my lad. I'm not going to leave yer. I don't want to know afterward as yer chucked yerself down that hole, despairing like. You're going away with me."

"I'm going to stay till help comes to get poor Gwyn out."

Hardock shook his head.

"Go and tell them what's happened."

"I dursent," said the man, with a shiver.

"You go at once."

"What! and tell the Colonel his boy's dead? That I won't, my lad. He'd be ready to kill me."

"Go to my father, and tell him. He'll break the news to Colonel Pendarve; and you go on then to the village, to collect men and ropes."

"They wouldn't come."

"Oh, have you no feeling in you, at such a time?" cried Joe. "You are only thinking about yourself. You must—you shall go on. What's that?"

The boy started and stood staring wildly at his companion, for a faintly-heard cry reached their ears, and Hardock's face grew mottled, sallow, white, red and brown.

"Sea-bird," he said at last hoarsely, after they had waited for a few moments, listening for a repetition of the cry.

"I never heard a sea-bird call like that," said Joe, in a husky whisper. "It wasn't a gull, nor a shag, nor a curlew."

"Nay, it warn't none o' they," said Hardock, in a whisper. "I know all the sea-fowl cries. I thought it was one o' they big black-backed gulls, but it warn't that."

"Can you make out what it was, then?"

"Yes; it was something we don't understand, making joy because some one as it don't like has been drownded."

The boy felt too much startled and excited to pause and ridicule his companion's superstitious notions, and he took a few steps quickly to the rough, square wall, from a faint hope that the sound might have come from there; but as he touched the wall, a strong grip was on his shoulder.

"No, yer don't," growled Hardock. "You keep back."

"But that cry!" panted Joe.

"It didn't come from there. It was sea way."

"Yes; there it is again!"

Sounding more faint and distant, the strange cry floated from away to their left, and a strange thrill ran through Joe Jollivet, as he yielded to the man's hand, and suffered himself to be drawn right away from the mouth of the hole.

"Yes, I heard it," said Hardock, in a low tremulous voice, and with a look of awe, which accorded ill with the man's muscular figure. "Don't you know what it was?"

"No; do you? Could it be Gwyn calling for help?" The man nodded his head and spoke in a low mysterious whisper, as if afraid of being overheard.

"I dunno about calling for help, my lad; but it was him."

"But where—where?" cried Joe, wildly.

"Out yonder. We couldn't see 'em, but they must ha' come sweeping out of the pit there, and gone right off with him, like a flock of birds, right away out to sea."

"Oh, you fool!" cried Joe. "It's horrible to listen to you great big fishermen and miners with your old women's tales. If it's Gwyn calling, he must be somewhere near, I know. There's another shaft somewhere, and he's calling up that. Come and see."

"There aren't no other shaft, my lad," said the man, mysteriously. "It's what I say. You'll know better some day, and begin to believe when you've seen and heard as much as me. There's things and critters about these cliffs sometimes of a night, and in a storm, as makes your hair stand on end to hear 'em calling to one another. Why, I've knowed the times when—"

"There it is again," cried Joe, excitedly. "Ahoy!" he yelled. "Where are you?"

There was no answer, and the boy stood staring about him with every sense strained, listening intently; but no further sound was heard, and the man laid his hand upon the boy's arm.

"Come away, lad," he whispered, "afore ill comes to us. Didn't you hear?"

"I heard the cry."

"Nay, I meant that there whispering noise as seemed to come up out o' the pit. Let's go while we're safe."

"Nonsense! What is there to be afraid of?" cried Joe, impatiently. "Listen!"

"I don't know what there is to be afraid of, my lad; but there's something unked about, and the gashly thing's given me the creeps. Come away."

"Ah, there! Why, it's towards the cliffs. A cry!" Joe shouted, for, very softly, but perfectly distinct, there was a peculiar distant wailing cry. "It's all right, Sam. He's alive somewhere, and he's calling to us for help."

Chapter Five
Fishing for a Boy

Sam Hardock looked at the boy with a mingling of horror and pity on his countenance.

"What yer talking about?" he cried. "Can't yer understand as it means trouble? Someone's deloodering of yer away so as you may be drownded, too."

But Joe Jollivet hardly heard him in his excitement. He was convinced that he had heard Gwyn calling for aid, and he dashed off in search of his comrade.

He felt that it was useless, but he stepped back to the mouth of the ancient mine, and shouted down it once, but without response, and then started to climb out of the gully in which he stood, mounting laboriously over the rugged granite masses which lay about, tangling and scratching himself among the brambles, and at last standing high up on the slope to gaze round and shout.

"What's the good o' that?" cried Hardock, who was following him. "Come back."

For answer Joe gazed round about him, wondering whether by any possibility there was another opening into the mine hidden by bramble and heath. He had been all over the place with Gwyn scores of times, and the walled-in mouth was familiar enough; and from the cliff edge to the mighty blocks piled up here and there he and Gwyn had climbed and crawled, hunting adders and lizards among the heath, chased rabbits to their holes in the few sandy patches, and foraged for sea-birds' eggs on the granite ledges and, by the help of a rope, over on the face of the cliffs. But never once had they come upon any opening save the one down into the old mine.

"But there must be—there must be," muttered Joe, with a feeling of relief, "and I've got to find it. It's blocked up with stones, and the blackberries have grown all over it. There!—All right. Ahoy! Coming."

For the faint halloa came now very distinctly.

"Are you comin' back?" shouted Hardock. "Don't stand hollering there in that mad way."

"He's here—he's here—somewhere," shouted back Joe, excitedly, and he waved to his companion to come on.

"Yah! stuff!" growled Hardock; but he followed up the side of the gully, while Joe went on away from the sea to where a wall of rock rose up some twenty feet and ran onward for seventy or eighty.

Joe came back hurriedly after a few moments and met Hardock.

"Well, where is he?" said the latter.

"I don't know," panted the boy; "somewhere underneath. I keep hearing him."

"You keep hearing o' them," said the man, with a look full of the superstition to which he was a victim.

"Ahoy!" came faintly from behind them.

"Now, then," cried Joe, excitedly; "he's up there."

He turned and ran up toward the wall of rock once more, followed more deliberately by Hardock, who hung the coil of rope on his shoulder.

"Well, where is he?" said the man, as he reached the spot where Joe was hunting about among the great pieces of stone.

"I don't know, but there must be another opening here." Hardock shook his head mysteriously.

"But you heard him shout."

"I heerd a voice," said the man; and as he spoke there came a querulous chorus from the gulls that were floating in the air close to the edge of the cliff.

"No, no, it was not a gull," cried Joe.

"I did not say it weer," replied Hardock. "You can think what you like, but I only says, 'Wheer is he?'"

"He must be somewhere here," cried Joe; and he climbed about in all directions for some time, and only gave up when he felt how impossible it was that his comrade could be anywhere near.

"Theer, come on down, my lad," said Hardock at last.

"It's impossible for anyone to be here. There aren't a hole big enough to hide a rabbit, let alone a boy."

They descended slowly toward the lower part of the slope, near the cliff edge. Here Joe stopped short, for faintly, but perfectly distinct, came the words, "Joe, ahoy!" and certainly from behind him.

"There, I knew he was up there!" cried the lad, excitedly; "come back. I was sure of it."

He scrambled back as fast as he could, and Hardock followed him, frowning, and stood looking on, while his companion searched once more in every possible direction without avail.

"Ahoy, Gwyn. Y-doll!" he shouted through his hands. "Where are you?"

There was no reply, and after more searching and shouting, and with the man's superstitious notions beginning to affect him, Joe stopped and gazed blankly in his face.

"Well, d'yer begin to believe me now, my lad?" whispered Hardock.

"I can't help—" began the lad; and then he burst out with an emphatic. "No, it's all nonsense! Gwyn must be here. Ahoy, Ydoll! Where are you?"

His voice died away, and in obedience to an order from the man, Joe began to descend the rugged slope again towards the green strip, which ran along near the cliff edge.

"It's of no use fighting again' it, my lad," said Hardock, solemnly; "they're a-mocking of you, and you might go on hunting all day long and couldn't find nought. Let's go; we aren't safe here."

"I won't go," cried the boy, "and I won't believe what you think is possible. Gwyn's somewhere about here. Now, think. Where is there that we haven't searched?"

"Nowheres," whispered Hardock, and in spite of the bright sunshine around them he kept on nervously glancing here and there.

"Why, if you go on like that in the middle of the day, Sam," cried the boy, angrily, "what would you do if it was dark?"

"Dark! You don't know a man in Ydoll Cove as would come up here after dark, my lad. It would be more than his life was worth, he'd tell you. Why, there's not only them in the old mine, but the cliffs swarm with them things as goes raging about whenever there's a storm. I never used to believe in them, but I do now."

"And I don't," said Joe, "and you won't frighten me. It's poor old Gwyn we heard shouting, and there must be an opening somewhere down into the mine."

"Wheer is it, then?" whispered the man. "You've been all over here times enough, and so have I, but I never found no hole 'cept the one big one down."

"No, I never saw one, but there must be. There!" For a faint hail came again from the wall of rock behind them.

"Gwyn, ahoy!" cried Joe as loudly as he could.

"Ahoy!" came back steadily.

"Why, it's an echo," cried Joe, excitedly. "Ahoy! Ahoy!"

"Oy—oy!" came back from the wall, and directly after, much more faintly—"Oy—help!"

"Oh, what fools—what idiots!" cried Joe, excitedly; and certain now of where his comrade was, he went quickly down the slope to the cliff edge and looked over down towards where the sea eddied among the fallen rocks three hundred feet below, and shouted,—"Gwyn!—Gwyn!"

His voice seemed lost there; but as he listened there came faintly a reply in the one appealing cry—"help!"

But it was away to his right, where the rocks rose up rugged and broken. Where he stood the grass ran right to the edge, but there the granite looked as if it had been built up with large blocks into a mighty overhanging bastion, which rose up fully fifty feet higher; and it was evident that Gwyn had worked his way somewhere out to the cliff face far below this mass.

"Why there must be an adit," cried Hardock, in a tone full of wonder. "I never knowed of that."

(Note; an adit is a horizontal shaft driven in from the cliff.)

"Yes, and he's safe—he's safe?" cried Joe; and his manliness all departed in his wild excitement, for he burst into a fit of hysterical sobbing. He mastered his emotion though, directly, and shouted,—

"Hold on! Coming," in the hope of being heard.

He was heard, for, faintly heard from below to their right, came the former appealing word—

"Help!"

"All right," he yelled. "Now, Sam, can I get down there?"

"You'll get to the bottom afore you know it," replied the man. "No."

"Then you must lower me with the rope."

"What, and one o' my knots!" said the man, maliciously.

"Oh, don't talk," cried Joe, "but come on. We must get along to where it's right over him, and then I'll go down. But did you ever see a hole along here?"

"Nay—never!"

"Come on."

Joe led the way inland, and then had to clamber over block after block of tumbled together granite for some fifty yards, when he turned to begin mounting to the hog-back-like ridge which ran out to the great bastion which overhung the sea.

It was an awkward climb—not dangerous, but difficult. Joe's heart was in his work though; and, free now from superstitious dread, Hardock toiled after him, keeping up so that he was at his shoulder when the boy lay down on his chest and looked over the edge.

For a few moments he could see nothing but ledge and jutting block, whitened by the sea-birds which here brought up their young in peace, for even the reckless boys had looked upon it as too hazardous to descend. The sea far below was just creaming among the rocks which peered above the water, and ran out in a reef causing a dangerous race; but though Joe searched the whole cliff face below him for nearly a minute he could see nothing, and at last he shouted with all his might and had a lesson in the feebleness of the human voice in that vast expanse.

"Ahoy!"

"Ahoy!" came up from below as faintly as the cry which evoked it.

"I can't see him," said Hardock, shading his eyes as he peered down.

"No; he must be under one of the blocks that jut out."

"Ay and all hings over, or he'd ha' climbed up. Now, my lad, what's to be done? Will you go down?"

"Yes, of course; but knot me fast this time, Sam."

"Ay, my lad, I will. You trust me."

"I will, Sam," said the boy, calmly. Then he strained outwards, put both hands, trumpet fashion, to his lips, and shouted,—

"Ahoy! Coming down.—Hardock, look! I can see him."

"Eh? Where? I can't see nought."

"There, nearly straight under us, about half-way down—look!"

"No; I can't see him. Can you?"

"Yes; only his hand. It's like a speck. He's waving it to us. There, I can just see a bit of his arm, too."

"I got it now. Yes, I can see it. He must be at the mouth of an adit where they threw out their waste stuff to be washed away by the sea."

"Ahoy! Rope!"

Those two words came up plainly now, and Joe answered through his closed hands.

"All—right—coming down!—Now, Sam, quick. Make me fast, and lower away."

"No! Rope!" came up from below.

"Says you aren't to go down," cried Hardock, excitedly. "And why should yer? I'll drop the rope, and you can help me haul him up. He'll make it fast enough, I know."

As he spoke the man rose up, threw the ring of rope on the rock by his side, set the end free, made a knot in it, and gave it to Joe to hold while, after a little examination to make sure that it would uncoil easily, he raised the ring, stood back a couple of yards, swung the coil to and fro horizontally on a level with his left shoulder and then launched it seaward with a vigorous throw, making a snatch directly after at the end close to where Joe held on with both hands.

Away went the rope with the rings gracefully uncoiling and straightening out as the stout hemp writhed like some long thin serpent, opening out more and more, till, far away below them, they saw it hang down, swaying to and fro like a pendulum.

"Not long enough," cried Joe, sadly.

"Good two hundred foot, my lad; nigh upon five-and-thirty fathom; p'raps he'll climb to it. Can you see the end?"

"No—no," said Joe; "it hangs over beyond that block that sticks out?"

"And it's below that he's a-lying, aren't it?"

"I don't know—I think so. It's of no use. I must slide down to him. Ah, stop a minute, let's give it a swing to and fro. Perhaps he can't see it. Hurrah! I've got a bite."

"Nay!" cried Hardock, excitedly.

"Yes, it's all right. Feel."

But there was no need, for at that moment there was a most unmistakable tug.

Chapter Six
At an Awkward Corner

"Hurrah!" yelled Joe, half mad with excitement. "It is long enough, and he has got it. He was trying if it was safe."

"Hooroar!" shouted Hardock, hoarsely, for he was as excited as the boy. "Hold tight, my lad; don't let him pull it out of your hands. But he won't, for I've got it, too. Why, it's all right, young Jollivet, and the old mine goblins had nothing to do with it, after all. We'll soon have him up."

"Yes, we'll soon have him up," cried Joe, hysterically, and he burst into a strange laugh. "I say, how he frightened us, though!"

And in those moments of relief from the tension they had felt, it seemed like nothing that the lad was two hundred feet down the terrible precipice, about to swing at the end of the rope which had played him so false but a short time before.

"He's making the line fast round him, Sam. I can feel it quiver and jerk. Shout down to him to be sure and tie the knots tight."

"Nay, nay, you let him be. He don't want no flurrying. Trust him for that. He knows how to make himself fast."

"Think so?" said Joe, hoarsely; and he felt the hands which held the rope grow wet.

"Nay, don't want no thinking, my lad. He'll manage all right."

"He has," cried Joe, excitedly. "Do you feel? He's signalling for us to haul him up."

For three sharp tugs were given at the rope.

"Ay, that means all right," said Hardock. "Now you hold on tight."

"I can't haul him all alone."

"Nay, not you. Nobody wants you to try; I only want you to hold while I get ready. It wouldn't do to let one end go loose, would it?"

As he spoke Hardock relinquished his hold of the rope, and began to strip off his jacket.

"What are you going to do? You're not going down, Sam?"

"You wait a bit: you'll see," said the man; and he folded his coat into a large pad, which he laid over the edge of the rock. "Now you lay the rope on that, my lad, and give me the end. That's the way; now it won't be cut."

"When we haul it over the rock? No; I see."

"But we aren't going to haul it over the rock," said Hardock, nodding his head. "I'll show you a way worth two of that."

He took the end and pulled it over, and made a loop, leaving just enough free line for the purpose; and slipping it over one shoulder and across his breast diagonally, he stood ready.

Meanwhile jerk after jerk was given to the rope, each signal which reached Joe's hands making him thrill with eagerness.

"There, he must be ready now," growled Hardock.

"Ready? Yes," cried the boy, impatiently. "Then you are going to walk away with the rope?"

"Ay, that's it; draw steadily as I go right along the Hog's Back. All right. Look out," he shouted as the word "Haul!" reached their ears. "There, you stand fast, my lad, ready to help him when he comes up to the edge. Now then—off!"

Hardock, who stood with his back now to the cliff edge, started off at a slow steady walk inland, and Joe dropped upon his breast and craned his neck over the edge of the precipice to watch the block below which hid his comrade from his sight.

But not for many moments now. All at once Gwyn's head appeared, then his chest, and his arms were busy as he seemed to be helping himself over the rock; and the next minute, as Hardock steadily walked away, the boy was hanging clear of the rock face, swinging to and fro and slowly turning round, suggesting that the layers of the rope were beginning to untwist.

To use a familiar expression, Joe's heart felt as if it were in his mouth, and he trembled with apprehension, dreading lest the rope should come untwisted or the hemp give way, the result of either of these accidents being that Gwyn must fall headlong on to the sea-washed rocks below. Consequently, Joe's eyes were constantly turning from the ascending figure to the rough pad over which the rope glided, and back again, while his heart kept on beating with a slow, heavy throb which was almost suffocating.

The distance to ascend was very short under the circumstances, but to both boys, as they found when they afterwards compared notes, it seemed to be interminable, and it is doubtful which of the two suffered the more—Joe, as he gazed down with strained eyes and his vacant hands longing to seize the rope, or Gwyn, as he hung with elbows squared, fists clenched on the knot of the rope to ensure its remaining fast, and his head thrown back and face gazing up at his comrade when he slowly turned breast inward, at the sky when he turned back to the rocky wall.

So short a distance for Hardock to continue—his tramp less than two hundred feet—and yet it seemed so great, for every nerve was on the strain, and no one spoke a word.

It was in Joe's heart to keep on saying encouraging words to Gwyn, and to utter warnings to Hardock, and advice as to going slow or fast, but not a word would come. He could only stare down at the upturned face or at the bare head to which the wet hair clung close.

But all the time Gwyn was steadily rising, and in a few seconds more Joe felt that he would have to act—catching hold of his comrade by the rope about his chest and helping him over the edge into safety.

"Will he never come?" groaned Joe, softly. "Oh, make haste, Hardock, make haste."

He turned to look round once to see the strained rope and Hardock bending forward like some animal drawing a load, and the rope looked so thin that he shivered. Then, as it did not part, he felt a pang of dread, for he felt that the risk for his comrade was doubled by the feet that he was dependent upon two knots now instead of one, the slipping of either meaning certain death.

The moisture in Joe's hands grew more dense, and the great drops gathered upon his forehead, ran together and glided down his nose with a horrible tickling sensation; and as he now gazed down once more at Gwyn's hard, fixed, upturned face and straining eyes, his own grew dim so that he could only see through a mist, while a strange, paralysing feeling began to creep through him, so that he knew that he would not be able to help.

And all the time Gwyn rose higher and higher, till he was not ten feet below the edge, and now the horrible, numbing chill which pervaded Joe's being was chased away, for he found that he was suddenly called upon to act—to do something to help.

For the action of the rope had told upon the jacket laid there to soften the friction, and it began to travel slowly from the edge, keeping time with the rope, which now ground over the edge, and, to Joe's horror, looked as if it were fraying.

Bending down, he seized the pad and tried to thrust it back in its place, but soon found that this was impossible, and, before he could devise some plan, the knot in front of Gwyn's breast reached the edge, and a greater call was made upon him for help.

The inaction had passed away, and he shouted to Hardock to stop.

"Keep it tight!" he roared; and he went down on his knees, leaned over, caught hold of the loop on either side close beneath Gwyn's arms, and essayed to lift him over the edge on to the rocky platform.

It was a bitter lesson in his want of power, for, partly from his position there on the extreme edge of the terrible precipice, partly from its being a task for a muscular man, he found out he could not stir Gwyn in the least, only hold him tighter against the rock, pressing the great knot of the rope into the boy's chest.

"Up with him, lad!" shouted Hardock from where he stood straining the rope tight. "Up with him—right over on to the rock!"

Joe's eyes dilated and he gazed horror-stricken into the eyes of his comrade, who hung there perfectly inert, while just overhead three great grey gulls wheeled round and round, uttering their screams, and looking as if they expected that the next minute the boy would have fallen headlong on to the stones beneath.

"Come, look sharp!" shouted Hardock; "this rope cuts. Up with him quick!"

"Can—can you get hold of anything and—and help?" panted Joe at last, hoarsely.

Gwyn stared at him as if he had heard him speak, but did not quite comprehend what he said.

"Quick, Ydoll! Do you hear! Do something to help. Get hold."

This seemed to rouse the boy, who slowly loosened his hold of the rope, and then, with a quick spasmodic action, caught hold of the collar of Joe's jacket on either side.

"Now—your feet," said Joe, in a harsh whisper. "Try and find foothold."

"Can you—hold?" said Gwyn, faintly.

"Yes, I'll try," was the reply, and Gwyn's toes were heard scraping over the rock again and again, but without result, and Joe uttered a piteous groan.

"Can't you do it?" cried Hardock from the other end. "Why, it's as easy as easy. Up with him."

"No—no! Can't move!" cried Joe, frantically.

"Hold tight of him then till I come," cried the man, and Joe uttered a piercing shriek, for the rope went down with a jerk which drew him forward upon his chest as his hands were torn from their hold, and he clutched wildly at the rock on either side to save himself from going down.

Just then one of the gulls swooped close to his head and uttered its strange querulous cry.

Chapter Seven
Sam Hardock laughs

Joe Jollivet must have gone over the cliff in another instant headlong down to destruction, for only one thing could have saved him, and in all probability the sudden jerk of his snatching at his comrade would have taken him, too.

But as it happened Samuel Hardock—"the Captain," as he was generally called in Ydoll Cove—saw the mistake he had made, and did that one special thing.

Turning suddenly, he stepped quickly back, tightening the line again, drawing Gwyn close up to the sharp edge of the cliff once more; and as in his agony Joe clutched at the moving cord, and clung to it with all his might, he too was drawn back from the edge.

"That was near," muttered Hardock. "What's best to be done?"

Fortunately the man could be cool and matter-of-fact in the face of real danger, though, as he had shown, he was a superstitious coward when it was something purely imaginary; and he did at once the very best thing under the circumstances.

"Put heart into 'em by making 'em wild," he muttered, and he burst into a hearty fit of laughter.

"Yah!" he cried. "Nice pair o' soft-roed 'uns you two are! Why, you aren't got no more muscle than a pair o' jelly-fishes. There, get, your breath, Master Joe, and have another try; and you see if you can't make another out of it, Colonel. You're all right if you've made that knot good. I could hold you for a week standing up, and when I get tired I can lie down. Now— hard, hard! I thought you meant to dive off the cliff, you, Master Joe."

The latter had risen to his knees with his wet hair clinging to his brow; and for a moment he felt disposed to rage out something furiously at the grinning speaker.

But he refrained, and turned to get a fresh grip of Gwyn, who seemed to have recovered somewhat, too.

"He's a beast!" cried Joe, angrily, for the anger was working in the right direction.

Hardock began again, —

"Rope cut, Master Gwyn?" he cried. "S'pose it does, though. Well, when you two are ready, just say. I've got him tight enough. But, hark ye, here; can you tell what I say?"

"Yes," cried Joe, in a choking voice.

"That's right. Well, first thing you do, my lad, you try and ease the rope over the edge. It checks you like, don't you see? Stretch your arms well over, Colonel, and get your fingers in a crack and find a place for your toes, while young Joe Jollivet eases the knot over. Take it coolly. There's nothing to mind. I've got yer, yer know. Ready?"

"Yes. Now, Ydoll, old chap," whispered Joe, "can you do what he says and find foothold?"

There was a peculiar staring look in the boy's eyes, but he began to search about with his toes; and almost at once found a crack that he had passed over before, forced in the end of one boot, and, reaching over, he gripped the rope with both hands.

"Get tight hold of my collar," he whispered rather faintly. "Can you do it kneeling?"

"No power," said Joe, huskily, "I must stand."

He rose to his feet, gripping the collar as he was told, gazing there into Gwyn's eyes, for he dared not look down beyond him into the dizzy depth.

"Now," said Gwyn, "when you're ready, I'll try and raise myself a bit, and you throw yourself back."

"Wait a moment," panted Joe. Then he shouted, "Now I am—all together!"

"Right! Hauley hoi!" came back, and with one effort Gwyn curved his body, forcing his breast clear of the edge, joined his strength to that of his comrade in the effort to rise, and the next moment Joe was on his back with Gwyn being dragged over him.

Then came an interval of inaction, for the three actors in the perilous scene lay prone upon the rough surface of the cliff, Hardock having thrown himself upon his face.

"Oh, Gwyn, old chap!—oh, Gwyn," groaned Joe.

"Hah! Yes; it was near," sighed the rescued boy, as he slowly rose to a sitting posture, and began to unfasten the rope. "I thought I was gone."

"It was horrid—horrid—horrid!" groaned Joe. "And I couldn't do anything."

He rose slowly, wiping his brow, which was dripping with perspiration, and the two boys sat there in the sunshine gazing at one another for a few minutes as if quite unconscious of the presence of Hardock at the end of the rope, where he lay spread-eagled among the heath.

Then Gwyn slowly held out his hand, which was gripped excitedly by Joe, who seized it with a loud sob.

"Thank ye, Jolly-wet," said Gwyn, quietly. "I felt so queer seeing you try so hard."

"You felt—about me? Ah, you don't know what I felt about you. Ugh! I could kick you! Frightening me twice over like that! I don't know which was worst—when you went down or when you came up."

"Going down was worst," said Gwyn, quietly. "But have a kick if you like; I don't feel as if I could hit back."

"Then I'll wait till you can," said Joe, with a faint smile. "Oh, dear, how my heart does keep on beating!"

He turned with hand pressing his side and looked toward Hardock, for the man had moved, and he, too, sat up and began searching in his pockets. And then, to the great disgust of the two boys, they saw him slowly bring out a short pipe and a brass tobacco-box, and then deliberately fill the former, take out his matches, strike a light, and begin to smoke.

"Look at that," cried Joe, viciously.

"Yes; I'm looking," said Gwyn, slowly, and speaking as if he were utterly exhausted. "I feel as if I wish I were strong enough to go and knock him over."

"For laughing at us when we were in such a horrible fix? Yes; so do I. He's an old beast; and when you feel better we'll go and tell him so."

"Let's go now," said Gwyn, rising stiffly. "I say, I feel wet and cold, and sore all over."

Joe rose with more alacrity and clenched his fists, his teeth showing a little between his tightened lips.

"Why, Jolly," said Gwyn, gravely, "you look as if you'd knocked the skin off your temper."

"That's just how I do feel," cried the boy—"regularly raw. I want to have a row with old Sammy Hardock. It's all his fault, our getting into such trouble; and first he stands there laughing at us when we were nearly gone, and now he sits there as if it hadn't mattered a bit, and begins to smoke. I never hated anyone that I know of, but I do hate him now. He's a beast."

"Well, you said that before," said Gwyn, slowly; and he shivered. "I say, Jolly, isn't it rum that when you're wet, if you stand in the sun, you feel cold?"

"Then let's go and give it to old Hardock; that'll warm you up. I feel red hot now."

Gwyn began to rub his chest softly, where the rope had cut into him, and the boys walked together to where Hardock sat with his back to them, smoking.

The man did not hear them coming till they were close to him, when he started round suddenly, and faced them, letting the pipe drop from between his lips.

The resentment bubbling up in both of the boys died out on the instant, as they saw the drawn, ghastly face before them.

"Ah, my lads! Ah, my dear lads!" groaned the man; "that's about the nighest thing I ever see; but, thank goodness, you're all safe and sound. Would you two mind shaking hands?"

The boys stared at him, then at each other and back.

"Why, Sam!" said Gwyn, huskily.

"Yes; it's me, my lad," he replied, with a groan, "what there is left on me. I've been trying a pipe, but it aren't done me no good, not a bit. I seem to see young Jollivet there going head first over the cliff; and the mortal shiver it did send through me was something as I never felt afore."

"Why, you laughed at us!" said Joe, with his resentment flashing up again.

"Laughed at yer? Course I did. What was I to do? If I'd ha' told yer both you was in danger, wouldn't it ha' frightened you so as you'd ha' been too froze up to help yourselves?"

"No; I don't think so," cried Joe.

"Don't yer? Well, I'm sure on it. I couldn't do anything but hold on to the rope, and no one could ha' saved you but yourselves."

"But you shouldn't have laughed," said Gwyn, gravely.

"What was I to do then, Colonel? It was the only thing likely to spur you up. I thought it would make you both wild like, and think you warn't in such a queer strait, and it did."

The boys exchanged glances.

"Yes," continued Hardock, as he shook hands solemnly with both, "there was nobody to help you, my lads, but yourselves, and I made you do that; but talk about giving a man a turn—Oh, dear! oh, dear! And now my pipe's gone right out."

"Light it again, then, Sam," said Gwyn, quietly, as he stooped stiffly to pick up the fallen pipe, and hand it to its owner.

"Thank ye, my lad, thank ye; but I don't feel in the humour for no pipes to-day, I'm just as if I've had a very gashly turn."

"But you might have tied the rope round me better, Sam," said Gwyn.

"Ay, I might, my lad, but somehow I didn't. Are you hurt much?"

"Only sore, with the rope cutting me."

"Nay, but I mean when you fell down the shaft. Did you hit yourself again' the sides?"

"No. It was very horrible, though. One moment I was turning slowly round and round and the next I was losing all the light; the rope slipped from round me and I was going down, down into the darkness. It was as if it lasted ever so long. Then there was a splash, the water was roaring in my ears, and I felt as if I were being dragged down lower and lower, till all at once my head shot up again. I never once felt as if I was coming up."

"How queer!" exclaimed Joe, who stood listening with his face all wrinkled over. "Didn't you feel, when you'd got as low as you went, that you were going up again?"

"No, not in the least. It was all confused like and strange, and I hardly knew anything till I was at the surface, and then I began to strike out, and swam along the sides of the slimy stones, trying to get a grip of them, but my hands kept slipping off."

"But you didn't halloa!" said Joe.

"No," continued Gwyn, still speaking in the same grave, subdued way, as if still suffering from the shock of all he had gone through. "I didn't shout; I felt stunned like, as if I'd been hit on the head."

"You must have been," cried Joe. "You hit yourself against the side."

"No, if I had it would have killed me. I can't explain it. Perhaps it was striking on the water."

"Nonsense; water's too soft to hurt you. But go on; what did you do then?"

"I hardly know, only that I kept on striking out, thinking how horribly dark it must be and wondering whether there were any live things to come at me; and then I hit my knee against the stones at the bottom."

"But you said it was deep."

"So it was in the shaft, but I must have swum into a passage where it was quite shallow; and almost directly after I'd hit my knee my hands touched the stones and I crawled out into the dark, and went on and on, feeling afraid to go back because of the water."

"But why didn't you shout to us?" cried Joe, excitedly.

"I don't know. I suppose I couldn't. It was like being in a dream, and I felt obliged to go crawling on. Then all of a sudden I began to feel better, for I could see a faint light, and this made me try to stand up, but I couldn't without hitting my head. But I could walk stooping like, and I went on toward the pale light, which was almost like a star. Directly after, I was there looking out of a square place like a window, trying to find a way up or a way down, but the rocks stood out overhead, and they were quite straight down below me, so I could do nothing but shout, and I began to think no one would come. Every now and then I could hear voices, but when I called my voice seemed to float out to sea. There, you know the rest. But that's an adit, isn't it, Sam Hardock?"

"Ay, my lad, and lucky for you it was there. You see, the water must run off by it out to sea when the top rises so high. But I never knew there was an opening from seaward into the mine. Being right up there, nobody could see it. Why it must be 'underd and fifty feet above the shore."

"It looked more," said Gwyn, with a shudder.

"There, I say, hadn't you better get home and change your things, my lad? You're pretty wet still. If you take my advice, you'll go off as fast as you can."

"Yes," said Joe, "you'd better. But we haven't done much to examine the mine."

"Eh?" cried Hardock, "I think we have. Found out that there's an adit for getting rid of the water and the spoil. Not bad for one day's work."

Chapter Eight
The Mine Fever

"You'll have to tell them at home, Ydoll," said Joe as they reached the rough stone-wall which enclosed the Colonel's estate. "What shall you say?"

"Oh, just what happened," replied Gwyn; "but the job is how to begin. It's making the start."

"Pst! Look out!" whispered Joe. "Here is your father."

"Good-morning, Hardock," said the Colonel, coming upon the group suddenly.

"I hope you haven't been filling my boy's head with more stuff about mining. Why, halloa, Gwyn; how did you get in that state? Where's your cap?"

"Down the mine-shaft, father," replied the lad; and he found no difficulty about beginning. In a few minutes the Colonel knew all.

"Most reckless—most imprudent," he cried. "You ought to have known better, sir, than to lead these boys into such a terrible position; and how dare you, sir—how dare you begin examining my property without my permission!"

"Well you see, Colonel," began Hardock, "I thought—be doing you good, like, and as a neighbour—"

"A neighbour, indeed! Confounded insolence! Be off, sir! How dare you! Never you show yourself upon my land again. There, you, Gwyn, come home at once and change your clothes; and as for you, Jollivet, you give my compliments to your father and tell him I say he ought to give you a good thrashing, and if he feels too ill to do it, let him send you down to me, and I will. Now, Gwyn; right face. March!"

The Colonel led off his son, and Hardock and Joe stood looking at each other.

"Made him a bit waxy," said the miner; "but he'll come round to my way of thinking yet; and it strikes me that he'll be ordering me on to his land again, when he knows all. I say, young Jollivet, mean to go down to him to be thrashed with the young Colonel?"

"Oh, he wouldn't thrash me," said Joe, quietly. "I know the Colonel better than that. I feel all stretched and aching like. I wish he hadn't taken Gwyn home, though."

"I don't feel quite square myself, lad," said the mining captain; "but you see if the Colonel don't go looking at the mine."

Hardock's prophecy was soon fulfilled, for that evening the Colonel was rowing in his boat with his son, who had a mackerel line trailing astern, and when they came opposite to the great buttress the Colonel lay on his oars, and let his boat rise and fall on the clear swell.

"Now, then; whereabouts is the mouth of the adit?"

"I can't quite make it out from down here, father," replied Gwyn. "Yes I can; there it is, only it doesn't look like an opening, only a dark shadowy part of the cliff. No one could tell it was a passage in, without being up there."

"Quite right; they could not," said the Colonel, thoughtfully. "And you were drawn up from there, and right over the top of the cliff?"

"Yes, father."

"Horribly dangerous, boy—hideous. There, your mother knows something about it, but she must never be shown how frightful a risk you ran. Come, let's get back."

Gwyn only caught one fish that evening, and his father was very thoughtful and quiet when they returned.

"Here, Gwyn," he said next morning; "come along with me, I want to have a look at the old pit-shaft, and the bit of cliff over which you were drawn."

"Yes, father," said Gwyn, and he led the way over their own ground; but before they reached the dwarf mine wall, he was conscious of the fact that they were observed; for, at the turn of the lane, Hardock's oilskin cap could be seen as if the man were watching there, and the next moment Joe Jollivet's straw hat was visible by his side.

Gwyn felt disposed to point out that they were not alone; but the next moment his father began talking about the slow progress made by the belt of pines he had planted between there and the house, so as to take off something of the barrenness of the place.

"Want of shelter, Gwyn," he said; "the great winds from the west catch them too much. I'm afraid they will always be stunted. Still, they would hide the mine buildings."

"The mine buildings, father?" said the boy, looking at his father inquiringly.

"Yes; I mean if I were to be tempted into doing anything of the kind — opening the mine again. Seems a pity, if it does contain wealth, to let it lie there useless. Money's money, my boy."

"But you don't want money, father, do you?" said Gwyn. The Colonel stopped short, and faced round to gaze in his son's face before bursting into a merry fit of laughter. "Have I said something very stupid, father?"

"No, not stupid — only shown me how inexperienced you are in the matters of everyday life, Gwyn. My dear boy, I never knew an officer on half-pay who did not want money."

"But I thought you had enough."

"Enough, boy? Someone among our clever writers once said that enough was always a little more than a man possessed."

"But you will not begin mining, father?"

"I don't know, my boy. Let's have a look at the place. Here have we been these ten years, and I know no more about this hole than I did when I came. I know it is an old mine-shaft half full of water, just like a dozen more about the district, and I should have gone on knowing no more about it if that man had not begun talking, and shown me, by the great interest he takes in the place, that he thinks it must be rich. Be rather a nice thing to grow rich, my boy, and have plenty to start you well in the world."

"But I don't want starting well in the world, father; it's nice enough as it is."

"What, you idle, young dog! Do you expect to pass all your life fishing, bathing, and bird's-nesting here?"

"No, father; but —"

"'No, father; but —' Humph! here's the place, then. Dear me, how very unsafe that stone-wall is. A strong man could push it down the shaft in half-an-hour."

As he spoke the Colonel strode up to the piled-up stones, and looked over into the fern-fringed pit.

"Ugh! horrible! Pitch one of those stones down, boy."

Gwyn took a piece of the loose granite, raised it over his head with both hands, and threw it from him with force enough to make it strike the opposite side of the shaft, from which it rebounded, and then went on down, down, into the darkness for some moments before there was a dull splash, which came echoing out of the mouth, followed by a strange swishing as the water rose and fell against the sides.

"Horrible, indeed!" muttered the Colonel. Then aloud: "And you let them lower you down by a rope, it came undone, and you fell headlong into that water down below, rose, swam to the side and then crept along a horizontal passage to where it opened out on the sea yonder?"

"Yes, father," said the boy, recalling his sensations as his father spoke.

"Bless my heart!" exclaimed the Colonel. "Well, Gwyn, you're a queer sort of boy. Not very clever, and you give me a good deal of anxiety as to how you are going to turn out. But one thing is very evident—with all your faults, you are not a coward."

"Oh, yes, I am, father," said Gwyn, shaking his head. "You don't know what a fright I was in."

"Fright! Enough to frighten anybody. I've faced fire times enough, my boy, and had to gallop helter-skelter with a handful of brave fellows against a thousand or more enemies who were thirsting for our blood! But I dared not have gone down that pit hanging at the end of a rope. No, Gwyn, my boy, you are no coward. There, show me now where you were drawn up."

Gwyn led the way to the foot of the granite ridge, fully expecting to hear his father say that he could not climb up there; but, to his surprise, the Colonel mounted actively enough, and walked along the rugged top to where it ended in the great buttress, and there he stood at the very edge gazing down.

"Where were you, Gwyn?" he said at last; and the boy pointed out the projection beneath which the adit opened out.

"To be sure. Yes, I couldn't quite make it out," said the Colonel, coolly, as he turned away; but Gwyn noticed that he took out his handkerchief to pass it over his forehead, and then wiped the insides of his hands as if they were damp.

"Let's go back by the road," said the Colonel, after shading his eyes and taking a look round; "but I want to pass the mouth of the mine."

Upon reaching the latter, the Colonel drew a hammer from his pocket, and after routing out a few grey pieces of stone from where they lay beneath the furze bushes, he cracked and chipped several, till one which looked red in the new cleavage, and was studded with little blackish-purple, glistening grains, took his fancy.

"Carry this home for me, Gwyn," he said. "I wonder whether that piece ever came out of the mine?"

"I think all that large sloping bank covered with bushes and brambles came out of the mine some time, father," said the boy. "It seems to have been all raised up round about the mouth there."

"Eh? You think so?"

"Yes, father; and as the pieces thrown out grew higher, they seem to have built up the mouth of the mine with big blocks to keep the stones from rolling in. I noticed that when I was being let down. The ferns have taken root in the joints. Lower down, fifteen or twenty feet, the hole seems to have been cut through the solid rock."

"Humph! you kept your eyes open, then?"

Crossing the wall where the lane ran along by the side of the Colonel's property, they turned homeward, and in a few minutes Gwyn caught sight of Joe Jollivet's cap gliding in and out among the furze bushes, as he made his way in the direction of his own house, apparently not intending to be seen. But a few hundred yards farther along the lane there was some one who evidently did intend to be seen, in the shape of Sam Hardock, who rose from where he was sitting on a grey-lichened block, and touched his hat.

"That's a nice specimen you've got there, Master Pendarve," he said, eyeing the block the boy carried.

"It's a very heavy one, Sam," replied Gwyn; and his father strode on, but stopped short and turned back frowning, unable, in spite of his annoyance, to restrain his curiosity.

"Here, you Hardock," he cried, tapping the block his son carried, with his cane. "What is it? What stone do you call that?"

"Quartz, sir," said the man, examining the piece, "and a very fine specimen."

"Eh? Good for breaking up to repair the roads with, eh?"

"No, sir; bad for that; soon go to powder. But it would be fine to crush and smelt."

"Eh? What for?"

"What for, sir?" said the man with a laugh; "why, that bit o' stone's half tin. I dunno where you got it, o' course; but if it came from the spoil bank of that old mine, it just proves what I thought."

"Tin? Are you sure?"

"Sure, sir? Yes," said the man, laughing. "I ought to know tin when I see it. If it comes out of the old Ydoll mine, you've only got to set men at work to go down and blast it out, sir, and in a very short time you'll be a rich man."

"Come along, Gwyn," said the Colonel, hastily; "it's time we got back. Hang the fellow!" he muttered, "he has given me the mining fever, and badly, too, I fear."

Chapter Nine
Doctor Joe

"Oh, dear! Oh, dear! What a life! what a state of misery to be in!"

"Shall I turn the pillow over, father?" said Joe to Major Jollivet, who was lying on the couch drawn before the window, so that he could have a good view of the sea.

"No," shouted the Major, whose face was contracted by pain; and he shivered as he spoke although his forehead was covered with perspiration. "Why do you want to worry me by turning the pillow?"

"Because it will be nice and cool on the other side."

"Get out. Be off with you directly, sir. Can't you see I'm shivering with cold? Oh, dear: who would have jungle fever?"

"I wouldn't father," said the boy; and in spite of the words just spoken, he softly thrust his arm under his father's neck, raised his head, and then turned and punched the pillow, smoothed it, and let the Major's head down again.

"How dah you, sir!" cried the sufferer, fiercely. "Did I not tell you, sir, that I did not want it done? Did I not order you to quit the room, sir? Am I not your superior officer, sir? And you dared to disobey me, sir, because I am on the sick list. How dah you, sir! How dah you, sir! If you were in a regiment, sir, it would mean court-martial, sir, and—Oh, dear me!"

"That's cooler and more comfortable, father, isn't it?" said Joe, calmly enough, and without seeming to pay the slightest attention to the fierce tirade of angry words directed against him.

"Yes," sighed the Major, "that's cooler and more comfortable; but," he cried, turning angry again and beginning to draw out and point his great fierce moustache with his long thin fingers, "I will not have you disobey my orders, sir. You're as bad as your poor mother used to be—taking command of the regiment, and dictating and disobeying me as if I were not fit to manage my own affairs. How dah you, sir, I say—how dah you!"

Joe leaned over his father in the most imperturbable way, screwed up his mouth as if he were whistling, and drew out the Major's clean handkerchief from his breast-pocket, shook it, and then gently dabbed the moist forehead.

"Don't! Leave off, sir!" roared the Major. "How dah you, sir! I will not be treated in this way as if I were a helpless infant. Joseph, you scoundrel, you shall leave home at once, and go to an army tutor. I will not have these mutinous ways in the house."

Joe smiled faintly, screwed up his lips a little more, turned the handkerchief, gave the forehead a light wipe over by way of a polish, and then lowered it.

"Want to blow your nose, dad?" he said.

"No, sir, I do not want to blow my nose; and if I did I could blow it myself. Oh, dear! Oh, dear. This pain—this pain!"

Joe thrust the handkerchief back, and laid his palm on his father's forehead.

"Not quite so hot, dad," he said.

"How dah you, sir! It's your rank mutinous obstinacy that makes you say so. Take away that nasty hot paw."

Joe went to the mantelpiece, took a large square bottle of eau-de-Cologne, removed the stopper, and once more drew out his father's pocket-handkerchief, moistened it with the scent, and softly applied it to the sufferer's forehead.

"Confound you!" cried the Major. "Will you leave me alone, sir, or am I to get up and fetch my cane to you?"

"What do they make eau-de-Cologne of, father?" said Joe, coolly. "Does it come from a spring like all those nasty mineral waters you take?"

"It's insufferable!" panted the Major.

"Time you had a drink, father," said Joe, quietly.

"It is not, sir. I take that medicine at eleven o'clock, military time. It wants quite half-an-hour to that yet. You want to be off to play with that idle young scoundrel of Pendarve's, I suppose; but I wish you to stay here till it is eleven. Do you hear that, sir? You disobey me if you dare."

"Five minutes past eleven now, dad," said Joe, after a glance at the clock over the chimney-piece.

"It's not, sir," cried the Major, turning his head quickly to look for himself, and then wincing from pain. "That clock's wrong. It's a wretched cheap fraud, and never did keep time. Fast! Nearly an hour fast!"

"Said it was the best timekeeper in Cornwall only yesterday," said Joe to himself, as he went to a side table on which stood a couple of bottles, a glass, and water-jug.

Here the boy busied himself for a few moments, with his father frowning and watching him angrily, and looking, in spite of his pain-distorted countenance, pallid look and sunken cheeks, a fine, handsome, middle-aged man.

The next minute Joe was coming back with a tumbler in his hand, and stirring it with a little glass rod.

"Here you are, dad. Shall I hoist you up while you tip it off?"

"No, sir; I can sit up. How much quinine did you put in?"

"Usual dose, father."

"Ho! How much lemon juice?"

"Wineglass full, and filled up with spring water."

Major Jollivet made an effort to sit up, but sank back again with a groan.

Joe might have smiled, but he did not. He could justly have said triumphantly: "There, I knew you could not manage it!" but he calmly drew a chair to the side of the couch, stood the glass within reach of his father's hand, and then went behind his head, forced his arm under the pillow, lowered his brow so that he could butt like a ram, and slowly and steadily raised the invalid's shoulders, keeping him upright till the draught had been taken and the glass set down.

"Bah! Horrible! Bitter as gall."

"Lower away!" said Joe; and he drew softly back till the pillow was in its old place, and the Major uttered a sigh of relief.

"I say, dad, you're getting better," said Joe, as he took away chair and glass after brushing his disordered hair from his forehead.

"How dah you, sir!" cried the Major, "when I'm in such a state of prostration!"

Joe laid his hand on the patient's forehead again, and nodded.

"Head's getting wet and cool, dad. You'll be right as a trivet again soon."

"Worse than your poor mother—worse than your poor mother. You haven't a bit of feeling, boy. It's abominable."

Joe took a sprayer, thrust it into the neck of the scent bottle, and blew an odorous vapour about the sufferer's head.

"Will you put that tomfool thing away, sir! You're never happy unless you're playing with it."

"I say," cried Joe, still without seeming to pay the slightest heed to his father's words—"what do you think, dad?"

"Think, sir? How can I think of anything but this wretched jungle fever. Oh, my bones, my bones!"

"Colonel Pendarve's going to open the old Ydoll mine."

"Eh? What?" cried the Major, turning his head sharply. "Say that again."

"Captain Hardock got talking to me and Gwyn about it, and Gwyn told his father."

"Told him what?"

"Sam Hardock said he was sure that there was plenty of tin in it, and that it was a pity for it to be there, and when the Colonel might make a fortune out of it."

"And—and what did Pendarve say?" cried the Major, excitedly.

"Said it was all nonsense, I believe. Then Sam Hardock took me—me and Gwyn—to have a look, and Ydoll went down."

"Look here, sir, I will not have you call Gwyn Pendarve by that idiotic nickname."

"No, father. When he was half down the rope came undone, and he went down plash."

"Killed?" cried the Major, excitedly.

"Oh, no, father, there was plenty of water, and he got out through a passage on to the cliffs, and Sam and I had to pull him up again."

"What mad recklessness!"

"He wasn't hurt, father, only got very wet; and since then the Colonel has been to have a look at the place and had a talk or two with Sam Hardock, and Ydoll—"

"What!" cried the Major, fiercely.

"Gwyn thinks his father is going to have machinery down, and the mine pumped out."

"Madness! Going to throw all his money away. He sha'n't do it. I won't have it. What does Mrs Pendarve say?"

"Gwyn says she doesn't like it at all."

"I should think not, sir. It means ruin spelt with a big letter. Why can't he be contented with his half-pay?"

"I dunno, father. I suppose he feels as if he'd like more."

"Yes, and get less. You never knew me tempted by these wretched mining schemes, did you, sir?"

"No, father."

"The man's mad. Got a bee in his bonnet. Going to ruin his son's prospects in life. He sha'n't do it. How can he be so absurd! I'll go to him as soon as I can move."

"Feel a little easier, father?" said Joe, going to the head of the couch, and pressing his hand upon his father's brow again.

"Yes, much easier, my boy," said the invalid, placing his hand upon his son's, and holding it down for a few moments. "Feels cooler, doesn't it?"

"Ever so much, dad, and not so damp."

"Yes, I feel like a new man again. Thank you, Joe—thank you, my boy. Haven't been fretful, have I?"

"Oh, just a little, father, of course. Who could help it?"

"I was afraid I had been, Joe. But, as you say, who could help it? Didn't say anything very cross to you, did I?"

"Oh, no, nothing to signify, dad. But, I say, I am glad you're better."

"Thank you, my boy, thank you," said the Major, drawing his boy's hand down to his lips and kissing it. "Just like your poor, dear mother, so calm and patient with me when I am suffering. Joe, my boy, you will have to be a doctor."

"I? Oh, no, father. I must be a soldier, same as you've been, and Gwyn is going to be."

"But I meant a military surgeon," said the Major.

"Wouldn't do, father. Why, if I were to tell Ydoll—I mean Gwyn—that I was going to be a doctor, he would crow over me horribly, and I should never hear the end of it. He'd christen me jalap or rhubarb, or something of that sort."

"Ah, well, we shall see, and—who's that coming up to the door?"

Joe looked out from the window, and came back directly.

"The Colonel, dad. Shall I go and let him in?"

"Yes, fetch him in, and stop here and give me a hint now and then if I get a little irritable. What you have told me makes me feel rather cross, and I shall have to give him a bit of my mind. I can't let him go and waste his money like that."

Joe hurried out to the front hall, and found that Gwyn had accompanied his father, the former having been hidden by the shrubs as they came up to the door.

Chapter Ten
Finding an Intruder

"Well, old man; on the sick list?" began the Colonel, shaking hands warmly with his friend. "What's the last bulletin?"

"Bad, bad," said the Major, sharply. "Just heard that a man I respected is going to make a fool of himself."

"Eh? What?" said the Colonel, flushing. "Who's been chattering about— ahem! Are you alluding to the mine on my property, Major Jollivet?"

"No, sir," said the Major, sitting up, "I was speaking about the hole by the cliff that was dug by a pack of greedy noodles who were not satisfied with their incomes, and I felt that I should not like to see an old friend of mine go shovelling his money down into it, and breaking his wife's heart."

"Then it was like your—ahem, ahem!" coughed the Colonel, checking himself. "No, no; don't go away, boys," for Gwyn was stealing out, followed by Joe.

"No, don't you boys go," cried the Major; "it will be a lesson for you both."

"Father been very bad, Joe?" said the Colonel.

"Very bad, indeed, sir," said the boy.

"Silence, sir!" cried the Major. "Nothing of the sort. Don't exaggerate, Joe."

"No, father."

"He doesn't, Dick. You've had a nasty touch this morning, or you wouldn't have spoken to me like that."

"I couldn't help it, old man," said the Major, warmly. "But surely you will never be so mad as to go pumping out that old place."

"H'm! I don't know about mad. Be useful to make a little money for the sake of the boy."

"Very bad to lose a great deal for the sake of the boy."

"Nothing venture, nothing win, Dick. I'm beginning to think that it would be worth while to put some money in the venture, and I came up this morning to make you the first offer of joining in."

"And throwing away my bit of money, too. No, sir, not if I know it. I'm not quite such an idiot as that."

"You mean as I am," said the Colonel, quietly.

"I did not say so," retorted the Major. "I should not dream of insulting an old friend by using such language."

"No, but you would think it all the same," cried the Colonel. "Now, look here, Jollivet; you and I have enough to live upon comfortably."

"Quite."

"But there's nothing left to start these two young dogs well in life; now is there?"

"Well—er—rum—er—no; there is not much, Pendarve, certainly."

"That's what I have been thinking, and though the idle, reckless young dogs do not deserve it—do you hear, you two? I say you don't deserve it."

"Joe doesn't," said Gwyn, with a mischievous grin at his companion.

"No, not at all," said Joe. "I'm nearly as bad as Gwyn."

"Ah, you're a nice pair," said the Colonel. "But we, as fathers, must, I suppose, give you both a good preparation for the army—eh, Jollivet?"

"Yes, of course that must be done," said the Major.

"Exactly! Well, I've been thinking a great deal about it this last day or two, and I have quite come to the conclusion that I must do something."

"Well, do something," said the Major, testily; "don't go and fling your money down a mine."

"But there are mines and mines, Jollivet, old fellow. If I were asked to join in some company to buy a mine or open a new one, I should of course hesitate; but in this case I have one of my own, one that is undoubtedly very ancient, and must have had a great deal of tin or copper or both in it."

"No doubt, and it was all dug out and sold long enough ago. The old people had the oyster, and you've got the shell."

"I don't know so much about that, sir," said the Colonel, earnestly. "I brought home a piece of old ore that was dug out, and it's very rich in tin. There's plenty of room down below for there to be an enormous amount, and as the only outlay will be for machinery for pumping and raising the ore, I have made up my mind to start a company of the owners to work that mine."

"And lose all your money."

"I hope not. The mine is already sunk, and I believe when it is pumped dry we shall find that there are drifts with plenty of ore in them, waiting to be worked—plenty to pay well for the getting."

"And if there turns out to be none at all?"

"Well, that's the very worst way of looking at it. If it turns out as bad as that, I shall have spent so many hundred pounds in new pumping machinery, and have it to sell for what it will fetch to some fresh company."

"But you would only get half the value."

"If I got half the value, I should be satisfied. Then the loss would not be so very severe."

"Severe enough to make you repent it to the last day of your life," said the Major, shortly.

"I hope not. Money is not worth so much repentance."

"But you talk as if you really meant to do this, Pendarve," said the Major, warmly.

"I do. I have quite made up my mind."

Gwyn looked at his father, with his eyes flashing with excitement.

"My dear Pendarve, I implore you not to do so for that boy's sake," cried the Major.

"It is for his sake I am going to venture upon what seems to me a very safe piece of business."

"No, no; a wild-goose chase, sir."

"Mining is not so reckless as that, if carried out on business principles, my dear Jollivet."

"There, we shall never agree. But in the name of all that is sensible, why did you come to me?"

"Partly because you are my oldest friend, and one in whom I should confide any important business."

"And partly," cried the Major, warmly, "because you thought I should be weak enough to join you."

"Quite right, all but the question of weakness," said the Colonel.

"Absurd! There, I am obliged to speak plainly; I could never dream of such a thing."

"I don't want you to dream," said the Colonel, smiling; "I want you to act—to join me; and upon this basis: I will find the mine, and half the money for the machinery, if you will find the other half."

"It would be folly. Look at the money we know to have been lost on mines."

"Yes, in companies, and over very doubtful affairs. In this case we have the proof of mining having been carried on. We have the mine, and we should not have to share profits with a number of shareholders."

"Nor losses neither," said the Major, testily.

"Nor the losses neither," assented the Colonel. "Then we live on the spot and could oversee matters."

"Bah! What do we know about mines? I could manage a regiment, not a hole underground."

"We could soon learn, my dear boy," said the Colonel; "and it would be very interesting to have such an occupation. I have felt for years past that you and I have been wasting time. No occupation whatever, nothing to do but think about our ailments. It's rusting, Jollivet—it's rusting out; and I'm sure that if we both worked hard, we should be healthier and better men."

"Humph! Well, there is something in that. But, no, no, no, I'm not going to be tempted to spend money that ought some day to come to Joe."

"Oh, I don't mind, father, if it's going to do you good," cried the boy, eagerly. "I should like for you to have a mine."

"Shall I have any money some day, father?" said Gwyn.

"I suppose so, my boy, what I leave when I die," said the Colonel, frowning.

"Oh, then, I'll give it to go into the mine, father," cried Gwyn; and the stern look passed off the Colonel's face. He nodded, and looked pleased.

"Think of the anxiety that such a venture would bring," said the Major.

"I have thought of it, and also of the anxieties and worries which come to a man who has nothing to do. Look here, Jollivet, I firmly believe in this adventure, and I should very much like it if you would join me, for I feel that it would do you good, and that we should get on well together."

"Oh, yes, I've no doubt about that," said the Major, "and if you really do make up your mind to venture, I don't say that I will not lend you some money if you need it."

"Thank you, I know that you would, Jollivet; but I don't want to take it in that way. Think it over for a few days, and see how you feel about it."

"No, I can give you my answer now without any hesitation. It is quite out of the question, Pendarve. Even if it were a gold mine, I should say—"

"Don't decide rashly, old fellow," said the Colonel. "A few days ago I should have answered you in the same way, if you had come and proposed the thing; but since I have thought it over, I have quite changed my mind. Do the same, and let me hear how you have concluded to act at the end of a week."

"But I tell you, my dear sir—"

"Yes; tell me at the end of a week," said the Colonel, smiling. "What do you think of these fellows beginning to investigate the mine for themselves? There, Gwyn, you need not stay for me if you want a run with Joe: I'll walk home alone."

"Father is not well enough to be left," said Joe.

"Yes, yes, my boy," cried the Major; "I don't want to make a prisoner of you. Go and have a run with Gwyn, by all means."

The boys required no second permission, but were off at once, their fathers hearing the beat of their feet on the road directly after.

"Where have they gone?" said the Major, turning on his couch.

"Over to the mouth of the mine, for certain," said the Colonel.

He was quite right. There was no proposal made by either of the boys, but as soon as they were outside the gate, they started off together at a rapid trot, making straight for the Colonel's land, springing over the stone-wall, and threading their way amongst stones and bushes, till they were compelled by the rough ground to go more slowly.

"Makes one want to see more of what it's like," said Joe.

"Yes; I didn't know father was thinking about it so seriously. Why, it'll be splendid, Joe. I say; you'll have to go down the mine first this time."

"Yes, I suppose so, but not your way."

"Hist!" whispered Gwyn, as they drew near. "What does that mean?"

"What? I don't see anything."

Gwyn ducked down behind one of the great, grey weathered lumps of granite, and signed to his companion to follow his example.

This was done on the instant, and then Joe looked inquiringly in his face.

"Something wrong," whispered Gwyn. "Trespassers. Got to know that father means to work the mine."

Gwyn raised his head slowly, so as to peer over the block of granite, and plainly made out a hand and arm working about at the side of the low protection wall of the old mine.

"Sam Hardock," whispered Joe, who had followed his example. "What's he doing? Measuring the depth?"

"'Tisn't Sam," whispered Gwyn, "it's someone else—stranger, I think. Then the mine must be valuable or he wouldn't be there. What shall we do?"

"He has no business there. It's on your father's property, perhaps it'll be ours, too," whispered Joe. "I say, Ydoll, we're not going to stand that; let's go and collar him."

"Agreed!" said Gwyn, excitedly. "We've right on our side. Come on."

Chapter Eleven
Fighting the Enemy

Gwyn Pendarve's "Come on!" was loyally responded to by Joe Jollivet, and the two lads made a hurried charge down the slope at the interloper so busy about the old mine-shaft.

Now, if you take two dogs out for a walk in the country, unless they are particularly well-behaved, spiritless animals, as soon as they see sheep, cow, or bullock grazing, they will make a furious dash, and if the grazing creature runs, they will have a most enjoyable hunt. But if the quarry stands fast and makes a show of attacking in turn, the probabilities are that the dogs will slacken speed, stop short a few yards away, give vent to their opinions upon the unnatural behaviour of the animal in barks, lower their triumphantly waving tails, and come back at a gentle trot, stopping at times, though, to turn their heads and make a few more remarks in dog language.

Truth to tell, when Gwyn and Joe made their charge, they fully expected to see the man leaning over the old wall start off and run; but, as it happened, he did not, but stood up, turned, and faced them, looking a big, sour-faced, truculent fellow, who scowled at them and stood his ground.

Whatever their inclinations might have been for the moment, not being dogs, and each having his prestige to keep up in his companion's eyes, Gwyn and Joe certainly stopped; but they did not turn, but stood firm, noting that the man had a large reel of sea-fishing line evidently of goodly length.

"Hullo!" he said, hoarsely. "What's for you?"

"What are you doing here?" cried Gwyn.

"What's that to you?"

"Everything. Do you know you are trespassing?"

"No. Am I?"

"Yes, of course."

"Thank ye for telling me. Good-morning."

Gwyn stared, and then looked at Joe.

For, instead of going at once, the man turned his back and drew upon his line, whose end—evidently weighted—was hanging down the shaft; but instead of continuing to draw it out, he let it run down again rapidly from a reel.

"Here, stop that," cried Gwyn. "What are you doing?"

The man turned upon them, scowling.

"Hullo!" he said; "aren't you gone? What are you waiting for?"

"To know what you're doing on our property."

"Your property!" said the man, scornfully. "Can't you see what I'm doing? Fishing."

"Fishing?" cried Joe, who felt staggered, and began wondering whether there might be any underground communication with the sea, through which some of the huge eels of the rocky cove might have made their way.

"Yes, fishing," growled the man. "Don't make that row, because I've got one at me. Be off!"

"Nonsense!" cried Gwyn, sharply. "There are no fish there."

"How do you know, youngster?" said the man. "Ever tried?"

"No," replied Gwyn; "but I do know that there are no fish in a hole like that."

"Ho! You're precious cunning. But never you mind, my young sharpshooter. You be off while your shoes are good."

"How dare you order me to go!" cried Gwyn, flushing. "I told you this was my father's property."

"No, you didn't," said the man, after giving a glance round. "You said it was yours. Consequently you must be a liar, for you tells two tales. Now be off, and don't bother me."

Joe looked inquiringly at Gwyn, and the silent question meant, "Hadn't we better go and fetch your father?" But Gwyn felt upon his mettle, and he cried angrily,—

"No, it's you who'll have to be off. You're on private grounds, and it's all nonsense about fishing. I know what you are about."

"Oh, do you?" said the man, sneeringly, as he looked sidewise at the lad, but went on busily all the same with his long line. "Well, what am I about, young clever shaver, if I'm not fishing?"

"You're trespassing, as I told you; and whoever you are, you've no right to be doing that."

"Anybody's got a right to fish."

"Yes, in the sea, but not on private grounds; so now be off at once."

"And suppose I say I won't," said the man, menacingly.

"But you won't now you're told. Be off, please, at once; we can't have you doing that."

"Why, you're never going to interfere with a stranger who's trying to ketch a few podnoddles," said the man, grinning.

"No, but I will with a stranger who has come spying and measuring that mine; so be off at once, and no more nonsense."

"Let's fetch the Colonel," whispered Joe.

"Yah! go and fetch your grandmother," snarled the man. "Look here, both of you, I didn't interfere with you; don't you come interfering with me, my lads, because I'm one of the sort who turns ugly when he's meddled with."

Gwyn hesitated for a few moments, and then stepped close up, clapped his hand on the man's shoulder, and pointed toward the wall.

"Come!" he cried; "that's the way, and don't you come here again."

The man turned upon him with a wild-beast-like snarl.

"Do you want me to pitch you down that hole?" he cried.

"No, and you daren't do it," cried Gwyn, whose temper rose at this. "Now, then, will you go?"

For answer the man swung round fiercely, bringing his right arm across Gwyn's chest and sending him staggering back for a yard or two.

"Come on, Gwyn, let's fetch the Colonel."

Gwyn's blood was up. He felt not the slightest inclination to run for help, but, big as the man was, he sprang forward with such energy that, in his surprise, the fellow gave way for the moment, and Gwyn seized the opportunity to make a snatch at the great reel he held, wrenched it from his hand, and threw it to Joe, who caught it as cleverly as if it had been a cricket ball.

"Run round the other side, Joe, and drag it out. Run off with it. Never mind me."

Joe obeyed on the instant, and, making for the other side, he dashed off up the side of the gully, dragging the line after him, and was some yards away before the man recovered from his surprise.

"Oh, that's your game, is it?" he cried savagely. "I'll 'tend to you directly, my lad," and he made to pass Gwyn, who tried to stop him, but received a thrust which sent him backward on the heath, while the man started to follow Joe.

But Gwyn's life on the rocky coast had made him as active as a cat, and as the fellow was passing he thrust out one leg, tripped him, and his adversary went down with a crash, while, before he could rise, Gwyn was upon him trying to hold him down.

The boy was strong for his years, and, gripping his adversary by the collar with both hands, he drove his knees into the man's ribs, and held on. For some moments the advantage of position was on his side, but it was like trying to ride a mad bull. For the man heaved and twisted, and Gwyn had hard work to maintain his place as long as he did. This was till the man gave a tremendous writhe, sending his rider over sidewise, and then dashing after Joe, who was running as hard as he could go, trailing the line after him.

Joe had a good start, and the advantage of being light and accustomed to make his way among the heath and stones; but he soon found that the weight at the end of the line kept on catching in the rough growth; and as he tore on, he saw that the fierce-looking fellow was in full pursuit. If he had dropped the line, he could easily have got away, but Gwyn had thrown that reel to him, and told him to run with it; and setting his teeth he ran on, jerking the weight free again and again, till all at once in one of the bounds it made after a heavy drag, it struck against a small post-like piece of granite which stuck up out of the ground, swung round and clasped it, as the bolas of a South-American Indian twine round the legs of a running animal, and the sudden jerk threw the boy down.

He was up again directly, and turned to run and untwist the line, but it was only to rush into the man's arms, and be thrown, when with a foot upon his chest the fellow began to try and tear the line from his hands.

But Joe's blood was up now, and he held on with all his might, turning himself over so as to get the reel beneath his chest. "Gwyn! Gwyn! Help!" he shouted.

"All right!" came from behind him, and his comrade, who had been in pursuit, pitched heavily on to the man's back, when a trio in struggling commenced, the boys holding on with stubborn determination, and their enemy beginning to strike out savagely with fist and elbow.

It was only a question of minutes, and then the boys would have been completely mastered. In fact, it had reached the pitch when the man had them both at his mercy and was kneeling between them, holding each by the throat, and forcing them back on the heather, when there was a loud whistle, the sound of a heavy blow, and the fellow uttered a savage yell as he sprang up and turned upon a fresh adversary. But *whish! crash!* the sounds were repeated, followed by a savage shout, and the man beat a retreat.

For Colonel Pendarve had come panting up at the sight of the struggle, and, bringing to bear his old cavalry officer's skill, delivered three slashing sabre cuts with his heavy cane, the first from the right, the second from the left shoulder, putting the enemy thoroughly to rout. For the man left the trophies of the fight in the boys' hands, made for the road, and disappeared over the wall.

Chapter Twelve
The Major has Strange Symptoms

"Whatever is the meaning of all this?" panted the Colonel, as Major Jollivet came up more slowly, looking weak and pale, but urged on by his excitement, to their side.

Gwyn blurted out something incoherent, for he was too much exhausted to speak plainly, and stared confusedly at his father.

"What?" cried the latter; "I can't understand you. Here, Joe Jollivet, what have you to say?"

"Blurr—blurr—bline!" babbled Joe.

"Splendid cuts, Pendarve. The grand old form," panted Major Jollivet. "You—you—you—sent—sent—the blood—der—der—dancing through—in—my veins."

"Yes, I flatter myself, he had them home," said the Colonel, smiling with satisfaction. "Regular old pursuing practice. Lucky for him it was not the steel. But what is it all about? Who is the fellow? Was he trying to rob you?"

"No—you, father," stuttered Gwyn. "C–caught him—mum—measuring the mine. Took away—his line."

"What? You boys did?"

Joe nodded, still too breathless to speak, and not feeling disposed to utter incoherent sounds again.

"Yes—father—Joe's got it."

"Ha! ha! ha!" laughed the Colonel. "It seems to me that you've both got it. Do you know that your nose is bleeding, sir?"

Gwyn gave that organ the aboriginal wipe, drawing the back of his hand across his face, looked at it and saw that it was covered with blood.

"No—didn't know, father," he said, taking out his handkerchief now. "Yes, it does bleed."

"Bleed, yes! Why, you have had a regular fight, then?"

"Running fight, seemingly," said the Major, grimly. "Tut—tut—tut! What a disreputable pair of young blackguards they look."

"Never mind," said the Colonel, suavely. "They did quite right to attack the enemy, even if he was in greater force. But I don't quite understand it, Gwyn. Did he say he was measuring the mine?"

"No, father; but we saw him doing it."

"But how could he know anything about it? The man was a stranger to me."

"I never saw him before, father?"

"Humph!" ejaculated the Colonel, turning to the Major, "I'm glad I brought you out to have a look. Pretty good proof that someone believes the old mine to be valuable, eh?"

"Yes, or a trick to make it seem so."

"Pooh! Impossible! It might be if someone wanted to sell the mine; but it is not for sale, and not likely to be. So you found him measuring—sounding, I suppose you mean?"

"Yes, sir," said Joe. "Here's the line, and it seems to have knots in it to show the depth."

For the boy was busily reeling up the loose cord, and walking back toward where the leaden weight had twined it round the piece of granite.

Joe set this free, and it proved to be a regular fishing sinker.

"But what did the fellow say to give you an excuse for attacking him as you did?"

"Said he was fishing, father," replied Gwyn; "but that was only his insolence."

"Might have been stupid enough to think he could fish there," said the Major.

"No; he meant to find out something about the place. It is being talked about the—"

"Yes, a good deal," said the Major, significantly. "Well, as you have brought me here to see it, you may as well show me the hole."

By this time the line was all wound up, and the Colonel led the way back to the mine, where, just as they reached the rough stone-wall, Gwyn ran forward and picked up a common memorandum book, which had fallen, to lie half-hidden amongst the heath.

A roughly pointed lead pencil was between the leaves, which opened to show that the owner had been making notes; but that he was not accustomed to the work was evident from the spelling, the first entry reading as follows:—

"Dounter warter 30 fathom."

The second,—

"Dounter botm 49 fathom an narf."

The third entry was,—

"Lot warter in thole as mus be pumpt out."

Then came a series of hieroglyphics which puzzled Gwyn; and, after a long trial, he handed the book to his father, who looked at it for some time, and then shook his head, as he passed it to the Major.

"I'm not scholar enough for this, Jollivet," he said. "Will you have a try?"

"No; I haven't brought my glasses. Here, Joe, what does this say?"

Joe, who had been all eagerness to begin, caught at the book, and tried to decipher the roughly-written words, but got on no better than the rest.

"Let me try again," cried Gwyn.

"No, no; I haven't done yet," said Joe; "but it looks all rubbish. No one can make this out."

"Spell it over," said his father, and the boy began.

"H-o-r-s-i-m-s-p-o-o-t-e-t-y-de-b-i-t-h-e-t-o-p-e."

"What does that spell? It's all one word."

"Read it again," said Gwyn, excitedly; and Joe repeated the letters.

"I know. Can't you see?" cried Gwyn, laughing.

Joe shook his head, and the two old officers looked nonplussed.

"What is it, Gwyn?" said his father. "Speak out, if you know."

"Ore seems pretty tidy by the top."

"No; nonsense!" cried the Colonel.

"It is, father," said Gwyn. "You read it over again, Joe."

The letters were once more repeated, and the Major exclaimed,—

"That's it, sure enough."

"Then there must be something in it," cried Colonel Pendarve. "The place is being talked about, and this fellow, who is evidently experienced in such matters, has been sent on to act as a spy. But how does he know about the depth?"

"Line's all knotted in six-feet lengths, sir," said Joe.

"Then I'm much obliged to him for taking the measures; but let's try for ourselves. You would like to see the depth tried, Jollivet."

"I? No, certainly not. Why should I?" cried the Major, testily.

"Because I presume you will take some interest in seeing me succeed if I go on with the venture."

"Oh! Well, yes, of course. Going to try now?"

"I am," replied the Colonel. "Will you boys let down the leaden sinker? Be careful, mind. Will you hold the reel, Joe? and then Gwyn can count the knots as the line runs down."

"All right, sir," cried Joe; and the Major took his place by the wall to look on while, after stationing themselves, Gwyn counted three knots, so as to get a little loose line, then took tight hold and pitched the lead from him, letting the stout cord run between his finger and thumb, and counting aloud as it went down, stopping at thirty by tightening his grasp on the line.

"He's wrong, father; thirty fathoms, and there's no water yet."

"Try a little lower, boy."

The line began to run again, and there was a faint plash before half of another fathom had been reeled off.

"Not so very far out," said the Major, as Gwyn went on counting and the reel turned steadily on, Joe turning one finger into a brake, and checking the spool so that it would not give out the line too fast.

On went the counting, the words coming mechanically from Gwyn's lips as he thought all the while about his terrible fall, and wondered how deep down he had gone beneath the black water.

"Forty-seven—forty-eight—forty-nine—fifty," counted Gwyn.

"Bottom?" cried the Colonel.

"No, father;·he must have let it catch on some ledge or piece that stuck out. Look, the lead's going steadily on. He said forty-nine: I've counted fifty, and there it goes—fifty-one—fifty-two," and to the surprise of all, the line ran out till another twenty fathoms had passed off the reel.

"Seventy fathoms, father. That's bottom," said Gwyn, hauling up and letting the line run again with the same result.

"Hah, yes," said the Colonel; "and that means so many thousand gallons more water to be pumped out. But try again. Jerk the lead, and let it shoot down. Perhaps you have not quite sounded the bottom yet."

Gwyn obeyed, and the result was again the same.

"Seventy fathoms. Well, that is not deep compared to some of the mines; but it proves that there must have been profitable work going on for the people, whoever they were, to have gone on cutting through the hard stone. A tremendous task, Jollivet."

"Hang it, yes, I suppose so. Well, there is nothing more to be done or seen, is there?"

"Not at present. Only to reel up the line our visitor has been so obliging as to lend us."

"Wind away, Joe," cried Gwyn; "and I'll let the string pass through my fingers, so as to wring off some of the water."

The boys began to gather in the sounding-cord, and the Major stood peering down over the wall into the black depths and poking at a loose stone on the top of the wall with his cane.

"Seems rather childish," he said suddenly; "but should you mind, Pendarve, if I dislodged this stone and let it fall down the shaft?"

"Mind? Certainly not. Go on. Here, shall I do it?"

"No. I should prefer doing it myself," said the Major; and standing his cane against the wall, he took hold of the stone and stood it upon the edge.

"Stop!" cried the Colonel as he noted that the under part of the stone glistened, as granite will.

"What's the matter?"

"That piece of stone," said the Colonel, excitedly. "Why, man, look; it is rich in tin ore."

"That blackish-purple glittering stuff?"

"Yes; those are tin grains. But there, it does not matter. Throw it in. We can have it sent up again when the mine is pumped out. In with it."

The Major raised the stone with both hands face high and threw it from him, while all watched him, and then stood waiting for the heavy hollow-sounding splash which followed, with the lapping of the water against the sides.

"It is strange," said the Major, "what a peculiar fascination a place like this exercises over me, Pendarve. I feel just as if I could leap down into—"

As he spoke, he leaned over the low wall as if drawn toward the place, and his son turned ghastly white and uttered a faint cry.

Chapter Thirteen
The Compact Sealed

"No, no, my boy, don't be alarmed," said the Major, turning to smile at his son. "It is only that I am a little nervous and impressionable from my illness. But it is strange how a depth attracts, and how necessary it is for boys to be careful and master themselves when tempted to do things that are risky. Upon my word, I marvel at the daring of you fellows in running such a risk as you did the other day."

"It was not Joe, sir," interposed Gwyn. "I went down."

"But I'll be bound to say my boy was ready to offer."

The pair of actors in the trouble glanced at each other, and Joe's cheeks grew red again.

"Take my advice," said the Major, "as boy or man never do anything risky unless it is for some good reason. One has no right to go into danger unless it is as an act of duty."

"Quite right," said the Colonel; "that's what I tell Gwyn; but boys have such terribly short memories. There, we may as well go back; but you had better wash your face at the first pool, Gwyn. You look horrible. I can't have you go home in that condition."

"No; he would frighten Mrs Pendarve out of her senses," said the Major. "Well, I've seen the wonderful mine, and it looks just like what it is: a big square hole, with plenty of room to throw down money enough to ruin the Queen. But you were right, Pendarve: the fresh air and the exertion have done me good. I must go back, though, now; the fever makes me weak."

That evening the Colonel had a long talk with his son, for he had come to the conclusion that they had not heard the end of the man's visit to the mine.

"It seems to me, Gwyn," he said, "that something must have been known about the place and caused this amateurish kind of inspection."

"I've been thinking so, too, father," said Gwyn. "Sam Hardock must have been talking about it to different people, and praised it so that someone wants to begin mining."

They had come to the right conclusion, for the very next day a dog-cart was driven to the Cove, stopped at the Colonel's gate, and a little fussy-looking gentleman, with sharp eyes, a snub nose, and grey hair, which seemed to have a habit of standing out in pointed tufts, came up to the door, knocked, and sent in his card.

"Mr Lester Dix, solicitor, Plymouth," said the Colonel, reading the card, as he and Gwyn were busy over a work on military manoeuvres. "I don't know any Mr Dix. Show him in."

"Shall I go, father?"

"No, I think not, my boy. I don't suppose it is anything important, unless it is someone come to claim damages for the assault you committed on the man at the mine, and for confiscating the reel and line."

"Oh, it would not be that, would it, father?" cried Gwyn, anxiously. "And besides—"

"He began it, eh? Well, we shall see. You had better stay."

The visitor was shown it, and entered with so smiling a countenance that at first Gwyn felt better; but a suspicion came over him directly after that the smile might mean a masking of the real attack.

For Gwyn's education was growing decidedly military, his father devoting a great deal of time to reading works on fortification and army matters.

But he was soon set at rest, for, after a few preliminary words of apology for the call, with some remarks on the fineness of the morning, and the pleasant drive over from the station, the visitor plunged at once into the object of his visit.

"The fact is, Colonel Pendarve, my professional business lies a great deal with mining companies, and one of those for whom I act have been for some time looking out for a spot here on the west coast, where they could exploit, so to speak, the land, and try with the newer machinery some of the old neglected workings. Now, I am instructed that you have on your estate one of these disused mines, and my company, for whom I act, are willing to run the risk of trying if anything can be made of it with the modern appliances. You see I am quite frank with you, sir. In other words, they are desirous of becoming the purchasers of your little estate here at a good advance upon the sum for which you purchased it."

"Indeed?" said the Colonel, smiling.

"Yes, sir; and I will not conceal from you the fact that they will be quite willing to agree to what would really be a most advantageous thing for you."

"Then the old mine must be very valuable," said Gwyn, excitedly.

"Eh?" ejaculated the visitor, turning his eyes sharply upon the boy. "Oh dear me, no, my dear young friend. That does not follow. It might turn out to be, of course; but mining is a terribly speculative, risky business, and the probabilities are that this mine—let me see, Ydoll, I think, is the old name, and eh, young gentleman, not badly named? Been lying idle for a very long time, I suppose? Eh? You'll excuse the joke. We may lose very heavily in this one, while we gain on others. But, of course, Colonel Pendarve, that is not my affair. My instructions, to be brief, are to ascertain whether you will sell, and, if you will take a reasonable price, to close with you at once."

"I wish father would ask him how he knows about the mine," thought Gwyn.

"May I ask how you became aware of the existence of this place, sir?" asked the Colonel.

"Maps and plans, sir. I have pretty well every property marked out all through the country; picturesque and geological features all set down. Quite a study, young gentleman. You have a nice place here Colonel Pendarve, but you must find it bleak, and I think I may venture to say this is an opportunity for parting with it most profitably."

"I suppose so, sir," said the Colonel, "for your clients would not be, I presume, particular about a few hundreds to obtain possession?"

"Well," replied the lawyer, smiling, "without committing myself, I think I may say that your wishes within reason would be met, sir, upon pecuniary points."

"Well that sounds satisfactory," said the Colonel, "but I have grown attached to the place, and so has my son."

"Oh, yes, father," said Gwyn, eagerly. "I don't want to go."

"Plenty of more beautiful places to be had, my dear sir," said the lawyer, "by the man who has money."

"I have improved the house, too, a great deal lately."

"So I should suppose, sir," said the lawyer; "but we should consider all that in the purchase money."

"And I have made my little garden one of the most productive in the county."

"All of which we will take into consideration, my dear sir. Now, not to take up your time, what do you say? I have a plan in my pocket of the estate, and I am quite prepared to come to terms at once."

"But is not this very sudden?" said the Colonel, smiling.

"Well, perhaps so, my dear sir; but I always advise the companies who intrust me with their affairs to be business-like and prompt. Let us have none of the law's delays, my dear sir, I say. It means waste of time; and as time is money, it is a waste of hard cash. Now, sir, you, as a military man, know the value of decision."

"I hope so," said the Colonel, who looked amused.

"Well, in plain English, sir, will you sell?"

"In plain English, Mr Dix," said the Colonel, promptly, "'No.'"

"Take time, my dear sir, take time," said the lawyer. "Don't, let me implore you, throw away a good chance. Name your terms."

"I have no terms to propose, sir. I like my house here, and I shall not part with it at any price.—Yes, Dolly? What is it?"

For the maid had tapped and entered, looking very round-eyed and surprised.

"Another gentleman to see you, sir."

"Indeed? You will not mind, Mr Dix?"

"Oh, by no means, my dear sir. But one moment, please. Why not close with my proposal? Come, my dear sir, to be plain, I will take the place at your own terms."

"You will not take the place at any terms, sir," said the Colonel, decisively. "Dolly, show the other gentleman in. But did he give you his card?"

"No, sir; said he'd like to speak to you himself."

"Show him in, then."

"Hah!" ejaculated the lawyer; "but you will alter your mind, Colonel Pendarve?"

"I hope not."

"But if you do, you will give me the first offer?"

"I will make no promises, sir," replied the Colonel.

At that moment a reddish-haired, sour-looking man was shown in, and he nodded shortly to the lawyer.

"You here?" he said.

"Yes, my dear Brownson, I am here. Business, my dear sir, business. You really do not mean to say that you have come on the same mission as I."

"I beg pardon, Colonel Pendarve," said the fresh visitor. "I was not aware that Mr Dix here proposed visiting you. Can I have the pleasure of a few words on business of great importance?"

"Certainly," said the Colonel, who now looked very much amused; "but may I ask if it is concerning the purchase of the mine?"

"To be frank, sir, yes, it is. On the behalf of a client, but—but you don't mean that I am too late?"

There was a look of misery in the newcomer's face that was comical, and before the Colonel could speak, he went on:—

"Don't be rash, sir, pray don't be rash. You cannot have closed yet, and I am here prepared, not merely to negotiate, but to come to the most advantageous terms for you."

Mr Dix chuckled, rubbed his hands, and gave the newcomer a look which seemed to sting him to the core.

"I need hardly say, gentlemen," said the Colonel, "that this visit has taken me quite by surprise. I did not expect these sudden offers from what seem to me to be rival companies."

"Hardly rival companies, sir; but I must say that Mr Dix has taken a very unfair advantage of me, after we had agreed to a truce."

"Yes, one which I knew you would break, Brownson," said Dix; "and so I came on first. Now, Colonel Pendarve you will come to terms with me."

"No, sir," said the Colonel, fiercely, "nor with your friend here. My mind is quite made up. I do not know to which party the visit of a spy is due, but you may take these words as final; I shall certainly not sell this little estate to either of you, nor," he added, after a pause, "to anyone else. What, another?" he cried, as Dolly re-appeared at the door.

"No, sir, it's only Major Jollivet, sir. But he says, if you're engaged, he'll call again."

"Show him in," cried the Colonel. "Ah, there he goes. Call him back, Gwyn."

The boy flew to the window, and, in answer to his call, the Major came back, and entered.

"Oh, I didn't wish to interrupt you, Pendarve, but I wanted to have a few words with you on business. Eh? Yes. Very much better. I shall be all right for a few months now."

"Let me introduce you," said the Colonel. "This is Mr Dix, solicitor, of Plymouth, and Mr Brownson, also a solicitor, I presume, of the same town. My old friend and brother officer, Major Jollivet."

Bows were exchanged, and the visitors scowled at each other.

"Jollivet, these two gentlemen, who represent different companies as clients, have come over to make me a very advantageous offer for this little estate."

"Indeed!" said the Major, starting. "What for?"

"They wish to reopen the mine, and are ready to give me my own price."

"Certainly," said Mr Dix.

"Yes, certainly," said Mr Brownson, "with, gentlemen, the addition of a royalty on our part on all the metal smelted. Come, Dix, that's trumps."

"Yes, sir, but this is the ace. Colonel Pendarve, I will guarantee you double the royalty Mr Brownson offers," said Dix.

"Come, that's business, gentlemen," said the Colonel, smiling, while Gwyn's face was scarlet with excitement. "Now, Jollivet, as the man whom I always consult on business matters, and irrespective of anything I may have said to these gentlemen, what would you advise me to do?"

"Ah," exclaimed Mr Dix, rubbing his hands, "what would you advise him to do, General?"

"Major, sir, Major," said the old officer, shortly.

"Yes, Major Jollivet," said Mr Brownson, "what would you advise him to do? Surely to take our fair and liberal offer. We are very old established, and shall carry that old mine to a triumphant success. What would you advise?"

"Oh, Major Jollivet, don't advise him to sell," whispered Gwyn.

"Silence, sir! How dah you interfere!" cried the Major. "Pendarve, if this boy speaks again, send him away."

"Oh, he will not hurt," said the Colonel. "Now, what do you say?"

"Ahem!" coughed the Major, and then he took out an India bandanna silk handkerchief, and blew his nose with a blast like that of a trumpet heralding a charge. "I say, gentlemen, that my old friend, Colonel Pendarve, and I, are very much obliged to you for your offer, which is one that we refuse without the smallest hesitation."

"I will increase my offer, gentlemen; I did not know that Colonel Pendarve had a partner," said Mr Dix.

"I will double mine, gentlemen," cried Brownson.

"Gwyn," said the Colonel. "Never mind the licence; you had better jump on the table and play auctioneer."

"By all means," cried Dix, "and knock it down to the highest bidder."

"No!" roared the Major. "Keep your place, boy. Out of the question. The mine is not for sale. Colonel Pendarve and I are going to carry it on ourselves."

"What!" cried the two lawyers in a breath.

"Jollivet and Pendarve of the Ydoll Mine," cried the Colonel, excitedly.

"That's it, the other way on," said the Major. "Your own proposal; do you hold to it? I came to ask you if you would, before I knew these people were here. Now, then, what do you say?"

"Jollivet and Pendarve."

"Pendarve and Jollivet, or I won't play," cried the Major.

"As you wish," said the Colonel, "There's my hand and seal."

"And mine," cried the Major, seizing the hand extended to him.

"Don't, don't say that, gentlemen," cried Dix, wildly, "It may mean ruin to you both."

"And destruction," cried Brownson.

"Very well," said the Major. "We're old soldiers, we'll face all as we've often faced death. Pen, old man, for the sake of the boys."

"For the sake of the boys," cried the Colonel.

And the next minute the two mining companies' agents were bowed out, while Gwyn leaped on a chair to shout "hurrah!" just as the French window was darkened, and a voice cried,—

"Is father here?"

Joe was not long before he heard the news.

Chapter Fourteen
A Suspicion of Evil

The result of the morning's work was that Sam Hardock received a message from the Colonel, delivered by Gwyn, and the man rubbed his hands gleefully.

"I thought he couldn't refuse such a chance," cried Hardock. "It's a big fortune for him."

"I hope so," said Gwyn. "But how came those people at Plymouth to hear about it?"

"I dunno, sir. But they got hold of the gashly news somehow."

"You did not send them word, of course?"

"Me? Not I, sir."

"But how could that man have heard of it, and come over to sound the mine and examine the place?"

"What man?" cried Hardock, anxiously.

Gwyn explained, and, in answer to questions, the lad gave a pretty good description of his awkward adversary.

Hardock struck his fist upon the table.

"That's the chap! I often wondered who he was. Been hanging about here these two months past."

"Then you did tell him."

"Me, Master Gwyn? Not a bit of it. I'm too close."

"Then you must have talked about it to other people, and he picked up what you said. But there, come along. He will not get it now."

"He must have been sent by someone out Plymouth way, that's for certain, sir. But come along. I want to hear what the Colonel has to say."

"And the Major, too."

"Why, he's not in it, sir, is he?"

"Of course. He will be my father's partner."

Hardock whistled, and was very silent all the way up to the house by Ydoll Cove.

He was talkative enough, though, when he came away, but in a very mysterious fashion.

"It's all right, Mr Gwyn," he whispered. "Going to be a very big thing. I mustn't talk about it; but you're like one of us, and I may tell you. I'm off to Truro this afternoon to talk to an old friend of mine—engineer, and a very big man on working mines. He'll advise on the best kind of pump to have."

The engineer came, examined the shaft, gave his opinions, and in a week's time masons were at work setting up an engine-house, ready for the steam machinery that was to come round by ship from Liverpool; and in a short time the wild slope at the top of the great cliffs was invaded by quite a colony of workmen. The masons' hammers were constantly chipping as they laboriously went on building and raising a platform above the mouth of the shaft, while, whenever a few rich pieces of ore, after possibly lying there many hundred years, were turned up, they were solemnly conveyed to the two old officers for examination.

Here the two boys were soon in their element, and began working away with a great deal of enthusiasm in a small, corrugated iron shed which had been erected in the garden, and dignified by the name of laboratory. For, to the boys' great delight, a model furnace had been made, with bellows, and a supply of charcoal was always ready. There was a great cast-iron mortar fitted on a concrete stand, crucibles of various sizes, and the place looked quite ship-shape.

Both the old officers worked hard at assaying the ore brought from about the mouth of the pit, dug no one knew when, and though they spent a good deal of time, they were very soon superseded by Gwyn and Joe. Hardock gave them a little instruction; everything about the work was interesting and fresh; and in a few weeks they were able to roughly declare how much pure metal could be obtained from a ton of the quartz which they broke up in the great mortar, powdering, and washing and drying, and then smelting in one of the plumbago crucibles of the laboratory.

"There's no telling yet what we may find in that mine, Joe," said Gwyn; "only we don't know enough chemistry to find out."

"It's metallurgy, father says," said Joe, correcting him.

"Never mind; it's chemistry all the same; and we must read more about it, and try experiments. Why, we might get gold and silver."

"What, out of a tin mine?" said Joe, derisively.

"Well, why not? I don't know about the gold, but we may, perhaps. Sam Hardock said there were some specks in one bit of quartz he brought up."

"But we shouldn't want specks; we should want lumps."

"There's sure to be silver."

"Why?" said Joe.

"Because there's lead, and I was reading with father about how much silver you can get by purifying the lead. It's going to be a wonderful business."

"Hope so," said Joe; "but they're a precious long while getting the machinery together, and my father says the cost is awful."

"Can't get a great pump in a mine ready to work like you can one in a back kitchen," said Gwyn. "See what an awkward job it is fitting the platforms for the tubing. I think they're doing wonders, seeing what a lot there is to get ready. Sam says, though, that he believes they'll begin pumping next month."

But next month came round, and they did not begin pumping, for the simple reason that the machinery was not ready. Still it was in fair progress, and an arrangement was fixed so that, when the beam began to rise and fall, the water would be sent gushing into the adit by which Gwyn had made his escape on that adventurous day; and as this little gully had a gentle slope towards the sea, the water would be easily got rid of by its own natural flow.

The boys were at the mouth of the shaft on one particular day, and as the news had been spread that the first steps for drying the mine were to be taken, half the people from the little village had sauntered up, many of them being fisherfolk, and plenty of solemn conversation went on, more than one weather-beaten old sage giving it as his opinion that no good would come of it, for there was something wicked and queer about this old mine, and they all opined that it ought not to have been touched.

Gwyn noticed the head-shakings, and nudged Joe.

"Talking about the goblins in the mine," he answered. "I say, if there are any, they'll come rushing up the big tube like the tadpoles did in the garden pump when it was first made."

Just then Joe caught hold of his companion's arm, and pinched it.

"Hullo!" cried Gwyn.

"Hush! don't talk—don't look till I tell you which way. I've just seen him."

"Seen whom?" said Gwyn, wonderingly.

"That big chap who was measuring the pit. He's over yonder with about a dozen more men. What does it mean?"

"Mischief," said Gwyn, huskily. "Quick! Let's go and warn my father."

"What about? He may only have come up to see."

"I don't know," said Gwyn, excitedly. "Someone who wanted to get the mine must have sent them up first of all, and, as they couldn't get it, I'm afraid they've turned spiteful, and may try to do us harm. What would they do, do you think?"

"Try and damage the machinery, perhaps," said Joe.

"Yes, that's it. We must warn father, and keep an eye on those fellows, or there's no knowing what they may do. Where are they now?"

"Can't see them," said Joe, after a glance round. "They must have gone."

"Yes, but where? Not to the engine-house, surely. Why, they might upset the whole thing, and do no end of mischief if they liked. Come on, and let's make sure that they are not there, and then tell Sam Hardock to keep watch."

Joe had another look round the now thoroughly transformed place, with its engine-house, sheds, and scaffold and wheel over the built-up shaft, but he saw nothing, and said so. Still Gwyn was not satisfied, for a peculiar feeling of dread oppressed him.

"It isn't easy to see for the people and the buildings— Ah, there's father; let's go and tell him what we think."

It was quite time: for the hero of the measuring and another sour-looking fellow were making their way round to where the two boilers were beginning to be charged with steam, and what was worse for all concerned, no one paid any heed to their movements, which were furtive and strange, suggesting that they had not come for the purpose of doing good, while their opportunities for doing a serious ill were ample; but Gwyn had just grasped that fact.

Chapter Fifteen
In the Engine-House

The boys hardly spoke as they made their way towards the engine-house, from whence came a loud hissing noise, and on hearing this, Joe exclaimed excitedly,—

"He's there."

For answer Gwyn ran to the door, and entered, hardly knowing what he was about to do, but with the feeling that this man was a natural enemy, whom it was his duty to attack; and, like a true comrade, Joe followed closely at his heels.

The hissing noise increased as they approached the door; and, fully alive as he was to the danger of meddling with steam, Gwyn's heart began to beat a little faster, for he felt that they were too late; that the mischief had been done, the steam was escaping, and that if they entered the house, it might be at the expense of a terrible scalding.

All else was silent, and as they reached the doorway of the place, the shrill, shrieking noise was piercing, and made their words difficult to hear.

"He has broken something, or turned on the steam, so that it may escape, Joe," said Gwyn. "Shall we go in and try to put it right?"

"If we must. But where's the engine-driver?—where's the stoker?"

Gwyn looked round, to see that the people were crowding about the shaft where the great pump was to be set in motion and where work-people were busy still trying to get it ready. Hammers were clinking, spanners and screw wrenches rattling on nuts, and the work in progress was being patiently watched, the engine-house and boilers being for the time unnoticed.

"Perhaps he's here, after all," said Gwyn at last, with a gasp. "Shall we go in?"

Joe hesitated while you might have counted ten, and he looked despairingly round, as if in the hope of seeing something that would check him and render the venture unnecessary, for there was the sound as of a thousand snakes hissing wildly, and to one unused to the behaviour of engine boilers all this seemed preliminary to a terrible explosion, with possible death for those who went inside.

"Yes, we must go in," said the boy at last; and as Gwyn made one effort to summon his courage, and dashed through the door, he followed.

The noise was now almost deafening, and at a glance they saw that the steam was escaping furiously from the two long boilers at the end farthest from where they stood, but the new bright engine, with its cylinders, pistons, rods, cranks, driving-wheel, governor, and eccentric, seemed to be perfectly safe.

"He has been in and driven a pickaxe into each of the boilers," cried Joe. "They'll blow up together. Shall we run?"

The boy's words were almost drowned by the fierce hissing, which was now mingled with a deep bass formed by a loud humming, throbbing sound such as might be made by a Brobdingnagian tea-kettle, just upon ready for use. Then came loud cracking and spitting sounds, and the dull roar of big fires.

But the man of whom they were in search was invisible, and Gwyn walked quickly round to the other side of the engine and looked sharply down that side of the long building.

Joe followed.

It was darker here, and the steam which filled the open roof, and was passing out of a louvre, hung lower, so that the far end was seen through a mist. "Not here," said Gwyn. "Think we could stop the steam escaping?"

"Don't know," shouted back Joe. "Sha'n't we be scalded to death?"

"Let's go and try."

That was enough for Joe, who felt as if he would have given anything for the power to rush out, but seemed held there by his companion's example.

"Go on, then," he panted out; and Gwyn had taken a couple of steps into the hot vapour, his heart throbbing violently with the great dread of ignorance, when, beyond the mist which was looking light in front of the door at the far end, there was a heavy, quick step. They could see a dark, shadowy figure, which looked of gigantic proportions through the hanging steam, and heard the crackling and crushing of coal under its feet, as it descended the stone steps into the stoke hole. This was followed by the rattling of an iron bar, quickly used, the rattle and clang of an iron door being thrown open, when a sudden glare of brilliant light turned the cloud of steam from grey to ruddy gold.

"Hullo! there," shouted a voice, evidently from the door by which the boys had entered; and in an instant there was a rush of feet, the crackling of the coal on the granite steps, and they saw the dark shadow once more, as it darted out through the far door.

At the same instant there were heavy steps going along on the other side of the boilers to the stoke hole, a loud exclamation heard above the hissing and shrieking of the steam. Then came the crackling of the coal dust, the rattle of an iron implement, the furnace was closed with a clang, and the steam between the boys and the far door changed back to grey once more.

The next instant, as they went on, they were face to face with the big bluff engine-driver, who shouted at them.

"Oh! it's you two young gents is it? Well, all I've got to say is that if you're to come here meddling and playing your larks, someone else may tend the bylers, for I won't."

"We haven't done anything," cried Gwyn, hotly.

"What!" roared the man, "when I come and ketched you fooling about with that furnace door! Do you know that you might have made the fire rage away if you got stoking hard, and perhaps blow up the whole place. There's too much pressure on now."

"Will you let me speak!" cried Gwyn angrily. "We came in because something was wrong, and no one near to see to the steam."

"Yes, there now; I only just went to that clumsy lot at the pump, to see if they meant to start it to-day, because, if they didn't soon, I should have to damp down. Twelve o'clock, they said, and as I told Sam Hardock, there was I ready for them, but I s'pose he means twelve o'clock to-morrow. And when I comes back, I find you young gents playing the fool. D'yer want a big burst?"

"No," cried Gwyn, who had striven twice to stop the indignant flow of words. "I tell you we came in because something was wrong—to try and stop—"

"Wrong? Yes, you meddling with the furnace."

"We did not, I tell you."

"What? Well, if you young gents can't tell a good slumper, I'm a Dutchman. Why, I heard you at the furnace door, and as soon as I shouted, I hears you both roosh up the steps. Then I came round, and here you are. Better say you didn't leave the door open."

"I do say so," shouted Gwyn, who had hard work to make himself heard above the steam.

"Oh, all right, then. You're the governors' sons. Burst the bylers if you like; they aren't mine."

"Will you listen?" cried Gwyn.

"Why, I am a-listening, aren't I?" cried the man. "All right, it warn't you, then, and it must ha' been one o' they big Cornish tom-cats."

"Don't talk like a donkey," cried Gwyn, who had lost his temper now. "I tell you we came in because something was wrong."

"Very," said the man.

"The steam was hissing horribly, as you hear it now. Aren't you going to try and stop it?"

"Stop it?" said the man. "What for? Want me to blow the place up?"

"Of course not; but I want you to stop up those holes."

"You don't know what you're talking about, squire, or else it's to throw me off the scent."

"I know the steam's escaping horribly."

"Yes; all waste, through them not finishing that pump."

"Then try and stop it."

"Stop it? Don't I tell you there's too much pressure on as it is?"

"It's the safety valves open, Ydoll," said Joe, with his lips to his companion's ear.

"Oh!" ejaculated Gwyn, as he grasped the truth. "I thought something was wrong."

"I know something was wrong, and without thinking, young squire," said the man. "But you take my advice, and don't you meddle with anything here again."

"I have told you we did not touch anything; but I suppose it's no use to talk to you," said Gwyn, warmly.

"No, sir, not a bit," replied the man, gruffly; "and I shall speak to the governors about you two coming meddling."

"And I shall speak to my father about your not being here taking care of the engines," said Gwyn, as a parting shot. "If you had been at your duty, no one would have had a chance to meddle. So we will see what he says."

Chapter Sixteen
An Attack of Heroes

"That was a topper for him, Ydoll," said Joe, as they stood outside. "Phew! what a hot, stuffy place it is!"

"We were the first there, Joe," said Gwyn, who had not heard his companion's words. "But what was he going to do?"

"Who going to do—that chap?"

"Yes. I'm sure he meant mischief of some kind. I'll speak to father. He won't interfere with the people coming to-day, because it's like a sight, this beginning: but afterwards he'll have to give orders for no one but the work-people to be about."

"Hullo, what's this?" cried Joe.

For a shout arose, and a man stood forward from the crowd, making signals.

"I know: they want the steam turned on."

Gwyn stepped back to the mouth of the temporary engine-house, told the driver, and he connected a band with the shaft; this started another long band, and the power was communicated to the pump, with the result that a huge wheel began to turn, a massive rod was set in motion, and a burst of cheers arose; for, with a steady, heavy, clanking sound, the first gallons of water were raised, to fall gushing into the cistern-like box, and then begin to flow steadily along the adit; the boys, after a glance or two down the deep shaft, now one intricacy of upright ladder and platform, hurrying off to where a series of ladders had been affixed to the face of the cliff, down which they went, to reach a strongly-built platform at the mouth of the adit.

It was rather different from the spot on which Gwyn had knelt a few months before, waiting for help to come and rescue him from his perilous position, and he thought of it, as he descended the carefully-secured ladders, connected with the rock face by means of strong iron stanchions.

"I say, Joe," he cried, as they descended, "better than hanging at the end of a rope. Why, it's safe as safe."

"So long as you don't let go," was the reply from above him.

"Well, don't you let go, or you'll be knocking me off. I say, I wonder what the birds think of it all."

"Don't seem to mind it much," replied Joe. "But I suppose we sha'n't leave these ladders here when the mine-shaft is all right."

"No, because we shall go along the adit, that way. Father says Sam Hardock wants the gallery widened a little, so that a tramway can be laid down, and then he'll run trucks along it, and tilt all the rubbish into the sea."

"Yes, young gentlemen, that's the way," said a voice below them. "So you're coming down to have a look?"

"I say, Sam, you startled me," cried Gwyn. "Well, how does the pump work?"

"Splendidly, sir; here's a regular stream of water coming along, and running into the sea like a cascade, as they call it. Only ten more steps, sir. That's it! Mind how you come there. None too much room. We must have a strong rail all round here, or there'll be some accident. Two more steps, Mr Joe. That's the way! Now then, sir, don't this look business-like?"

The boys were standing now on the platform, whose struts were sloping to the rock below, and through an opening between them and the mouth of the adit the water came running out, bright and clear, to plunge down the face of the cliff in a volume, which promised well for draining the mine.

"Why, it won't take long to empty the place at this rate," cried Joe, as he knelt upon the platform and gazed down at the falling water, which dropped sheer for about twenty feet, then struck the rock, glanced off, and fell the rest of the way in a broken sheet of foam, which rapidly changed into a heavy rain.

"No, sir, it won't take very long," said Hardock. "A few weeks, I suppose; because, as it lowers, we shall have to put down fresh machinery to reach it, and so on, right to the sumph at the bottom."

"Oh, not a few weeks," said Gwyn, in a tone of doubt. "Well, say months, then, sir. Nobody can tell. If you gave me a plan of the mine on paper, with the number and size of the galleries, I could tell you pretty exactly; but, of course, we don't know. There may be miles of workings at different levels; and, on the other hand, there may be not—only the shaft, and that we can soon master."

"But suppose that there's a hole into it from the sea," said Joe, looking up from where he knelt, with a droll look of inquiry in his eyes.

"Why, then we shall want more pumps, and a fresh place to put the water in," cried Gwyn, laughing. "Rather too big a job for you, that, Sam Hardock."

"Oh, I don't know, sir. We might p'r'aps find out where the gashly hole was, and put a big cork in it. But let's try first and see. What do you say to coming through to the shaft, and having a look whether the water's beginning to lower?"

"But we shall get out feet so wet."

"Bah! what's a drop o' water, my lad, when there's a big bit o' business on? Have off your shoes and stockings, then. I've got a light."

"Will you come, Joe?"

"Of course, if you're going," said the boy, sturdily, as if it were a matter beyond question. "But you haven't told Sam about the engine-house."

"What about it?" said the man, anxiously. "What!" he continued, on hearing what they had noticed. "That's bad, my lads, that's bad, and they mean mischief. But I don't see what harm he could have done to the fire, only burnt himself—and sarve him right. Wanted to see, perhaps, how our bylers was set. I know that chap, though—met him more than once, when I've been here and there in different towns, talking to folk of a night over a pipe—when I was looking for work, you know. One of those chaps, he seemed to be, as is always hanging about with both ears wide open to see what they can ketch. I fancy he had something to do with the two gents as came over to buy the mine. I aren't sure, but I think that's it."

"I feel quite sure," said Gwyn, emphatically. "Very well, then, sir; what we've got to do is to keep him off our premises, so that he don't get picking up our notions of working the old mine. He's after something, or he wouldn't be here to-day. Regular old mining hand, he is; and I daresay he was squinting over our machinery, and he wants to see the pumping come to naught. Just please him. But look at this; isn't it fine?"

He pointed to the steady stream of clear water rushing toward them, and falling downward, glittering in the sunshine. "Ready to go in with me?"

For answer the two boys took off their boots and socks, and stood them in a niche in the rock, while Hardock passed in through the mouth of the adit; and directly after he had disappeared in the darkness, he re-appeared in the midst of a glow of light produced by a lanthorn he had placed behind a piece of rock.

"Come on, my lads," he cried, and the two boys stepped in, with the cold water gurgling about their feet, and stooping to avoid striking their heads against the roof of the low gallery.

"One o' the first things I mean to have done is to set the men to cut a gully along here for the water to run in, for I daresay we shall always have to keep the pump going. Then the water can keep to itself, and we shall have a dry place for the trucks to run along."

"But this place won't be used much," said Gwyn, as he followed the man, and kept on thinking about his strange feelings, as he crept along there in the darkness toward the light, after his terrible fall.

"I don't know so much about that, my lad. Don't you see, it will be splendid for getting rid of our rubbish? The trucks can be tilted, and away it will go; but what's to prevent us from loading ships with ore out below there in fine weather? But we shall see."

It was a strange experience to pass out of the brilliant sunshine into the black, cold tunnel through the rock, with the water bubbling about their feet, and a creepy, gurgling whispering sound coming toward them in company with a heavy dull clanking, as the huge pump worked steadily on. Try how they would to be firm, and forcing themselves to fall back upon the knowledge of what was taking place, there was still the feeling that this little stream of water was only the advance guard of a deluge, and that at any moment it might increase to a rushing flood, which would sweep them away, dashing them out headlong from the mouth of the gallery to fall into the sea.

But there in front was the black outline of Hardock's stooping figure, with the lanthorn held before him, and making the water flash and sparkle, while from time to time the man held up the lanthorn, and pointed to a glittering appearance in the roof, or on the walls.

"Ore," he said, with a chuckle. "I didn't come to your father, Master Gwyn, with empty hands, did I? Well, I'm glad he woke up to what it's all worth. Here we are."

He stopped short, for they had come to the shaft, and his light showed up the strong beams and wet iron ties which held the machinery in place. There were a couple of men here, too, with lanthorns hanging from what seemed to be a cross-beam. On their right, was a wet-looking ladder, whose rounds glistened, and this ran up into darkness, where a great beam had been fixed, with a square hole where the top of the ladder rested, the light from above being almost entirely cut off.

The men said something to Hardock, but their words were almost inaudible in the rattle and clank of the great pump, and the wash and rush of the water as it was drawn into a huge trough, and rushed from it into the adit.

Hardock gave them a nod in reply, and then signed to the boys as he swung his lanthorn.

"Come and look here," he shouted; and, with their bare feet slipping on the wet planks that were just loosely laid across the beams fitted into the old holes, cut no one knew when, in the sides of the shaft, they went down to where Hardock dropped on his knees and held the lanthorn through an opening, so that the light was reflected from the water, whose level was about a foot below where they now stood.

"See that?" he shouted, so as to make his voice heard.

"What, the water?" cried Gwyn. "Yes."

"No, no; my mark that I made in the wall with a pick?"

"Oh, yes; the granite looks quite white," said Gwyn, as he looked at the roughly-cut notch some six inches long.

"How far is the water below it?" cried Hardock.

"About seven inches, eh, Joe?"

"Nearly eight."

"Then you may go up and tell your father the good news. He'll like to hear it from you. Tell him that we've lowered the water seven inches since the pump started, and if nothing goes wrong, we shall soon be making a stage lower down."

"But what should go wrong?" cried Joe, who looked full of excitement.

"A hundred things, my lad. Machinery's a ticklish thing, and as for a mine, you never know what's going to happen from one hour to another. Go on, up with you both, my lads; it's news they'll be glad to hear, and you ought to be proud to take it."

"We are," cried Gwyn, heartily. "It's splendid, Sam. You have done well."

"Tidy, my lad, tidy. Will you go up the ladder here?"

"No," said Gwyn, "we've left our shoes and stockings outside."

"Very well; go that way, then."

"Yes," said Joe, "it's better than going up the shaft; the ladders look so wet, and the water drops upon you. I saw it dripping yesterday. Come on."

He stepped into the adit, and Gwyn followed.

"Don't want a light, I s'pose?" said Hardock.

"Oh, no; we shall see the sunshine directly," said Gwyn; and the two boys retraced their wet steps, soon caught sight of the light shining in, and made their way out to the platform, where they sat down in the sunshine to wipe their feet with their handkerchiefs, and then put on socks and boots, each giving his feet a stamp as he rose erect.

"Isn't the water cold! My feet are like ice," said Joe.

"They'll soon get warm climbing up these ladders," said Gwyn. "But steady! Don't jump about; this platform doesn't seem any too safe. I'll ask father to have the stout rail put round. Shall I go first?"

"No; you came down first," said Joe. "My turn now. But I say, I'd a deal rather go up and down in a bucket. What a height it seems."

"Well, make it less," said Gwyn. "Up with you! don't stand looking at it. I want to be at the top."

"So do I," said Joe, as he stood holding on by one of the rounds of the ladder, they two and the platform looking wonderfully small on the face of that immense cliff; the platform bearing a striking resemblance to some little bracket nailed against a wall, and occupied by two sparrows.

Then, uttering a low sigh, Joe began to mount steadily, and as soon as he was a dozen feet up, Gwyn followed him.

"It doesn't do to look upwards, does it?" said Joe, suddenly, when they had been climbing for about half-a-minute.

"Well, don't think about it, then. And don't talk. You want all your breath for a job like this."

Joe was silent, and the only sounds heard were the scraping of their boots on the wooden spells, and the crying of the gulls squabbling over some wave-tossed weed far below.

Then, all at once, when he was about half-way up, Joe suddenly stopped short, but Gwyn did not notice it till his cap was within a few inches of the other's boots.

"Well, go on," he cried cheerily. "What's the matter—out of breath?"

"No."

"Eh? What is it—what's the matter?" said Gwyn, for he was startled by the tone in which the word was uttered.

"I—I don't know," came back in a hoarse whisper, which sent a shudder through Gwyn, as he involuntarily glanced down at the awful depth beneath him. "It's the cold water, I think. One of my feet has gone dead, and the other's getting numb. Gwyn! Gwyn! Here, quick! I don't know what I'm—Quick!—help! I'm going to fall!"

Chapter Seventeen
Gwyn shows his Mettle

Too much horrified for the moment even to speak, Gwyn grasped the sides of the ladder with spasmodic strength; his eyes dilated, his jaw dropped, and he clung there completely paralysed. Then his mental balance came back as suddenly as he had lost it, and feeling once more the strong, healthy lad he was, it came to him like a flash that it was impossible that Joe Jollivet, his companion in hundreds of rock-climbing expeditions—where they had successfully made their way along places which would have given onlookers what is known as "the creeps,"—could be in the danger he described, and with a merry laugh, he cried,—

"Get out! Go on, you old humbug, or I'll get a pin out of my waistcoat and give you the spur."

There was no response.

"Do you hear, old Jolly-wet? I say, you know, this isn't the sort of place for playing larks. Wait till we're up, and I'll give you such a warming!"

Then the chill of horror came back, for Joe said in a whisper, whose tones swept away all possibility of his playing tricks,—

"I'm not larking. I can't stir."

"I tell you you are larking," cried Gwyn, fiercely. "Such nonsense! Go on up, or I'll drive a pin into you right up to the head."

The cold chill increased now, and Gwyn shuddered, for Joe said faintly,—

"Do, please; it might give me strength."

The vain hope that it might be all a trick was gone, and Gwyn was face to face with the horror of their position. He too looked down, and there was the platform, with the water splashing and glittering in the sunshine as it struck upon the rock; and he knew that no help could come from that direction, for Hardock was at the pump in the shaft. He looked up to the edge of the cliff, but no one was there, for the people were all gathered about the top of the mine, and were not likely to come and look over and see their position. If help was to come to the boy above him, that help must come from where he stood; and, with the recollection of his own peril when he was being hauled up by the rope, forcing itself upon him, he began to act with a feeling of desperation which was ready to rob him of such nerve as he possessed.

A clear and prompt action was necessary, as he knew only too well, and, setting his teeth hard together, he went on up without a word, step by step, as he leaned back to the full stretch of his arms, and reached to where he could just force his feet, one on either side of his companion's, the spell of the ladder just affording sufficient width, and then pressing Joe close against the rounds with his heavily-throbbing breast, he held on in silence for a few moments, trying to speak, but no words would come.

Meanwhile, Joe remained silent and rigid, as if half insensible; and Gwyn's brain was active, though his tongue was silent, battling as he was with the question what to do.

"Oh, if those gulls would only keep away!" he groaned to himself, for at least a dozen came softly swooping about them, and one so close that the boy felt the waft of the air set in motion by its wings.

Then the throbbing and fluttering at his heart grew less painful, and the power to speak returned.

With a strong endeavour to be calm and easy, he forced himself to treat the position jauntily.

"There you are, old chap," he cried; "friend in need's a friend indeed. I could hold you on like that for a month—five minutes," he added to himself. Then aloud once more. "Feel better?"

There was no reply.

"Do you hear, stupid—feel better?"

A low sigh—almost a groan—was the only answer, and Gwyn's teeth grated together.

"Here, you, Joe," he said firmly. "I know you can hear what I say, so listen. You don't want for us both to go down, I know, so you've got to throw off the horrible feeling that's come over you, and do what I say. I'm going to hold you up like this for five minutes to get your wind, and then you've got to start and go up round by round. You can't fall because I shall follow you, keeping like this, and holding you on till you're better. You can hear all that, you know."

Joe bent his head, and a peculiar quivering, catching sigh escaped his lips.

"It's all nonsense; you want to give up over climbing a ladder such as we could run up. 'Tisn't like being on the rocks with nothing to hold on by, now, is it? Let's see; we're half of the way up, and we can soon do it, so say when you feel ready, and then up you go!"

But after a guess at the space of time named, Joe showed no inclination to say he was ready, and stood there, pressed against the ladder, breathing very feebly, and Gwyn began to be attacked once more by the chill of dread.

He fought it back in his desperation, and in a tone which surprised himself, he cried, —

"Now, then! Time's up! Go on!"

To his intense delight, his energy seemed to be communicated to his companion; and as he hung back a little, Joe reached with one hand, got a fresh hold there with the other, and, raising his right foot, drew himself slowly and cautiously up, to stand on the next spell.

"Cheerily ho!" sang out Gwyn, as he followed. "I knew, I knew you could do it. Now then! Don't stop to get cold. Up you go before I get out that pin."

Joe slowly and laboriously began again, and reached the next step, but Gwyn felt no increase of hope, for he could tell how feeble and nerveless the boy was. But he went on talking lightly, as he followed and let the poor fellow feel the support of his breast.

"That's your sort. Nine inches higher. Two nine inches more—a foot and a half. But, I say, no games; don't start off with a run and leave me behind. You'd better let me go with you, in case your foot gives—gives way again."

That repetition of the word gives was caused by a peculiar catching of Gwyn's breath.

"I say," he continued, as they paused, "this is ever so much better than going up those wet ladders in the shaft. I shall never like that way. Don't you remember looking down the shaft of that mine, where the hot, steamy mist came up, and the rounds of the ladder were all slippery with the grease that dropped from the men's candles stuck in their caps? I do. I said it would be like going down ladders of ice, and that you'd never catch me on them. Our way won't be hot and steamy like that was, because there'll always be a draught of fresh sea air running up from the adit. Now then, up you go again! I begin to want my dinner."

Joe did not stir, and Gwyn's face turned ghastly, while his mouth opened ready for the utterance of a wild cry for help.

But the cry did not escape, for Gwyn's teeth closed with a snap. He felt that it would result in adding to his companion's despair.

He was once more master of himself.

"Now then!" he cried; "I don't want to use that pin. Go on, old lazybones."

The energy was transferred again, and Joe slowly struggled up another step, closely followed by Gwyn, and then remained motionless and silent.

"You stop and let yourself get cold again," cried Gwyn, resolutely now. "Begin once more, and don't stop. You needn't mind, old chap. I've got you as tight as tight. Now then, can't you feel how safe you are? Off with you! I shall always be ready to give you a nip and hold you on. Now then, off!"

But there was no response.

"Do you hear! This isn't the place to go to sleep, Joe! Wake up! Go on! Never mind your feet being numb. Go on pulling yourself up with your hands. I'll give you a shove to help."

No reply; no movement; and but for the spasmodic way in which the boy clung with his hands, as if involuntarily, like a bird or a bat clings in its sleep, he might have been pronounced perfectly helpless.

"Now, once more, are you going to begin?" cried Gwyn, shouting fiercely. "Do you hear?"

Still no reply, and in spite of appeal, threat, and at last a blow delivered heavily upon his shoulder, Joe did not stir, and Gwyn felt that their case was desperate indeed. Each time he had forced his companion to make an effort it was as if the result was due to the energy he had communicated from his own body; but now he felt in his despair as if a reverse action were taking place, and his companion's want of nerve and inertia were being communicated to him; for the chilly feeling of despair was on the increase, and he knew now that poor Joe was beyond helping himself.

"What can I do?" he thought, as he once more forced himself to the point of thinking and acting. To get his companion up by his own force was impossible. Even if he could have carried the weight up the ladder, it would have been impossible to get a good hold and retain it, and he already felt himself growing weak from horror.

What to do?

It would have been easy enough to climb over his companion and save his own life; but how could he ever look Major Jollivet or his father in the eyes again? The momentary thought was dismissed on the instant as being cowardly and unworthy of an English lad. But what to do?

If he could have left him for a few minutes, he could have either gone up or gone down, and shouted for help; but he knew perfectly well that the moment he left the boy to himself, he would fall headlong.

"What shall I do? What shall I do?" he groaned aloud, and a querulous cry from one of the gulls still floating around them came as if in reply.

"Oh, if I only had a gun," he cried angrily. "Get out, you beasts! Who's going to fall!"

Then he uttered a cry for help, and another, and another; but the shouts sounded feeble, and were lost in space, while more and more it was forced upon him that Joe was now insensible from fear and despair, his nerve completely gone.

What could he do? There seemed to be nothing but to hold on till Joe fell, and then for his father's sake, he must try and save himself.

"Oh, if I only had a piece of rope," he muttered; but he had not so much as a piece of string. There was his silk neckerchief; that was something, and Joe was wearing one, too, exactly like it; for the boys had a habit of dressing the same.

It was something to do—something to occupy his thoughts for a few moments, and, setting one hand free, he passed it round the side of the ladder, leaned toward it, as he forced it toward his neck; his fingers seized the knot—a sailor's slip-knot—and the next minute the handkerchief was loose in his hands.

A few more long moments, and he had taken his companion's from his neck. Then came the knotting together, a task which needed the service of both hands, and for a time he hesitated about setting the second free.

Free he could not make it, but by clinging round the sides of the ladder with both arms, he brought his hands together, and with the skill taught him by the Cornish fishermen, he soon, without the help of his eyes, had the two handkerchiefs securely joined in a knot that would not slip, and was now possessed with a twisted silken cord about five feet long.

But how slight! Still it was of silk, and it was his only chance unless help came; and of that there seemed to be not the slightest hope.

He twisted the silk round and round in his hands for some seconds after the fashion that he and Joe had observed when making a snood for their fishing lines, and then passing one end round the spell that was on a level with Joe's throat, he drew till both ends were of a length, and then tied the silken cord tightly to the piece of stout, strong oak, letting the ends hang down.

Joe's hands were grasping the sides of the ladder—how feebly Gwyn did not know till he tried to move the left, when it gave way at once, and would have fallen to his side but for his own strong grasp. Holding it firmly, he passed it round the left side of the ladder, placing it along the spell, and then passing one of the silken ends round the wrist, he drew it tight to the spell and kept it there, while he loosened the boy's right-hand, passed that round the other side, so that wrist rested upon wrist, and the next minute the handkerchief was slipped round it, and drawn tightly, binding both together.

They were safely held so long as he kept up a tension upon the end of the silk; and this with great effort he was able to do with his left hand, while, working in the opposite way, he passed the second end round the two wrists once, dragged it as hard as he could, and then tied the first portion of a simple knot. Then he dragged again and again, bringing his teeth to bear in holding the shorter end of the handkerchief, while he tugged and tugged till the silk cut into the boy's flesh, and his wrists were dragged firmly down upon the spell. There the second portion of the knot was tied; and, feeling that Joe could not slip, he bound the longer end round again twice, brought the first end to meet it, and once again tied as hard as he could.

Breathless with the exertion of holding on by his crooked arms while he worked, and with the perspiration streaming down his face, he stood there panting for a few moments, holding on tightly, and peering through the spells to make sure that his knots were secure, and the silken cord sufficiently tight to stay Joe's wrists from being dragged through. Then he tried the fastening again, satisfying himself that Joe was as safe as hands could make him, and that his arms could not possibly be dragged away from the spell to which they were tied, even if his feet slipped from the round below.

Satisfied at this, Gwyn's heart gave a throb of satisfaction.

"You can't fall, Joe," he said. "I don't want to leave you, but I must go for help."

There was no reply.

"Can you hear what I say?" cried Gwyn.

Still no reply; and, feeling that he might safely leave him, Gwyn hesitated for a moment or two as to whether he should go up or down.

The latter seemed to be the quicker way, and, after descending a step or two, he threw arms and legs round the sides of the ladder, and let himself slide to the platform.

Here he stood for a moment to look up and see Joe hanging as he had left him. Then, stooping down, he entered the adit, out of which the clanging sound of the huge pump went on volleying, while the water kept up its hissing and rushing sound.

"Hardock!" he shouted, with his hands to his lips, and the cry reverberated in the narrow passage; but, though he shouted again and again, his voice did not penetrate, for the sound of the pumping and rushing of water, and the boy had to make his way right to where Hardock was anxiously watching the working of the machinery; and as Gwyn reached him, he was once more holding his lanthorn down to see how much the water had fallen.

The man gave a violent start as a hand was laid upon his shoulder.

"Come back!" shouted Hardock, to make himself heard, and he gazed wonderingly at the boy, whose face was ghastly. "Here, don't you go and say young Master Joe has fallen."

Gwyn placed his lips to the foreman's ear.

"Can't fall yet. Send word—ropes—top of ladder at once. Danger."

Hardock waited to hear no more, but dragged at the wire which formed the rough temporary signal to the engine-house, and the great beam of the pump stopped its work at once, when the silence was profound, save for a murmur high up over them at the mouth of the shaft.

"What is it there?" came in a familiar voice, which sounded dull and strange as it was echoed from the dripping walls.

"Help!" shouted Gwyn. "Long ropes to the head of the outside ladders."

"Right!" came back.

"What's wrong?" came down then in another voice.

"Joe Jollivet—danger," shouted Gwyn, stepping back to reply. "Now, come on!" he cried to Hardock; and he led the way along the adit from which, short as had been the time since the pump ceased working, the water had run off.

No more was said as they hurried along as fast as the sloping position necessary allowed; and on stepping out on to the platform, Gwyn looked up in fear and trembling, lest the silken cord should have given way, and fully anticipating that the ladder would be vacant.

Hardock uttered a groan, but Gwyn had already begun to climb.

"What are you going to do, lad?" shouted the man, excitedly.

"Go up and hold him on."

"No, no; I'm stronger than you." But Gwyn was already making his way up as fast as he could, and Hardock, after a momentary hesitation, followed.

Before they were half way, voices at the top were heard. "Hold tight!" shouted the Colonel, in his fierce military fashion. "Rope!"

Then an order was heard, and a great coil of rope was thrown out, so that it might fall clear of the climbers, whizzed away from the rock with the rings opening out, and directly after, was hanging beside the ladder right to the platform.

There was a clever brain at work on the top of the cliff, for, as Gwyn climbed the ladder, the rope was hauled in so as to keep the end close to his hands; and, seeing this, the boy uttered a sigh of relief, and climbed on, feeling that there was hope of saving his comrade now.

"Shall I send someone down?" shouted the Colonel, who was evidently in command at the top.

"No. We'll do it," cried Gwyn, breathlessly. "All right, Joe. We're here."

There was no response from above him, and at every step Gwyn felt as if his legs were turning to lead, and a nightmare-like sensation came over him of being obliged to keep on always clambering a tremendous ladder without ever reaching to where Joe was bound.

And all this in the very brief space of time before he reached to where he had tied the insensible lad.

Gwyn uttered a sigh like a groan as he touched Joe's feet. Then, without hesitating, he went higher, till he was on a level, with his feet resting on the same spell, fully expecting moment by moment, as he ascended, that the silk would give way and Joe's fall dash them both down. And, as at last he thrust his arms through the ladder on either side of the boy's neck and then spread them out, so as to secure them both tightly pressed against the spells, his head began to swim, and he felt that he could do no more.

His position saved him, for in those moments he could not have clung there by his hands, his helplessness was too great.

But this was all momentary, and he was recalled to himself by the voice of Hardock.

"I say, lad, hope this ladder's strong enough for all three. Now, then; what's next? Will you tie the rope round him and cast him free?"

Gwyn made no reply. His lips parted, and he strove to speak, but not a word would come.

"D'yer hear?" said Hardock. "I say, will you make the rope fast round him?"

"Below there!" came from above. "Make the rope fast round Joe's chest—tight knots, mind, and send him up first. Be smart!"

"All right, sir," shouted back Hardock, as he took hold of the rope swinging close to his hand. "Now, then, Master Gwyn, don't stand there such a gashly while thinking about it. Lay hold and knot it round him. They'll soon draw him away from under you."

Gwyn uttered an inarticulate sound, but only wedged his arms out more firmly.

"Ready?" came from above in the Colonel's voice.

"No, nothing like," roared Hardock. "Hold hard. Now, my lad, look alive. Don't think about it, but get hold of the rope, and draw it round his chest. Mind and not tie him to the ladder. Steady, for it's all of a quiver now."

Still Gwyn made no sign.

"Hi! What's come to you?" growled Hardock.

"Are you asleep, below there?" shouted the Colonel. "Hold fast, and I'll send someone down."

"Nay, nay!" yelled Hardock, "the ladder won't bear another. I'll get it done directly. Now, Master Gwyn, pull yourself together, and make this rope fast. D'yer hear?"

"Yes," gasped the boy at last. "Wait a minute and I'll try."

"Wait a minute and you'll try," growled the man. "We shall all be down directly. My word! What is the use o' boys. Hi! hold fast and I'll try and get up above you and tie the rope myself."

"No, no!" cried Gwyn, frantically. "You can't climb over us."

"But I must, lad, I aren't going to get round inside and try it that way. I aren't a boy now."

"No, don't try that," panted Gwyn, breathlessly. "You'd pull us off. I'm coming round again. I'll try soon, but I don't seem to have any breath."

"Hi! below there! what are you about?" shouted the Colonel. "Make that rope fast."

"Yes, sir; yes, sir; directly," yelled Hardock. "You, must wait."

"Make it fast round Jollivet," shouted the Colonel.

"All right, sir. Now, Master Gwyn, you hear what your guv'nor says?"

"Yes, I hear, Sam," panted the lad; "and I'm trying to do it. I'll begin as soon as ever I can, but I feel that if I let go, Joe would come down on you. He has no strength left in him, and—and I'm not much better."

"And you'll let go, too," growled the man to himself, "and if you do, it's all over with me." Then aloud: "Hold tight, my lad; I'm coming up."

Chapter Eighteen
An Ignominious Ascent

"Am I to send someone down?" cried the Colonel, angrily.

"No, father," shouted Gwyn, his father's voice seeming to give him new force. "The ladder won't bear four."

"Then make fast that knot, sir. Quick, at once!"

"Yes, father," said the boy, as a thrill of energy ran through him, and he felt as if he could once more do something toward relieving himself from the strange feeling of inertia which had fettered every sense.

"You get up higher," growled Hardock, "and hold on, my lad."

"No. Keep where you are," cried Gwyn, whose voice now sounded firm. "If I leave him, he'll go."

"Nay, you go on; I'll take care o' that," said Hardock. "Up with you!"

"Keep down, I say," cried Gwyn, fiercely.

"Are you ready?" shouted the Colonel.

"In another minute, father," cried Gwyn; and, drawing out one arm, he made a snatch at the rope, drew it from Hardock's hand, and then hauled it higher by using his teeth as well as his right-hand.

"Better let me come, my lad."

"No," said Gwyn, shortly.

"Ready?" came from above.

"Not quite, father. I'll say when."

That last demand gave the final fillip to the lad's nerves, and, taking tightly hold of the spell above Joe's head with both hands, he raised his own legs till they came level with Joe's loins, and bestriding him as if on horseback, he crooked his legs and ankles round the sides of the ladder, held on by forcing his toes round a spell, and then, with his hands free, he hung back, and quickly knotted the rope about Joe's chest.

"Steady, my lad! Be ready to take hold," said Hardock, whose face was now streaming with perspiration, and his hands wet, as he looked up at the perilous position of Gwyn. Then, obeying a sudden thought, he loosened one hand, snatched off his cap, threw it down, and took three steps up the ladder, raising himself so that he could force his head beneath the lad, with the result that he gave him plenty of support, relieving him of a great deal of the strain on his muscles, for during the next minute he was, as it were, seated upon the mining captain's head.

"That's better," panted Gwyn.

"Make a good knot, lad," growled Hardock; and all was perfectly silent at the edge of the cliff above them, for every movement was being attentively watched.

"Hah!" sighed Gwyn, as he tightened the last knot.

"Quite safe?" asked Hardock.

"Yes, quite."

"What next?"

"Get down!"

"Are you right?"

"Yes."

Hardock yielded very slowly for a while, and then stopped and raised himself again.

"What yer doing?"

"Getting out my knife. He's lashed to the spell."

"Oh!"

Gwyn's hands were dripping wet, and, as he tried to force his right into his pocket, he had a hard struggle, for it stuck to the lining, the strain of his position helping to resist its passage. But at last he forced it in, to find to his horror that the knife was not in that pocket, and he had a terrible job to drag out his hand.

"Can't get at my knife," he panted.

"All right; have mine," was growled, and Hardock took out and opened his own. "Here you are."

The boy blindly lowered his hand for the knife, and not a whisper was heard in those critical moments. For every movement was scanned, and the Colonel was lying on his chest, straining his eyes, as he waited to give the order to haul up.

'Gwyn forced the knife-point steadily through the silk.'

Gwyn gripped the knife, a sharp-pointed Spanish blade, and raised it, bending forward now, so as to look over Joe's shoulder to see where to cut.

His intention was to thrust the point in between the silken cord and the boy's wrists; but he found it impossible without having both hands, and there was nothing for it but to saw right down.

This he began to do just beneath the knots, hoping that the last part would yield before the knife could touch the boy's skin.

"Take care, my lad," growled Hardock.

"Yes; I'm trying not to cut him," panted Gwyn.

"Nay, I mean when you're through. Hold tight yourself."

"Yes, I'll try."

"Tell 'em to make the rope quite taut."

"Haul and hold fast," cried Gwyn.

"Right!" came promptly from above, and a heavy strain was felt.

"I—tied it—so tight," muttered Gwyn, as he sawed away.

"Ay, and his weight. Steady, my lad, steady!"

"Hah! that's through," cried Gwyn. "Be ready to haul."

"Right!" came from above.

"Shall I get lower?" said Hardock.

"Yes!—No! The other knot holds him," panted Gwyn; and he had to begin cutting again; but this time he found that by laying the blade of the knife flat against the spell, he could force the point beneath the handkerchief. "Now, steady, Sam," he said, "I'm going to have one big cut, and then hold on."

"All right, my lad. I'll support you all I can, but you must hold tight."

The strain on the rope was firm and steady, as Gwyn drew a deep breath, forced the knife point steadily through beneath the silk, raised the edge of the blade a little more and a little more, and then, in an agony of despair, just as he was about to give one bold thrust, he let go, and snatched at the ladder side.

For all at once there was a sharp, scraping sound. The silk, which had been strained like a fiddle-string over a bridge, parted on the edge of the keen knife, and, as Joe's arms dropped quite nerveless and inert, down went the knife, and Gwyn felt that he was going after.

For in those brief moments he seemed to be falling fast.

But he was not moving; it was Joe being drawn upward, and the next minute Gwyn was clinging with his breast now on the spells of the ladder, against which he was being pressed, Hardock, with a rapid movement, having forced himself up so as to occupy the same position as Gwyn had so lately held with respect to Joe.

"He's all right—if your knots hold," said Hardock, softly. "How is it with you, my lad?"

"Out of breath, that's all. I can't look, though, now, Sam. Watch and see if he goes up all right."

"No need, my lad," said the man, bitterly. "We should soon know if he came down. Come, hold up your chin, and show your pluck. There's nothing to mind now. Why, you're all of a tremble."

"Yes; it isn't that I feel frightened now," said the boy; "but all the muscles in my legs and arms are as if they were trembling and jerking."

"'Nough to make 'em," growled Hardock. "Never mind, the rope'll soon be down again—yes, they've got him, and they're letting another down. I'll soon have you fast and send you up."

"No, you won't, Sam," said Gwyn, who was rapidly recovering his balance. "I haven't forgotten the last knot you made round me."

"Well, well! I do call that mean," growled the man. "You comes and fetches me to help, and I has to chuck my cap away; then you chucks my best knife down after it; and now you chucks that there in my teeth. I do call it a gashly shame."

"Never mind. I don't want the rope at all," said Gwyn. "There, slacken your hold. I'm going to climb up."

"Nay; better have the rope, my lad."

"I don't want the rope. I'm tired and hot, but I can climb up."

"Gwyn!" came at that moment.

"Yes, father."

"Just sarves you right," growled Hardock. "Take some of the gashly conceit out of you, my lad. Now, then, I'm going to tie you up."

"No; I shall do it myself," said Gwyn, making a snatch at the line lowered down. "Now, get out of my way."

"Oh, very well; but don't blame me if you fall."

"No fear, Sam."

"Nay, there's no fear, my lad; but I hope we're not going to have no more o' this sort o' thing. There's the pumping stopped and everything out o' gear, but it's always the way when there's boys about. I never could understand what use they were, on'y to get in mischief and upset the work. We sha'n't get much tin out o' Ydoll mine if you two's going to hang about, I know that much. Now, then, the rope aren't safe."

"Yes, it is," said Gwyn, who had made a loop and passed it over his head and arms. "I'm not going to swing. I'm going to walk up."

"Ready, my lad?" cried the Colonel.

"Yes, father; but I'll climb up, please. You can have the rope hauled on as I come."

"Come on, then," cried the Colonel.

"Yes, father, coming."

"Hor, hor!" laughed Hardock, derisively, as he drew back to the full extent of his arms so as to set Gwyn free. "Up you goes, my lad, led just like a puppy-dog at the end of a string. Mind you don't fall."

"If it wasn't so dangerous for you, I'd kick you, Sam," said Gwyn.

"Kick away, then, my lad; 'taint the first time I've been on a ladder by a few thousand times. My hands and feet grows to a ladder, like, and holds on. You won't knock me off. But I say!"

"What is it?" said Gwyn, who was steadily ascending, with the rope held fairly taut from above.

"You'll pay for a new hat for me?"

"Oh, yes, of course."

"And another knife, better than the one you pitched overboard?"

"Oh, we can come round in a boat and find that when the tide's down."

"Rocks are never bare when the tide's down here, my lad. There's always six fathom o' water close below here; so you wouldn't ha' been broken up if you'd falled; but you might ha' been drownded. That were a five-shilling knife."

"All right, Sam, I'll buy you another," shouted Gwyn, who was some distance up now.

"Thank ye. Before you go, though," said Sam Hardock.

"Go? Go where?"

"Off to school, my lad; I'm going to 'tishion your two fathers to send you both right away, for I can't have you playing no more of your pranks in my mine, and so I tell you."

Gwyn made no reply, but he went steadily up, while, on casting a glance below, he saw that the mine captain was making his way as steadily down; but he thought a good deal, and a great deal more afterwards, for, on reaching the top of the cliff, there lay Joe on the short grass, looking ghastly pale, and his father, with Joe's, ready to seize him by the arm and draw him into safety.

"There must be no more of this," said the Colonel, sternly. "You two boys are not fit to be trusted in these dangerous places. Now, go home at once."

The little crowd attracted by the accident had begun to cheer wildly, but the congratulatory sound did Gwyn no good. He did not feel a bit like the hero of an adventure, one who had done brave deeds, but a very ordinary schoolboy sort of personage, who was being corrected for a fault, and he felt very miserable as he turned to Joe.

"Are you coming home, too?"

"Yes. I suppose so," said Joe, dismally.

There was another cheer, and the boys felt as if they could not face the crowd, till an angry flush came upon Gwyn's cheeks; for there stood, right in the front, the big, swarthy fellow who had been caught plumbing the depth of the mine, and he was grinning widely at them both.

"Ugh!" thought Gwyn, "how I should like to punch that chap's head. Here, Joe, let's tell our fathers that this fellow is hanging about here."

"No," said Joe, dismally. "I feel as if I didn't mind about anything now. My father looked at me as if I'd been doing it all on purpose to annoy him. Let's go home."

Chapter Nineteen
A Brutal Threat

Gwyn did not see Joe for a whole week, and he did not go over to the mine, for the Colonel had called him into his room the next morning, and had a very long, serious talk with him, and this was the end of his lesson, —

"Of course, I meant you to go and read for the army, Gwyn, my lad, but this mine has quite upset my plans, and I can't say yet what I shall do about you. It will seem strange for one of our family to take to such a life, but a man can do his duty in the great fight of life as well whether he's a mine owner or a soldier. He has his men to keep in hand, to win their confidence, and make them follow him, and to set them a good example, Gwyn. But I can't say anything for certain. It's all a speculation, and I never shut my eyes to the fact that it may turn out a failure. If it does, we can go back to the old plans."

"Yes, father," said the boy, rather dolefully, for his father had stopped as if waiting for him to speak.

"But if it turns out a successful, honest venture, you'll have to go on with it, and be my right-hand man. You'll have to learn to manage, therefore, better than ever I shall, for you'll begin young. So we'll take up the study of it a bit, Gwyn, and you shall thoroughly learn what is necessary in geology, and metallurgy and chemistry. If matters come to the worst, you won't make any the worse officer for knowing such matters as these. It's a fine thing, knowledge. Nobody can take that away from you, and the more you use it the richer you get. It never wastes."

"No, father," said Gwyn, who began to feel an intense desire now to go on with his reading about the wars of Europe, and the various campaigns of the British army, while the military text-book, which it had been his father's delight to examine him in, suddenly seemed to have grown anything but dry.

"Begin reading up about the various minerals that accompany tin ore in quartz, for one thing, and we'll begin upon that text-book, dealing with the various methods of smelting and reducing ores, especially those portions about lead ore, and extracting the silver that is found with it."

"Yes, father," said Gwyn, quietly; and the boy set his teeth, wrinkled his brow, and looked hard, for Colonel Pendarve treated his son in a very military fashion. He was kindness and gentleness itself, but his laws were like those of the Medes and Persians done into plain English.

But the whole week had passed, and Mrs Pendarve took him to task one morning.

"Come, Gwyn," she said, "I am quite sure your father does not wish you to mope over your books, and give up going out to your old amusements."

"Doesn't he, mother?" said the boy, drearily.

"Of course not. What has become of Joe Jollivet? He has not been near you."

"In the black books, too, I suppose," said Gwyn, bitterly. "Major's been giving it to him."

"Gwyn, I will not have you talk like that," said his mother. "You boys both deserve being taken to task for your reckless folly. You forget entirely the agony you caused me when I heard of what had taken place."

"I didn't want to cause you agony, mother," pleaded the boy.

"I know that, my dear, but you have been growing far too reckless of late. Now be sensible, and go on as if there had been no trouble between your father and you. I wish it. Try and grasp the spirit in which your father's reproofs were given."

"All right, mother, I will," said Gwyn; and his face brightened up once more.

The consequence was that he went out into the yard, and unchained the dog, with very great difficulty, for the poor beast was nearly mad with excitement directly it realised the fact that it was going out with its master for a run; and as soon as they entered the lane, set off straight for the Major's gates, stopping every now and then to look round, and to see if Gwyn was going there.

But half-way up the hill Gwyn turned off on to the rough granite moorland, and Grip had to come back a hundred yards to the place where his master had turned off, and dashed after him.

It didn't matter to the dog, for there was some imaginary thing to hunt wherever they went; and as soon as he saw that he was on the right track, he began hunting most perseveringly.

For Gwyn did not want to go to the Major's. He felt that he would like to see Joe and have a good long talk with him, as well as compare notes;

but if he had gone to the house, he would have had to see the Major, and that gentleman would doubtless have something to say that would not be pleasant to him—perhaps blame him for Joe getting into difficulties.

No, he did not want to go to the Major's.

"Like having to take another dose," he said to himself, and he went on toward the old circle of granite stones which had been set up some long time back, before men began to write the history of their deeds.

It lay about a mile from the cove, high up on the windy common among the furze bushes, and was a capital place for a good think. For you could climb up on the top of the highest stone, look right out to sea, and count the great vessels going up and down channel, far away on the glittering waters—large liners which left behind them long, thin clouds of smoke; stately ships with all sail set; trim yachts; and the red-sailed fishing fleet returning from their cruise round the coast, where the best places for shooting their nets were to be found.

It was quite a climb up to the old stones, which were not seen from that side till you were close upon them, for they stood in a saucer-like hollow in the highest part of the ridge, and beyond, there was one of the deep gullies with which that part of Cornwall was scored—lovely spots, along which short rivulets made their way from the high ground down to the sea.

Grip knew well enough now where his master was making for, and dashed forward as if certain that that mysterious object which he was always hunting had hidden itself away among the stones, and soon after a tremendous barking was heard.

"Rabbit," muttered Gwyn; and for a few moments he felt disposed to begin running and join the dog in the chase. But he did not, for, in spite of being out there on the breezy upland, where all was bright and sunny, he felt dull and disheartened. Things were not as he could wish, for he had just begun to feel old enough to bear upon the rein when it was drawn tight, and to long to have the bit in his teeth and do what he liked. The Colonel had been pleasant enough that morning, but he had not invited him to go to the mine; and it felt like a want of trust in him.

So Gwyn felt in no humour for sport of any kind; he did not care to look out at the ships, and speculate upon what port they were bound for; he picked up no stones to send spinning at the grey gulls; did not see that the gorse was wonderfully full of flower; and did not even smell the wild thyme as he crushed it beneath his feet. There were hundreds of tiny blue and copper butterflies flitting about, and a great hawk was havering overhead;

but everything seemed as if his mind was out of taste and the objects he generally loved were flavourless.

All he felt disposed to do was to turn himself into a young modern ascetic, prick his legs well in going through the furze, and then take a little bark off his shins in climbing twenty feet up on to the great monolith, and there sit and grump.

"Bother the dog, what a row he's making!" he muttered. "I wish I hadn't brought him."

Then his lips parted to shout to Grip to be quiet, but he did not utter the words, for he stopped short just as he neared the first stone of the circle, on hearing the dog begin to bark furiously again, and a savage voice roar loudly,—

"Get out, or I'll crush your head with this stone!"

Chapter Twenty
A Doubtful Acquaintance

Gwyn recognised the voice, and knew what was the matter, and his first aim was to make a rush to protect his dog from the crushing blow which would probably be given him with one of the many weather-worn fragments of granite lying about among the great monoliths. But he was just where he could not make such a rush, for it would have been into a dense bed of gorse as high as himself, and forming a *chevaux de frise* of millions of sharp thorns.

The next best plan was to shout loudly, "You hurt my dog if you dare—" though the man might dare, and cast the stone all the same.

But Gwyn did neither of these things, for another familiar voice rose from beyond the furze, crying loudly,—

"You let that dog alone! You touch him and I'll set him to worry you. Once he gets his teeth into you, he won't let go. Here, Grip! Come to heel!"

"Well done, Joe!" muttered Gwyn, who felt that his dog was safe; and he ran to the end of the bank of prickly growth, where there was an opening, and suddenly appeared upon the scene.

It was all just as he had pictured; there was Joe Jollivet, with Grip close to his legs, barking angrily and making short rushes, and there, a few yards away, stood the big, swarthy stranger who had been caught at the mine mouth, and whom Gwyn believed to have tampered with the furnace door, now standing with a big stone of eight or ten pounds' weight, ready to hurl at the dog if attacked.

"Here, you put down that stone," cried Gwyn, angrily. "How dare you threaten my dog!"

"Stone aren't yours," said the man, tauntingly. "This ground don't belong to you. Keep your mongrel cur quiet."

"My dog wouldn't interfere with you if you let it alone."

"Oh, it's your dog, is it?" said the man. "Well, take him home and chain him up. I don't want to flatten his head, but I jolly soon will if he comes at me."

"He couldn't hit Grip," said Joe, maliciously, as he bent down to pat and encourage the dog. "Set him at the fellow—he has no business here."

"What!" cried the fellow, who looked a man of three or four-and-thirty, but talked like a boy of their own age. "Much right here as you have. You let me alone, and I'll let you alone. What business have you to set your beastly dog at me?"

"Who set him at you?" cried Joe. "He only barked at you—he saw you were a stranger—and you picked up a stone, and that, of course, made him mad."

"So would you pick up a stone, if a savage dog came at you. Look at him now, showing his sharp teeth. On'y wish I had his head screwed up in a carpenter's bench. I'd jolly soon get the pinchers and nip 'em all out. He wouldn't have no more toothache while I knew him."

"There, you be off," said Gwyn, "while your shoes are good."

"Don't wear shoes, young 'un. Mine's boots."

"You're after no good hanging about here."

"Er—think I want to steal your guv'nor's pears off the wall, now, don't yer?"

"How do you know we've got pears on our wall?"

"Looked over and see," said the man, grinning.

"Yes, that's it; you're a regular spy, looking for what you can steal," cried Joe. "Be off!"

"Sha'n't. Much right here, I tell you, as you have. But I like folks to talk about stealing! Who nipped off with my fishing line and sinker? You give 'em back to me."

"No; they're confiscated, same as poachers' nets," said Gwyn. "Who sent you here?"

"Sent me here? Sent myself."

"What for?"

"Wants a job. I'm mining, and I heared you was going to open the old mine. Think your guv'nors'll take me on?"

"You put down that stone before you ask questions," said Gwyn.

"You shut up your dog's mouth, then. I don't want to kill him, but I aren't going to have him stick his teeth into me."

"The dog won't hurt you if you don't threaten him. Throw away that stone."

"There you are, then; but I warn you, if he comes at me, I'll let him have my boot, and if he does get it, he won't have any more head."

"Quiet, Grip!" said Gwyn, as the man threw away the stone, and the dog whined and said, "Don't talk to me like that; this fellow isn't to be trusted; make me drive him away." At least not in words, for the dog spoke with his eyes, which seemed to suggest that this course should be taken.

"Who are you, and where do you come from?" said Gwyn, looking at the man suspiciously.

"Truro. All sorts o' places wherever there's mines open and—work."

"And you heard that this one was going to be opened?"

"Yes, that's just what I did hear."

"Then why did you come spying about the place?"

"Never came spying about; only wanted to know how deep she was. I don't like mines as is two hundred fathom deep. Too hot enough, and such a long way up and down. Takes all the steam out of you. Will your guv'nors give me a job?"

"Go to the office and ask them; that's the best way," said Gwyn, looking at the man suspiciously, as he took off his cap, and began to smooth it round and round.

"Well, p'r'aps that won't be a bad way," said the fellow. "But you two won't say anything again' me, will you, 'cause of that row we had when you smugged my line and sinker?"

"I don't think I shall say any more than what happened," replied Gwyn.

"'Cause it was all over a row, now, warn't it? Of course, a chap gets his monkey up a bit when it comes to a fight. That's nat'ral, ar'n't it?"

Gwyn nodded, and felt as if he did not like the look of the man at all; but at the same time he was ready to own that there might be a good deal of prejudice in the matter.

"Wouldn't like to go and say a good word for me, would you?" said the man.

"Of course, I should not like to," said Gwyn, laughing. "How can I go and speak for a man whom I only know through our having two rows with him. That isn't natural, is it?"

"No, I s'pose not," said the man, frankly. "Well, I'll go myself. I say, I am a wunner to work."

"You'd better tell Colonel Pendarve so," said Gwyn, smiling.

"Think so? Well, I will, and good luck to me. But, I say, hadn't you two better make your dog friends with me?"

"No," said Gwyn, promptly. "Grip will know fast enough whether he ought to be friends with you or no."

"Would he? Is he clever enough for that?"

"Oh, yes," said Gwyn; "he knows an honest man when he sees him, doesn't he, Joe?"

"To be sure he does."

"Think o' that, now," said the man. "All right, then. Don't you two go again' me. I'll start for the office at once."

"Here, what's your name?"

"Dinass—Thomas Dinass," said the man, with a laugh, "but I'm mostly called Tom. That all?"

"Yes, that's all," said Gwyn, shortly; and the man turned to go, with the result that Grip made a rush after him, and the man faced round and held up his boot.

"Come here, sir! Come back!" shouted Gwyn; and the dog obeyed at once, but muttering protests the while, as if not considering such an interruption justifiable.

Then all three stood watching till the man had disappeared, the dog uttering an angry whine from time to time, as if still dissatisfied.

At last the two boys, who had met now for the first time since the adventure on the ladder, turned to gaze in each other's eyes, and ended in exchanging a short nod.

"Going up?" said Gwyn at last.

"Yes; I came on purpose, and found Grip here."

"So did I come on purpose," said Gwyn. "Wanted a good think. Lead on."

Joe went to the tallest of the old stones, and began to climb—no easy task, but one to which he seemed to be accustomed; and after a little difficulty, he obtained foothold, and then, getting a hand well on either side of one of the weather-worn angles, he drew himself higher and higher, and finally perched himself on the top.

Before he was half up, Gwyn began to follow, without a thought of danger, though he did say, "Hold tight; don't come down on my head."

Up he went skilfully enough, but before he was at the top, Grip uttered a few sharp barks, raised his ears, became excited, and jumped at the monolith, to scramble up a few feet, drop, and, learning no wisdom from failure, scramble up again and again, and fall back.

Then, as he saw his master reach the top, he threw back his head, opened his jaws, and uttered a most doleful, long-drawn howl, as full of misery and disappointment as a dog could give vent to.

"Quiet, will you!" cried Gwyn, and the dog answered with a sharp bark, to which he added another dismal, long-drawn howl.

"Do you hear!" cried Gwyn; "don't make that row. Lie down!"

There was another howl.

"Do you want me to throw stones at you?" cried Gwyn, fiercely.

Doubtless the dog did not, for he had an intense aversion to being pelted; but, as if quite aware of the fact that there were no stones to cast, he threw his head up higher than ever, and put all his force into a dismal howl, that was unutterably mournful and strange.

"You wretch! Be quiet! Lie down!" cried Gwyn; but the more he shouted the louder the dog howled, while he kept on making ineffectual efforts to mount the stone.

"Let him be; never mind. He'll soon get tired. Want to talk."

The boys settled themselves in uncomfortable positions on the narrow top, where the felspar crystals stood out at uncomfortable angles, and those of quartz were sharper still, and prepared for their long confab. As a matter of course, they would have been ten times as comfortable on the short turf just beyond the furze; but then, that would have been quite easy, and there would have been no excitement, or call upon their skill and energy. There was nothing to be gained by climbing up the stone—nothing to see, nothing to find out; but there was the inclination to satisfy that commonplace form of excelsiorism which tempts so many to try and get to the top. So the boys sat there, thoughtfully gazing out to sea, while the dog, after a good many howls, gave it up for a bad job, curled himself into an ottoman, hid his nose under his bushy collie tail, and went to sleep.

Some minutes elapsed before either of the boys spoke, and when one did, it was with his eyes fixed upon the warm, brown sails of a fishing-lugger, miles away.

It was Gwyn who commenced, and just as if they had been conversing on the subject for some time, —

"Major very angry?"

Joe nodded.

"Awfully. Said, knowing what a state of health he was in, it wasn't fair for me to go on trying to break my neck, for I was very useful to him when he had his bad fever fits—that it wasn't pleasant for him to stop at home, expecting to have me brought back in bits."

"He didn't say that, did he?"

"Yes, he did—bits that couldn't be put together again; and that, if this was the result of having you for a companion, I had better give you up."

Gwyn drew a deep breath, and kicked his heels together with a loud clack. Then there was a long pause.

"Well," said Gwyn, at last; "are you going to give me up?"

Joe did not make a direct answer, but proposed a question himself.

"What did the Colonel say?"

"Just about the same as your father did; only he didn't bring in about the fever, nor he didn't say anything about my being brought home in bits. Said that I was a great nuisance, and he wondered how it was that I could not amuse myself like other boys did."

"So we do," said Joe, sharply. "I never knew of a boy yet who didn't get into a scrape sometimes."

Gwyn grunted, and frowned more deeply.

"Said it was disgraceful for me to run risks, and cause my mother no end of anxiety, and—"

"Well, go on: what a time you are!" cried Joe, for Gwyn suddenly paused. "What else did he say?"

"Oh, something you wouldn't like to hear."

"Yes, I should. Tell me what it was."

Gwyn took out his knife, and began to pick with the point at a large crystal of pinkish felspar, which stood partly out of the huge block of granite.

"I say, go on. What an aggravating chap you are!"

Gwyn went on picking.

"I say, do you want me to shove you off the top here?"

"No; and you couldn't, if I did."

"Oh, couldn't I?—you'd see. But I say, go on, Ydoll; tell us all about it. I did tell you what my father said."

"Said he supposed it was from associating with such a boy as you; for he was sure that I was too well-meaning a lad to do such things without being prompted."

"Oh, my! What a shame!" cried Joe. "It was too bad."

"Well, I didn't want to tell you, only you bothered me till I did speak."

"Of course. Isn't it better to know than have any one thinking such things of you without knowing. But I say, though, it is too bad; I couldn't help turning like I did. It came on all at once, and I couldn't stir."

"He didn't mean about that so much. He bullied me for not taking care of you, and stopping you from going up the ladder."

"Did he? Why, you couldn't help it."

"He talked as if he supposed I could, and said if we went out again together, I had better take Grip's collar and chain, put the collar round your neck, and lead you."

"Oh I say! Just as if I was a monkey."

"No; father meant a dog, or a puppy." Joe gave himself a sudden twist round to face his companion, flushing with anger the while, and as the space on the top of the stone was very small, he nearly slipped off, and had to make a snatch at Gwyn to save himself from an ugly fall.

"There!" cried Gwyn, "you're at it again. You've made up your mind to break your neck, or something else."

"It was all your fault," cried Joe, "saying things like that. I don't believe your father said anything of the kind. It was just to annoy me."

"What, do you suppose I wanted to go home with fresh trouble to talk about?"

"No, but it's your nasty, bantering, chaffing way. Colonel Pendarve wouldn't have spoken about me like that."

Gwyn laughed.

"I suppose he didn't say I had better give you up as a companion—"

"Did he?"

"If I was always getting into some scrape or another."

"No; but I say, Ydoll, did he?"

"Something of the kind. He said it was getting time for me to be thinking of something else beside tops and marbles."

"Well, so we do. Whoever thinks about tops and marbles now? Why, I haven't touched such a thing for two years."

"So I suppose you and I will have to part," continued Gwyn.

Joe glanced at him sidewise.

"It's no use for us to be companions if it means always getting into scapes at home."

Joe began to whistle. His face became perfectly smooth, and he watched his companion, as he picked away at the crystal, while Gwyn looked puzzled.

"I say, you'll break the point of your knife directly," said Joe.

"Well, suppose I do?"

"Be a pity. It's a good knife."

"Well, you won't see it when it's broken if we're going to part."

"Of course not; and you could get to the big grindstone they've set up under that shed for the men to grind their picks. Soon give it a fresh point. I say, how jolly that is—only to put on the band over the wheel shaft from the engine, and the stone goes spinning round! I tried it one day on my knife. It was splendid."

"You seem precious glad that we've got to part," said Gwyn.

"Not a bit of it. It's all gammon."

"Eh? What is?"

"Talking about separating. It doesn't mean anything. I know better than that. Come, let's talk sense."

"That's what I have been doing," said Gwyn, stiffly.

"Not you; been bantering all the time. They didn't mean it, and you didn't mean it. We're to be partners over the mine some of these days, Ydoll, when we grow up, and they're tired of it. I say, though, I don't think I shall like having that Tom Dinass here."

"No," said Gwyn, thoughtfully. "He looks as if he could bite. Think what he said about getting work was all true?"

"I suppose so. Seems reasonable. I don't like to disbelieve people when they speak out plainly to you."

"No," said Gwyn, thoughtfully. "If they've told you a crammer at some time, it makes all the difference, and you don't feel disposed to believe them again. Perhaps it's all right, and when he's taken on, he may turn out a very good sort of fellow."

"Yes; we shall have to chance it. I say, though, Ydoll, we must be more careful for the future about not getting into scrapes together."

"Won't matter if we're not to be companions any more. We can't get into any, can we?"

"Gammon! They didn't mean it, I tell you. We've only got to mind."

"And we begin by getting up here, and running the risk of breaking our legs or wings."

"Well, it was stupid, certainly," said Joe, thoughtfully. "But then, you see, we were so used to climbing up it that it came quite natural."

"Father says one has got to think about being a man now, and setting to work to understand the mining."

"Yes," said Joe, with a sigh; "that's what my father said. Seems rather hard to have to give up all our old games and excursions."

"Then don't let's give them up," said Gwyn, quickly. "They don't want us to, I know—only to work hard sometimes. There, let's get down and go and see how they're getting on at the mine."

"Shall we?" said Joe, doubtingly.

"Yes. Why not? We needn't do anything risky. I haven't been there since the day the pump was started. Have you?"

"No; haven't been near it."

"Then come on!"

Gwyn set the example of descending by lowering his legs over the side, gripping the angle with his knees, and let himself down cleverly, Joe following directly after; while Grip, who had uncurled himself, bounded away before them full of excitement.

A week had resulted in a good deal of work being done by the many men employed; the roughly-made office had been advanced sufficiently for the two old officers to take possession, and spend a good deal of time in consultation with Hardock, who was at work from daylight to dusk, superintending, and was evidently most eager for the success of the mine. The tall granite shaft was smoking away, and the puffs of steam and the whirring, buzzing noises told that the engine was fully at work, while a dull heavy *clank, clank,* came to the boys from the mouth of the shaft.

The first person almost that they set eyes upon was Hardock, who came bustling out of the building over the mouth of the shaft, and stopped short to stare. Then, giving his leg a heavy slap, his face expanded into a grin of welcome.

"There you are, then, both of you at last. Why, where have you been all this time?"

"Oh, busy at home," said Gwyn, evasively.

"Come to knock up an accident of some kind!" said the man, with the grin on his face expanding.

"No, I haven't," said Gwyn, shortly.

"You, then?" cried Hardock, turning to Joe, who coloured like a girl.

"Ah, well, we won't quarrel now you have come, my lads: but the Colonel made my ears sing a bit the other day for not looking more sharply after you both. Well, aren't you going to ask how the mine is?"

"Yes," said Gwyn, glad to change the subject. "Got all the water out?"

"Nay, my lad, nor nothing like all."

"Then you never will," said Joe. "Depend upon it, there's a way in somewhere from the sea, and that's why the old place was forsaken."

"Sounds reasonable," said Hardock, "'specially as the bits of ore we've come across are so rich."

"Yes, that's it," said Gwyn. "What a pity, though. How far have you got down?"

"Oh, a long way, my lad, and laid open the mouths of two galleries. Wonderful sight of water we've pumped out. Don't seem to get much farther now."

"No, and you never will," said Joe again, excitedly. "I'm sorry, though. Father will be so disappointed."

"What makes you say that there's a way in from the sea?" said Hardock, quietly.

"Because the shaft's so near. It's a very bad job, though."

"But look ye here," said Hardock, laying his hand on Gwyn's shoulder, "as you have come, tell me this: how should you try to find out whether it was sea-water we were pumping out?"

"Why, by tasting it, of course," said Gwyn. "It would be quite salt."

"Of course!" said Hardock, with a chuckle, "that's what I did do."

"And was it salt?" asked Joe.

"No, it warn't. It was fresh, all fresh; only it warn't good enough to make tea."

"Why?" asked Gwyn.

"'Cause you could taste the copper in it quite strong. We shall get the water out, my lads, in time; but it's a big mine, and goodness knows how far the galleries run. Strikes me that your guv'nors are going to be rich men and— Hullo! What's he been doing there?"

The boys turned, on seeing the direction of the mine captain's gaze, and they saw Tom Dinass's back, as he stood, cap in hand, talking to someone inside the office door—someone proving to be the Colonel.

"Been to ask to be taken on to work at the mine," said Gwyn.

"But that won't do, my lads," cried Hardock, excitedly. "We want to be all friends here, and he belongs to the enemy. They can't take him on! It would mean trouble, as sure as you're both there. Oh, they wouldn't engage he."

Hardock said no more, for Dinass had seen them as he turned from the office door, and came toward them at once.

"Are you?" he said to Hardock, without the 'How'; and the captain nodded in a sulky way.

"What do you want here?" he said.

"Just whatever you like, captain. I'm an old hand, and ready for anything. The guv'nors have took me on, and I'm come to work."

Chapter Twenty One
Sam Hardock Disapproves

Clank, clank! and *wash, wash*! The great pump worked and the water came up clear and bright, to rush along the channel cut in the floor of the adit and pour from the end like a feathery waterfall into the sea, the spray being carried like a shower of rain for far enough on a breezy day. But there seemed to be no end to it, and the proprietors began to look anxious.

Still Hardock's face was always cheery.

"Only because she's so big underground, and there's such a lot to get out, you see, my lads. She's right enough. Why, that water's been collecting from perhaps long before I was born. We shall get her dry some day."

But Dinass, who somehow always seemed to be near when the boys were about the mine, looked solemn, and as soon as Hardock's back was turned he gave Gwyn a significant wink.

"I only hope he's right," said the man.

"Then you don't know he is?" said Joe, sharply.

"I don't say nothing, young gents, nothing at all; but that pump's been going long enough now to empty any mine, and yet, if you both go and look at the water, you'll see it's coming as fast as ever and just as clear."

"Because they haven't got to the bottom of it yet," said Gwyn.

"It aren't that, young gentleman," said Dinass, mysteriously. "Of course it aren't my business, but if the mine belonged to me I should begin to get uncomfortable."

"Why?" asked Joe.

"Because I should be thinking that the old folks who digged this mine had to come up it in a hurry one day."

"Why?—because there were bogies and goblins in it?"

"No, sir, because they broke through one day into an underground river; and you can't never pump dry a place like that. But there, I don't know, gentlemen—that's only what I think."

The man went about his work, over which he was so assiduous that even Hardock could not complain, and the latter soon after encountered the lads.

"Don't say Dinass told us," whispered Gwyn. "Sam hates him badly enough as it is. Let him think that it's our own idea."

"Not got to the bottom of the water yet, then?" said Gwyn.

"No, sir—not yet, not yet," replied the captain, blandly; "and it won't come any the quicker for you joking me about it."

"But aren't you beginning to lose heart?"

"Lose heart? Wouldn't do to lose heart over a mine, sir. No, no; man who digs in the earth for metals mustn't lose heart."

"But we're not digging, only pumping."

"But we might begin in one of these galleries nearly any time, sir. I've been down, and I've seen better stuff than they're getting in some of the mines, I can tell you, sir. But we'd better have the water well under first."

"But suppose you are never going to get it under?"

"Eh? No, I don't s'pose anything of the kind. It's fresh water, and we must soon bottom it."

"But suppose it's an underground river, Sam?" said Joe, sharply.

"Underground river, my lad? Then that will be a fine chance for you two. I should be for getting my tackle ready, and going fishing as soon as the water's low enough. Who knows what you might ketch?"

"Nothing to laugh at, Sam," said Gwyn, sternly. "If there should prove to be an underground stream, you'll never pump the mine dry."

"Never, sir, and I shouldn't like to try; but," the man continued with a twinkle of the eye, "the steam-engine will. That's the beauty of these things—they never get tired. Here's the guv'nors."

Colonel Pendarve came up with the Major, both looking very serious, and evidently troubled by the slow progress over the water.

"Been down the shaft, Hardock?" said the former.

"Yes, sir; just come up."

"Any better news?" said the Major, quickly.

"No, sir; it's just about the same. Couldn't be better."

"Not be better, man! The anxiety is terrible."

"Oh, no, sir," said Hardock; "that's only because you worry yourself over it. Water's been steadily sinking ever since we began to pump."

"But so slowly—so slowly, man."

"Yes, sir, but there's the wonder of it. Place is bigger than we expected."

"Then the water is falling, Hardock?" said the Colonel.

"Yes, sir, steady and sure; and whenever the pump has been stopped, the water hasn't risen, which is the best sign of all."

"Yes; we must have patience, Jollivet, and wait."

"Yes, sir," put in Hardock; "and if I might make so bold as to speak I wouldn't engage anyone else for the present. When the mine's dry it will be time enough."

"No; better get recruits while we can," said the Colonel.

"But you have ideas on paying wages, sir, and I fancy I know the best sort of men we want."

"Ah, you don't like the man Dinass," said the Colonel.

"No, sir, I don't; not at all."

"But you said he worked well and knew his business."

"Yes, sir; but I don't like him none the more."

"Petty jealousy, my man, because you did not have a word in the business. Come along, Major, and let's see how the pump's getting on."

"Jealousy," grunted Hardock; "just as if I'd be jealous of a chap like that. What yer laughing at, Mr Gwyn?"

"You, Sam. Why, you're as jealous of Dinass as you can be."

"Think so, sir? What do you say, Mr Joe Jollivet?"

"Didn't say anything, but I thought so. You're afraid of his taking your place as foreman or captain."

"Me?" cried the man, indignantly. "'Fraid of an odd-job sort of a chap, took on like out of charity, being able to take my place? Come, I do like that, Master Joe. What do you think of it, Mr Gwyn?"

"Think Joe Jollivet's right," said Gwyn, hotly; and Hardock turned upon him angrily,—

"Well, aren't it enough to make me, sir. Here was I out of work through mine after mine being advertised, and none of 'em a bit of good. And what do I do but sit down and puzzle and think out what could be done, till I hit upon Ydoll and went up and examined it, and looked at bits of stuff that I found on the bank and round about the mouth, till I was sure as sure that it was a good thing that had never been properly worked, or they wouldn't have pitched away the good ore they did. Though what could you expect from people ever so long ago who had no proper machinery to do things with; and the more I work here the more I'm sure of there being heaps of good stuff to be got. Well, what do I do? Talks to you young gents about it, don't I? and then your fathers laugh at it all, and I'm regularly upset till they took the idea up. Then I set to and got the place in going order, and it's bound to be a very big thing, and all my doing, as you may say; and then up comes Mr Dinass to shove his nose in like the thin edge of a wedge. How would you both like it if it was you?"

"Well, I shouldn't like it at all," said Gwyn.

"Of course, you wouldn't, sir, nor Mr Joe neither; and I just tell Mr Tom Dinass this: so long as he goes on and does his work, well and good—I sha'n't quarrel with him; but if he comes any underhanded games and tries to get me out of my place, I'll go round the mine with him."

"You'll do what?" cried Joe.

"See how deep the mine is with him, sir, and try how he likes that."

Sam Hardock gave the lads a very meaning nod and walked away, leaving the pair looking inquiringly at each other.

"He'd better mind what he's about," said Joe. "That Tom Dinass is an ugly customer if he's put out."

"Yes, but it's all talk," said Gwyn. "People don't pitch one another down mines; and besides, you couldn't pitch anyone down our mine on account of the platforms. Why, you couldn't drop more than fifteen or twenty feet anywhere."

"No, but it would be very ugly if those two were to quarrel and fight."

Chapter Twenty Two
A Mental Kink

The time went on, with the carpenters and engineers hard at work. As fast as the water was lowered enough, fresh platforms were placed across the shaft. After a little consideration and conference with Hardock, it was decided not to let the men go up and down the mine by means of ladders on account of the labour and loss of time, but to erect one of the peculiar beams used in some mines, the platforms being at equal distances favouring the arrangement.

The boys were present at the consultation, and when it was over they went off for a stroll, Grip following in a great state of excitement, and proceeding to stalk the gulls whenever he saw any searching for spoil on the grassy down at the top of the cliffs.

But the dog had no success. The gulls always saw him coming, and let him creep pretty near before giving a few hops with outstretched wings, and then sailing away just above his head, leaving him snapping angrily and making his futile bounds.

After a time the boys threw themselves on the grass at the top of one of the highest cliffs, from whence they could look down through the transparent sea at the purply depths, or at the pale-green shallows, where the sand had drifted, or again, at where all the seaweed was of a rich golden brown.

It was a lovely day, and in the offing the tints on the sea were glorious, but the boys had no eyes for anything then. So to speak, they were looking back at the meeting which had just taken place at Colonel Pendarve's.

"Father looked very serious about these lift things," said Gwyn, at last.

"Enough to make him; it's nothing but pay, pay, pay. I want to see them get to work and make money. It will be skilly and bread for us if the mine fails."

"'Tisn't going to fail. Don't be a coward. See what a grand thing this new apparatus will be."

"Will it?" said Joe. "I don't understand it a bit."

"Why, it's easy enough."

"I can understand about a bucket or a cage, let up and down by a rope running over a wheel, but this seems to me to be stupid."

"Nonsense! It's you who are stupid. Can't you see that a great beam is to go from the top to the bottom of the mine?"

"That's nonsense. Where are they going to get one long enough?"

"Can't they join a lot together till it is long enough, old Wisdom teeth? Of course, it will have to be made in bits, and put together."

"Well, what then?" cried Joe.

"What then? Sam Hardock and the engineer explained it simply enough. The beam is to have a little standing-place on it at every eighteen feet."

"Yes, I understand that, and it's to be attached to an engine lever which will raise it eighteen feet, and then lower it eighteen feet."

"Of course. Well, what's the good of pretending you did not understand?"

"I didn't pretend; I don't understand."

Gwyn laughed.

"You are a fellow! There'll be a ledge for a man to stand on, all down the beam from top to bottom exactly opposite the regular platform."

"Yes, I understand that."

"Well, then, what is it you don't understand?" cried Gwyn, smiling.

"How it works."

"Why, you said you did just now. Oh, I say, Jolly-wet, what a foggy old chap you are. You said as plain as could be, that the beam rose and fell eighteen feet."

"Oh, yes, I said that, but I don't understand about the men."

"Well, you are a rum one, Joe. Is it real, or are you making believe?"

"Real. Now, suppose it was us who wanted to go down."

"Well, suppose it was us."

"What do we do?"

"Why, we—"

"No, no, let me finish. I say, what do we do? We step on the ledge attached to the beam?"

"Of course we do, only one at a time."

"Very well, then, one at a time. Then down goes the beam eighteen feet to the next platform."

"Yes, and then up it rises again eighteen feet, and most likely there'd be a man on every ledge, from top to bottom."

"Well, what's the good of that?"

"Good? Why, so that the men can ride up or down when they're tired, and do away with the ladders."

"Isn't that absurd? I'm sure my father never meant to put a lot of money into this thing so as to give the men a ride up and down on a patent see-saw."

"Oh I say, Joe, what a chap you are! What have you got in your head?"

"This old see-saw that Hardock and the engineer want us to have, of course."

"Well, can't you see how good it will be?"

"No, I can't, nor you neither."

"But don't you see it sends the men all down eighteen feet into the mine?"

"Of course I can. Never mind the men. Suppose it's me, and I step on. It sends me down eighteen feet."

"Yes, at one stride, and then comes up again; can't you see that?"

"Of course, I can. It comes up again, and brings me up with it, ready to go down again. Why, it's no good. It will be only like a jolly old up-and-down."

Gwyn stared at his companion.

"What are you talking about?" he said, but in a less confident tone.

"You know, this gimcrack thing that was to do so much. Why the idea's all wrong. Don't you see?"

Gwyn stared at his companion again.

"Nonsense!" he cried, "it's all right. There'll be a man step on to it at every platform, and then down he'll go."

"Of course, and when he has gone down eighteen or twenty feet, up he'll come again. It sounds very pretty, but it's all a muddle. It's just like the story of the man who wanted to go to America, so he went up in a balloon and stayed there for hours and waited till the world had turned round enough, so as to come down in America."

"Oh, but this is all right; they explained it exactly to my father, and I saw it all plainly enough then: it was as clear as could be," said Gwyn, thoughtfully. "A man stepped on and went down."

"Yes, and the beam rose and he came up again."

Gwyn scratched his head and looked regularly puzzled, and the more he tried to see the plan clearly, the more confused he grew.

"Here, I can't make it out now," he said at last.

"Of course you can't, my lad; it's all wrong."

"But if it is, there will be a terrible loss."

"To be sure there will."

"Let's go and talk to my father about it."

"Or mine," said Joe.

"Our place is nearest, or perhaps father's in the office," cried Gwyn, excitedly. "Mind, I don't say you're right, because I seemed to see it all so clearly, though it has all turned misty and stupid like now."

"I know how it was," said Joe. "Sam Hardock had got the idea in his head, and he explained it all so that it seemed right; but it isn't, and the more I think about it, the more I wonder that no one saw what a muddle it was before."

"Gammon!" cried Gwyn, springing up, and the two lads started back toward the mine; but they were not destined to reach it then, for they had not gone above a hundred yards along by the edge of the cliff, when they came upon Dinass seated with his back to a rock, smoking his pipe and gazing out to sea between his half-closed eyelids.

"Hallo!" shouted Gwyn; "what are you doing here?"

"Smoking," said the man, coolly.

"Well, I can see that," cried Gwyn. "How is it you are not at work?"

"'Cause a man can't go on for ever without stopping. Man aren't a clock, as only wants winding up once a week; must have rest sometimes."

"Well, you have the night for rest," said Gwyn, sharply.

"Sometimes," said Dinass; "but I was working the pump all last night."

"Oh, then you're off work to-day?"

"That's so, young gentleman, and getting warm again in the sun. It was precious cold down there in the night, and I got wet right through to my backbone. I'm only just beginning to get a bit dried now."

"Look here, Ydoll," said Joe, sharply; "he'll have been talking to Sam Hardock about it, I know. Here, Tom Dinass, what about that hobby up-and-down thing Sam Hardock wants to have in the mine?"

"'Stead of ladders? Well, what about it?"

"It's all nonsense, isn't it?"

"Well, I shouldn't call it nonsense," said the man, thoughtfully, as he took his pipe out of his mouth and sat thinking.

"What do you call it, then?" said Joe.

"Mellancolly, sir, that's what I call it—mellancolly."

"Because it won't work?" cried Joe.

"But it would work, wouldn't it?" said Gwyn.

"Oh, yes, sir, it would work," said the man, "because the engine would pump it up and down."

"Of course it would," said Joe; "but what's the use of having a thing that pumps up and down, unless it's to bring up water?"

"Ay, but this is a thing as pumps men up and down," said Dinass.

"Gammon! It's impossible."

Dinass looked at him in astonishment.

"No, it aren't," he said gruffly. "I've been pumped up and down one times enough, so I ought to know."

"You have?" said Gwyn, eagerly.

"Ay, over Redruth way."

"There, then it is right," cried Gwyn. "I knew it was. What an old jolly wet blanket you are, Joe!"

"But it can't be right," cried Joe, stubbornly. "Here you get on a bit of a shelf and stand there and the beam goes down twenty feet."

"Nay, it don't," said Dinass, interrupting; "only twelve foot."

"Well it's all the same—it might be twenty feet, mightn't it?"

"I s'pose so, sir. Ones I've seen only goes twelve foot at a jog."

"Twelve feet, then; and then it jigs up again," cried Joe.

"Ay, just like a pump. Man-engines they call 'em," said Dinass; "but I have heard 'em called farkuns."

(Note: *Fahr-Kunst*. First used in the Harz Mountain mines.)

"Then you've seen more than one?" cried Gwyn.

"More than one, sir! I should think I have!"

"And they do go well?"

"Oh, yes, sir, they go well enough after a fashion."

"Can't," cried Joe.

"But they do, sir," said Dinass. "I've seen 'em and gone down deep mines on 'em."

"Now you didn't—you went down twelve feet," said Joe, more stubbornly than ever.

"Yes, sir, twelve foot at a time."

"And then came up twelve feet."

"That's right, sir."

"Then what's the good of them if they only give you a ride up and down twelve feet?"

"To take you to the bottom."

"But they can't," cried Joe.

"I dunno about can't!" said the man, gruffly; "all I know is that they do take 'em up or down whenever you like, and saves a lot of time, besides being (I will say that for 'em) a regular rest."

"What, through just stepping on a shelf of the beam and stopping there?"

"Who said anything about stopping there?" cried the man, roughly. "You steps on to the shelf and down goes the beam twelve foot, and you steps off on to a bit o' platform. Up goes the beam and brings the next shelf level with you, and on you gets to that. Down you go another twelve foot, or another twenty-four. Steps off, up comes the next shelf, and you steps on. Down she goes again, and you steps on and off, and on and off, going down twelve foot at a time, till you're at the bottom, or where you want to be part of the way down at one of the galleries."

"Of course," cried Gwyn, triumphantly. "I knew it was German, all right, only I got a bit foggy over it when you said it wasn't."

"But—"

"I knew there was something. We forgot about stepping off and letting the beam rise."

Joe scratched his head.

"Don't you see now?" cried Gwyn.

"Beginning to: not quite," said Joe, still in the same confused way. Then, with a start, he gave his leg a hearty slap. "Why, of course," he cried, "I see it all clearly enough now. You step on and go down, and then step on and go up, and then you step on—and step on. Oh, I say, how is it the thing does work after all?"

"Why you—" began Gwyn, roaring with laughter the while, but Joe interrupted him.

"No, no; I've got it all right now. I see clearly enough. But it is puzzling. What an obstinate old block you were, Ydoll."

"Eh? Oh, come, I like that," cried Gwyn. "Why you—" Then seeing the mirthful look on his companion's face he clapped him on the shoulder. "You did stick to it, though, that it wouldn't go, and no mistake."

"Well, I couldn't see it anyhow. It was a regular puzzle," said Joe, frankly. "But I say, Tom Dinass, what made you call these man-engines melancholy things?"

"'Cause of the mischief they doos, sir. I do hope you won't have one here."

"Why? What mischief do they do?" cried Gwyn.

"Kills the poor lads sometimes. Lad doesn't step on or off at the right time, and he gets chopped between the step and the platform. It's awful then. 'Bliged to be so very careful."

"Man who goes down a mine ought to be very careful."

"O' course, sir; but they things are horrid bad. I don't like 'em."

"But they can't be so dangerous as ladders, or going down in a bucket at the end of a string or chain; you might fall, or the chain might break. Such things do happen," said Gwyn.

"Ay, sir, they do sometimes; but I don't like a farkun. Accident's an accident, and you must have some; but these are horrid, and we shall be having some accident with that dog of yours if we don't mind."

"Accident?" said Gwyn. "What do you mean?"

"He'll be a-biting me, and I shall have to go into horspittle."

"Oh, he won't hurt you," cried Gwyn.

"Don't know so much about that, sir," said the man, grinning. "I should say if he did bite he would hurt me a deal. Must have a precious nice pair o' legs, or he wouldn't keep smelling 'em as he does, and then stand licking his jaws."

"I tell you he won't hurt you," cried Gwyn. "Here, Grip—come away."

The dog looked up at his master, and passed his tongue about his lower jaw.

"Look at that, sir," said Dinass, laughing; but there was a peculiar look in his eyes. "Strikes me as he'd eat cold meat any day without pickles."

"I'll take care he sha'n't bite your legs, with or without pickles," said Gwyn, laughing. "Come along, Joe, and let's go and have a talk to Sam Hardock about the—what did he call it—far—far—what?"

"I don't know," replied Joe; "but somehow I wish Master Tom Dinass hadn't been taken on."

"Going to have a man-engine, are they?" muttered Dinass, as he sat watching the two lads from the corners of his eyes. "Seems to me that things have gone pretty nigh far enough, and they'll have to be stopped. Won't eat my legs with or without pickles, won't he? No, he won't if I know it. Getting pretty nigh all the water out too. Well, I daresay there'll be enough of it to drown that dog."

Chapter Twenty Three
Grip takes an Interest

"Now, Joe, this ought to be a big day," said Gwyn, one bright morning. "Father's all in a fidget, and he looked as queer at breakfast as if he hadn't slept all night."

"Wasn't any as if," replied Joe; "my father says he didn't sleep a wink for thinking about the mine."

"Oh, but people often say they haven't slept a wink when they've been snoring all the night. See how the fellows used to say it at Worksop. I never believed them."

"But when father says it you may believe him, for when he has fits of the old jungle fever come back, I'm obliged to give him his doses to make him sleep."

"Well I woke ever so many times wondering whether it was time to get up. Once the moon was shining over the sea, and it was lovely. It would have been a time to have gone off to Pen Ree Rocks congering."

"Ugh, the beasts!" exclaimed Joe. "But, I say, what a thing it will be if the place turns out no good after all this trouble and expense."

"Don't talk about it," said Gwyn. "But Sam says it's right enough."

"And Tom Dinass shakes his head and says—as if he didn't believe it could be—that he hopes it may turn out all right, but he doubts it."

"Tom Dinass is a miserable old frog croaker. Sam knows. He says there's no doubt about it. The mine's rich, and it must have been worked in the old days in their rough way, without proper machinery, till the water got the better of them, and they had to give it up."

"I hope it is so," said Joe, with a sigh. "But, I say, what about going down?"

"Your father won't go down."

"Oh, yes, he will. He says he shall go in the skep if your father does."

"Oh, my father will go, of course; but he said I'd better not go till the mine was more dry, and the man-engine had been made and fitted."

"Hurrah! Glad of it!"

"What do you mean by that?" cried Gwyn, angrily.

"What I say! I don't see why you should be allowed to go, and me stay up at grass."

"Humph! Just the place for you," said Gwyn.

"And what do you mean by that?" cried Joe, angrily in turn.

"Proper place for a donkey where there's plenty of grass."

"Ah, now you've got one of your nasty disagreeable fits on. Just like a Cornishman—I mean boy."

"Better be a Cornish chap than a Frenchy."

"Frenchy! We've been long enough in England to be English now," cried Joe. "But it's too hard for us not to go."

"Regular shame!" said Gwyn. "I've been longing for this day so as to have a regular examination. It must be a wonderful place, Joe. Quite a maze."

"Oh, I don't know," said Joe, superciliously; "just a long hole, and when you've seen one bit you've seen all."

"That's what the fox said to the grapes," said Gwyn, with a laugh.

"No, he didn't; he said they were sour."

"Never mind; it's just your way. The place will be wonderful. There are sure to be plenty of crystals and stalactites and wonderful caverns and places. Oh, I do wish we were going down."

"I don't know that I do now—the place will be horribly damp."

"Fox again."

"Look here, Gwyn Pendarve, if you wish to quarrel, say so, and I'll go somewhere else."

"But I don't want to quarrel, Joseph Jollivet, Esquire," said Gwyn, imitating the other's stilted way of speaking. "What's the good of quarrelling with you?"

Joe picked up a stone and threw it as far as he could, so as to get rid of some of his irritability; and Grip, who had been sitting watching the boys, wondering what was the matter, went off helter-skelter, found the stone, and brought it back crackling against his sharp white teeth, dropped it at Joe's feet, and began to dance about and make leaps from the ground, barking, as if saying, "Throw it again—throw it again!"

"Lie down, you old stupid!" cried Gwyn.

"Let him have a run," said Joe, picking up the stone and jerking it as far as he could over the short grassy down, the dog tearing off again.

"Ugh! Look at your hand," said Gwyn, "all wet with the dog's 'serlimer,' as the showman called it."

"Oh, that's clean enough," said Joe; but he gave his hand a rub on the grass all the same.

The dog came back panting, and Joe picked up the stone to give it another jerk, but, looking round for a fresh direction in which to throw it, he dropped the piece of granite.

"Come on!" he shouted, as he started off; "they're going to the shaft."

Gwyn glanced in the direction of the mine, and started after Joe, raced up to him, and they ran along to the building over the mouth, getting there just at the same time as the Colonel and Major Jollivet, the dog coming frantically behind.

"Well, boys," cried the Colonel, "here we are, you see. Wish us luck."

"Of course I do, father," said Gwyn. "But you'd better let us come, too."

"No, no, no, no," said the Colonel, "better wait a bit. Besides, you are not dressed for it. We are, you see."

He smilingly drew attention to their shooting caps and boots and long mackintoshes.

"Yes," said the Major, laughing, "we're ready for a wet campaign."

Gwyn was not in the habit of arguing with his father, whose quietest words always carried with them a military decision which meant a great deal, so he was silent, and contented himself with a glance at Joe, who took his cue from him and remained quiet.

Several of the men were there standing about the square iron-bound box attached by a wire rope to a wheel overhead, and known as the skep, which, with another, would be the conveyances of the ore that was to be found, from deep down in the mine to the surface, or, as the miners termed it, to grass; and until the man-engine was finished this was the ordinary way up and down.

There was Sam Hardock, muffled up in flannel garments, and wearing a leather cap like a helmet, with a brim, in front of which was his feather represented by a thick tallow candle. He was armed with a stout pick in his belt, and the Colonel and Major both carried large geological hammers.

Tom Dinass was there, too, in charge with the engineer of the skep, to ensure a safe descent.

Then there were lanthorns, and Hardock, in addition, bore by a strap over his shoulder what looked like a large cartouche box, but its contents were to re-load the lanthorns, being thick tallow candles.

"Got plenty of matches, Hardock?" said Gwyn, eagerly.

"Oh yes, sir, two tin boxes full."

"We have each a supply of wax matches, too, my boy," said the Colonel. "All ready, I think," he continued, turning to the Major, who nodded, and then said to him in a low tone of voice, overheard by the boys in addition to him for whom it was addressed, —

"If anybody had told me six months ago that I should do this, I should have called him mad."

"Never mind, old fellow," said the Colonel, laughingly; "better than vegetating as we were, and doing nothing. It sets my old blood dancing in my veins again to have something like an adventure. Well," he said aloud, "we may as well make a start. By the way, have you any lunch to take down?"

"Oh, yes," said the Major, tapping a sandwich-box in his coat pocket; "too old a campaigner to forget my rations."

"Right," said the Colonel, tapping his own breast. "Well, boys, if we get lost and don't come up again by some time next week, you will have to organise a search-party, and come down and find us."

"Better let us come with you, father, to take care of you both."

The Colonel laughed, and shook his head.

"Now, Major," he cried, "forward!"

The Major stepped into the great wooden bucket, the Colonel followed, and then Sam Hardock took his place beside them.

"All ready!" cried the Colonel. "Now, Hardock, give the word."

The mining captain obeyed, there was a sharp, clicking noise, as the engineer touched the brake, and the wheel overhead began to revolve; then the skep dropped quickly and silently down through the square hole in the rough plank floor formed over the great open shaft, the pump being now still. Then, all at once, as the boys caught at the stout railing about the opening and looked down, the lanthorns taken began to glow softly and grew brighter for a time; then the light decreased, growing more and more feeble till it was almost invisible, and Gwyn drew a deep breath and looked up at the revolving wheel.

"Seems precious venturesome, doesn't it?" observed Joe.

"Not half so bad as going down with a rope round you, and feeling it coming undone," said Gwyn.

"No, but you did have water to fall into," said Joe. "If the wire rope breaks, they'll fall on the stone bottom and be smashed."

"Ah, yes," said Dinass, in solemn tones. "Be a sad business that."

"Will you be quiet, Tom Dinass!" cried Gwyn, irritably. "You're always croaking about the mine."

"Nay, sir, not me," replied the man. "It were Mr Joe here as begun talking about the rope breaking and their coming down squelch."

"Well, don't let anybody talk about such things," said Gwyn, who spoke as if he had been running hard. "Nearly down now, aren't they?"

"About half, sir," said the engineer.

"Oh, I don't want to talk," said Dinass; "only one can't help thinking it's queer work for two gents to do. It's a job for chaps like me. Howsoever, I hope they won't come to no harm."

Grip growled at something, as if, in fact, he were resenting the man's words, but it might have only been that he was being troubled by the flea which he had several times that morning tried to scratch out of his thick coat.

"You'd better not let them come to harm. I say, mind they don't come down bang at the bottom," said Gwyn, after what seemed to be a long time.

"He'll see to that, sir," said the man, nodding his head in the direction of the engineer.

"Yes, young gentlemen, that's all right. I've got the depth to an inch, and they'll come down as if on to a spring."

"I say, how deep it seems," said Joe, who also was rather breathless.

"Deep, sir!" said Dinass, with a laugh; "you don't call this deep? Why, it's nothing to some of the pits out Saint Just way—is it, mate?"

"Nothing at all," said the engineer. "This is a baby."

"Rather an old baby," said Gwyn, smiling. "Why, this must be the oldest mine in Cornwall."

"Dessay it is, sir," said the man; and he checked the wheel as he spoke, just as an empty skep of the same size as that which had descended made its appearance and came to a standstill.

"Right!" came up from below, in a hollow whisper, and Gwyn drew a deep breath.

"You two ought to have gone with 'em," said Dinass, "and had a look round."

"Oh, don't bother," cried Gwyn, petulantly. "I suppose we shall have our turn."

"No offence meant, sir," said the man. "Better let me go down with you. Dessay I can show you a lot about the mine."

"I suppose it will be all one long passage from the bottom," said Joe.

"Not it, sir," said Dinass, holding out his bare arm, and spreading his fingers. "It'll go like that. Lode runs along for a bit like my wrist, and then spreads out like my fingers here, or more like the root of a tree, and they pick along there to get the stuff where it runs richest. But you'll see. We don't know yet; but, judging from the water pumped out, this mine must wander a very long way. There's no knowing how far."

"I say, how long will they stop down?" said Joe.

"Oh, I don't know," replied Gwyn. "Hours, I daresay."

"Plenty of time for you young gents to take a boat and have half-a-day with the bass. There's been lots jumping out of the water against Ydoll Point. I should say they'd be well on the feed."

"That's likely!" said Gwyn. "You don't suppose we shall leave here till they come up?"

"Oh, I didn't know, sir. Makes no difference to me; only it'll be rather dull waiting."

Grip uttered a low, uneasy growl again, and looked up at his master, and then went to the opening and peeped down.

"Like us to send him down in the skep, sir?" said Dinass, grinning. "Better not, p'r'aps, as he might lose his way."

"No fear of Grip losing his way—eh, Joe?"

Joe shook his head.

"He'd find his way back from anywhere if he had walked over the ground. Wouldn't you, Grip?"

The dog gave a sharp bark as he turned his head, and then looked down again, whining and uneasy.

"What's the matter, old boy?" said Gwyn. "It's all right, old man, they've gone down. Will you go with me?"

The dog uttered a volley of barks, then turned to Dinass and growled.

"Quiet, sir!" cried Gwyn. "Look here, Tom Dinass, you must tease him, or he wouldn't be so disagreeable to you."

"Me? Me tease him, sir! Not me."

"Well, take my advice," said Gwyn, "don't. He's a splendid dog to his friends; so you make good friends with him as soon as you can."

Chapter Twenty Four
Anxious Times

An hour glided by and not a sound was heard from below. Then another hour, and the boys began to grow impatient.

"Why, the place must be very big," said Gwyn, after straining over the rail and looking down for some time. "Shall I shout?"

"Couldn't do no harm," said Dinass; and Gwyn hailed several times, and then gave place to Joe, who was beginning to look uncomfortable.

But the second series of shouting produced nothing but a dull smothered echo, and the lad spoke quite hoarsely when he turned to Gwyn, who was looking angrily at Dinass and the engineer, both of whom sat coolly enough close to the skep shaft, waiting the signal to lift.

"Think there's anything wrong?" said Joe in a whisper to the engineer.

"Oh, no, the place is big. See what a while it took to pump it out."

"But there may be deep holes here and there, and it would be horrible if they had slipped down one."

"They wouldn't all slip down a hole. If one did, the others would come for help. No; they're thoroughly exploring the place and chipping off specimens. I daresay they'll bring up quite a load."

"I hope so," said Joe, solemnly, and Gwyn, who felt very uncomfortable, tried to cheer him up, but in a low voice, so that the others should not hear.

"I say, how strange it is that if anyone doesn't come back when you expect him you are sure to think he has met with an accident."

"I don't, if they've only gone out," said Joe, with a shiver. "This isn't like that. This place seems to me now quite awful."

"Pooh! I say, I believe you'd go down and look for them if you might."

"Yes," said Joe, quickly; "I shouldn't like to, but I would."

"I wonder what it's like down below—all long, narrow passages roughly-cut through the rock," said Gwyn; "they wouldn't cut so carefully as they do now."

"No, as they say, the old people would only cut where the lode of ore ran, of course. But I hope there's nothing wrong."

"Of course you do; so do I. What's the good of fidgeting."

Joe did not say what was the good of fidgeting, but he fidgeted all the same; and Gwyn noted, as the time went on, that his companion looked quite hollow-cheeked, while at the same time he felt a peculiar sinking sensation that was very much like dread; and at last, as over two hours and a-half had passed, he began to feel that something ought to be done.

Joe not only felt, but said so, and frowned angrily as he spoke.

"It's too bad," he said; "those two sit there as coolly and contentedly as if nothing could be the matter. I say, Dinass," he cried aloud, "do you think there is anything wrong?"

"No, sir," said the man, coolly, "I don't. They're only having a good long prowl. You'll hear 'em shout to be taken up directly."

But the boys did not feel satisfied, and hung about the opening, growing more and more uneasy, though Gwyn kept the best face on the matter.

"Don't you fidget," he said, "father was only joking, of course, about time; but he knew they'd be down a long while, and he meant to be. They're all right."

"They're not all right," said Joe, quickly. "They can't be, or we should have heard from them. They've either fallen down some hole, or the roof has come down and crushed them, or they've lost their way in some wild out-of-the-way part of the mine. Let's call for volunteers, and go down and search for them."

"Hush! Be quiet! Don't be hysterical," whispered Gwyn; "there's no need to call for volunteers. I feel sure I know what it means; this old mine must be very big, perhaps winds about for miles in all directions; and they're only having a good long hunt now they are down. They'd laugh at us if we were to send volunteers."

"Send volunteers down!" said Joe.

"Well, lead them then. Wait a bit and see."

"They've been overcome by choke-damp."

"Nonsense! that's only in coal pits. Don't let these two see what a fright we're in."

"Don't see that you're in any fright," said Joe, bitterly. "You take it coolly enough."

"Outside," said Gwyn; "perhaps I feel as much as you do, only I don't show it. Joe, I wouldn't have my mother know about this for all the world—it would frighten her to death; and if we get talking about volunteers going down, someone is sure to go and tell her that we're in trouble, and she'll come on."

"But we must do something; they may be dying for want of help."

"Don't," whispered Gwyn, angrily; "you're as bad as a girl; try and think about how they are situated. Perhaps there are miles of passages below there, and they would be hours wandering about. Of course they go slowly."

"Couldn't be miles of passages," said Joe, piteously.

"Think the mine's very big, Dinass?" said Gwyn, quietly.

"Oh, yes, sir, bigger than I thought for."

"Some mines are very far to the end, aren't they?"

"Miles," said the man calmly, and Gwyn gave his companion a nudge. "I've been in some of 'em myself. Why, I know of one long 'un—an adit as goes from mine to mine to get rid of the pumpings—and it's somewhere about thirty miles."

"Hear that, Joe?" whispered Gwyn.

"Yes, I hear," said the lad, breathlessly.

"I don't say there's anything of the kind here, of course; but I know one place where there's more than sixty miles o' workings, and it would take some time to go all over that, wouldn't it?"

The boys were silent, and the engineer went on.

"Oh yes, that's right enough," he said; "and to my mind it's rather bad for any folk strange to go down a mine they know nothing about."

Joe started violently.

"You see it's all noo to 'em," continued the engineer, "and they may wander away into places they know nothing about, and never find their way out again."

"Gwyn!" groaned Joe.

"Hush! Be quiet!" was whispered back.

"I have heard of such things."

"But that was in deserted mines," said Gwyn, sharply.

"Yes, I believe it was in deserted mines, now you say so, sir."

"Of course it was, Joe, where nobody knew that they had gone down."

"How could they have gone down without anyone knowing?" cried Joe. "There must have been someone to let them down."

"Nay, they might have been venturesome and gone down by ladders, same as the old ones used to be from sollar to sollar."

"What's a sollar?" said Gwyn, more for the sake of saying something than from a desire to know.

"What you calls platforms or floors," said Dinass. "Well, I will say one thing; I do hope the guv'nors haven't lost their way."

"Of course, mate," said the engineer; "so do I; but if I was you young gents, I should begin to feel a little uncomfortable about them below."

"We are horribly," cried Joe, wildly.

"Exactly so, sir, for you see it must be getting on for four hours since they started."

"Nay, not so much as that," cried Dinass.

"I didn't say it was, mate—I only said it was getting on for four hours. There mayn't be nothing wrong, but there may be; and there wouldn't be no harm in doing something now. What do you say to getting some of the lads to go? They was talking about it when I went outside, as I told mate Dinass here—didn't I, my son?"

"Ay, you did— What do you say, Mr Gwyn?"

"It is time to act," cried Joe, excitedly.

"Yes," said Gwyn, as he drew a deep breath, "we must do something. Get lanthorns and candles."

"Shall I call to some of the men, sir," said Dinass, "and hear what they say?"

The answer came from the doorway, where three or four heads appeared, and one of the owners said:

"I say, mates, aren't it time we heerd something about them as is gone down?"

"Yes," said Gwyn, firmly; "we're going down to see. Will you come with me, Joe?"

The boy's lips parted, though no words came; but he put out his hand and gripped his companion's fast.

"Get lights, some of you, quick!" cried Gwyn; and a murmur was heard outside, a murmur that increased till it was a loud cheer; and then, distinctly from outside, a voice was heard to say, —

"Hear that, mates? The young masters are going down."

And as if to endorse this, Grip, who had suddenly grown excited, burst into a loud bark.

Chapter Twenty Five
True to the Core

"Do you mean it, Master Gwyn?" said Dinass, sharply.

"Mean it? Of course. You'll come with us and help."

The man's mouth opened widely, and he stared for a few moments before he spoke,—

"Help to get lanthorns and candles, sir? Yes, of course."

"Come down with us," said Gwyn, sharply. "You can't let us go alone."

"Not let you go alone, sir," growled the man, surlily. "Well, you see—"

"Yes, we see," cried Gwyn, "you have been used to mines, we have not."

"Much used to this one as I am, sir. I don't know no more about it than you do."

"'Course you don't, matey," said the engineer, "but you can't say you won't go with 'em to look for the guv'nors and our mate."

"Can't I? Yes, I can," cried Dinass, fiercely; "easy; I won't go—there!"

"Yah!" came in a fierce growl from the men outside.

"Ah, but you don't mean it," cried the engineer.

"Yes, I do," cried Dinass. "Don't you be so precious handy sending people where they don't want to go. Why don't you go yourself?"

"How can I go?" said the engineer, sharply. "My dooty's here. Can you manage the skep and rope?"

"How do I know till I try?" growled Dinass.

"Try? Why, you'd be doing some mischief. I've no right to leave my work while anyone's down, and I won't leave it; but I'd go if I was free."

"Tom Dinass will go," said Joe. "You can't leave us in the lurch like this."

"'Course not: it's his gammon," cried a man at the opening into the shed-like place. "You'll go, mate."

"Ay, he'll go," rose in chorus.

"No, he won't," said Dinass, angrily. "I get five-and-twenty shilling a week for working here, not for going to chuck away my life."

"Gahn!" shouted a man. "Your life aren't worth more nor no one else's. Who are you?"

"Never you mind who I am," growled Dinass, "I aren't going to chuck away my life, and so I tell you."

"Who wants you to chuck away your life? Go on down, like a man," said the engineer.

"You go yourself; I'll take care of the engines," cried Dinass.

"That will do," said Gwyn, quietly. "Let us have candles, please, quick."

"Oh, you're not going down alone, young gen'lemen," said the man at the doorway who had spoken the most. "Some on us'll go with you if he won't, but the guv'nors made him second like to Master Hardock, and he ought to go, and he will, too, or we'll make him."

"Oh, will you?" cried Dinass, fiercely; "and how will you make me?"

"Why, if you don't go down like a man along with the young masters, we'll tie you neck and crop, and stuff you in the skep, and two more of us'll come, too, and make you go first. What do you say to that?"

"Say you daren't," cried Dinass.

"What do you say, lads?" cried the man.

"Oh, we'll make him go," came in chorus.

By this time, as Dinass stood there angry and defiant, the engineer had produced a candle-box and lit a couple of lanthorns, when Gwyn and Joe each took one, and stepped into the empty skep, followed by Grip, who curled up by their feet.

"Can't go like that, young gents. Them caps won't do. Here, come out. Who'll lend young masters hats?"

A couple of the strong leathern hats were eagerly offered, but only one would fit, and a fresh selection had to be made.

"'Keep back, you cowards. You're afraid to go yourselves, and you want to force me!'"

"Better have flannel jackets, sir," said the engineer to Gwyn.

"No, no, we can't wait for anything else. Come, Joe. Now let us down."

He raised the iron rail which protected the hole, and again stepped into the skep, followed by Joe, lanthorn in hand, and with the candle-box slung from his shoulder.

"Now, Tom Dinass," cried the engineer, "I'm with you."

"Nay, I don't go this time," was the surly reply, as Dinass looked sharply round at the men who had crowded into the shed, and in response to a meaning nod from the engineer began to edge nearer to him.

"Are you quite ready, Joe? Lower away," cried Gwyn.

"Wait a minute, sir," said the engineer, "you aren't quite ready. Now, then, Dinass, be a man."

"Oh, I'm man enough," said the miner, taking out his pipe and tobacco, "but I don't go down this time, I tell you."

"Yes, you do," said the man who had spoken. "Ready?"

"Nay," cried Dinass, thrusting back his pipe and pouch and catching up a miner's pick, which he swung round his head; "keep back, you cowards. You're afraid to go yourselves, and you want to force me. Keep off, or I'll do someone a mischief. There isn't one of you as dare tackle me like a man."

"Oh, yes, there is," cried the first speaker; "any of us would. Now, once more, will you go down with the young gentlemen?"

"Go yourself. No!"

"Oh, I'd go, but it's your job. You're made next to Master Sam Hardock, so just show that you're worth the job."

"Lower away there," cried Dinass, "and let the boys go down theirselves."

"Not me," said the engineer.

"Right," said the leader of the men. "Now, Tom Dinass, this time settles it: will you go down?"

"No!"

"Then here goes to make you."

The man dashed at Dinass, who struck at him with the pick, but the handle was cleverly caught, the tool wrested from his grasp and thrown on the floor, while, before the striker could recover himself, he was seized, there was a short struggle, and his opponent, who was a clever Cornish wrestler, gave him what is termed the cross-buttock, lifted him from the ground, and laid him heavily on his back.

The men raised a frantic cheer of delight, which jarred terribly on the two boys in their anxious state, though all the same they could not help feeling satisfied at seeing Dinass prostrated and lying helpless with the miner's foot upon his chest.

"Let him get up," said Gwyn; "we'd sooner go alone than with him; but if you'll come with us I should be glad."

"I'd come with you, sir, or any on us would—"

"Ay, ay," chorused the men.

"But we feel, as miners, that when a man's got his dooty to do, he must do it. So Master Tom Dinass here must go by fair means or foul."

"I'll go," cried Dinass. "Set o' cowards—ten or a dozen on you again' one."

"Nay, there was only one again' you with bare hands and without a pick. You go down, mate, and when you come up t'others'll see fair, and I'll show you whether I'm a coward."

"Don't I tell you I'll go?" growled Dinass. "Let me get up."

"Do you mean it? No games, or it'll be the worse for you," said the miner, sternly.

"I said I'd go with them," growled Dinass. "I aren't afraid, but I warn't engaged to do this sort of thing."

"You'll go, then?"

"Are you deaf? Yersss!" roared Dinass; and as the miner took his foot from the prostrate man's chest another moved to the doorway to guard against retreat.

But if Dinass had any intention of breaking away he did not show it. He rose to his feet, shook himself, and picking up his hat, which had been knocked off, put it on, took it off again, glanced round for one he considered suitable, snatched it from its wearer's head, put it on his own and pitched the one he had worn to the miner he had robbed, and then stepped into the skep.

"There you are," he said. "Now, then, lower away;" and as he spoke he stooped down quickly seized the dog by the collar, and swung him out of the skep.

"Don't! Don't do that," cried Gwyn. "Let the dog come."

But his words were too late; the rail was clapped down, the engineer had seized the handle; there was a clang, a sharp blow upon a gong, and it seemed to the boys that the floor they had just left had suddenly shot up to the ceiling. Then it gave place to a glow of light dotted with heads, and amidst a low murmur of voices there rose the furious barking of a dog.

Directly after, they were conscious of the singular sensation that is felt when in a swing and descending after the rise, but in a greatly intensified way. Then the glow overhead grew fainter and smaller, and the lanthorns they held seemed to burn more brightly, while a peculiar whishing, dripping noise made itself heard, telling of water oozing from some seam.

"For we always are so jolly, oh! So jolly, oh!" sang Dinass in a harsh, discordant voice. "How do you like this, youngsters?"

Neither of the boys answered, but the same thought came to them both—"that their companion was singing to make a show of his courage."

"I didn't want to fight," continued Dinass; "but I could have knocked that fellow Harry Vores into the middle of next week if I'd liked. I'd have come down, too, without any fuss if they'd asked me properly; but I'm not going to be bullied and driven, so I tell 'em."

Still neither Gwyn nor Joe spoke, but stood listening to the dripping water, and wondering at the easy way in which the skep went down past platform and beam, whose presence was only shown by the gleam of the wet wood as the lanthorns passed. And still down and down for what seemed to be an interminable length of time.

They knew that they must have passed the openings of several horizontal galleries, but they saw no signs of them, as they stood drawing their breath hard, till all at once the skep stopped, and Dinass shouted boisterously,—

"Here we are; bottom. Give's hold o' one o' them lanthorns, or we shall be in the sumph."

He snatched the lanthorn Joe carried, held it down, and stepped off the skep.

"It's all right," he said; "there's some planking here."

The two boys followed, and looked down into the black thick water of the sumph, a great tank into which the drainings of the mine ran ready for being pumped up; and now Gwyn held up his light to try and penetrate the gloom, but could only dimly trace the entrance of what appeared to be a huge, arch-roofed tunnel, and as they stepped over the rough wet granite beneath it, Dinass placed a hand to the side of his mouth and uttered a stentorian hail, which went echoing and rolling along before them, to be answered quite plainly from somewhere at a distance.

A load fell from Gwyn's breast, and he uttered a sigh of relief.

"It's all right, Joe," he said. "There they are, but some distance in. Come on."

He led the way, Joe followed, and Dinass came last with the other lanthorn; and in a few minutes the great archway contracted and grew lower and lower, till it very nearly met their heads, and the sides of the place were so near that they could in places have been touched by the extended hands.

"Hold hard a moment," said Dinass, after they had gone on a short distance; and as the boys turned to him wonderingly, he continued, "this here's the main lead of course, but it's sure to begin striking out directly right and left like the roots of a tree. What you've got to do's to keep to the main lead, and not go turning off either side. It's not very easy, because they're often as big as one another. That's what I wanted to say to you as one thing to mind. T'other's to keep a sharp look-out for ways downward to lower leads. There would be no railings left round here, 'cause the wood'll all have rotted away. I'd keep your light low down, and if you see a place like a square well don't step into it. You won't break your neck, 'cause it will be quite full of water, for the pumping hasn't reached down there, but you might be drowned, for it aren't likely I'm coming down after you."

"I'll take care," said Gwyn, with his voice sounding husky; and Joe nodded, with his eyes looking wild and dilated.

"That's all I wanted to say," said Dinass, "so on you go."

"Give another shout," said Gwyn, "and let them know we're here."

"What for?" said the man, roughly.

"You heard what I said—to let them know we're here. They answered before, but I suppose voices travel a long way."

"Sometimes," said the man, with a strange laugh.

"Shout, then; your voice is louder than ours," said Gwyn.

"What's the good o' shouting? They're miles away somewhere."

"No, no, you heard them answer."

"No I didn't," said the man, contemptuously; "that was only eckers."

"What?" cried Gwyn, with his heart seeming to stand still.

"Eckers. Hark here."

He put his hand to his mouth, and proved the truth of his words.

"Sam!"

"*Sam!*" very softly.

"Har!"

"*Har!*"

"Dock!"

"*Dock!*"—the echo coming some moments after the calls in a peculiar weird way.

"Sam 'Ardock!" shouted Dinass then, with a loudness and suddenness which made the boys start.

"*Dock!*" came back from evidently a great distance, giving such an idea of mystery and depth that the boys could hardly repress a shudder.

"Only eckers," said the man; "and as old Sam Hardock would say, 'it's a gashly great unked place,' but I think there's some tin in it. Look there and there!"

He held up the lanthorn he carried close to the roof, which sparkled with little purply-black grains running in company with a reddish bloom, as if from rouge, amongst the bright quartz of the tunnel.

"Oh, never mind the tin," cried Joe. "Pray, pray go on; we're losing time."

"Yes, make haste," said Gwyn. "We'd better keep straight along here, and stop and shout at every opening or turning."

"Yes, that will be right," said Joe. "Only do keep on. My father is so weak from his illnesses, that I'm afraid he has broken down. I ought not to have let him come."

The words seemed strangely incongruous, and made Gwyn glance at his companion; but it was the tender nurse speaking, who had so often waited upon the Major through his campaign-born illnesses, and there was no call for mirth.

Onward they went along the rugged tunnel, which wound and zigzagged in all directions, the course of the ancient miners having been governed by the track of the lode of tin; and soon after they came to where a vein had run off to their left, and been laboriously cut out with chisel, hammer, and pick.

They shouted till the echoes they raised whispered and died away in the distance; but there was nothing to induce them to stay, and they went on again, to pause directly after by an opening on their right, where they again shouted in turn till they were hoarse, and once more went on to find branch after branch running from the main trunk, if main trunk it was; but all efforts were vain, and an hour must have gone by, nearly a quarter of which, at the last, had been here and there along the rugged gallery, without encountering a branch which showed where another vein had been followed.

It was very warm, and the slippery moisture of the place produced a feeling of depression that was fast ripening into despair. At first they had talked a good deal concerning the probabilities of the exploring party coming out into the main trunk from one of the branches they had passed, but, as Gwyn said, they dared not reckon upon this, and must keep on now they were there. And at last they went trudging on almost in silence, the tramping of their feet and the quaint echoes being all that was heard, while three black shadows followed after them along the rugged floor, like three more explorers watching to see which way they went.

All at once the silence was broken by Joe, who cried in a sharp, angry way,—

"Stop! Your candle's going out."

Gwyn stopped without turning, opened the door of the lanthorn, and uttered an ejaculation.

"Quite true," he said; "burned right down. I'll put in another candle."

The box was opened, a fresh one taken out, its loose wick burned and blown off in sparks, and then it was lit and stuck in the molten grease of the socket.

"You had better have another candle in yours, Dinass," said Joe; and he watched Gwyn's actions impatiently, while the lad carefully trimmed the wick, and waited till the grease of the socket cooled enough to hold the fresh candle firm.

"Now," said Joe, "you ought to give another good shout here before we start again."

There was no reply.

"Well, did you hear what was said?" cried Gwyn, closing and fastening his lanthorn.

Still there was no answer.

"Here, Tom Dinass," cried Gwyn, raising his lanthorn, as he turned to look back; "why don't you do what you're told?"

His answer was a sudden snatch at his arm by Joe, who clung to it in a fierce way.

"What's the matter? Aren't you well? Oh, I say, you must hold up now. Here, Tom Dinass."

"Gone!" gasped Joe, in a low whisper, full of horror.

"Gone? Nonsense! he was here just now."

"No. It's ever so long since he spoke to us. Gwyn, he has gone back and left us."

"Left us? What, alone here!" faltered Gwyn, as the grey, sparkling roof seemed to revolve before his eyes.

"Yes, alone here, Gwyn! Ydoll, old chap, it's horrible. Can we ever find our way back?"

Chapter Twenty Six
To the Bitter End

If ever an awful silence fell upon two unfortunate beings, it was upon those lads, deep down in the strange mazes of the ancient mine. For some moments neither could speak, but each stood gazing at his companion, with the two shadows strangely mingled upon the rugged, faintly-glittering wall.

Joe was the first to speak again, for his passionately-uttered question was not answered.

"He warned us to beware of the holes and places, and he must have slipped down one."

"Not he," said Gwyn, bitterly, as he stood scowling into the darkness. "He warned us when he was making up his mind to hang back and leave us. A miserable coward!"

"You think that?"

"I'm sure of it. A sneak! A miserable hound! Oh, how could anyone who calls himself a man act like this!"

"Perhaps he is close at hand after all. Let's try," cried Joe, and he uttered a long piercing hail, again and again, but with no other result than to raise the solemn echoes, which sounded awe-inspiring, and so startling, that the lad ceased, and gazed piteously at his companion.

"Feel scared, Joe?" said Gwyn at last.

Joe nodded.

"So do I. It's very cowardly, of course, but the place is so creepy and strange."

"Yes; let's get back. We can't do any more, can we?"

Gwyn made no reply, but stood with his brows knit, staring straight before him into the darkness beyond the dim halo cast by the lanthorn.

"Why don't you speak? Say something," cried Joe, half hysterically; but, though Gwyn's lips moved, no sounds came. "Gwyn!" cried Joe again, "say something. What's the good of us two being mates if we don't try to help each other?"

"I was trying to help you," said Gwyn at last, in a strange voice he hardly knew as his own; "but I was thinking so much I couldn't speak—I couldn't get out a word."

"Well, think aloud. Keep talking, or I shall go mad."

"With fright?" said Gwyn, slowly.

"I don't know what it is, but I feel as if I can't bear it. Say something."

"Well, that's just how I feel, and I want to get over it, but I can't."

There was another pause, and then, as if in a rage with himself, Gwyn burst out,—

"We're not babies just woke up in the dark, and ready to call for our mothers to help us."

"I called for mine to help me, though you could not hear," said Joe, simply; and his words sounded so strangely impressive that Gwyn uttered a sound like a gasp.

"What is there to be afraid of?" he cried passionately. "We ought to be savagely angry, and ready to feel that we could half kill that cowardly hound for forsaking us like this. I know what you feel, Joe; that we must hurry back as fast as we can to the foot of the shaft, and shout to them to haul us out."

"But do you really think Tom Dinass has sneaked away?"

"I'm sure he has, out of spite because he was forced to come; and when we got back he would be one of the first to grin and sneer at us. I want to run back as fast as I can, but you'll stand by me, won't you?"

"Of course I will."

"I know that, old chap. Well, what did we come for?"

"You know; to try and find them."

"Yes, and I'm getting better now. I couldn't help feeling scared. We're alone here, but we won't give up. We've got to find them somehow, and we will. I sha'n't turn back, for mother's sake. How could I go and tell her I came down to try and find them, and was afraid to go on in the dark!"

"Do you mean it?" said Joe, whose face was of a ghastly white.

"Yes; and you won't turn like you did on the ladder?"

"No."

"There was something to be afraid of then, but there isn't now."

"No," said Joe, with a gasp.

"We've got a light and can avoid any pit-holes; the water has all been pumped out, and there are only the pools we passed here and there. Nothing can hurt us here, for the roof won't fall; it's too strong, cut all through the rock as it is."

"Yes, but if we go on and lose ourselves as they have done—"

"Well, we must find our way again; and if we can't we must wait till somebody comes."

"Here! Alone?"

"We sha'n't be alone, because we're together."

"But do you think anyone would come?"

"Do you think all those men would stop hanging about the mouth, knowing we're lost, and not come and help us? I don't."

"No. Englishmen wouldn't do that," said Joe, slowly. "Let's go on. I'm not so scared now, but it is very horrible and lonely. Suppose the light went out."

"Well, we'd strike a match, and start another candle."

"Ah, you've got some matches then?"

"Yes; a whole box. No, I haven't; not one."

"Ydoll!" cried Joe in a despairing voice.

"But we've got plenty of candles, and we'll take care to keep them alight. Now then, if we stand still we shall lose heart again. Ready?"

"Yes."

"Come on, then;" and, setting his teeth and holding the lanthorn well above his eyes, Gwyn led the way further into the solemn darkness of the newly dried-out mine.

Chapter Twenty Seven
Reversal of Position

The afternoon had glided by, and evening was approaching fast, as the men gathered about the mouth of the mine sat and chatted over the place and its prospects. Work had been suspended for the greater part of the day, to allow the owners to make an inspection, and the men held quite a discussion meeting as to how matters would prove.

Some were of opinion that they would have perhaps a few weeks' work, and then be dismissed; but among those who took the opposite view was Harry Vores, the miner who had behaved so well that day.

"I don't think it will be so," he said. "This is a gashly old mine; and depend upon it when it was worked they didn't get half out of it. I begin to think that we shall soon find a lot; more men will be wanted; and I hope it will be so, for the pluck these two gentlemen have shown. We want a few more good mines to be going in the country, for things have been bad enough lately."

Others took his side, and as the time went on and there was no signal from the bottom of the shaft, that was discussed as well.

"Oh, they'll be all right," said Harry Vores. "The place is bigger than we thought; but we ought to have known, seeing what a sight of water was pumped out. They've only gone farther than they expected, and we shall be having them all up in a bunch directly."

He had hardly uttered these words when the gong arranged for signalling gave three tings, and the engineer responded by standing by to hoist.

Another signal was sent up, and the wheel began to revolve, the wire rope tightened, and the empty skep descended.

"Won't bring 'em all up at once, will you, mate?" said Harry Vores.

"No; two lots," said the engineer; and the men all eagerly gathered round the place to see the explorers of a mine which had not been entered probably for hundreds of years when they came up, and to learn what report they would have to give of the prospects of the place.

The rope ran over the wheel almost silently, for the work had been well done; and as they were waiting, Grip, who had passed the greater part of his time watching the place where he had seen his master disappear, grew more and more excited. He kept on bursting into loud fits of barking till the ascending skep appeared, when he bounded away among the men, barking, snarling and growling savagely, for the only occupant of the skep was Dinass.

"Hullo!" cried Vores, as the man stepped out, muddy and wet, with his cheeks reddened by the minerals which had discoloured his hands, and looking as if he had rubbed his face from time to time.

"Hullo, to you," he said sourly; and he sat down at once upon a rough bench, with the water slowly dripping from his legs and boots.

"Where are the young guv'nors? Lie down, dog!"

"Young guv'nors?" said Dinass, looking wonderingly round as he slowly took the lanthorn from where it swung from his waist by a strap.

"Yes, where are they?" cried Vores.

"How should I know?" growled Dinass. "Aren't they up here?"

"Here? No; we haven't seen them since they went down with you," cried Vores.

"More aren't I, hardly; I thought they'd come up again."

"Come up again!" cried the miner, as a low murmur arose from the men around. "You don't mean to say that you've come up and left them two poor boys in the lurch!"

"Lurch be hanged!" cried Dinass, fiercely, and now subsiding with a groin, as it were in pain. "It's them left me in the lurch. They started a game on me; I saw 'em whispering together, but I didn't think it meant anything till we'd got some ways in, and my candle wanted a bit o' snuffing to make it burn; so I kneels down and opens the lanthorn, and it took a bit o' time, for I wetted my thumb and finger to snuff it, and the wick spluttered after, and the light went out. Course I had my box o' matches, but it took ever so long to light the damp wick. At last, though, I got it to burn, but it went out again; and I turns to them, where they was waiting for me when I see 'em last. 'Give's a fresh candle, sir,' I says, 'for this here one won't burn.' But there was no answer. So I spoke louder, never thinking they was playing me any larks, but there was no answer; and I shouted, and there was no answer; and last of all I regularly got the horrors on me, for I was all alone."

"Well?" said Vores, scornfully, "what then?"

"Oh, then I begun wandering about in the dark banks and lanes, shouting and hollering, and going half mad. It's a horrid place, and I must have gone about for miles before I found my way back to the sumph, and nearly fell into it. But haven't they come up again?"

"No," said Vores, who had stepped up and opened the lanthorn as the man went on talking. "But how was it, when your candle wouldn't light again, that it's all burnt down in the socket?"

"Oh, I did get it to light at last of all," said Dinass; "but I had to burn all my matches first, and hadn't one left for a pipe."

"But you said you went about all in the dark."

"Yes, that was afterwards, and it soon burned out."

"Soon burned out!" cried Vores, fiercely. "Look here, mates; this fellow's a stranger here, and I don't know why he should have been set over us, for he's a liar, that's what he is. He didn't want to go down, and as soon as he could he hung back, and let those two poor boys go on all by themselves."

"What!" cried Dinass, as a murmur arose; "it's you that's the liar;" and he rose scowling.

"Dessay I am," said Vores as fiercely; "but I'm a honest sort of liar, if I am, and not a coward and a sneak, am I, lads?"

"Nay, that you aren't, Harry Vores," cried another miner. "We'll all say that."

"Ay! Shame, shame!" cried the miners.

"I'll lay a halfpenny he's been waiting at the bottom of the shaft all the time, and then come up."

"Get out of the way," roared Vores, "this is men's work, not cowards'. Here, lads, come on, we must go and fetch those boys up at once."

He gave Dinass a heavy thrust with his hand as he spoke, and the man staggered back against Grip, who retaliated by seizing him by the leg of the trousers and hanging on till he was kicked away.

But this incident was hardly noticed, for the men were busily arming themselves with lanthorns and candles ready for the descent.

"Four of us'll be enough," said Vores, every man present having come forward to descend. "Perhaps Tom Dinass, Esquire, would like to go too, though. If so, we can make room for him."

There was a roar of laughter at this, and Dinass glared round at the men, as he stood holding one leg resting on the bench, as if it had been badly bitten by the dog.

"Ready?" cried Vores.

"Ay, ay," was answered.

"Come on, then, and let's get the boys up. Dessay they've found their fathers before now."

Vores stepped to the skep and laid his hand on the rail just as the last lanthorn was lit and snapped to, when there was the sharp ting on the gong again—the signal from below—and the men gave a hearty cheer.

"Give another, my lads," cried Vores; and instead of taking their places in the empty skep, the men stood round and saw it descend, while they watched the other portion of the endless wire rope beginning to ascend steadily with its burden.

"I wouldn't stand in your boots for a week's wage, my lad," said Vores, banteringly, as he looked to where Dinass stood, still resting his leg on the bench and holding it.

"You mind your own business," he growled.

"Ay, to be sure, mate; but when a brother workman's in trouble it is one's business to help him. You're in trouble now. Like a man to run and get a doctor to see to that hole the dog made in your trousers?"

There was a roar of laughter.

"Don't grin, mates," said Vores; "they're nearly a new pair, and there's a hole made in the leg. He thinks it's in his skin."

There was another roar of laughter which made Dinass look viciously round, his eyes lighting sharply on the dog, which had gone close up to the opening where the skep would rise, and kept on whining anxiously.

"Smells his master," said Vores; and the dog then uttered a sharp bark as the top of the skep appeared with the link and iron bands attached to the wire rope.

Then, to the surprise of all, Colonel Pendarve, the Major, and Sam Hardock stepped wearily out, their trousers wet, their mackintoshes and flannels discoloured, and their faces wet with perspiration.

"Here you are, then, gentlemen," said Vores; "we thought you were lost. The young gents are waiting to come up, I s'pose."

"Young gents?—waiting to come up?" cried the Colonel, who had just looked round with a disappointed air at not seeing his son waiting. "What do you mean?"

"We all got tired o' waiting, and scared at your being so long, sir; and the young gents went down with Tom Dinass to seek for you."

"What? I don't understand you," cried the Colonel, excitedly. "Dinass is here."

"Yes, sir, he come up," said Vores; "but—the young gents are down still."

"My son—my son—down that place!" cried the Colonel, while the Major uttered a groan.

"Yes, sir, and we were just going down to search for 'em when you come up."

"Horrible!" groaned the Major.

"The place is a dreadful maze," cried the Colonel; "we were lost, and have had terrible work to find our way up. You're quite exhausted, Jollivet. Stay here. Now, my lads; volunteers: who'll come down?"

"All on us, sir," said Vores, sturdily; "they've got to be found."

"Thank you," cried the Colonel, excitedly; and the look of exhaustion died out of his face. "But you, Dinass—they say you went down with them. Why are you here?"

"'Cause they give me the slip, sir. For a lark, I suppose."

"When they were in great anxiety about their fathers?" cried the Colonel, scornfully. "Do you dare to tell me such a lie as that? Explain yourself at once. Quickly, for I have no time to spare."

It was the stern officer speaking now, with his eyes flashing; and literally cowed by the Colonel's manner, and in dead silence, Dinass blundered through his narrative again, but with the addition of a little invention about the way in which his young companions had behaved.

"Bah!" roared the Colonel at last; "that will do. I see you turned poltroon and shrank back, to leave them to go on by themselves. Man, man! if you hadn't the honest British pluck in you to go, why didn't you stay up?"

"'Cause he funked it at fust, sir," said Vores; "but then, being second after Sam Hardock, we said it was his dooty, and made him go!"

"Bah! he is of no use now. Hah! You have candles ready, I see. How many will the skep take?"

"Six on us, sir," said Vores.

"Follow me, then, some of you," said the Colonel. "Hardock, you're fagged out, and had better stay."

"What! and leave them boys down there lost, sir?" cried Hardock, sharply. "Not me."

"Then head a second party; I'll go on with five."

"Right you are, sir," said Hardock. "Down with you, then; and we'll soon be after you. Will someone give me a tin o' water?"

Two men started up to supply his wants, as the Colonel and his party stepped into the skep to stand closely packed—too closely for Grip to find footing; and as the great bucket descended, the dog threw up his muzzle and uttered a dismal howl.

"Quickly as you can," shouted the Colonel, as the skep went down; but the engineer shook his head.

"Nay," he said to the remaining men present; "none o' that, my lads: slow and steady's my motter for this job. One reg'lar rate and no other."

In due time the other skep came to the surface, and Hardock, with a lump of bread in his hand and a fresh supply of candles and matches, stepped in, to be followed by five more, ready to dare anything in the search for the two lads; but once more poor Grip was left behind howling dismally, while Tom Dinass nursed his leg and glared at him with an evil eye.

Chapter Twenty Eight
Down in the Depths

"You lead with the lanthorn, Hardock," said the Colonel, as the man and his companions stepped out of the second skep and had to wade knee-deep for a few yards from the bottom of the shaft, the road lying low beneath the high, cavernous entrance to the mine, at one side of which a tiny stream of clear water was trickling. There the bottom began to rise at the same rate as the roof grew lower; and soon they were, if not on dry land, walking over a floor of damp, slimy rock.

"Keep straight on, sir?" said the captain.

"Yes, right on. They would not have entered the side gallery, or we should have met them as we came out."

The first side gallery, a turning off to the left, was reached, and, but for the fact that the Colonel's party had strayed into that part by accident, it would have been passed unseen, as it was by the boys and Dinass, for the entrance was so like the rock on either side, and it turned off at such an acute angle, that it might have been passed a hundred times without its existence being known.

The men were very silent, but they kept on raising their lanthorns and glancing at the roof and sides as they tramped on behind the Colonel.

"There's good stuff here," whispered Vores to his nearest companion.

"Yes, I've been noticing," was the reply. "It's a fine mine, and there's ore enough to keep any number of us going without travelling far."

"Yes," said Vores. "Worked as they used to do it in the old days, when they only got out the richest stuff."

Just then Hardock stopped, and, upon the others closing up, they found themselves at an opening on the right—one which struck right back, and, like the other, almost invisible to anyone passing with a dim light.

"Shall we give a good shout here, sir?" said Hardock.

"Yes," was the reply; and the men hailed as with one voice, sending a volume of sound rolling and echoing down the passage of the main road and along its tributary.

Then all stood silent, listening to the echoes which died away in the distance, making some of the experienced miners, accustomed as they were to such underground journeys, shiver and look strange.

"Vasty place, mate," whispered Vores to Hardock, after they had all hailed again and listened vainly for a reply.

"Vasty?" said Hardock. "Ay! The gashly place is like a great net, and seems to have no end."

"Forward," said the Colonel. "No, stop. We have plenty of candles, have we not?"

"Yes, sir, heaps," was the reply.

"Light one, then, and stick it in a crevice of the rock here at the corner."

While the man was busily executing the order, the Colonel took out his pocket-book, wrote largely on a leaf, "Gone in search of you. Wait till we return," and tore it out to place it close to the candle where the light could shine on the white scrap of paper.

Then on they went again, with the experienced miners talking to one another in whispers, as with wondering eyes they took note of the value of the traces they kept on seeing in the rugged walls of the main gallery they traversed—tokens hardly heeded by the two boys in their anxiety to gain tidings of their fathers.

"It's going to be a grand place, my son," whispered Vores; "and only to think of it, for such a mine to have lain untouched ever since the time of our great-great-gaffers—great-great-great-great, ever so many great-gaffers, and nobody thinking it worth trying."

"Ay, but there must have been some reason," said the other.

"Bah! Old women's tales about goblin sprites and things that live underground. We never saw anything uglier than ourselves, though, did we, all the years we worked in mines?"

"Nay, I never did," said the man who walked beside Vores; "but still there's no knowing what may be, my lad, and it seems better to hold one's tongue when one's going along in the dark in just such a place as strange things might be living in."

Hardock stopped where another branch went off at a sharp angle, his experienced eyes accustomed to mines and dense darkness, making them plain directly; and here another shout was sent volleying down between the wet gleaming walls, to echo and vibrate in a way which sounded awful; but when the men shouted again the echoes died away into whispers, and then rose again more wildly, but only to die finally into silence.

Without waiting for an order, Hardock lit and fixed another candle against the glittering wall of the mine passage, the Colonel wrote on a slip of paper, and this too was placed where it must be seen; but the Colonel hesitated as if about to alter the wording.

"No," he said, "I dare not tell them to make for the sumph, they might lose their way. You feel sure that you can bring us back by here, Hardock?"

The man was silent for a few moments, and then he spoke in a husky voice.

"No, sir," he said, "I can't say I am. I think I can, but I thought so this morning. The place is all a puzzle of confusion, and it's so big. Next time we come down I'll have a pail of paint and a brush, and paint arrows pointing to the foot of the shaft at every turn. But I'll try my best."

"Ay, we'll all try, sir," said Harry Vores.

"Forward!" cried the Colonel, abruptly; and once more they went on till all at once, after leaving candle after candle burning, they reached a part where the main lode seemed to have suddenly broken up into half-a-dozen, each running in a different direction, and spreading widely, the two outer going off at very obtuse angles.

Here they paused, unconscious of the fact that they had passed the spot, only a couple of hundred yards back, where the boys had made their heroic resolve to go on.

"Let me see," said the Colonel, excitedly; "it was the third passage from the left that we took this morning."

Hardock raised his lanthorn and stared vacantly in his employer's face.

"No, sir, no," he cried breathlessly; "the third coming from the right."

"No, no, you are wrong. The third from the left; I counted them this morning—six of these branches. Why, Hardock, there are seven of them now."

"Yes, sir, seven, and that one running from the right-hand one makes eight. I did not see those two this morning by our one lanthorn. There are—yes—eight."

"What are we all to do? My head is growing hopelessly confused."

He gazed piteously at Hardock, who seemed to be in a like hopeless plight, suffering as they both were from exhaustion.

"I—I'm not sure, sir, now. We went in and out of so many galleries, all ending just the same, that I'm afraid I've lost count."

"Oh, Hardock! Hardock!" groaned the Colonel, "this is horrible. We must not break down, man. Try and think; oh, try and think. Remember that those two boys are lost, and they are wandering helplessly in search of us. They will go on and on into the farther recesses of this awful place, and lie down at last to die—giving their lives for ours. There, there, I am babbling like some idiot. Forward, my men; there is no time to lose. We must find them."

"Yes, sir; we must find them," cried Hardock; "which passage shall we take?"

"Stop a moment," said the Colonel, in a voice which seemed to have suddenly grown feeble; and he signed to the mining captain to light a candle and place it where they stood, while he tremblingly wrote on another leaf of his pocket-book,—

"Make for the pit-shaft."

He tore out the leaf, and the men noticed how his hand trembled; and he stood waiting for it to be taken by Hardock, who had sunk on his knees and was holding the candle sidewise, so that a little of the grease might drip into a crack where he meant to stick the candle close to the side.

Hardock groaned as he rose and took the paper, staggering as he stooped again to place it by the candle. But he recovered his steadiness again directly, and looked, to the Colonel for orders.

"Which branch, sir?" he said.

"The largest," said the Colonel in a hollow voice; "it is the most likely because it goes nearly straight. Forward then."

They obeyed in silence, and for another couple of hours they went on, finding the gallery they had taken branch and branch again and again; but though they sent shout after shout, there was no reply but those given by the echoes, and they went on again, still leaving burning candles at each division of the way.

Then all at once, as the Colonel was writing his directions on the pocket-book leaf, Vores saw the pencil drop from his hand; the book followed, and he reeled and would have fallen had not the miner caught him and lowered him gently to the rocky floor.

"I knew it, I knew it," groaned Hardock. "He was dead beat when we got back, for we've had an awful day. It's only been his spirit which has kept him up. And now I'm dead beat, too, for I had to almost carry the Major when we were nearly back. It's like killing him to rouse him to go on again. Harry Vores, you're a man who can think and help when one's in trouble. There's miles and miles of this place, and the more we go on the more tangled up it gets. Which way are we going now:— east, west, north, or south? Of course, nobody knows."

"What's that?" cried Vores, for a low deep murmur came upon their ears, and was repeated time after time. "I know; water falling a long way off. Then that's how it was so much had to be pumped out."

"Yes," said Hardock; "that's water, sure enough. I thought I heard it this morning. But look here, what shall, we do—carry the Colonel forward or go back?"

There was no reply; but the murmur, as of water falling heavily at a great distance, came once more to their ears.

Chapter Twenty Nine
The Position Darkens

"Isn't a flood coming to sweep us away, is it?" said Vores, in a low voice full of the awe he felt.

"Nay, that's no flood," said Hardock. "There'll be no flood, lads, that I can't master with my pumping gear. Now, look here, all of you; I want to try and find those boys, but we can't carry the guv'nor farther in. What do you all say?"

The men gathered round him, a weird-looking company with their lanthorns, turned to Vores as their spokesman, and the latter took off his hat and wiped his streaming brow.

"And I want to find those two poor lads," he said; "but I want to go back, for it's turrerble work searching a place that you don't know, and in which you seem to lose your way. It's just madness to go on carrying the guv'nor with us; and the captain here is dead beat, so it's nonsense to let him go on."

"Then what must we do?" said Hardock, who looked quite exhausted.

"'Vide into two parties," said Vores. "One, headed by Sam Hardock, 'll take the guv'nor back to grass; t'other party, all volunteers, 'll choose a leader and go on searching till a fresh gang comes down and brings some grub for 'em. That's all I can say. If some 'un 'll make a better plan I'd be glad to hear it and follow it out."

There was a dead silence, during which every man thought of the frank lads, who had won the hearts of those who knew them, but no one spoke.

"Well, boys," said Hardock at last, "has anyone anything to say? As for me, I don't feel like sneaking out of it; I think I'll be for leading the search-party if anyone volunteers."

"Oh, some on us'll volunteer," said one of the men. "I don't feel like going home to my supper and bed—to can't eat, and to can't sleep for thinking of those two merry lads as I've often gone out to fish with and shared their dinner with 'em. Not me. I'll volunteer."

"Same here, my lads," said Vores; "I'm with you. That's two of us. Anyone else say the word?"

"Ay!—ay!—ay!" Quite a chorus of 'ays' broke out as the miners volunteered to a man.

"Well done," cried Vores, "that's hearty; I feel just as if I'd had a good meal, and was fresh as a daisy. But we can't all stay. Sam Hardock, how many do you want to help carry the guv'nor back?"

"Three twos," said Hardock, "for I'm no use yet. I can only just carry myself."

"That's seven then, so pick your men and we'll stay, five of us, and find the lads somehow."

"I say that Harry Vores leads us," said the man who had first volunteered.

"Hear, hear!" was chorused, and a few minutes only elapsed before Hardock had chosen his party and turned to raise the Colonel, to go back.

"What's limpet-shells and sand doing down here?" said Vores, as he held a lanthorn to light the men.

"Forsils," said Hardock, glancing at a couple Vores had picked up.

"Nay, they aren't stony shells," said Vores. "I know; they used to eat 'em, and they're some the old chaps as did the mining brought down for dinner."

"Ready?" said Hardock.

"Ay, ay," cried the men, who had made what children call a dandy chair with their hands, and supported the Colonel, whose arms were placed about their necks.

"Then as he says, and I wish I could hear him say it now, 'Forward!'"

The men started, and Hardock turned to Vores.

"Seems like acting Tom Dinassy, my lad," he said bitterly. "I don't feel as if I could go."

"Do you want to get up a row?" said Vores, sourly. "Be off and look after the guv'nor; don't stop putting us chaps out of heart and making us think you jealous of me doing your work."

Hardock held out his hand to his fellow-workman.

"Thank ye, my lad," he said. "Go on, then, and take care. I've kept just enough candle to last us to the shaft foot; don't go farther than you can find your way out."

"We're going to find those two boys," said Vores through his set teeth. "By-and-by, if we don't come back, you send a fresh shift, and let 'em bring us some prog and some blankets; but I'm hoping you'll find them up at grass when you get there. Now off you go, and so do we."

They parted without another word, and the next minute the dim light of the lanthorns borne by the men were dying away in two directions— the party bearing the Colonel progressing slowly till he recovered himself somewhat and ordered them to stop.

"Nay, sir, there's no need," said Hardock; "we keep on taking you in three shifts, and can go on for long enough."

"Thank you, my lads, thank you," said the Colonel; "but I am better now. Anxiety and fatigue were too much for me. I'm stronger, and can walk."

"Nay, sir, you can better ride."

"If I am overdone again I will ask you to carry me," said the Colonel. "I am not a wounded man, my lads; only at the heart," he added bitterly to himself. "How am I to face his mother if he is not found?"

They set him down, and he walked on slowly for a few hundred yards; but after that one of the men saw him display a disposition to rest, and in his rough way offered his arm.

"May help you a bit, sir, like a walking stick," said the man, with a smile.

"Thank you, my lad. God bless you for your kindness," said the Colonel as he took the man's arm; and they went on again for some time till far ahead there was the faint gleam of a light reflected from the wet granite rock, and the Colonel uttered a cry—

"Ah! Quick! quick! My poor boys! At last! at last!"

He hastened his steps, and the men exchanged glances and then looked at Hardock, expecting him to speak.

But Hardock felt choking, and remained silent as they went on, till, turning about an angle in the zigzagging gallery, they came suddenly upon a nearly burned-out candle stuck against the wall, and beneath it, plainly to be seen, one of the leaves of the Colonel's pocket-book.

It was some moments before the old officer spoke, for the finding of the light confused him.

"Why, what's this?" he said, in an agitated voice; "you have taken some turning by mistake, and worked round to the way we came. Then very likely my poor boys have done the same, and found their way out by now."

No one spoke.

"Don't you think so, my lads?"

Still no one answered; and now he began to grasp the truth.

"Why, what's this?" he cried angrily. "Surely you men have not dared— have not been such cowards—as to turn back! Halt!"

The last word was uttered in so commanding a tone of voice that the little party stopped as one man.

"Hardock! Explain yourself, sir. Did you dare to change the arrangements during my temporary indisposition?"

"Beg your pardon, sir, you were completely beat out, and we felt that we must carry you back to the shaft."

"What insolence!" roared the Colonel. "Right about face. Forward once more. But," he added bitterly, "if any man among you is too cowardly to help me, he can go back."

He turned and strode off into the darkness, and Hardock followed just in time to catch him as he reeled and snatched at the side of the gallery to save himself from falling.

"You can't do it, sir, you can't do it," said Hardock, with his voice full of the rough sympathy he felt. "We did it all for the best. We'd have carried you farther in, but it seemed like so much madness, and so we decided. Part's gone on with Harry Vores, and we're going to send in another shift as soon as we get back."

The Colonel looked at him despairingly, for he knew that the man's words were true, and that it would be impossible to go on.

"We did what we thought were right, sir," continued Hardock; "and it's quite likely that the young gents have got safely back by now."

The Colonel made no reply, but suffered himself to be led back to where the men were waiting, and then, growing more helpless minute by minute, he was conducted, after a long and toilsome task, which included several pauses to rest, to the foot of the shaft.

The water had increased till it was nearly knee-deep when they waded to where the skep was waiting, and the Colonel was half fainting from exhaustion; but the feeling that the boys might be safely back revived him somewhat, and he strove hard to maintain his composure as they all stepped in, the signal was given, and they began to rise. But he was hanging heavily upon the arm of one of the men before the mouth of the shaft was reached, and he looked dazed and confused, feeling as if in a dream, when the engineer cried,—

"Well, found 'em?"

"Then they've not come back?" said Hardock.

The Colonel heard no more, but just as his senses left him he was conscious of a trembling hand being thrust into his, and a voice saying,—

"Our poor lads, Pendarve; can nothing more be done?"

Something more could be done, for the work-people about the place—carpenters, smiths and miners—volunteered freely enough; and in the course of the night two more gangs went down, and Vores and his party gave them such advice as they could, after returning utterly wearied out; but it became more and more evident that the lads had either fallen down some smaller shaft, as yet undiscovered, in one of the side drifts of the mine, or wandered right away—how far none could tell until the place had been thoroughly explored.

And at this time anxious watchers in the shed over the mouth of the mine had been recruited by the coming of one who said little, her pale, drawn face telling its own tale of her sufferings as she sat there, ready to start at every sound, and spring up excitedly whenever the signal was given for the skep to be raised.

But there was no news, and she always shrank back again, to seat herself in a corner of the shed, as if desirous of being alone, and to avoid listening to the words of comfort others were eager to utter.

"Not a word, Jollivet, not a word," whispered the Colonel once during the horrors of that long-drawn night. "She has not spoken, but her eyes are so full of reproach, and they seem to keep on asking me why I could not be content without plunging into all the excitement and trouble connected with this mine."

The Major groaned.

"Don't you look at me like that," said the Colonel, appealingly. "I am doing everything I can; and as soon as I can stir, I will head a party to go right on as far as the mine extends."

Chapter Thirty
In Darkness

Gwyn Pendarve opened his eyes, feeling sore and in grievous pain. A sharp point seemed to be running into his side, and he was hurting his neck, while one shoulder felt as if it had become set, so that, though it ached terribly, he could not move.

He did not know how it was or why it was, for all was confused and strange; and he lay trying to puzzle out clearly why Caer Point light should be revolving so quickly, now flashing up brightly, and now sinking again till all was nearly dark.

It seemed very strange, for he had often looked out to sea on dark nights, over to where the great lighthouse stood up on the Jagger Rock ten miles away, seeing the light increase till it seemed like a comet, whose long, well-defined tail slowly swept round over the sea till it was hidden by the back of the lanthorn, and he waited till it flashed out again; but it had never given him pains in the body before, neither could he recall that it smelt so nasty, just like burnt mutton-chops.

That was the strangest part of it, for he remembered when the fishermen sailed over there with them so that they could have some conger fishing off the rocks, the light keepers took them round, and among other things showed them the store-room in the lower part of the building, where the great drums of crystal oil for trimming the lamps were lifted into the tank. Yes, of course they burned paraffin oil in the great optical lanthorn; but though it was tremendously hot there, when the light was in full play, there was scarcely any odour, while now it smelt of burnt mutton fat.

Gwyn could not make it out. There, in the far distance, was the light, now flashing out brightly, now dying; out into darkness, smelling horribly, making him very hot, and giving him all those aching pains from which he was suffering.

There was another problem, too, that he had to solve; why was it that a lighthouse lanthorn ten miles away on a dark night should make him so hot that the perspiration stood out all over his face, and the collar of his shirt was soaked?

Why was it?—why was it? He puzzled and puzzled in a muddled way, but seemed to get no nearer the solution. There was the light still coming and going and smelling badly, and making him so hot that he felt as if he could not breathe.

Then the solution came like a flash, which lit up his mind just as all was black darkness; and in spite of the agony he felt as soon as he moved, he started up into a sitting posture, and then made for the light.

For he knew now that it was not the lighthouse lanthorn on Jagger Rock ten miles away, but the common lanthorn he had brought down into the mine some time before, and set about ten feet off, where it could not be kicked over when they turned over in their sleep—the sleep into which he had plunged at once as if into a stupor.

It was from this stupor that he had now awakened to turn from the sultry heat of the mine, chilled to the heart with horror, for the fresh candle he had lit had burned down into the socket, and was giving the final flickers before going out, and they had not a match to strike and light another.

Stretching out his trembling hands, he felt in the black darkness for the lanthorn, touched it after two or three ineffectual trials, and snatched it back, feeling his fingers burnt, just as the light gave a final flare, the jar of his touch upon the lanthorn being sufficient to quench the tiny flame.

In the horror of the moment Gwyn uttered a loud cry, and the result was a quick movement close at hand, followed by a voice saying,—

"Yes, father, all right. I'll get up and fetch it. Is the pain so bad?"

Gwyn tried to speak, but no words came.

"Did you call, father?"

There was perfect silence in the stifling place, and Joe Jollivet spoke again, drowsily now.

"Must have dreamt it. But—hallo—Oh, my back! What ever's the matter with it, and—here! hallo! What does it all mean? I must have been walking in my sleep."

"Oh, Joe, Joe!" cried his companion.

"Ydoll! You there? I say—what—what—where are we?"

"Don't you understand?—where we lay down when we could get no farther."

There was the sound of some one drawing a long gasping breath, and then silence again, till Joe spoke in a piteous voice.

"I was dreaming that father was taken ill in the night, and he called me. Oh, Ydoll, old chap, my head feels so queer. Then we haven't found them? I don't feel as if I could recollect anything. It's all black like. We came down to find them, didn't we?"

"Yes," said Gwyn, "and walked till you stumbled and fell."

"I did? Yes, I recollect now. I was regularly beaten. We came such a long way for hours and hours. Then we've both been to sleep?"

"I suppose so."

"But why is it so dark?"

"The candle I set up burned out."

"Well, light another. You have some more."

"What am I to light one with?" groaned Gwyn.

"Oh! I'd forgotten," cried Joe, piteously, "you've no matches."

"No, I've no matches."

"But you had some, I know—you had a box; feel in your pockets again."

There was a faint rustling sound as in obedience to his companion's imperative words, Gwyn felt in each pocket vainly, and then uttered a sigh like a groan.

"No, no, no!" he cried, "there is a hole in my pocket, and the box must have gone through."

"Oh," cried Joe, angrily; "how could I be such a fool as to trust you to carry them?"

"You mean how could you be such a fool as to come without a box yourself," said Gwyn, bitterly.

"Yes, that's it, I suppose. Here, I know—we must strike a light from the rock with the backs of our knives."

"What for?" said Gwyn, bitterly. "Where are the tinder and matches?"

Joe uttered a sigh, and they both relapsed into silence once more.

"What are we to do?" said Joe, at last. "It is horrible, horrible to be in this black darkness. Say something, Ydoll—we can't lie down here and die."

"We can't go on in the black darkness," said Gwyn, bitterly.

"We must feel our way."

"And suppose we come to some hole and go down?"

Joe drew his breath sharply through his teeth as he winced at the horrible idea.

"Better lie down again and go to sleep," said Gwyn, despondently. "We can do no more."

"Lie down till they come with lights and find us?"

"Yes," said Gwyn, who gathered courage from these words of hope. "It's of no use to give up. Father must have found his way out by this time. Sam Hardock knows so much about mines; he is sure not to be lost for long."

"But if they don't find us? I'm so faint and hungry now I don't know what to do."

"Yes, I suppose what I feel is being hungry," sighed Gwyn, "but we mustn't think about it. I say, how far do you think we wandered about yesterday?"

"Miles and miles and miles," said Joe, dismally; "and for nothing at all but to lose ourselves. But I say, Ydoll, it wasn't yesterday. We couldn't have slept long."

"I felt as if I slept all night."

"But we couldn't; because we only slept as long as our candle burned."

"Of course not. How stupid! But I'm so done up that my head doesn't seem as if it would go; let's lie down and go to sleep till they find us."

"And perhaps that will be never. Someone will find our bones, perhaps."

"Ha, ha!" cried Gwyn, bursting into a mocking laugh. "We're a nice pair of miserable cowards! I did think you had more pluck in you, Joe."

"That's what I thought about you, Ydoll."

"So did I," said Gwyn, frankly; "and all the time I'm as great a coward as you are. I say, though, doesn't it show a fellow up when he gets into trouble? Can't show me up in the dark, though, can it?"

"Oh, I don't know; I only know I feel horribly miserable. Let's go to sleep and forget it all."

"Sha'n't," shouted Gwyn, making an effort over himself. "I won't be such a jolly miserable coward, and you sha'n't neither. We'll do something."

"Ay, it's all very well to talk, but what can we do?—cooey?"

"No good, or I'd cooey loud enough to bring some of the stones down. I say, though, isn't it wonderful how solid it all is—no stones falling from the roof."

"How could they fall when there are none to fall? Isn't it all cut through the solid rock?"

"Humph! yes, I suppose so; but we have found scarcely anything to fall over."

"No," said Joe, sarcastically, "it's a lovely place. I wish the beastly old mine had been burnt before we had anything to do with it."

"Oh, I say, what a plucked 'un you are, Joey. Breaking down over a bit of trouble. I feel ever so much better now, for I'm sure the dad has found his way out."

"I was thinking about my father."

"Well, so was I. My father wouldn't go out without yours. They're too good old chums to forsake one another; and you see if before long they don't both come with a lot of men carrying baskets—cold roast chicken, slices of ham, bread and butter, and a kettle and wood to light the fire and make some tea."

"I say! don't, don't, don't," cried Joe. "I was bad enough before, now you're making me feel savagely hungry. But I say, Ydoll, do you really think they've got out?"

"I'm sure of it."

"And not lost themselves so that they won't be found till it's too late?"

"Get out! Too late? They'll be all right, and so shall we; we're only lost for a bit in the dark, and we don't mind a bit. I don't now. I feel as plucky as a gamecock. And I say, Joe."

"Well?"

"Tom Dinass?"

"What about him?—a beast!"

"What we're going to do when we see the sneak again. I say, it won't be the first time we've had a set-to with him."

"Oh, I should like to—"

"Ah!"

Gwyn uttered a wild cry, as if something from out of the darkness had seized him; and as the cry went echoing down the long zigzag passage in which they were, Joe uttered a gasp, and in spite of his desire to stand by his friend, dashed off from the unknown danger by which they were beset.

Chapter Thirty One
Gwyn gives it up

There came a dull sound out of the darkness, as if Joe had struck against the wall of the mine; but he gave vent to no exclamation, and Gwyn cried to him to stop.

"Where are you? Don't run off like that, Joe!—Joe! Where are you?"

"Here," said the lad, hoarsely. "What is it? What has hurt you?"

"Hurt me? I thought something had hurt you. What made you rush off?"

"You shouted. What was it?"

"Enough to make me shout. Where are you?"

Guided by their voices, the lads approached till they were close together.

"Now what was it?" panted Joe, who was still trembling from the nervous alarm and shock.

"Give me your hand."

Joe obeyed shrinkingly, and felt it passed along the skirt of his companion's jacket.

"Feel it?"

"Yes, I feel something inside the lining. What is it—a box?"

"Yes, the matches. They got through the hole into the lining. Wait till I get them out."

This was only achieved with the help of a knife.

"Ah!" ejaculated the boy, as he at last dragged out the box, struck a match, and held it over his head to see where the candle-box had been laid; and then by quick manipulation he managed to get a wick well alight before the tiny deal splint was extinct.

In his excitement and delight, Joe clapped his hands as the candle was forced into the empty socket, and the lanthorn door closed.

"Oh, what a beautiful thing light is!" he cried.

"And what a horrible thing darkness, at a time like this! There, one feels better, and quite rested. Let's go on, and we may come to them at any time now."

Joe said nothing, for fear of damping his companion's spirits; but he knew that they were not rested — that they would soon be forced to stop; and as he gazed right away before them, and tried to pierce the gloom beyond the circle of light shed by the candle, the hopeless nature of their quest forced itself upon him more and more.

But Gwyn's spirits seemed to be now unnaturally high, and as they went on following the narrowed tunnels, and passing along such branches as seemed to be the most likely from their size, he held up the lanthorn to point out that the ore seemed to have been cut out for ten or twenty feet above their heads in a slanting direction. In another place he paused to look into a narrow passage that seemed to have been only just commenced, for there was glittering ore at the end, and the marks of picks or hammers, looking as if they had been lately made.

"There's nothing to mind, Joe," he said; "only I do want to get back to the shaft now."

"Then why not turn?"

"We did, ever so long ago. Don't you remember seeing that beginning of a passage as we came along?"

"I remember stopping to look into two niches like this one but they were ever so far back, and we are still going on into the depths of the mine."

"No, no; we took a turn off to the left soon after I lit the fresh candle, and we must be getting back towards the entrance."

Joe said nothing, but he felt sure that he was right; and they went on again till at the end of another lane Gwyn stopped short.

"I say, I felt sure we were going back. Do you really believe that we are going farther in?"

"I felt sure that we were a little while ago, but I am not so sure now, for one gets confused."

"Yes, confused," said Gwyn, sadly. "We seem to have been constantly following turnings leading in all directions, and they're all alike, and go on and on. Aren't you getting tired?"

"Horribly; but we mustn't think of that. Let's notice what we see, so as to have something to tell them when we get home."

"Well, that's soon done; the walls are nearly all alike, and the passages run in veins, one of which the people who used to work here followed until they had got out all the ore, and then they opened others."

"But the ore seems to be richer in some places than in others."

"Yes, and the walls seem wetter in some places than in others; and sometimes one crushes shells beneath one's feet, and there's quantities of sand."

"But how far should you think we are now from the entrance?"

"I don't know. Miles and miles."

"Oh, that's exaggeration, for we've come along so slowly; and being tired makes you feel that it is a long way."

They went on and on, at last, as if in a dream, following the winding and zigzagging passages, and speaking more and more seldom, till at last they found themselves in a place which they certainly had not seen before, for the mine suddenly opened out into a wide irregular hall, supported here and there by rugged pillars left by the miners; and now confusion grew doubly confused, for, as they went slowly around over the rugged, well-worn floor, and in and out among the pillars, they could dimly see that passages and shafts went from all sides. The roof sparkled as the light was held up, and they could note that in places the marks of the miners' picks and hammers still remained.

Roughly speaking, the place was about a hundred feet across, and the floor in the centre was piled up into a hillock, as if the ore that had been brought from the passages around had been thrown in a heap—for that it was ore, and apparently rich in quality, they were now learned enough in metallurgy to know.

Gwyn had a fancy that, this being a central position, if the party they sought were still in the mine they would be somewhere here; and he made Joe start by hailing loudly, but raised so strange a volley of echoes that he refrained from repeating his cry, preferring to wait and listen for the answer which did not come.

"It's of no use," he said; "let's turn back; they must have got out by now."

"Yes, I hope so; but what an awfully big place it is. I say, though, where was it we came in—by that passage, wasn't it?"

Gwyn looked in the direction pointed out, but felt certain that it was not correct. At the same time, though, he fully realised that he was quite at fault, for at least a dozen of the low tunnels opened upon this rugged, pillared hall, so exactly alike, and they had wandered about so much since they entered, and began to thread their way in and out among the pillars, that he stared blankly at Joe in his weariness, and muttered despairingly,—

"I give it up."

Chapter Thirty Two
A Novel Nightmare

From that hour they both "gave it up"—in other words, resigned themselves in a hopeless weary way to their fate, and went on in an automatic fashion, resting, tramping on again over patches of sand and clean hard places where the rock had been worn smooth. The pangs of hunger attacked them more and more, and then came maddening thirst which they assuaged by drinking from one of the clear pools lying in depressions, the water tasting sweet and pure. From time to time the candles were renewed in the lanthorn, and the rate at which they burned was marked with feverish earnestness; and at last, in their dread of a serious calamity, it was arranged that one should watch while the other slept. In this way they would be sure of not being missed by a body of searchers who might come by and, hearing no sound, pass in ignorance of their position.

Gwyn kept the first watch, Joe having completely broken down and begun to reel from side to side of the passage they were struggling along in a hopeless way; and when Gwyn caught his arm to save him from falling, he turned and smiled at him feebly.

"Legs won't go any longer," he said gently; and, sinking upon his knees, he lay down on the bare rock, placed his hand under his face as he uttered a low sigh, and Gwyn said quietly,—

"That's right; have a nap, and then we'll go on again."

There was no reply, and Gwyn bent over him and held the lanthorn to his face.

"How soon anyone goes to sleep!" he said softly. "Seems to be all in a moment."

The boy stood looking down at his companion for a few moments, and then turned with the light to inspect their position.

They were in a curve of one of the galleries formed by the extraction of the veins of tin ore, and there was little to see but the ruddy-tinted walls, sparkling roof, and dusty floor. A faint dripping noise showed him where water was falling from the roof, and in the rock a basin of some inches in depth was worn, from which he refreshed himself, and then felt better as he walked on for a hundred yards in a feeble, weary way, to find that which gave him a little hope, for the gallery suddenly began to run upward, and came to an end.

"But it may only be the end of this part," muttered Gwyn; "there are others which go on I suppose, but one can't get any farther here, and that's something."

He walked back to where Joe lay sleeping heavily, after convincing himself of the reason why the turning had come to an end where it did, for the vein had run upward, gradually growing thinner till, at some thirty feet up, as far as he could make out by his dim light, the men had ceased working, probably from the supply not being worth their trouble.

Joe was muttering in his sleep when Gwyn reached his side, but for a time his words were unintelligible. Then quite plainly he said, —

"Be good for you, father. The mine will give you something to do, and then you won't have time to think so much of your old wounds."

"And if he has got out safely and they never find us, this will be like a new wound for the poor old Major to think about," mused Gwyn. "How dreadful it is, and how helpless we seem! It's always the same; gallery after gallery, just alike, and that's why it's so puzzling. I wonder whether any of the old miners were ever lost here and starved to death."

The thought was so horribly suggestive that the perspiration came out in great drops on the boy's face, and he glanced quickly to right and left, even holding up his lanthorn, fancying for the moment that he might catch sight of some dried-up traces of the poor unfortunates who had struggled on for days, as they had, and then sunk down to rise no more.

"How horrible!" he muttered; "and how can Joe lie there sleeping, when perhaps our fate may be like theirs?"

But he had unconsciously started another train of thought which set him calculating, and took his attention from the imaginary horrors which had troubled him.

"Wandered about for days and days," he mused. "It seems like it, but that's impossible. It can't be much more than one, or we couldn't have kept on. We should have been starved to death. We couldn't have lived on water."

He wiped his wet brow, and it seemed to him that the gallery they were in was not so stifling and hot, unless it was that he had grown weaker. Still one thing was certain; he could breathe more freely.

"Getting used to it," he thought; and, putting down the lanthorn, he seated himself with his back close to the wall.

Joe slept heavily, and the lad looked at him enviously.

"I couldn't sleep so peaceably as that," he said half aloud. "How can a fellow sleep when he doesn't know but what his father may be dying close by from starvation and weakness. It seems too bad."

Gwyn opened the lanthorn and found that the candle was half burned down, and for a moment he thought of setting up another in its place, for fear he should go to sleep and it should burn out.

"Be such a pity," he said, "we don't want light while we're asleep; only to wake up here in this horrible place is enough to drive anybody mad."

Then he closed the lanthorn again.

"I sha'n't go to sleep," he muttered. "In too much trouble." And he began thinking in a sore, dreary way of his mother seated at home waiting for news of his father and of him.

"It'll nearly kill her," he said. "But she'll like it for me to have come here in search of poor dad. It would have been so cowardly if I hadn't come, and she would have felt ashamed of me. Yes, she'll like my dying like this."

He paused, for his thoughts made him ponder.

"We can't be going to die," he said to himself, "or we shouldn't be taking it all so easily and be so quiet and calm. If we felt that we really were going to die, we should be half mad with horror, and run shrieking about till we dropped in a fit. No," he said softly, "it isn't like that. People on board ship, when they know it's going to sink, all behave quite calmly and patiently. There was that ship that was being burned with the soldiers on board. They all stood up before their officers, waiting for the end, and went down at last like men. But I don't feel despairing like, and as if we were going to die."

Then he began to think of his peaceful home life, and of the days at school till about a year ago, when he had come home to study military matters with his father and Major Jollivet, prior to being sent to one of the military colleges in about a year's time.

"And now this mining has altered everything," mused Gwyn, "and—"

He started violently, sprang up, and looked about him, for his name had been uttered loudly close to his ear.

But all was still now, and a curious creepy sensation ran through him and made him shiver with apprehension—a strange, superstitious kind of apprehension, as if something invisible were close to him.

"What a cowardly donkey!" he muttered, for his name was uttered again, and plainly enough it came from Joe.

"Talking in his sleep; and I was ready to fancy it was something 'no canny.' Why I must have been dropping off to sleep, too, and it startled me into wakefulness. This won't do. Sentries must not sleep at their posts."

He began to do what the soldiers call "sentry go." But in a few minutes he grew so weary and hot that he was glad to stop by his sleeping companion, and stand looking down at him lying so peacefully there with his head upon his hand.

"Just as if he were in a feather bed and with a soft pillow under his cheek. Wish I could lie down and have a nap for half-an-hour. I will, and then he can have another."

Gwyn bent down to waken his companion, who just then burst out with a merry laugh.

"Oh, I say, father, you shouldn't," he said. "Just as if I didn't take care. It isn't—"

"Isn't what, Joe?" said Gwyn, softly.

"The wrong bottle. You're always thinking I give you the wrong medicine, and saying it tastes different. Hah!"

He ended with a long deep sigh of content, and lay perfectly silent.

"I can't wake him," muttered Gwyn; and with a weary groan he seated himself once more, supporting his back against the side of the gallery, for he was too weak and tired to stand, and in an instant he was out in the bright sunshine, with the water making the boat he was in dance and the sail flap, as he glided along out of the cave into the open sea. Then with a violent start he was awake again, drawing himself up and fighting hard against terrible odds, for Nature said that he was completely exhausted, and must rest.

And as he set his teeth and stared hard at the faintly glittering wall opposite, where the great vein of milk-white quartz was spangled with grains of tin, his head bowed down and dropped forward till his chin touched his chest.

Again he sprang up, to prop his head back against the rock, but it had been hacked away so that it curved over and seemed to join Nature in her efforts to master him and force him to sleep, bending down his head and sending it in the old direction, so that his brow seemed heavier than lead, and he bent it lower and lower, while once more he was out on the glittering waters of the sea, the boat bounding rapidly along and all trouble at an end. For the darkness of the cavernous mine was gone, with all its weary horrors—there was nothing to mind, nothing to do, but sink lower and lower in the boat, and rest.

Hard—angular—stony? The granite chipped by hammer and pick felt like the softest down, as Gwyn swayed slowly over to his left, his shoulders rubbing against the wall and his half-braced muscles involuntarily acting in obedience to his will to keep him upright, so that he did not fall, but gently subsided till he was lying prone close to the lanthorn, which shed its faint yellowish light and cast dim shadows which, there in that gloomy spot, looked like a couple of graves newly banked up to mark the spots where the two lads had lain down to die or to be found and live, whichever fate ordained.

Joe must have slept for what was guessed to be a couple of hours; but they had passed, and he still slept on, with his rest growing more and more sweet and restful, while for Gwyn there was nothing but profound silence and vacancy. He did not dream—only plunged deeper and deeper into the stupor till six hours had passed away, and then the dream came.

A terrible wild dream of being somewhere in great danger—a place from which there was no escape from a dangerous wolf-like beast, which had followed him for hours, and was slowly hunting him down.

And every moment the vision grew more real, and the fierce beast came closer and closer in spite of his efforts to escape—mad, frantic efforts— while every limb was like lead, and held him back so that he might be the monster's prey.

He felt that it was a delusion, and that he must soon wake and find relief; but when he did, the relief did not come for the horrors of the dream were continued in the reality, and his lips parted to utter a wild cry; but lips, tongue, and throat were all parched and dry, and he lay there in an agony which seemed maddening.

There was no question now of where he was, for though it was intensely dark he knew well enough, for he had awakened into full consciousness with every sense unnaturally sharpened, and making things clear. His limbs were like lead still, but it was not from nightmare, for they were numbed and helpless. There was the unpleasant odour of the burnt-out candle, and the sickly smoke hanging about him, as if the light had but lately gone out, and he could hear Joe's stertorous breathing as if he too were in trouble; and simultaneously with it came the knowledge that, after all, the cavernous place out of which the water had been drained was inhabited by strange beasts, one of which had attacked him.

For the moment he was ready to explain it as a form of nightmare, but it was too real. It was the hard stern reality itself. There was the weight upon his chest, but not the heavy inert mass of a hideous dream, but that of some creature full of palpitating life extended upon him. He could feel the motion as it breathed, the heavy pulsations of its heart, and, worst horror of all, the hot breath from its panting jaws not many inches from his brow.

Chapter Thirty Three
Man's Good Friend

Gwyn tried hard to cry aloud to his companion for help—to make an effort for life; but for what seemed to him to be a long space of time he could not stir. At last, though, when he could bear the horror no longer, and just as the creature moved as if gathering its legs beneath it like some cat about to spring, the boy made a sudden heave, and threw the beast from his chest, at the same time struggling to rise and make for where he felt that Joe was lying; but with a strange, hollow cry the animal sprang at him with such force that he was driven backwards, while the creature regained its position upon his chest, and Gwyn lay back half paralysed.

But not from fear. Astonishment and delight had that effect, and, weak and prostrated as he was for some moments, he could not speak.

At last one word escaped from his lips, and in an instant—throb, throb, throb, throb—there was a heavy beating on his ribs, a joyous whining sound greeted his ears, and a cold nose and wet tongue were playing about his face.

"Oh, Grip! Grip! Grip!" he sobbed out at last, half hysterical with excitement; and seizing the dog by the neck he held him fast, while Grip burst now into a frantic paroxysm of barking.

"You good old dog, then you have found us," cried Gwyn, as he sat up now and held on tightly to the dog's collar, for fear he should be left again. "Why, there must be someone with him! Here, Grip, Grip, old chap, your master! Where is he, then?"

There was another frantic burst of barking, and Joe's voice was heard out of the darkness.

"What's that? What does it mean? Hi! Ydoll, are you there?"

"Yes, yes. Here's Grip! And—and—they must be—Oh, Joe, Joe, I can't—"

What it was that Gwyn Pendarve could not do was never heard, for he pressed his lips together and clenched his teeth to keep back all sound. He had no longer any control over himself, and in those anguished moments he felt, as he afterwards declared to himself, that he was acting like a girl.

Joe was nearly as bad, but it was in the darkness and there was no one to witness their emotion, as he too kept silence, fearing to hear even his own voice; so that Grip had the whole of the conversation to himself—a repetition that at another time would have been monotonous, but which now sounded musical in the extreme.

At last Gwyn recovered his equanimity to some extent, and, taking out the matches, struck one, but the moisture of his fingers prevented it from igniting, and he had to try two more before he could get anything but soft phosphorescent streaks on the box; and as the damp matches were thrown down, Grip sniffed at them and whined loudly.

Then one flashed out brilliantly, lighting up the darkness, was watched excitedly, and began to blaze up and transfer its illuminating powers to the one candle the boys had left, one which was directly after safely sheltered by the glass of the lanthorn.

At this point the joy of the dog was unbounded, and was shown in leaps, bounds and frantic barking, accompanied by rushes and sham worryings of his master's legs; and when driven off, he favoured Joe in the same way.

"Only to think of it," cried Joe, "that dog following us and running us down in the dark! How could he have done it? I never heard that dogs could see in the dark like cats."

"They can't," said Gwyn, going down on his knees to give the dog a hug. "A jolly old chap—they see with their noses; don't you, old Grip?"

"*Whuf!*" cried the dog; and he made a frantic effort to lick his master's face.

"It's wonderful!" cried Joe, excitedly.

"Yes, makes a fellow wish he had a nose like a dog. Why, Jolly, we could have found our way out, then."

"Don't see it," said Joe, who was in a peculiarly excited state, which made him ready to laugh or cry at the slightest provocation.

"Don't see it! Of course you don't. Couldn't we have smelt our way out by our own track, same as he did? But bother all that. Why, Jolly, if I could only feel sure that the dads were safe out, I shouldn't care a bit."

"No; I shouldn't either. Oh, I say, isn't it a relief?"

"Yes, and so I feel all right. They're out: I'm sure of it."

"How do you know?"

"By Grip being here."

"That doesn't prove it."

"Yes it does. I know! Father said, 'I'll send Grip down; he'll find them.'"

"Well, it does sound likely; but I say, Ydoll, isn't it queer?"

"What, being here?"

"No; while I was so miserable and feeling as I did, I was only faint; now I feel so hungry I could eat anything."

"Same here," said Gwyn; "but it's all right; they're out; father sent Grip—didn't he, Grip?"

The dog barked loudly and leaped up at him.

"There, hear him? He understands," cried Gwyn; but Joe shook his head.

"I don't know," he said. "The dog found us right enough, but that doesn't prove that he'll find his way back."

"He'd better," said Gwyn with mock earnestness; "if he doesn't we'll eat him. Do you hear, sir?"

The dog barked again.

"It's all right," said Gwyn, merrily. "Now then, pack up, and let's go home—do you hear, Grip?"

The dog threw up his head and barked loudly.

"Ready, Joe?"

"Ready—of course."

"Come on, then. Now, Grip, old fellow, lead the way. Go home!"

The dog barked again, and trotted in the opposite direction to which they had expected, making for the partly driven gallery where the roof ran up, showing how the lode of tin had ascended; and when he reached the blank end beginning to bark loudly.

"Come back, stupid!" cried Gwyn; "we found that out ourselves. That's the end of the mine. All right. Now, lead the way home."

But the dog barked again loudly; and it was not until Gwyn followed to the end and seized his collar that he gave up. "Now then, off with you, but don't go too fast. Forward! Quick march!"

The lad had straddled across the dog, holding him between his knees, with head pointed as he believed in the direction of the shaft; and at the last sound he unloosed him from the grip of his knees, and the dog started steadily off, and they followed, but in a few minutes had to take to running, for, after looking back several times to see if he was followed, Grip increased his pace, and directly after disappeared in the darkness beyond the glow shed by the lanthorn.

"You've done it now," cried Joe. "Why didn't you make your handkerchief fast to his collar? He's gone home."

"Think so?" said Gwyn, blankly.

"Yes; that's certain enough; and we're just as badly off as ever."

"No," said Gwyn, in a tone full of confidence; "Grip found us, and he'll come back again for certain."

"But we shall have to stop where we are, perhaps for another day or two."

"Oh, no, he will not be long," said Gwyn; but there was less confidence in his tones, and he stopped short, and began to call and whistle, with the sounds echoing loudly along the tunnel-like place; but for some moments all was silent, and Joe gave vent to a groan.

"Oh, why did you let him go, Ydoll? It was madness."

"Well," said the lad, bitterly, "you were as bad as I—you never said a word about holding him."

"No, I never thought of it," said Joe, with a sigh. "But how horrid, after thinking we were all right!"

"Yet it is disappointing," said Gwyn, gloomily; "but he'll soon come back when he finds that we are not following him; and even if he went right back to them, they'd send him in again."

"I don't believe they did send him in," said Joe, despairingly.

"They must. He couldn't have climbed down the ladders or got into the skep of his own accord, and, if he had, they wouldn't have let him down. They sent him, I'm sure."

"No, I'm afraid not," said Joe, piteously; "they didn't send him."

"How do you know?"

"Because if they had, they would have done what people always do under such circumstances—written a note, and tied it to the dog's collar. He had no note tied to his collar, I'm sure."

"No, I didn't see or feel any," said Gwyn, thoughtfully.

"No; we should have been sure to see it if he had one; so, for certain, the dog came of his own will, and I don't think it's likely he'll come again. He may or he may not."

Gwyn did not feel as if he could combat this idea, for Joe's notion that a note would have been tied to the dog's collar—a note with a few encouraging words—seemed very probable; so he remained silent, listening intently for the faintest sound.

But the silence was more terrible than ever, and, saving the musical dash of water from time to time, and an occasional rustle as of a few grains of earth or sand trickling down from the walls, all was still.

"Hear him coming back?" said Gwyn, at last, very dismally.

"No, but there is something I keep hearing. Can't you?"

"I? No," said Gwyn, quickly. "What can you hear?—footsteps?"

"Oh, no; not that. It's a humming, rolling kind of noise, very, very faint; and I can't always hear it. I'm not sure it is anything but a kind of singing in my ears. There, I can hear it now. Can you?"

Gwyn listened intently.

"No. Perhaps it is only fancy. Listen again. Oh, that dog must come back."

Joe sat down, with the lanthorn beside him.

"Oh, don't give up like that!" cried Gwyn. "Let's make a fresh start, and try and find our way out."

"It's impossible—we can't without help."

"Don't I always tell you that a chap oughtn't to wait to be helped, but try to help himself?"

"Yes, you often preach," said Joe, dismally.

"Yes, and try too. Why, I— Ah! hear that?" cried Gwyn, excitedly.

"No," said Joe, after a pause.

"Don't be so stupid! You can— Listen!"

They held their breath, and plainly now came the barking of a dog.

"There!" cried Gwyn. "Here, here, here!" and he whistled before listening again, when there was the pattering of the dog's nails on the rocky floor, and almost directly after Grip bounded up to them.

"Ah, we mustn't have any more of that, old fellow," cried Gwyn, seizing the dog's collar, and patting him. "Get on, you old rascal; can't you see we've only got two legs apiece to your four?"

The dog strained to be off again, barking excitedly; but Gwyn held on while their neckerchiefs were tied together, and then fastened to the dog's collar.

"Now, then, forward once more. Come on, Joe, you must carry the lanthorn and walk by his head. Steady, stupid! We can't run. Walk, will you? Now, then, forward for home."

The dog barked and went off panting, with his tongue out and glistening in the light as the red end was curled, and he strained hard, as if bound to drag as much as he could behind him, while the boys' spirits steadily rose as their confidence in the dog's knowledge of the way back began to increase.

Chapter Thirty Four
Too Eager by Half

"Think the candle will last, Jolly?" said Gwyn, after they had progressed for some time and the lanthorn door was opened.

"Plenty—yes," said Joe.

"Wish I knew there was enough and to spare," said Gwyn.

"Why?"

"Because I'd have a bite off the end. I'm so faint and hungry, it's quite horrible."

"Horrid!" exclaimed Joe.

"Not it. Nothing's horrid when you're starving. But I don't suppose it's very far as the crow flies."

"Crows don't fly in tin mines," said Joe, who was in better spirits now.

"Well, then, in a straight line."

"I don't believe there's a straight line in the place."

"I say, don't chop logic, Jolly, and don't— I say, look here, Grip, steady! don't pull a fellow's arm off!" interpolated Gwyn, for the dog tugged heavily at the neckerchiefs. "Look here, Joe, old chap, do talk gently to me, for I'm so hungry that I feel quite vicious, and just as if I could bite. Ah, would you get away! Steady, sir! We want to get home as badly as you do—for 'hoozza! we're homeward bound—bound; hoozza, we're homeward bound!'" sang the boy wildly.

"Don't you holloa till you're out of the wood."

"I wasn't holloaing," cried Gwyn, with hysterical merriment. "I was singing, only you've no ear for music."

"Not for such music as that. Hark at the echoes!—they sound just like howls."

"All right, but don't talk about getting out of the wood when we're like moles underground."

"Who's chopping logic now?"

"Oh, anybody. Steady, Grip, slow march."

"Does he pull so hard?"

"Horribly; but I don't mind—it shows he knows his way."

Grip barked and dragged at the improvised leash as if determined to hasten their pace.

"It's just like the greyhounds do over the coursing. But pull away, old chap! I say, though, isn't it hot now?"

"Yes, I'm bathed in perspiration. We must be very deep down."

"Oh, no, it's just about on a level; sometimes we go down, and sometimes up."

Splash, splash, splash, and then the dog's progress seemed to be checked, as the boys followed into a pool of water which filled all the tunnel to the sides.

"Stop!" cried Joe, as he waded to his knees.

"Why? What for?"

"Because we're going wrong."

"So I thought; but Grip ought to know."

"He can't, because we never came along here."

"No; but that proves he's right, for we never came along here, and we always lost ourselves."

"But it's getting deeper, and there's no knowing how deep it will be."

"Never mind; we must wade."

Joe went on, and the water was soon up to their waists, while the dog swam on.

"I'm sure Grip's going wrong," said Joe, excitedly, as the light of the lanthorn gleamed from the surface of what was now a narrow canal.

"Get on. Grip knows."

"He can't. It's impossible that he could have scented us over water."

"Yes, so it is," said Gwyn, anxiously; and he stopped, naturally checking the dog, who began to splash and to howl and bark angrily.

"Well, we must go on now. Perhaps it's the way he came."

'Holding the light well up they waded on.'

"Couldn't be, because he was not wet."

"Well, I am right over my waist," said Gwyn. "Shall we go on? We can swim if it gets deeper."

"I say, let's try it a little farther." And holding the light well up, they waded on, with the water growing deeper, till it reached their chests and soon after their chins.

"Now then—go back or swim?" asked Gwyn.

"Oh, go on; Grip must know. I suppose the floor has gone down a good deal here."

"Can you keep the lanthorn out of the water? If you can't we must not go on; because it would be too horrible to swim here in the dark, and I don't know whether I could keep on with only one hand swimming and holding Grip with the other."

"He'd tow you along," said Joe.

"Halt! Hold the light higher," shouted Gwyn, and his words reverberated strangely.

Grate, grate, scratch, came a strange sound.

"Do you hear what I say?" cried Gwyn, excitedly.

"I can't, I can't—there isn't room."

"Then give it to me," said Gwyn, fiercely, from where he stood a few yards now in advance of his companion. "How am I to see what I'm doing?—and I know you'll have it in the water directly."

"Don't I tell you I can't?" cried Joe, wildly. "Can't you see there isn't room? I'm holding it close up to the roof now." And at a glance Gwyn saw that the roof was so low where they were that the gallery was nearly filled by the water.

"Oh, hang the dog!" cried Gwyn, desperately. "Quiet, sir! Come back!" for with the water steadily deepening it seemed madness to let the animal lure them on into what appeared to be certain death.

"Yes, yes, come back," panted Joe; "it's horrible. Here, Grip, Grip, Grip! Here, here, here!"

But the dog only whined and swam on, and then began to beat the water wildly as if he were drowning, for in his excitement and dread, Gwyn had now begun to haul upon the leash, dragging the dog partly under water in his efforts to get hold of its collar.

It was no easy task; for as the dog rose again, it was evidently frightened by its immersion beneath the surface, and began barking, whining, and struggling to escape from its master's grasp.

"What is it? What are you doing?" cried Joe, as he held the light close to the roof.

"Doing? Can't you see the dog's half mad. Quiet, Grip! What is it! Hold still, will you?"

But this seemed to be the last thing the poor beast was disposed to do; for the tie, drag under the surface, and the seizure by the collar were all suggestive to its benighted intellect of death by drowning; and just as Gwyn, chin-deep in the water now and hardly able from his natural buoyancy to keep his footing, was backing towards the light, holding by the collar with both hands, the dog gathered itself together with its hind-legs resting against its master's breast, and made a tremendous bound as if for life.

Gwyn had had some experience of the muscular power in a collie dog, but never till that moment did he fully realise what strength a desperate animal does possess; for that bound sent the dog forward and him backward; and completely off his balance, his head went down, his legs rose from his buoyancy in the water, and as he made a desperate effort to regain his feet, there came a sharp drag at the neckerchief he had twisted round his hand, and he was dragged under in turn and towed along for some moments before he could get his head above the surface of the black water again. Then, obeying his natural instinct, he struck out and began to swim, feeling himself drawn steadily along by the dog farther and farther from the light which gleamed from the water, and into the black darkness and the unknown depths.

Chapter Thirty Five
The Help at Last

Joe uttered a groan, and began to wade after his companion, scraping the lanthorn against the roof from time to time in his agitation. He would have called to Gwyn to come back, but he could not find the words. He felt, though, that he must follow to help him, and began to wonder whether he could keep the light above water with one hand as he swam; and he prepared to try, for he felt that he must strike out as soon as the water touched his chin.

Then he paused, for from out of the darkness, and loud above the splashing, came Gwyn's angry words to the dog.

"You wretch! Come back!" he roared. "Wait till I get out of this, and I'll give you such a licking as will make your coat rougher than ever. Come back, will you!"

Grip made no sign of hearing, but swam on with all his might, and as he swam with one hand, Gwyn kept on lowering his feet to try for the bottom; but the dog's swimming was so energetic that the boy lost his balance again and again, and had a lesson in a man's helplessness in the water.

At last, and just when a feeling of dread was beginning to freeze his nerves, Gwyn, on lowering his legs, touched the rock, and giving an angry drag at the kerchiefs to check the dog, he regained his feet, and found the water little above his waist.

"It's all right," he panted. "Come on, Joe; the floor dips down there, and you're nearly in the deepest part, I think. I don't suppose you'll have to swim. I shouldn't if this wretch of a dog had not pulled me over."

Joe waded on very slowly and cautiously, finding his companion's words quite correct, and that, after just keeping his mouth above water, the level sank during the next few paces to his chin, then to his chest, and soon after to his waist, after which he easily reached his dripping companion.

"Nice mess, isn't it?" said Gwyn. "I wish old Sam Hardock was in it—pretending that the mine was pumped out. Will you be quiet, Grip? There, get on! It's all right if we're going in the proper direction;" and then, after wading on about a couple of hundred yards with the water still falling, Grip was able to walk, and uttering a joyous bark, he splashed along for a little way, and then stopped short, and gave himself a regular canine water-distributing shake which made him seem as if about to throw off his skin.

"Look at that," cried Gwyn now. "Only just wet above one's shoes."

Another fifty yards and they were upon the dry rocky floor, which they liberally bedewed with the water which trickled from their clothes as they were hurried on by the dog, who strained more than ever at his leash.

"It must be a good sign for him to tug like this," said Gwyn.

"Yes; he seems to know the way. It's of no use to try and stop him, for we know that we were all wrong, and perhaps he's right."

"Yes; look at him," said Gwyn; "there can't be a doubt about it. See how he tugs to get along."

"Yes; and now I think of it," said Joe, eagerly, "we haven't come through that hall-like place with the pillars all about."

"Haven't come to it yet, perhaps."

Joe shook his head, and gave his companion a meaning look.

"It isn't that," he said. "We've come quite a different way."

"Well, it doesn't matter," said Gwyn, so long as we get to the foot of the shaft; "and I shall be very glad, for, wet, tired, and hungry, it's very horrible being here."

They went on, led by the dog like two blind beggars Gwyn said, as he tried to look cheerfully upon their position, when he received another mental check, for Joe cried suddenly, "Stop a moment, for there's something wrong with this candle;" and a shudder worse than that which had attacked the boy when the water first rose to his breast ran through his nerves.

Joe opened the door of the lanthorn with a jerk, and the candle, which had fallen over on one side and was smoking the glass, dropped out on to the rocky floor; but Gwyn stooped quickly and saved it from becoming extinct, while the dog uttered an impatient bark and dragged at the leash again.

And it was always so as they proceeded, that the boys' strength, which had flickered up at the hope of rescue brought by the dog, rapidly burned down now like the candle, which quickly approached its end; while the dog seemed to be untiring and toiled and tugged away, as if trying to draw his master onward. They spoke less and less, and dragged their feet, and grew more helpless, till at the end of a couple of hours Joe suddenly said,—

"It's of no use, Ydoll; I can go no farther, and he's only taking us more into the mine. There isn't a bit of it we've passed before."

"Never mind; we must trust him now," said Gwyn, sadly; "we can't go back."

"No, but we oughtn't to have trusted him at all. We ought to have felt that we knew better than a dog."

"Stop! What are you going to do?" cried Gwyn, angrily.

"This," said Joe; and he let himself sink down on the rocky floor, and laid his head on his hand.

"No, no; get up! You sha'n't turn coward like this. Get up, I say!"

"I—can't," said Joe. "I'm dead beat. You go on, and if Grip takes you out try and find me again. If you can't, tell father I did my best."

"I won't; I sha'n't," cried Gwyn, furiously. "Think I'm going to leave you?"

"Yes. Save yourself."

"You get up," cried Gwyn; and stooping down, he caught one of his companion's arms, dragged at it with a heavy jerk, and found that he had miscalculated his strength, for he sank upon his knees, felt as if the lanthorn was gliding round him, and then subsided close by where Joe lay, while just then the dog gave a furious tug at the leash, freed itself, and dashed off into the darkness, barking apparently with delight.

"It's of no good, Joe; I'm as bad as you," said Gwyn, slowly; "I can't get up again."

"Never mind, Ydoll; we have done our duty, old chap, as the dads said we ought to as soldiers' sons. We have, haven't we?"

"No, not quite," cried Gwyn. "Let's have one more try—I will, and you shall."

He made an effort to rise, but sank back and nearly fainted, but recovered himself to feel that Joe had got hold of his hand, and he uttered a piteous sigh.

"Light's going out, Jolly, and if they don't find us soon our lights'll go out, too. I wouldn't care so much if it wasn't for the mater, because it will nearly kill her," he continued drearily. "She's ever so fond of me, though I've alway been doing things to upset her. Father won't mind so much, because he'll say I died like a man doing my duty."

"How will they know that?" mused Joe, whose eyes were half-closed. "Let's write it down on paper."

Gwyn was silent for a few moments as he lay thinking, but at last he spoke.

"No," he said; "that would be like what father calls blowing your own trumpet. He used to say to me that if he had gone about praising himself and telling people that he was a great soldier and had done all kinds of brave deeds, he would have been made a general before now; but he wouldn't. 'If they can't find out I've done my duty, and served my Queen as I should, let it be,' he said. And that's what we ought to do when we've fought well. If they don't find out that we've done what we should, it doesn't much matter; let it go. I'm tired out and faint, as you are, and—so's the candle, Joe. There, it has gone out."

Joe uttered a low, long, weary sigh, as, after dancing up and down two or three times, the light suddenly went out.

"Frightened?" said Gwyn, gently, as the black darkness closed them in.

"No, only sleepy," was the reply. "Good-night."

"Good-night," said Gwyn, softly; and the next minute they were sleeping calmly, with their breath coming and going gently, and the dripping of water from somewhere close at hand sounding like the beating of the pendulum of some great clock.

Once more the loud barking of a dog, long after the boys had lain down to rest, and Grip was dragging first at Gwyn, then at Joe, seizing their jackets in his teeth and tugging and shaking at them, but with no greater effect than to make Gwyn utter a weary sigh.

The dog barked again and tugged at him, but, finding his efforts of no avail, he stood with his paws resting on his master's breast, threw up his head, and uttered a dismal long-drawn howl which went echoing along the passages, and a faint shout was heard from far away.

The dog sprang from where he stood, ran a few yards, and stood barking furiously before running back to where Gwyn lay, when he seized and shook him again, and howled, ending by giving three or four licks at his face. Then he threw up his head once more, and sent forth another prolonged, dismal howl.

This was answered by a faintly-heard whistle, and the dog barked loudly over and over again, till a voice nearer now called his name.

All this was repeated till a gleam was seen on the wall, and now the dog grew frantic in his barking, running to and fro, and finally, as voices were faintly heard, and the gleaming of lights grew plainer, he crouched down with his head resting on Gwyn's breast, panting heavily as if tired out.

"Here, Grip! Grip! Grip! Where are you?" rang out in the Colonel's voice; and the dog answered with a single bark, repeated at intervals till the lights grew plainer, shadows appeared on the walls, there was the trampling of feet, and a voice said,—

"Hold up, sir; he must be close at hand. The dog keeps in one place, so he must have found them. Here, here, here!"

There was a long whistle, but the dog did not leave his place, only gave a sharp bark; and the next minute lights were being held over the Major and Colonel Pendarve, as they knelt beside their sons, trying all they knew to bring them back to their senses.

Their efforts were not without effect, for after a time Gwyn opened his eyes, stared blankly at the light, and said feebly,—

"Don't! Let me go to sleep."

Shortly after the two boys were being carefully carried in a semi-unconscious state by the willing hands of the search-party, through the bewildering mazes of the old mine, with Grip trotting on in front as if he were in command; and in this way the foot of the shaft was reached and they were safely taken to grass.

Chapter Thirty Six
Grip's Antipathy

"I really think you ought to stay in, Gwyn," said Mrs Pendarve, anxiously.

"Oh, I'll stay in if you like, mother," said the boy, patting the hand that was laid upon his arm, and looking affectionately in his mother's eyes; "but don't you think it would be all nonsense?"

"Yes," said the Colonel, firmly, as he looked up from the work he was reading. "He's quite well, my dear."

"No, no, my love; he's too pale to be well."

"Fancy, my dear; but perhaps he may be. Describe your symptoms, Gwyn, my boy."

"Haven't got any to describe, father," said Gwyn, merrily.

"Well, then, to satisfy your mother, how do you feel?"

"Ashamed of myself, father, for having had the doctor."

"Exactly. He's quite well, my dear. It was bad for him, of course; but a strong, healthy boy does not take long to recover from a long walk and some enforced abstinence— There, you can go, Gwyn, and—"

"Yes, father?" said the boy, for the Colonel paused.

"There's young Jollivet coming over the hill, so Major Jollivet and I would feel greatly obliged if you two lads did not get into another scrape for some time to come."

"Oh, I say," cried Gwyn, "I do call that too bad. Isn't it, mother? Father lets the Major take him down and get lost in the mine—"

"Nothing of the kind, sir. We found our way back—you did not."

"And then when we go down," continued Gwyn, without heeding his father's words, "to try and find them, father calls it getting into a scrape."

"Ah, well, never mind what I called it," said the Colonel, smiling; "but be careful, please. We don't want any more exploring."

Gwyn went off, met Joe, and they made for a favourite place on the cliff where they could look down on the sea and the sailing gulls to have a chat about their late adventure, this being their first meeting since they were carried home from the mine.

"You're all right, aren't you, Ydoll?" said Joe.

"Never felt better in my life, only I don't feel as if I could sit still here. Let's go to the mine."

"To go down? No, thank you—not to-day."

"Who wants to go down. I mean to have a talk to Sam and the men. I want to hear more about it. Oh, I say, though, it's too bad to have left old Grip chained up. Let's go and fetch him and, after we've been to the mine, give him a good run over the down and along the cliff."

"Yes," said Joe, quietly; and Gwyn led the way back toward the house by the cove.

"That dog ought to have a golden collar," said Gwyn. "No; I tell you what—he shall have one made of the first tin that is smelted."

"Too soft; it would bend," said Joe.

"Very well, then, we'll have some copper put with it to make it hard, and turn it to bronze."

"What's the good? Dogs don't want ornaments. He'd be a deal happier with his old leather strap."

"I don't care; he shall have one of bronze."

He told Grip this when he reached the yard, and the dog rushed toward them, standing on his hind-legs and straining against his collar at the full extent of his chain till he was unfastened, when he went half mad with excitement till they were out of the grounds and on their way toward the mine. Then as he trotted on before them straight for the buildings they heard the panting of the engine, and came in sight of the smoke.

For the pump was steadily at work again, clearing out the water which had begun to gather, consequent upon the enforced inaction.

Sam Hardock caught sight of them before they reached the mine, and came to meet them, smiling largely.

"How are you, gentlemen?—how are you?" he cried. "Not much the worse, then, from your trip underground?"

"Oh, no, Sam, we're right enough," said Gwyn; "but I say, I can't understand about our only being in the mine two days. It seemed to me like a week."

"Fortnight," said Joe, correcting him.

"Well, fortnight, then."

"Ay, it would," said Hardock, looking serious now. "I mind being shut up in one of the Truro mines by a fall; and we were only there about thirty hours, but it seemed to me just like thirty days."

"But hasn't there been a mistake? We must have been there more than forty-eight hours."

"No, my lad; that was the time, and quite long enough, too; but I'm afraid it would have been twice as long if it hadn't been for this dog. It was a fine idea to send him down to try and find you."

"A splendid idea! Who's was it?"

"Oh, never mind about that," said Hardock, stooping down to pat the dog in the most friendly way. "Someone said after we'd got back along of your father, Mr Gwyn, that the dog was more likely to find you than anyone; but just then the Colonel ordered a fresh search, and a party went down, and then another, and another, for there was no stopping; they hunted for you well. But at last him who proposed the dog said he was sure that was the way to go to work; and then at last the Colonel says, 'Well, Hardock,' he says, 'I believe you're right. Try the dog!'"

"Then it was you who proposed it," said Gwyn, catching the miner's arm.

"Me? Was it? Well, perhaps it was," said Hardock; "but lor' a mussy, I was all in such a flurry over the business I don't half recollect. Sort o' idee it was Harry Vores. Maybe it was."

"No, it wasn't," said Gwyn; "I'm sure it was you, Sam. Now, wasn't it?"

He caught the man's hand in his, and there was a dim look in his eyes which went straight to the miner's heart, and he said huskily—

"Well, s'pose it was, Master Gwyn, wouldn't you ha' been ready to jump at anything as a last sort o' chance, when there was two lads lost away down in a place like that? Why, I'd ha' done anything, let alone depending on a dog. It warn't as if I didn't want to go myself: I did go till I dropped and couldn't do no more, and begun to wish I'd never said a word about the gashly old mine."

"Well, don't go on like that," cried Gwyn, laughing, as he warmly shook the mine captain's hand, while Joe caught hold of the other and held on.

"Here, hi, don't you two go on like that," cried the man; "what's the good o' making such a fuss. It was the dog saved your lives, not me, my lads; and do leave off, please. You're making me feel like a fool."

"No, we're not; we're trying to make you feel that we're grateful for what you did, Sam," said Gwyn.

"Why, of course, I know that," said the man, with his voice sounding husky and strange; "but don't you see what you're doing, both of you?"

"Yes; shaking hands," said Joe.

"Nay; pumping my arms up and down till you've made the water come. Look here, if, if my eyes aren't quite wet. Ah!"

Hardock gave himself a shake, as if to get rid of his feeling of weakness, and then indulged in one of his broadest smiles.

"There," he said, "it's all over now; but my word, me and Harry Vores— ay, and every man-Jack of us—did feel bad. For, as I says to Harry, I says, it warn't as if it had been two rough chaps like us reg'lar mining lads. It was our trade; but for you two young gents, not yet growed up, to come to such an end was more than we could bear. But we did try, lot after lot of us. It warn't for want o' trying that we didn't find you. Wonderful place, though, aren't it?"

"Horrible!" said Joe.

"Oh, I don't know, sir; not horrible," said the man in a tone that was half-reproachful; "it's wonderful, I call it, and ten times as big as I expected."

"So big and dangerous that it will be no good," said Joe.

"What!" cried Hardock, laughing. "Did you look about you when you were down there?"

"As much as we could for the darkness."

"And so did I, sir," said the man, with a chuckle. "Of course, most when I was wandering about with your fathers. No good because it's so big? Wait a bit, and you'll see. Why, I shall begin to make a regular map plan of that place below. It will take months and months perhaps, but we shall explore a bit at a time, and mark the roads and drifts with arrows, and we shall all get more and more used to it."

"One could hardly get used to such a place as a tin mine, Sam," said Gwyn.

"Oh, yes, we could, sir, and we shall. But I see you didn't make the use of your eyes that I did, or you'd have more to say."

"What do you mean?" cried Gwyn.

"Didn't you see how rough all the mining had been?"

"Well, yes."

"And don't you see what that means?"

"No."

"Then I'll tell you, both of you—there's ore there enough to make your fathers the richest gentlemen in these parts; and there isn't a company in Cornwall as wouldn't do anything to get it. New-fashioned machinery will do what the old miners couldn't manage, and we won't have any more losing our way. There, I'm busy; so good-bye, and good luck to you both. Some day, when you grow to be men, you'll thank me for what I've done, for I've about made you both."

"That means we're both going to be very rich some day," said Gwyn; "but it doesn't matter. Come on, and let's give old Grip a jolly good run. Come on, old dog."

Grip did not come, but led off; and they made for the edge of the cliff, which ran along, on an average, three hundred feet above where the waves beat at their feet, but they had not gone far before Joe, who had glanced back, said quickly,—

"What's Tom Dinass following us for out here?"

Gwyn glanced back, too.

"Not following us," he said quickly; "he's making for the bend of the rock yonder."

"Yes," said Joe; "but that's where he knows we shall have to pass. What does he mean? He must have seen us at the mine and followed."

"I don't know," said Gwyn, thoughtfully; and a peculiar feeling of uneasiness attacked him. "But never mind; let's go on, or he'll think we're afraid of him."

"I am," said Joe, frankly.

"Well, then, if you are, you mustn't show it. Come on. Quiet, Grip."

For though the man was several hundred yards away, Grip had caught sight of him, set up all the thick hair about his neck, and uttered a low, deep growl.

Chapter Thirty Seven
Gwyn's Error

All at once, as the boys went along near the cliff edge, they found that Dinass had disappeared, and Joe expressed himself as being relieved.

"Went back beyond that ridge of rocks, I suppose," said Gwyn; "but I certainly thought he wanted to cut us off for some reason. Well, it's a good job he has gone."

But a little later they found that Dinass had not gone, for all the while Grip had had an eye on his movements and had acted after the manner of a dog.

For, after about five minutes, there was a sharp barking heard as the boys trudged on.

"Why, where's Grip?" said Gwyn. "I thought he was here."

The barking was repeated, and the dog was seen close to the edge of the cliff a hundred yards away, barking at something below him.

"What's he found?" said Joe.

"Oh, it's only at the gulls lower down. There's that shelf where it looks as if the granite had slipped down a little way. Let's see what he is about."

The dog kept up his barking, and the boys walked up, to find no gull below, but Tom Dinass seated in a nook smoking his pipe, with a couple of ominous-looking pieces of stone within reach of his hand, both evidently intended for Grip's special benefit should he attack, which he refrained from doing.

"Mornin', gentlemen," said the man. "Wish you'd keep that dawg chained up when you come to the mine; you see he don't like me."

"He won't hurt you if you don't tease him," said Gwyn. "Come to heel, Grip."

The dog uttered a remonstrant growl, but obeyed, and Dinass drew himself back against the cliff.

"Safer down here," he said.

"Yes, you are safer there," said Gwyn. "Good-morning."

"One minute, sir, please. Don't go away yet; I want just a word with you."

"Yes, what is it?" said Gwyn, shortly, while Joe gazed from the man to the depths below, troubled the while by some confused notion that he meant mischief.

"Only just a word or two, Mr Gwyn, sir," said the man in a humble manner, which accorded badly with his fierce, truculent appearance; and for the moment the lad addressed thought that he meant treachery, and he, Joe, could not help glancing at the precipice so close at hand. "You see, I'm an unlucky sort of fellow, and somehow make people think wrong things about me. You and me got wrong first time you see me; but I didn't mean no harm, and things got better till the other day over the bit o' fuss about going down."

"When you behaved like a cur and left us to take our chance. Quiet, Grip?"

"Look at that now!" cried Dinass, appealing to nobody—"even him turning again' me. Why, I ought to say as you two young gents went and forsook me down the old pit. Sure as goodness, I thought you both did it as a lark. Why, it warn't in me to do such a thing; and if you'd only waited a few minutes till I'd got my candle right, I'd perhaps ha' been able to save you from being lost. Anyhow I would ha' tried."

"Do you expect us to believe that you did not sneak back and leave us?" said Gwyn.

"Well, as young gents, I do hope you will, sir. Why, I'd sooner have cut my head off than do such a thing. Forsake yer! Why I was half mad when I found you'd gone on, and I run and shouted here and there till I was hoarse as a crow; and when I found I was reg'lar lost there, I can't tell you what I felt. That's a true word, sir; I never was so scared in my life."

"Ah, well, perhaps we'd better say no more about it, Dinass."

"Tom Dinass, sir. Don't speak as if you was out with me, too."

"We both thought you had left us in the lurch; but if you say you did not, why, we are, bound to believe you."

"*Bah!*" said Grip, in a growl full of disgust.

"Quiet, sir!"

"Ay, even that dawg don't take to me," said Dinass, in an ill-used tone. "But there, I don't care now you young gents believe me."

"All right; good-morning," said Gwyn, shortly. "Come along, Joe."

"Nay, nay, don't go away like that, Mr Gwyn, you'll think better of me soon, when you aren't so sore about it. For I put it to you, sir, as a gentleman as knows what the mine is, and to you, too, Master Joe Jollivet, you both know— Aren't it a place where a man can lose himself quickly?"

"Well, yes, of course," said Gwyn.

"Exactly; well, I lost myself same as you did; and because I warn't with you, everybody's again me—Sam Hardock and Harry Vores, and all the men, even the engine tenter; and that aren't the worst of it."

"What is, then?" said Joe.

"Why this, sir," said the man, earnestly: "They've made a bad report of me to the guv'nors just when I was getting on and settling down to a good job in what seems like to be a rich mine with regular work, and I'm under notice to leave."

"Serve you right for being such a sneak," said Joe, angrily.

"Oh, Master Joe, you are hard on a man; but you'll try and believe me, sir. I did work hard to find you both."

"I daresay we're wrong, Joe," said Gwyn; and the dog uttered another growl which sounded wonderfully like the word "*Bah!*"

"Yes, sir, wrong you are; and seeing how scarce work is, and so many mines not going, you won't mind putting a word in for me to the Colonel and the Major."

"What for? What about?" said Gwyn, sharply. "Your character?"

"Nay, sir, I don't want no character. Sam Hardock says the mine's rich, and I want to stay on. You say the right word to the Colonel, and he'll keep me on."

"I don't feel as if I could, Dinass," said Gwyn, thoughtfully.

"Not just this minute, sir," said the man, humbly; "but if you think about it, and how hard it is for a man to lose his bread for a thing like that, you'll feel different about it. Do try, sir, please. I'm a useful man, and you'll want me; and I'll never forget it if you do."

"Well," said Gwyn, "I'll think about it; but if I do ask my father, he may not listen to me."

"Oh, yes, he will, sir; he'd do anything you asked him; and so would yours, Master Joe. Do, please, gentlemen, and very thankful I'll be."

"Come along, Joe," said Gwyn.

"And you will speak a word for me, sir—both of you?"

"I'll see," said Joe; and with Grip trotting softly behind them, the two lads hurried off.

"You won't ask for him to stay, Ydoll?" said Joe, earnestly, as soon as they were out of earshot.

"Why not? Perhaps we're misjudging him after all."

"But I never liked him," said Joe.

"Well I didn't, and I don't; but that's no reason why we should be unfair. He isn't a pleasant fellow, and nobody seems to take to him; I believe he is right about all the men being set against him."

"Well, then, it's right for him to go."

"Oh, I say, Jolly, don't be hard and unfair on a fellow. One ought to stick up for the weaker side. Let's go and see if father's in the office."

"And you are going to speak for him?"

"Yes; and so are you;" and Gwyn led the way to the new mine buildings where the carpenters and masons were still busy, passing the shaft where the pump was steadily at work, but going very slowly, for there was very little water to keep down.

As the boys approached the doorway they saw Hardock come out and go on to the mine, while on entering they found the Colonel and the Major examining a rough statement drawn up by the captain who had just left.

"Well, boys," said Major Jollivet, "have you come in to hear about it?"

"No," said Gwyn, staring; "about what, sir?"

"The venture, my boy. Hardock reports that the mine is very rich in ore, and that we have entered upon a very good speculation."

"Yes, that is so, Gwyn," said his father; "and we are going to begin work in real earnest now—I mean, begin raising ore; and we must engage more men. Well; you were going to say something."

"Yes, father," said Gwyn, rushing into his subject at once. "We have just seen Dinass."

"Yes," said the Colonel, frowning; "he goes in about ten days, and we want someone in his place. What about him?"

"He has been telling us about his trouble—that he is dismissed."

"He need not worry you about it, boy. He should have behaved better."

"Yes; rank cowardice," said Joe's father, shortly.

"No, Major; he has been explaining how it was to us, and he tells me it was all accidental. He says we left him behind, and that he searched for us for long enough afterwards, till he was quite lost. It is an awkward place to miss your way in."

"Yes, you boys ought to know that," said the colonel. "Then this man has been getting hold of you to petition to stay?"

"Yes, father; he asked us to speak for him."

"Well, and are you going to?" said the Major.

"Yes, sir; I should like you and my father to give him another trial."

"But you don't like the man, Gwyn," said the Colonel.

"No, father—not at all; but I don't like to be prejudiced."

"And you, Joe," said the Major, "don't you want to be prejudiced?"

"No, father; Ydoll here has put it so that I'm ready to back him up. Dinass says he wants to get on, and doesn't like the idea of leaving a good rich mine."

"Humph!" said the Colonel. "We don't want to dismiss men—we want to engage them. What do you say, Jollivet; shall we give him another trial?"

"I think so," said the Major. "He's a big, strong, well set up fellow. Pity to drum a man out of the regiment who may be useful."

"Yes," said the Colonel, sharply. "Well, Gwyn, perhaps we have been too hard on him. He is not popular with the other men, but he may turn out all right, and we can't afford to dismiss a willing worker; so you may tell him that, at the interposition of you two boys, we will cancel the dismissal, and he can stay on."

"And tell him, boys," said the Major, "that he is to do your recommendation credit."

"Yes, of course," came in duet, and the boys hurried out to look for Dinass and tell him their news.

"Thank ye, my lads," he said, smiling grimly. "I'll stay, and won't forget it."

That night Dinass wrote a letter to somebody he knew—an ill-spelt letter in a clumsy, schoolboyish hand; but it contained the information that the old mine was rich beyond belief, and that he was beginning to see his way.

Gwyn did not know it then, but he had committed one of the great errors of his life.

Chapter Thirty Eight
Sam Hardock brings News

Time went on, and at the end of a year Ydoll Mine was in working order, with a good staff, the best of machinery for raising the ore, a man-engine for the work-people's ascent and descent, a battery of stamps to keep up an incessant rattle as the heavily-laden piles crushed the pieces of quartz, and in addition a solid-looking building with its furnaces for smelting the tin.

They were busy days there, and Gwyn and his companion found little time for their old pursuits—egging, rabbiting and fishing—save occasionally when, by way of a change, they would spend an evening on the rocky point which formed one of the protecting arms of Ydoll Cove, trying with pike rods, large winches and plenty of line, for the bass which played in silvery shoals in the swift race formed at the point by the meeting of two currents, and often having a little exciting sport in landing the swift-swimming, perch-finned fish.

For the fishing was too good off that part of the Cornish coast to be neglected, and the Colonel made allusions to the old proverb about all work and no play making Jack a dull boy.

One afternoon Gwyn loosened Grip for a run, to the dog's great delight, and, after seeking out Joe, who had been at home for days attending on his father, who was troubled with one of his old fits—Joe called them fits of the Jungle demon—the boys went down to the mine, Grip trotting behind them, save when some rustle to right or left attracted him for a frantic hunt to discover the cause.

At the mine Tom Dinass was found, looking very sour and grim, for he was still not the best of friends with his fellow-workmen; but as he was one of the most steady in his devotion to his work he stood well with the owners.

Gwyn caught sight of him first, and Dinass saw him at the same moment, but, instead of coming forward, he pretended to have something to do elsewhere, and went off into the smelting-house.

"What has he gone off like that for?" said Gwyn; and the boys followed just in time to hear some blows being struck in the gloomy place where a fierce fire was roaring and sending thin pencils of light through cracks in the furnace door.

The next minute some pieces of hard burned clay crumbled beneath the blows, and there was a dazzling stream of molten metal poured out, to run along channels made in the floor to form flat, squarish ingots of tin, and display the colours of the rainbow, intensified to a brilliancy that was almost more than the eye could bear.

"Please father when he hears of the casting," said Joe. "So much money has been laid out that he likes to hear of anything that will bring a return."

"Well, there's plenty of return coming in now," said Gwyn. "We've got one of the richest mines in Cornwall. Here, Tom Dinass! What's he mean by sneaking away? Here, Tom Dinass!"

"Want me, sir?" said the man, looking from one to the other suspiciously as he came up, his face shining in the wonderful glow shed by the molten tin.

"Yes, of course. Didn't you see us coming to you before?"

"Me, sir? No, I didn't know as you wanted me," and he seemed to draw himself up for defence.

"Well, we do," said Gwyn. "We want to have out the seine to-night; the tide will fit, and there have been mullet about."

"Oh, that's it, sir," said the man, who seemed much relieved. "Here, keep off with you," he growled, "my legs aren't roast meat."

"Come here, Grip!" cried Gwyn. "To heel, sir! I wish you two would be better friends."

"'Taren't my fault, sir; it's Grip. He's always nasty again' me."

"Well, never mind the dog. What time will you be off duty to-night?"

"Five, sir."

"That will do. See that the net is ready. I'll speak to the others. We'll be down there at five—no, half-past, because of tea."

"I'll be there, sir," said Dinass; and the boys went off, with the man watching them till the door swung close after them. "Nay, my legs aren't roast meat, but," he continued, as he glanced towards the molten metal still glowing, "it would soon be roast dog if I had my chance."

Meanwhile the boys went on to continue their preparations, and then hurried home for their meal; then for the first time Gwyn thought of Grip, and whistled to him to come and be tied up, but the dog did not come.

"Smelt a rabbit somewhere," said Gwyn, and thought no more about the dog.

In due time Dinass appeared down by the sandy cove, and after the long seine had been carefully laid in the stern of the boat, and the end lines left in charge of a couple of miners on one of the points, the boat was rowed straight out, with Gwyn paying out the net with its lead line and cork line running over a roller in the stern. Then at a certain distance the boat was steered so as to turn round to the right, and rowed in a curve, with the net still being paid out, till the rocks on the other side by the race were reached, and the sandy cove shut in by a wall of net, kept stretched by the leads at the bottom and the line of corks at the top.

At this point the boys landed with their trousers tucked up to the highest extent, jackets off, and arms bare as their legs, to start inland dragging the lines, the men on the other point starting at the same time, and bringing the dot-like row of corks to a rounder curve as the strain on the ropes grew heavier.

Tom Dinass now started for the point at the head of the cove to run the boat well ashore, and then go to the help of the boys as they toiled steadily on, stepping cautiously over the rocks, which were slippery with reddish-yellow fucus, till the broken part gave place to the heavy, well-rounded boulders which rattled and rumbled over one another in times of storms. Then the boulders gave place to shingle, which was rather better for the fishers, and lastly to the fine level sand over which the seine was to be dragged.

But this took some time and no little labour, for it was slow, hard work, full of the excitement of speculation; for the net, after enclosing so wide an area, might come in full of fish, or with nothing but long heavy strands of floating weed torn by the waves from the rocks perhaps miles away.

Experience and hints given by the blue-shirted bronzed fishers of the cove had taught the boys when was the best time for shooting the seine, however, so they generally were pretty successful; and as the net was drawn inland the bobbing of the line of corks and sundry flashes told that fish of some kind had been enclosed, when the excitement began.

It was a bright scene that summer's evening, when the sea was empurpled by the reflections of the gorgeous western sky, the smoke from the smelting-house looking like a golden feather.

But neither Gwyn nor Joe had eyes for the beauties of Nature which surrounded the nook where their fathers had made their home, for the excitement of the seine drawing was gaining in intensity.

Dinass, after running up the boat by the help of a couple of the men who had strolled down to see, was hurrying to pass the boys and wade out with an oar over his shoulder behind the line of corks, ready to splash and beat the water should there, by any chance, be a shoal of mullet within—no unlikely event, for these fish swam up with the tide to feed upon the scraps and odds and ends which came from the village down the little streamlet. And often enough their habit was, when enclosed, to play follow-my-leader, and leap the cork line and get out again to sea.

It was well that the precaution was taken, for upon this occasion a little shoal had been drawn in, to swim about peaceably enough for a time; but when the water shallowed, and their leader found that the wall of net was in its way, a frantic rush was made, and Dinass brought down his oar with a tremendous splash, making them dart in another direction; but there the top and bottom of the net were drawing together, forming a bag into which the shoal passed, and their effort to shoot out of the water was frustrated.

Again they appeared at the surface, but the splashing of the oar checked them; and this happened over and over, till their chance was gone, and, mingled with the other fish enclosed, they swam wildly about, seeking now for a hole or a way beneath the line of leads.

The fish sought in vain; and as the ends of the net were drawn in more and more, Dinass waded behind about the centre of the great bag, taking hold of the cork line and helping it along till the sandy beach was neared, and relieving some of the strain, till slowly and steadily the seine was drawn right up with its load, after cleanly sweeping up everything which had been enclosed, this being a great deal more than was wanted.

For the contents of the net were curious; and as the cork line was drawn back flat on the sands, there was plenty of work for the men to pick off the net the masses of tangled fucus and bladder-wrack which had come up with the tide. Jelly-fish—great transparent discs with their strangely-coloured tentacles—were there by the dozen; pieces of floating wood, scraps of rope and canvas, and a couple of the curious squids with their suckers and staring eyes.

All these were thrown off rapidly upon the sands right and left, and then the baskets were brought into play for the gathering of the spoil, while, scurrying away over net and sand, and making rapidly for the water, dozens of small crabs kept escaping from among the flapping fish, strangely grotesque in their actions, as they ran along sidewise, flourishing their pincers threateningly aloft.

In its small way it proved to be a fortunate haul, including as it did the whole of the little shoal of grey mullet, some three dozen, in their silvery scale armour, and running some three or four pounds weight each. Then there was nearly a score of the vermilion-and-orange-dyed red mullet, brilliant little fellows; a few small-sized mackerel; a few gurnard, a basketful of little flat fish, and a number of small fry, which had to be dealt with gingerly, for among them were several of the poisonous little weevels, whose sharp back fins and spines make dangerous wounds.

At last all were gathered up; and after giving orders for the seine to be carefully shaken clear and spread out to dry upon the downs, the two lads proceeded to select a sufficiency of the red and grey mullet for home use, and a brace for Sam Hardock, and then made a distribution of the rest, the men from the mine having gathered to look on and receive. Gwyn and Joe took a handle each of their rough basket, and began to trudge up the cliff path, stopping about half-way to look down at the people below.

"I say, how Tom Dinass enjoys a job of this kind," said Gwyn, as he turned over their captives in the basket, and noted how rapidly their lovely colours began to fade.

"Yes, better than mining," said Joe, thoughtfully. "I say, why is he so precious fond of hunting about among the rocks at low-water?"

"I don't know. Is he?"

"Yes. I've watched him from my window several times. I can just look over that rocky stretch that's laid bare by the tide."

"Why, you can't see much from there," said Gwyn.

"Yes I can. I've got father's field-glass up, and I can see him quite plain. I saw him yesterday morning just at daylight. I'd been in father's room to give him his medicine, for his fever has been threatening to come back."

"Trying to find a lobster or a crab or two."

"People don't go lobstering with a hammer."

"Expected to find a conger, then, and wanted the hammer to knock it down."

Joe laughed.

"You've got to hit a conger before you can knock it down. Not easy with a hammer."

"Well, what was he doing?"

"Oh, I don't know, unless he was chipping the stones to try whether a vein of tin runs up there."

"Well, it may," said Gwyn, thoughtfully. "Why shouldn't it?"

"I don't know why it shouldn't, but it isn't likely."

"Why not, when the mine runs right under there."

"What? Nonsense!"

"It does. I was down that part with Sam Hardock one day when the wind was blowing hard, and Sam could hear the waves beat and the big boulders rumble tumbling after as they fell back."

"How horrid!" said Joe, looking at his companion with his face drawn in accord with his words. "Why didn't you tell me?"

"Forgot all about it afterwards; never remembered it once till you began to talk like this."

"But how strange!" said Joe.

"Oh, I don't see why it should be strange. The old folks found a rich vein, and when they did they followed it up wherever it went; and that's, of course, why it's such a rambling old place. But that's what old Dinass is after. He thinks that if he can find a new vein, he'll get a reward."

"What a game if he finds one running out through the rocks!"

"I don't see how it's going to be a game."

"Don't you? Why, to find that he has discovered what already belongs to us; for of course the foreshore's ours, and even if it wasn't he couldn't go digging down there for ore."

"Why?"

"Because, for one thing, the waves wouldn't let him; and for another, we shouldn't allow him to dig a hole down into our mine. There, come on, and let's take them some fish; and I want to get on my dry clothes. What are you thinking about?"

"Eh?"

"I said what are you thinking about?"

"Tom Dinass."

"Not a very pleasant subject either. I get to like him less and less, and it's my opinion that if he gets half a chance he'll be doing something."

"Hallo!"

"Oh, here you are, Master Gwyn."

"Yes; what's the matter, Sam?"

"You'll know quite soon enough, sir. Come on up to the mine. Harry Vores has just gone back there. It was him brought me the news."

Chapter Thirty Nine
Grip's Bad Luck

"Why don't you speak?" cried Gwyn, angrily. "Has there been an accident? Surely father hasn't gone down!"

"Oh, the Colonel's all right, sir," said Hardock, genially. "The gov'nor hasn't gone and lost himself."

"But there has been an accident, Sam," cried Joe.

"Nor the Major aren't gone down neither, sir," said the man. "Here, let me carry that fish basket. Didn't remember me with a couple o' mullet, did you?"

"Yes, two of those are for you, Sam; but do speak out? What is wrong?"

"Something as you won't like, sir. Your dog Grip's gone down the mine."

"What for? Thinks we're there? Well, that's nothing; he'll soon find his way up. Why did they let him go down?"

"Couldn't help it, sir," said the man, slowly.

"What—he would go? I did miss him, Joe, when I went home. I remember now, we didn't see him after we went to the mine. He must have missed us, and then thought we had gone down."

"Sets one thinking of being lost and his coming after us," said Joe, slowly. "Well, he can't lose his way."

"But how do you know he went down, Sam?" asked Gwyn, as they approached the mine.

"Harry Vores heerd him."

"What, barking?"

"'Owlin'."

"Oh, at the bottom of the shaft. Dull because no one was down. Then why did you suggest that there was an accident? You gave me quite a turn."

"'Cause there was an accident, sir," said Hardock, quietly; and he led the way into the great shed over the pit mouth, where all was very still.

Gwyn saw at a glance that something serious had happened to the dog, which was lying on a roughly-made bed composed of a miner's flannel coat placed on the floor, beside which Harry Vores was kneeling; and as soon as the dog heard steps he raised his head, turned his eyes pitifully upon his master, and uttered a doleful howl.

"Why, Grip, old chap, what have you been doing?" cried Gwyn, excitedly.

"Don't torment him, sir," said Vores; "he's badly hurt."

"Where? Oh, Grip! Grip!" cried Gwyn, as he laid his hand on the dog's head, while the poor beast whined dolefully, and made an effort to lick the hand that caressed him, as he gazed up at his master as if asking for sympathy and help.

"Both his fore-legs are broken, sir, and I'm afraid he's got nipped across the loins as well."

"Nay, nay, nay, Harry," growled Hardock; "not him. If he had been he wouldn't have yowled till you heerd him."

"Nipped?" said Gwyn. "Then it wasn't a fall?"

"Nay, sir; Harry Vores and me thinks he must ha' missed you, and thought you'd gone down the mine, and waited his chance and jumped on to the up-and-down to go down himself."

"Oh, but the dog wouldn't have had sense enough to do that."

"I dunno, sir. Grip's got a wonderful lot o' sense of his own! 'Member how he found you two young gents in the mine! Well, he's seen how the men step on and off the up-and-down, and he'd know how to do it. He must, you know."

"But some of the men would know," said Gwyn.

"Dessay they do, sir, but they're all off work now, and we don't know who did. Well, he must have had a hunt for you, and not smelling you, come back to the foot o' the shaft, and began to mount last thing, till he were close to the top, and then made a slip and got nipped. That's how we think it was—eh, Harry?"

"Yes, sir; that's all I can make of it," said Vores. "I was coming by here when the men were all up, and the engine was stopped, and I heard a yowling, and last of all made out that it was down the shaft here; and I fetched Master Hardock and we got the engine started, and I went and found the poor dog four steps down, just ready to lick my hand, but he couldn't wag his tail, and that's what makes me think he's nipped."

But just then Grip moved his tail feebly, a mere ghost of a wag.

"There!" cried Hardock, triumphantly; "see that? Why, if he'd been caught across the lines he'd have never wagged his tail again."

"Poor old Grip," said Gwyn, tenderly; "that must have been it. He tried too much. Caught while coming up. Here, let's look at your paw."

The boy tenderly took hold of the dog's right paw, and he whined with pain, but made no resistance, only looked appealingly at his masters to let them examine the left leg.

"Oh, there's no doubt about it, Joe; both legs have been crushed."

Joe drew a low, hissing breath through his teeth.

"It's 'most a wonder as both legs warn't chopped right off," said Vores. "Better for him, pore chap, if they had been."

"Hadn't we better put him out of his misery, sir?" said Hardock.

"Out of his misery!" cried Gwyn, indignantly. "I should like to put you out of your misery."

"Nay, you don't mean that, sir," said the captain, with a chuckle.

"Kill my dog!" cried Gwyn.

"You'll take his legs right off, won't you, sir, with a sharp knife?" said Vores.

"No, I won't," cried Gwyn, fiercely.

"Better for him, sir," said Vores. "They'd heal up then."

"But you can't give a dog a pair of wooden legs, matey," said Hardock, solemnly. "If you cuts off his front legs, you'd have to cut off his hind-legs to match. Well, he'd only be like one o' them turnspitty dogs then; and it always seems to me a turnspitty to let such cripply things live."

"We must take him home, Joe," said Gwyn, who did not seem to heed the words uttered by the men.

"Yes," said Joe. "Poor old chap!" and he bent down to softly stroke the dog's head.

"Better do it here, Master Gwyn," said Hardock. "We'll take him into the engine-house to the wood block. I know where the chopper's kept."

"What!" cried Gwyn, in horror. "Oh, you wretch!"

"Nay, sir, not me. It's the kindest thing you can do to him. You needn't come. Harry Vores'll hold him to the block, and I'll take off all four legs clean at one stroke and make a neat job of it, so as the wounds can heal."

Gwyn leaped to his feet, seized the basket from where it had been placed upon the floor, tilted it upside down, so that the fish flew out over to one side of the shed, and turned sharply to Joe, — "Catch hold!" he said, as he let the great basket down; and setting the example, he took hold of one end of the flannel couch on which poor Grip lay. Joe took the other, and together they lifted the dog carefully into the basket, where he subsided without a whine, his eyes seeming to say, —

"Master knows best."

"I'll carry him to the house, Mr Gwyn, sir," said Vores.

"No, thank you," said the boy, shortly; "we can manage."

"Didn't mean to offend you, sir," said the man, apologetically. "Wanted to do what was best."

"Ay, sir, that we did," said Hardock. "I'm afeard if you get binding up his legs, they'll go all mortificatory and drop off; and a clear cut's better than that, for if his legs mortify like, he'll die. If they're ampitated, he'll bleed a bit, but he'll soon get well."

"Thank you both," said Gwyn, quietly. "I know you did not mean harm, but we can manage to get him right, I think. Come along, Joe."

They lifted the basket, one at each end, swinging the dog between them, and started off, Grip whining softly, but not attempting to move.

"Shall we bring on the fish, sir?" shouted Hardock.

"Bother the fish!" cried Gwyn. "No; take it yourselves."

Chapter Forty
A Bit of Surgery

"Oh, Gwyn, my dear boy," cried Mrs Pendarve, who was picking flowers for the supper-table as the boys came up to the gate, "what is the matter?"

"Grip's legs broken," said the boy, abruptly. "Where's father?"

"In the vinery, my dear. What are you going to do? Let me see if—"

"No, no, mother, we'll manage," said Gwyn; "come along, Joe."

They hurried down the garden, and up to where the sloping glass structure stood against the wall, from out of which came the sound of the Colonel's manly voice, as he trolled out a warlike ditty in French, with a chorus of "Marchons! Marchons!" and at every word grapeshot fell to the ground, for the Colonel, in spite of the suggestions of war, was peacefully engaged, being seated on the top of a pair of steps thinning out the grapes which hung from the roof.

"Here, father, quick!" cried Gwyn, as they entered the vinery.

"Eh? Hullo! What's the matter?"

"Grip's been on the man-engine and got his fore-legs crushed."

"Dear me! Poor old dog!" said the Colonel, descending from the ladder and sticking his long scissors like a dagger through the bottom button-hole of his coat. "Then we must play the part of surgeon, my boy. Not the first time, Joe. Clap the lid on the tank."

The wooden cover was placed upon the galvanised-iron soft-water tank, and poor Grip, who looked wistfully up in the Colonel's eyes, was lifted out and laid carefully upon the top, while the Colonel took off his coat and turned up his sleeves in the most business-like manner.

"I remember out at Bongay Wandoon, boys, after a sharp fight with a lot of fanatical Ghazis, who came up as I was alone with my company, we had ten poor fellows cut and hacked about and no surgeon within a couple of hundred miles, which meant up there in the mountains at least a week before we could get help. It was all so unexpected, no fighting being supposed to be possible, that I was regularly taken by surprise when the wretches had been driven off, and I found myself there with the ten poor fellows on my hands. I was only a young captain then, and I felt regularly knocked over; but, fortunately, I'd a good sergeant, and we went over to my lieutenant, who had been one of the first to go down. But he wouldn't have a cut touched till the men had been seen to. I'm afraid my surgery was a very bungling affair, but the sergeant and I did our best, and we didn't lose a patient. Our surgeon made sad fun of it all when he saw what we had done, and he snarled and found fault, and abused me to his heart's content; but some time after he came and begged my pardon, and shook hands, and asked me to let him show me all he could in case I should ever be in such a fix again. Consequently, I often used to go and help him when we had men cut down. I liked learning, and it pleased the men, too, and taught me skill. Poor old dog, then; no snapping. The poor fellow's legs are regularly crushed, as if he had been hit with an iron bar used like a scythe."

"Crushed in the man-engine, father," said Gwyn.

"Ah, yes, that must have done it. Well, Gwyn, my boy, a doctor would say here in a case like this—'amputation. I can't save the limbs.'"

"Oh, father, it is so horrible!"

"Yes, my boy, but you want to save the poor fellow's life."

"Can't anything be done, sir?" said Joe.

"Humph! Well, we might try," said the Colonel, as he tenderly manipulated the dog's legs, the animal only whining softly, and seeming to understand that he was being properly treated. "Yes, we will try. Here, Joe Jollivet, go and ask Mrs Pendarve to give you about half-a-dozen yards of linen for a bandage, and bring back a big needle and thick thread."

"Yes, sir," and Joe hurried out; but soon poked his head in again. "Don't get it all done, sir, till I've come back. I want to see."

"Can't till you come, boy. Off with you. Now, Gwyn, fill the watering-pot. I'll lift the lid of the tank."

The pot was filled and the dog placed back again.

"Now fetch that bag of plaster-of-Paris from the tool-house," said the Colonel.

This was soon done, and a portion of the white cement poured out into a flower-pot.

"Is that good healing stuff, father?" asked Gwyn.

"No, but it will help. Wait a bit, and you'll see," said the Colonel; and he once more softly felt the dog's crushed and splintered legs, shaking his head gravely the while.

"Don't you think you can save his legs, father?" asked Gwyn.

"I'm very much in doubt, my boy," said the Colonel, knitting his brows; but dogs have so much healthy life in them, and heal up so rapidly, that we'll try. Now, then, how long is that boy going to be with those bandages? Oh, here he is.

Gwyn opened the door, and Joe hurried in.

"Hah! that will do," said the Colonel; and cutting off two pieces a yard long, he thrust them into the watering-pot, soaked them, wrung them out, and then rolled both in the flower-pot amongst the plaster-of-Paris.

Then washing his hands, he took one of the injured legs, laid the broken bones in as good order as he could; and as Gwyn held the bandage ready, the leg was placed in it and bound round and round and drawn tight, the dog not so much as uttering a whimper, while after a few turns, the limp lump seemed to grow firmer. Then the bandaging was continued till all the wet linen was used, when the Colonel well covered the moist material with dry plaster, which was rapidly absorbed; and taking a piece of the dry bandage, thoroughly bound up the limb, threaded the big needle, and sewed the end of the linen firmly, and then the dog was turned right over for the other leg to be attacked.

"Well, he is a good, patient beast," said Gwyn, proudly. "But you don't think he's dying, do you, father?" he added anxiously.

"Speak to him, and try," said the Colonel.

Gwyn spoke, and the dog responded by tapping the cistern lid with his tail very softly, and then whined piteously, for the Colonel in placing the splintered bones as straight as he could was inflicting a great deal of pain.

"Can't help it, Canis, my friend," said the Colonel. "If you are to get better I want it to be with straight legs, and not to have you a miserable odd-legged cripple. There, I shall soon be done. That bandage is too dry, Gwyn; moisten it again. Wring it out. That's right; now dip it in the plaster."

"What's that for, sir?" said Joe, who was looking on eagerly.

"What do you think?" replied the Colonel. "Now, Gwyn, right under, and hold it like a hammock while I lay the leg in. I'm obliged to hold it firmly to keep the bones in their places. Now, right over and tighten it.

That's it. Round again. Now go on. Round and round. Well done. Now I'll finish. Well," he continued, as he took the ends of the bandage and braced the dog's leg firmly, "why do I use this nasty white plaster, Joe?"

"Because it will set hard and stiff round the broken leg."

"Good boy," said the Colonel, smiling, "take him up; Gwyn didn't see that."

"Yes I did, father; but I didn't like to bother you and speak."

"Then stop where you are, boy. Keep down, Joe; he behaved the better of the two. You are both right; the plaster and the linen will mould themselves as they dry to the shape of the dog's legs, and if we can keep him from trying to walk and breaking the moulds, Nature may do the rest. At all events, we will try. When the linen is firm, I'll bind splints of wood to them as well, so as to strengthen the plaster, though it is naturally very firm."

"It will be a job to keep him quiet, father," said Gwyn.

"I'm afraid so, my boy. Not, however, till the plaster sets; that cannot take very long, and we shall have to hold him down if it's necessary; but I don't think it will be. Poor fellow, he'll very likely go to sleep."

As he spoke, the Colonel was busily employed finishing the bandaging, and when this was done he stood thinking, while the dog lay quiet enough, blinking at those who had been operating upon him.

"We might secure his legs somehow," said the Colonel, thoughtfully; "for all our success depends upon the next hour."

But Grip solved the difficulty by stretching himself out on one side with his bandaged legs together, and, closing his eyes, went off fast asleep, with the boys watching him—the Colonel having gone into the house, for it had turned too dark for him to go on grape-thinning long before the canine surgery was at an end.

Chapter Forty One
A Man's Pursuits

The boys watched beside the dog till past ten o'clock, when the Colonel came in and examined the bandages.

"Set quite hard," he said, "and he's sleeping fast enough. Nature always seems kind to injured animals. They curl up and go to sleep till they're better."

"Then you think he'll get better, sir?" said Joe.

"Can't say, my boy; but you had better be off home to bed."

"Yes, sir," said Joe. "Coming part of the way with me, Gwyn?"

Gwyn glanced at his father before saying yes, for he expected to hear an objection.

But the Colonel's attention was fixed upon the dog.

"Let him sleep," he said; "he'll be all right here till morning."

"But if he stirs, he may fall off the cistern and hurt himself again, father."

"No fear, my boy. I don't suppose he will attempt to move all night. There, off with you, Gwyn, if you are going part of the way."

The boys followed the Colonel out of the vinery, the door was shut, and the ascending lane leading to the Major's house was soon reached, and then the rugged down.

"Precious dark," said Gwyn; but there was no answer. "Sleep, Jolly?" said Gwyn, after a few moments.

"Eh? No; I was thinking. I say, though, how precious dark it is;" for they could not see a dozen yards.

"Yes, but what were you thinking about?"

"The dog."

"Oh, yes, of course, so was I; but what about him?" said Gwyn, sharply.

"How he got hurt?"

"Chopped in the man-engine. You heard."

"Yes, but I don't believe it."

"Here's a miserable unbeliever," said Gwyn, mockingly. "How did he get hurt, then?"

"Someone did it."

"Oh, nonsense! It isn't likely. The machine did it, same as it would you or me if we weren't careful."

"But that wasn't how poor old Grip was hurt."

"How then?"

"I feel sure he was hurt with an iron bar."

"Why, who would hurt him in that brutal way?"

"Someone who hated him."

"Gammon!"

"Very well—gammon, then. But when did we see him last?"

"Last? Last? Oh, I know; when we went to the smelting-house to find Tom Dinass."

"Well, we left him behind there. The door must have swung-to and shut him in."

"Then you think Tom Dinass did it."

"Yes, I do."

"Then I say it's all prejudice. Tom's turning out a thoroughly good fellow. See how willing he was over the fishing, and how he helped us this evening. You're always picking holes in Tom Dinass's coat. What's that?"

A peculiar loud sneeze rang out suddenly from across the rough moorland to their right, where the blocks of granite lay thick.

"Tom Dinass," said Joe, in a whisper; and he stepped quickly behind a block of stone, Gwyn involuntarily following him. "That's his way of sneezing," whispered Joe. "What's he doing over here to-night?"

The boys stood there perfectly silent; and directly after there was a faint rustling, and the figure of a man was seen upon the higher ground against the skyline for a minute or so, as he passed them, crossing their track, and apparently making for the cliffs.

Their view was indistinct, but the man seemed to be carrying something over his shoulder. Then he was gone.

"Going congering," said Gwyn. "He's making for the way down the rocks, so as to get to the point."

"He wouldn't go congering to-night," said Joe. "We gave him as much fish as he'd want."

"Going for the sport of the thing."

"Down that dangerous way in the dark?"

"I daresay he knows it all right, and it saves him from going round by the fishermen's cottages—half-a-mile or more."

"'Tisn't that," said Joe.

"What an obstinate old mule you are, Jolly," cried Gwyn, impatiently; "you don't like Tom Dinass, and everything he does makes you suspicious."

"Well, do you like him?"

"No; but I don't always go pecking at him and accusing him of smashing dogs' legs with iron stoking-bars. It wouldn't be a man who would do that; he'd be a regular monster."

"Let's go and see what he's after," said Joe.

"What, late like this in the dark?"

"Yes; you're not afraid are you? I want to know what he's about. I'm sure he's doing something queer."

"I'm not afraid to go anywhere where you go," said Gwyn, stoutly; "but of all the suspicious old women that ever were, you're getting about the worst."

"Come along, then."

"All right," said Gwyn; "but if he finds us watching him throwing out a conger-line, he'll break our legs with an iron bar and pitch us off the cliff."

"Yes, you may laugh," said Joe, thoughtfully, "but I'm sure Tom Dinass is playing some game."

"Let's go and play with him, then. Only make haste, because I must get back."

Joe led the way cautiously off to their left, in and out among the stones and patches of furze and bramble, till they neared the edge of the cliff, when they went more and more cautiously, till a jagged piece of crag stood up, showing where the precipice began; and to the left of this was the rather perilous way by which an active man could get down to the mass of tumbled rocks at the cliff foot, and from there walk right out on the western point which sheltered the cove from the fierce wind and waves.

"All nonsense, Jolly," whispered Gwyn after they had stood for a few moments gazing down at where the waves broke softly with a phosphorescent light. "I won't go."

But as the boy spoke there was a loud clink from far below, as if an iron bar had struck against a stone, and the lad's heart began to beat hard with excitement.

Then all was silent again for nearly five minutes, and the darkness, the faint, pale, lambent light shed by the waves, and the silence, produced a strange shrinking sensation that was almost painful.

"Shall we go down?" said Joe, in a whisper.

"And break our necks? No, thank you. There, come back, he has only gone to set a line for conger."

"Hist!" whispered Joe, for at that moment, plainly heard, there came up to where they stood a peculiar thumping sound, as of a mason working with a tamping-iron upon stone.

"Now," whispered Joe. "What does he mean by that?"

Chapter Forty Two
Mining Matters

The boys stayed there some time listening to the clinking sound, and then, feeling obliged to go, they hurried away.

"Tell you what," said Gwyn, as they parted at last, "we'll wait till he has gone down the mine to-morrow morning, and then either go by the cliff or round by the cove head, and see what he has been about. I say it's a conger-line, and we may find one on."

"Perhaps so," said Joe, thoughtfully. "Ydoll, old chap, I don't like Tom Dinass."

"Nor I, neither. But what's the matter now?"

"I'm afraid he broke poor Grip's legs."

"What? Nonsense! He wouldn't be such a brute. No man would."

"Well, I hope not; but I can't help thinking sometimes that he did. You see, the smelting-house door might have swung-to and shut him in with Dinass and he might have flown at him, and Dinass might have struck at him with one of the stoking-irons and broken his legs, and then been afraid and thrown him down the mine."

"And pigs might fly, but they're very unlikely birds."

"Well, we shall see," said Joe; and he hurried home to find his father asleep, while Gwyn, before going in, went on tiptoe to the vinery and crept in, to hear the dog snoring. Satisfied with this, he walked round the house fully prepared to receive a scolding for being so long, and feeling disposed to take refuge in the excuse that he had been to see the dog; but no lights were visible, everyone having retired to rest, the leaving of doors unfastened not being considered a matter of much moment at that secluded place.

So Gwyn crept to bed unheard, and had no need to make a shuffling excuse, and slept late the next morning, to find at breakfast time his father had been out to the dog.

"How is he? Oh, better than I expected to find him? He is not disposed to eat, only to sleep—and the best thing for him. The bandages are as hard as stone. Storm coming, I think, my dear."

"We must not complain," said Mrs Pendarve. "We have had lovely weather."

"I don't complain, and should not unless the waves washed up into the mine, and gave us a week's pumping; but we should want monsters for that."

The Colonel was right, for there was nearly a month's bad weather, during which the waves came thundering in all along the coast, and no fishing-boats went out; and as no opportunity occurred for getting down to the point, which was a wild chaos of foam, the strange behaviour of Tom Dinass was forgotten.

There were busy days, too, in the mine, stolen from those passed in superintending the tremendous output of tin ore. The men worked below and above, and the Colonel and Major shook hands as they congratulated themselves upon their adventure, it being evident now that a year of such prosperity would nearly, if not quite, recoup them for their outlay in machinery, they having started without the terribly expensive task of sinking the mine through the rock. All that they had had to do was to pump out the first excavation, and then begin raising rich tin ore for crushing, washing, and smelting.

The stolen days were devoted to making explorations and mapping out the mine. There were no more goings astray, for gallery after gallery was marked in paint or whitewash with arrows, so that by degrees most of the intricacies, which formed a gigantic network, were followed and marked, and in these explorations abundant proof was given of the enormous wealth waiting to be quarried out.

There was no wonder felt now that those who had gone down first should have lost themselves.

"Wonder to me is, Mr Gwyn," said Hardock one day, "that we any on us come up again alive."

So they kept on exploring, and, well furnished with lights, the lads found the great hall with its pillars of quartz veined with tin, and strange passages going in different directions, far less horrible now. There was the gallery which dipped down too, one which they found their way to now from both ends. It looked gloomy and strange, with the whispering sounds of falling water and the reflections from the candles on the shining black surface; but knowledge had robbed it of its horrors.

"Go through it again?" said Gwyn, as they stood looking along it; "to be sure I would, only I don't want to get wet through for nothing. When we did wade through, Sam, one was always expecting to put one's foot in a shaft or in a well, and go down, never to come up again."

"Ay, that would make you feel squirmy, sir."

"It did," said Gwyn, laughing. "But, I say, wasn't Grip a splendid old fellow? and how he knew! Fancy his swimming right along here!"

"Ay, he is a dog," said Sam. "How is he, sir?"

"Oh, he'll soon be out again; but father wants to keep him chained up till his bones are properly grown together."

"He'll have to run dot and go one, I suppose, sir?"

"What, lame?" cried Gwyn. "Very little, I think. We can't tell yet, because his legs are stiff with so much bandaging. I say, Sam, you fall down the shaft and break your legs, and we'll put 'em in plaster for you."

"No thank ye, sir," said the man, grinning, as he stopped to snuff his candle with Nature's own snuffers. "I never had no taste for breaking bones. Now, then, we'll go round by a bit I come to one day, if you don't mind a long walk back. Take us another two hours, but the floor's even, and I want to have a look at it."

"What sort of a place is it?" said Gwyn; "anything worth seeing?"

"Not much to see, sir, only it's one of the spots where the old miners left off after going along to the west. Strikes me it's quite the end that way. And I want to make sure that we've found one end of the old pit."

"Does the place seem worn out?" said Joe, who had been listening in silence.

"That's it, sir. Lode seems to have grown a bit narrower, and run up edge-wise like."

"Why, we went there," said Joe, eagerly. "Don't you remember, Ydoll?"

"Yes, I remember now. I'd forgotten it, though. I say! Hark; you can hear quite a murmuring if you put your ear against the wall."

"Yes, sir, you can hear it plainly enough in several places."

"Don't you remember, Ydoll, how we heard it when we were wet?"

"Now you talk about it, I do, of course," said Gwyn; "but, somehow, being down here as we were, I seemed to be stunned, and it has always been hard work to recollect all we went through. I'd forgotten lots of these galleries and pools and roofs, just as one forgets a dream, while, going through them again, they all seem to come back fresh and I know them as well as can be. But what makes this faint rumbling, Sam? Is it one of the little trucks rumbling along in the distance?"

"No, sir," said Hardock, with a chuckle. "What do you say it is, Master Joe?"

The lad listened in silence for a few moments, and then said slowly,—

"Well, if I didn't know that it was impossible, I should say that we were listening to the waves breaking on the shore."

"It aren't impossible, sir, and that's what you're doing," said Hardock; and the boys started as if to make for the foot of the shaft.

"What's the matter," said Hardock, chuckling. "'Fraid of its bursting through?"

"I don't know—yes," said Gwyn. "What's to prevent it?"

"Solid rock overhead, sir. It's lasted long enough, so I don't see much to fear."

"But it sounds so horrible," cried Joe, who suddenly found that the gallery in which they were standing felt suffocatingly hot.

"Oh, it's nothing when you're used to it. There's other mines bein' worked right under the sea. There's no danger so long as we don't cut a hole through to let the water in; and we sha'n't do that."

"But how thick is the rock over our heads?"

"Can't say, sir, but thick enough."

"But is it just over our heads here?"

"Well, I should say it warn't, sir; but I can't quite tell, because it's so deceiving. I've tried over and over to make it out, but one time it sounds loudest along there, another time in one of the other galleries. It's just as it happens. Sound's a very curious thing, as I've often noticed down a mine, for I've listened to the men driving holes in the rock to load for a blast, and it's quite wonderful how you hear it sometimes in a gallery ever so far off, and how little when you're close to. Come along. No fear of the water coming in, or I'd soon say let's get to grass."

The boys did not feel much relieved, but they would not show their anxiety, and followed the mining captain with the pulsation of their hearts feeling a good deal heavier; and they went on for nearly an hour before they reached the spot familiar to them, one which recalled the difficulty they had had with Grip when he ran up the passage, and stood barking at the end, as if eager to show them that it was a *cul-de-sac*.

Hardock went right to the end, and spent some time examining the place before speaking.

Then he began to point out the marks made by picks, hammers, and chisels, some of which were so high up that he declared that the miners must have had short ladders or platforms.

"Ladders, I should say," he muttered; "and the mining must have been stopped for some reason, because the lode aren't broken off. There's plenty of ore up there if we wanted it, and maybe we shall some day, but not just yet. There's enough to be got to make your fathers rich men without going very far from the shaft foot; and all this shows me that it must have been very, very long ago, when people only got out the richest of the stuff, and left those who came after 'em to scrape all the rest. There, I think that will do for to-day."

The boys thought so, too, though they left this part rather reluctantly, for it was cooler, but the idea of going along through galleries which extended beneath the sea was anything but reassuring.

That evening the Major came over to the cottage with his son, and the long visit of the boys underground during the day formed one of the topics chatted over, the Major seeming quite concerned.

"I had no idea of this," he said. "Highly dangerous. You had not been told, Pendarve, of course."

"No," said the Colonel, smiling, "I had not been told; but I shrewdly suspected that this was the case, especially after hearing the faint murmuring sound in places."

"But we shall be having some catastrophe," cried the Major—"the water breaking in."

The Colonel smiled.

"I don't think we need fear that. The galleries are all arch-roofed and cut through the solid rock, and, as far as I have seen, there has not been a single place where the curves have failed. If they have not broken in from the pressure of the millions of tons of rock overhead, why should they from the pressure of the water?"

"Oh, but a leak might commence from filtration, and gradually increase in size," said the Major.

"Possibly, my dear boy," replied the Colonel; "but water works slowly through stone, and for the next hundred years I don't think any leakage could take place that we should not master with our pumping gear. Oh, absurd! There is no danger. Just try and think out how long this mine has been worked. I am quite ready to believe that it was left us by the ancient Britons who supplied the Phoenicians."

"May be, we cannot tell," said the Major, warmly; "but you cannot deny that we found the mine full of water."

"No, and I grant that if we leave it alone for a hundred years it will be full again."

"From the sea?"

"No; from filtration through the rock. The water we pumped out was fresh, not salt. There, my dear Jollivet, pray don't raise a bugbear that might scare the men and make them nervous. They are bad enough with what they fancy about goblins and evil spirits haunting the mine. Even Hardock can't quite divest himself of the idea that there is danger from gentry of that kind. Don't introduce water-sprites as well."

The subject dropped; but that night, impressed as they had been by what they had heard, and partly from partaking too liberally of a late supper, both Gwyn and Joe had dreams about the sea breaking into and flooding the mine, Gwyn dreaming in addition that he behaved in a very gallant way. For he seemed to find the hole through which the water passed in, and stopped it by thrusting in his arm, which stuck fast, and, try how he would, he could not extricate it, but stood there with the water gradually stifling him, and preventing him from calling aloud for help.

The heat and darkness at last rescued him from his perilous position— that is to say, he awoke to find himself lying upon his back with his face beneath the clothes; and these being thrown off, he saw that the morning sunshine was flooding the bedroom, and the memory of the troublous dream rapidly died away.

Chapter Forty Three
After a Lapse

"That makes the fourth," said Colonel Pendarve, tossing a letter across to his son in the office one morning when the mine was in full work; "four proposals from Mr Dix, and I have had three at intervals from that other legal luminary, Brownson. Seven applications to buy the mine in two years, Gwyn. Yes, it will be two years next week since we began mining, and in those two years you and Joe Jollivet have grown to be almost men—quite men in some respects, though you don't shave yet."

"Yes, I do, father," said Gwyn, smiling.

"Humph!" ejaculated the Colonel, "then it's an utter waste of time. There, answer that letter and say emphatically No."

The Colonel left the office, and Gwyn read the letter.

"Look here, Joe," he said; and Joe Jollivet, who had climbed up to six feet in the past two years, slowly rose from his table at the other side of the office, unfolding himself, as it were, like a carpenter's double-hinged rule, and crossed to where Gwyn was seated with his table covered with correspondence.

Joe read the letter, and threw it back.

"Well," he said, "it's a pity they don't sell it; but it's the old story: father says 'No,' as he has started mining and it pays, he shall go on, so that I may succeed him."

"And Colonel Pendarve, ex-officer of cavalry and now half-proprietor of Ydoll Mine, says precisely the same on behalf of his fine, noble, handsome son Gwyn. Look here, Joe, why don't you drop it, and swell out the other way?"

"Going to begin that poor stuff again?" said Joe, sourly.

"You make me. I declare I believe you've grown another inch in the night. What a jolly old cucumber you are! You'll have to go on your knees next time you go down the mine."

"You answer your letter, and then I want to talk to you."

"What about?"

"I'll tell you directly you've written your letter. Get one piece of business out of your way at a time."

"Dear me; how methodical we are," said Gwyn; but he began writing his answer, while, instead of going back to his table, Joe crossed to the hearthrug, where Grip was lying curled up asleep, and bending down slowly he patted the dog's head and rubbed his ears, receiving an intelligent look in return, while the curly feathery tail rapped the rug.

"There you are, Mr Lawyer Dix, Esquire," said Gwyn, after dashing off the reply; "now, don't bother us any more, for we are not going to sell—Hi! Grip, old man, rabbits!"

The dog sprang to his feet uttered a sharp bark, and ran to the door before realising that it meant nothing; and then, without the sign of a limp, walked slowly back and lay down growling.

"Ha, ha!" laughed Gwyn; "says 'You're not going to humbug me again like that,' as plain as a dog can speak."

"Well, it's too bad," said Joe. "Think of the boy who cried 'wolf.' Some day when you want him he won't come."

"Oh, yes, he will; Grip knows me. Come here, old man."

The dog sprang to him, rose on his hind-legs, and put his fore-paws on his master's hands.

"Only a game, was it, Grippy? You understand your master, don't you?"

The dog gave a joyous bark.

"There; says he does."

"Don't fool about, I want to talk to you," said Joe, sternly.

"All right, old lively. How was the governor this morning? You look as if you'd taken some of his physic by mistake. Now, Grip, how are your poor legs?"

"*Ahow–w–ow!*" howled the dog, throwing up his muzzle and making a most dismal sound.

"Feel the change in the weather?"

A bark.

"Do you, now? But they are quite strong again, aren't they?"

"*How-how-ow-ow*" yelped the dog.

"Here, what made you begin talking about that?"

"What? His broken legs?"

"Yes."

"Pride, I suppose, in our cure. Or nonsense, just to tease the dog. He always begins to howl when I talk about his legs. Don't you, Grip? Poor old cripple, then."

"Ahow!" yelped the dog.

"Why did you ask?"

"Because it seemed curious. I say, Gwyn, I believe I did that man an injustice."

"What man an injustice?" said Gwyn, who was pretending to tie the dog's long silky ears in a knot across his eyes.

"Tom Dinass."

The dog bounded from where he stood on his hind-legs resting on his master's knees, and burst into a furious fit of barking.

"Hark at him!" cried Gwyn. "Talk about dogs being intelligent animals? It's wonderful. He never liked the fellow. Hi! Tom Dinass there. Did he break your legs, Grip?"

The dog barked furiously, and ended with a savage growl.

"Just like we are," said Gwyn, "like some people, and hate others. I begin to think you were right, Joe, and he did do it."

"Oh, no—impossible!"

"Well, it doesn't matter. He's gone."

"No, he has not," said Joe, quietly. "He has been hanging about here ever since he left six months ago."

"What! I've never seen him."

"I have, and he has spoken to me over and over again."

"Why, you never told me."

"No, but I thought a good deal about it."

"What did he say to you?"

"That it was very hard for a man who had done his best for the mine to be turned away all of a sudden just because Sam Hardock and the fellows hated him."

"He wouldn't have been turned away for that. But as father said, when a man strikes his superior officer he must be punished, or there would be no discipline in a corps."

"I daresay Sam Hardock exasperated him first."

"Well, you often exasperate me, Jolly, but I don't take up a miner's hammer and knock you down."

"No," said Joe, thinking in a pensive way; "you're a good patient fellow. But he said it was very hard for a man to be thrown out of work for six months for getting in a bit of temper."

"Bit of temper, indeed! I should think it was! I tell you it was murderous! Why don't he go and get taken on at some other mine? There are plenty in Cornwall, and he's a good workman. Let him go where he isn't known, and not hang about here."

"He says he has tried, and he wants to come back."

"And you and me to put up a petition for him!"

"Yes, that's it."

"Then we just won't—will we, Grip? We don't want any Tom Dinass here, do we?"

The dog growled furiously.

"Don't set the dog against him, Ydoll. I did accuse him of having done that, but he looked at me in a horrified way, and said I couldn't know what I was saying, to charge him with such a thing. He said he'd sooner cut his hand off than injure a dog like that."

"And we don't believe him, do we, Grip? Why, you've quite changed your colours, Jolly. You used to be all against him, and now you're all for, and it's I who go against him."

"But you don't want to be unjust, Ydoll?"

"Not a bit of it. I'm going to be always as just as Justice. There, let's get to work again. I've a lot of letters to write."

"One minute, Ydoll. I want you to oblige me in something."

"If it's to borrow tuppence, I can't."

"Don't be stupid. I've spoken to father about Tom Dinass."

The dog growled furiously.

"There, you've set him off. Quiet, sir!" cried Gwyn.

"It's your doing. You worry the dog into barking like that. But look here; father said he did not like to see men idle, and that Dinass had been well punished, and he would consent if the Colonel agreed. So I want you to help me."

"I can't, Jolly, really."

"Yes you can, and you must," said Joe, glancing uneasily towards the door. "For I told him he might come and see the Colonel; and if we ask him, I'm sure he'll give way. Say you'll help me."

'With one furious growl the dog leaped at him.'

"I can't, old man."

"Yes, you can, and will. Let's be forgiving. I told him he might come and see you and talk to you as he did to me, and it's just his time. Yes; there he is."

For there was a step at the outside, and Joe went quickly to the door.

"Come in, Tom," said Joe.

The man, looking very much tattered and very humble, came in, hat in hand.

"Mornin', sir," he said softly. Then his eyes seemed to lash fire, and with a savage look he threw out his arms, for with one furious growl the dog leaped at him, and fastened upon the roll of cotton neckerchief which was wrapped about his throat.

Chapter Forty Four
Tom Dinass shows his Teeth

Gwyn sprang from his seat, dashed at the dog, and caught him by the collar.

"Grip! Down!" he roared. "Let go—let—go!"

He dragged at the furious beast, while Dinass wrenched himself away. Then there was a struggle, and Gwyn roared out,—

"Open the door, Joe. Quick! I can't hold him."

The door was flung open, and, with the dog fighting desperately to get free, Gwyn hung on to the collar, passed quickly, and dragged the dog after him right out of the office; then swung him round and round, turning himself as on a pivot, let go, and the animal went flying, while, before he could regain his feet, Gwyn had darted inside and banged-to the door, standing against it panting.

"I don't think you need want to come back here, Master Tom Dinass," he cried.

Bang!

The dog had dashed himself at the door, and now stood barking furiously till his master ran to the window and opened it.

"Go home, sir!" he roared; but the dog barked and bayed at him, raised his feet to the sill, and would have sprung in, had not Gwyn nearly closed the sash. "Go home, sir!" he shouted again; and after a few more furiously given orders, the dog's anger burned less fiercely. He began to whine as if protesting, and finally, on receiving a blow from a walking cane thrust through the long slit between sash and window-sill, he uttered a piteous yelp, lowered his tail, and went off home.

"Don't seem to take to me somehow, Mr Gwyn, sir," said the man. "The chaps used to set him again' me."

"Are you hurt?"

"No, I aren't hurt, but I wonder he didn't get it. Puts a man's monkey up and makes him forget whose dorg it is."

"Look here, Tom Dinass," said Gwyn, quickly. "Did you ever forget whose dog he was, and ill-use him?"

"Me, Mr Gwyn, sir? Now is it likely?" protested the man.

"Yes; very likely; he flew at you. Did you hurt him that time when he was found down the man-engine?"

"Why, that's what Mr Joe Jollivet said, sir, ever so long ago, and I telled him I'd sooner have cut off my right-hand. 'Taren't likely as I'd do such a thing to a good young master's dog."

"Now, no cant, sir, because I don't believe in it. Look here, you'd better go somewhere else and get work."

"Can't, sir," said the man, bluntly; "and as for the dog, if you'll let me come back and tell him it's friends he'll soon get used to me again. I seem to belong to this mine, and I couldn't be happy nowheres else. Don't say you won't speak for a poor fellow, Mr Gwyn, sir. You know I always did my work, and I was always ready to row or pull at the net or do anything you young gen'lemen wanted me to do. It's hard; sir—it is hard not to have a good word said for a poor man out o' work. I know I hit at Sam Hardock, but any man would after the way he come at me."

"We're not going to argue that," said Gwyn, firmly; "perhaps there were faults on both sides; but I must say that I think you had better get work somewhere else."

"No good to try, sir. Some o' the mines aren't paying, and some on 'em's not working at all. Ydoll's in full fettle, and you want more men. Ask the guv'nors to take me on again, sir."

"Yes, do, Gwyn," said Joe. "It must be very hard for a man to want work, and find that no one will give him a job."

"Hard, sir? That aren't the word for it. Makes a man feel as if he'd like to jump off the cliff, so as to be out of his misery. Do ask 'em, sir, and I'll never forget it. If I did wrong, I've paid dear for it. But no one can say I didn't work hard to do good to the mine."

"Well, I'll ask my father when he comes back to the office."

"Won't you ask him now, sir?"

"I don't know where he is. And as for you, I should advise you not to go near my dog; I don't want to hear that he has bitten you."

"Oh, he won't bite me, sir, if you tell him not. We shall soon make friends. Do ask soon, and let me stop about to hear, and get out of my misery."

"You will not have to stop long, Tom Dinass," said Gwyn, as a step outside was heard—the regular martial tread of the old soldier, who seemed to be so much out of place amongst all the mining business.

"Yes; here comes the Colonel," said Joe, quickly; and he went and opened the door to admit the stiff, upright, old officer.

"Thank you, Jollivet," he said. "Hallo! What does this man want?"

"He has come with his humble petition, father, backed up by Joe Jollivet and by me, for him to be taken on again at the mine."

"No," said the Colonel, frowning; "it's impossible, my boy."

"Beg pardon, sir, don't say that," said the man.

"I have said it, my man," said the Colonel, firmly.

"But you'll think better of it, sir. I'll work hard for you."

"No," said the Colonel; "you had a fair chance here for doing well, and you failed. The men would be ready to strike if I took you on again."

"Oh, but you've no call to listen to what a lot of men says."

"I am bound to in a certain way, my man. You made yourself universally unpopular among them, and all that culminated in your savage assault upon the captain. Why, my good fellow, many a man has gone into penal servitude for less than that."

"Yes, sir, I know I hit him; but they was all again' me."

"I cannot go into that," said the Colonel.

"Give him a trial, father," said Gwyn, in answer to Joe's appealing look.

"Do, sir. I've been out o' work a long time, and it's precious hard."

"Go right away, and try somewhere else, my lad."

"I have, sir," said Dinass, imploringly. "I served you well, sir, and I will again."

"I have no fault to find with your working, my man, but I cannot re-engage you."

"Do, sir; it's for your good. Do take me on, sir. I want to do what's right. It is for your good, sir, indeed."

The Colonel shook his head.

"No; I cannot alter my decision, my man," said the Colonel. "Do as I said: go right away and get work; but I know it is hard upon a man to be out of work and penniless. You are a good hand, and ought not to be without a job for long, so in remembrance of what you did—"

"You'll take me on, sir? I tell you it's for your good."

"No," said the Colonel, sternly. "Gwyn, give this man a sovereign for his present necessities, and for the next few weeks, while he is seeking work, he can apply here for help, and you can pay him a pound a week. That will do."

"Better do what I said, sir," said Dinass, with a grim look, "I warn you."

"I said that will do, sir," cried the Colonel, firmly. "Gwyn, my boy, pay him and let him go."

Joe's chin dropped upon his chest, and he rested his hand upon the back of the nearest chair.

Then he started and looked at the door wonderingly, for, scowling savagely, Tom Dinass stuck on his hat very much sidewise, and, without pausing to receive the money, strode out of the place and went right away.

"Specimen of sturdy British independence," said the Colonel, sternly. "I'm sorry, but he is not a man to have about the place. He is dangerous; and when it comes to covert threats of what he would do if not engaged, one feels that help is out of the question. Be the better for me if I engage him—means all the worse for me if I do not. There, it is not worth troubling about; but if he comes back for the money, when he has cooled down, let him have it."

"Yes, father," said Gwyn, and he went on with his letters, but somehow, from time to time the thought of the man's fierce manner came back to him, and he could not help thinking how unpleasant a man Dinass could be if he set himself up for an enemy.

Chapter Forty Five
Crystal, but not Clear

Tom Dinass did not come back for the money Colonel Pendarve had ordered to be paid him, but he started off the very next day, as if he had shaken the Ydoll dust from off his feet, and made for the Plymouth road.

The news was brought to Sam Hardock at the mine by Harry Vores, and Sam chuckled and rubbed his hands as he went and told the two lads.

"Gone, and jolly go with him, Mr Gwyn, sir. We're well quit of him. I was going to warn you to keep Grip always with you, for I have heared say that he swore he'd have that dog's life; but perhaps it was all bounce. Anyhow he's gone, and I'm sure I for one shall feel a bit relieved to be without him."

Gwyn said very little, but he thought a great deal for a few minutes about how much better it would have been if Sam Hardock had treated Dinass with a little more amiability. He quite forgot all about the matter for three days, and then he had fresh news, for Sam Hardock came to him chuckling again.

"It's all right, sir," he said.

"What is—the pumping?"

"Tchah!—that's all right, of course, sir; I mean about Tom Dinass. Harry Vores' wife has just come back from staying at Plymouth, and she saw Tom Dinass there. He won't come back here. Do you know, sir, I've got a sort o' suspicion that he broke Grip's legs."

"Eh! Why do you think that?" said Gwyn, starting. "Did anybody suggest such a thing?"

"No, sir; but he always hated the dog, and he might have done it, you know."

"Oh, yes, and so might you," said Gwyn, testily.

"Me, sir?"

"Yes, or anybody else. Let it rest, Sam. Grip's legs are quite well again."

"That's what you may call snubbing a chap," said Hardock to himself as he went away. "Well, he needn't have been quite so chuff with a man; I only meant—Well, I am blessed!"

Sam Hardock said "blessed," but he looked and felt as if it were the very opposite; and he hurried back to the office where Gwyn had just been joined by Joe, who had been back home to see how his father was getting on, for he was suffering from another of his fits.

Hardock thrust his head in at the door, and without preface groaned out,—

"You'd better go and chain that there dog up, sir," and he nodded to where the animal he alluded to had made himself comfortable on the rug.

"Grip? Why?" said Gwyn.

"He's back again, sir."

"Who is?" said Gwyn, though he felt that he knew.

"Tom Dinass, sir. Talk about bad shillings coming back—why, he's worse than a bad sixpence."

"Then it was him I saw crossing the moor toward the Druid Stones," said Joe.

"Then why didn't you say so?" cried Gwyn, sourly.

"Because I wasn't sure."

"Never sure of anything, since you've grown so tall," grumbled Gwyn. "No, I sha'n't chain up Grip; and I tell him what it is—I'm not going to interfere if the dog goes at him again, for he must have done something bad, or Grip wouldn't be so fierce."

The dog pricked up his ears on hearing his name, and gave the rug a few taps with his tail.

"He never so much as growls at any of the other men. Pretty state of things if one can't have one's dog about because some man hates him. Pooh! I know, Joe."

"Know what?"

"He hasn't got a job yet, and he's coming for the money father said he was to have till he got an engagement."

"Did the guv'nor say that, sir?" cried Hardock.

"Yes."

"Then Tom Dinass won't never get no engagements, but set up for a gentleman, and I think I shall do the same, for work and me aren't the best of friends."

"Get out!" said Gwyn, laughing; "why, you're never happy unless you are at work—is he, Joe?"

"No, he's a regular nuisance. Always wanting to do something else, and stop late in the mine wasting the candles."

"What a shame, Mr Joe!" said Hardock, grinning.

"It's quite true, Sam," cried Gwyn. "Done all that painting up of arrows on the walls near the water gallery?"

"Not quite, sir; I'm going to have a good long day at it on Friday."

"Friday's an unlucky day," said Joe.

"Not it, sir, when you want to get a job done. And I say, Mr Gwyn, come down with me. There's a long drift you've never seen yet, where there's some cracks and hollows chock full of the finest crystals I ever see."

"Crystals?" cried Gwyn.

"In a new gallery?" said Joe, excitedly.

"Well, you may call it a new gallery if you like, sir," said Sam, with a chuckle; "I calls it the oldest drift I was ever in."

"I should like to see that," said Joe.

"Come down then, sir, but aren't it a bit strange that you've taken to like going down of late."

"No; I like going down now, for it's all strange and interesting in the unexplored parts, when one can go down comfortably and not feel afraid of being lost."

"Nay, but you might be still, sir," said the captain, wagging his head. "There's a sight of bits yet that would puzzle you, just as they would me. I have got a deal marked with directions, though, sir, and I sha'n't be quite at rest till I've done all. Then you gents'll come down on Friday?"

"Yes," said Gwyn, "and I'll bring a basket and hammer and chisel. Are they fine crystals?"

"Just the finest I've ever seen, sir; some of 'em's quite of a golden-black colour like peat water."

"But I don't want to come down all that way and find that someone has been and chipped them off."

"Chipped 'em off, sir, when I gave orders that they weren't to be touched!" said the captain, fiercely. "There aren't a man as would dare to do it 'cept Tom Dinass, and he's gone. Leastwise, he was gone, and has come back. They're all right, sir; and I tell you what, if I were you gen'lemen, I'd bring down a basket o' something to eat, for you'll be down most of the day, and it wouldn't be amiss if you brought some o' that rhubarb and magneshy wire to light up in the crystal bit, for the roof runs up wonderful high—it's natural and never been cut like. Regular cave."

"We'll come, Sam. This is going to be interesting, Joe. We won't forget the rhubarb wire neither."

"That's right, sir. What do you say to d'rectly after breakfast—say nine o'clock, if it's not too soon for you, Friday—day after to-morrow?"

"We'll be there, Sam. All right down below?"

"Never more regular, sir. She's dry as a bone, and the stuff they're getting's richer than ever. Only to think of it! What a job I had to get the Colonel to start! I say, Mr Gwyn, sir, when he's made his fortune, and you've made yours, I shall expect a pension like the guv'nor's giving Tom Dinass."

"All right, Sam. I'll see that you have it."

"Thankye, sir," said the mining captain, in all seriousness, and he left the office.

No sooner was he gone than Gwyn turned to his companion.

"I say, Joe," he said; "you'd better not come."

"Why not?"

"You've grown too much lately; you'll be taking all the skin off the top of your head, and grow bald before your time."

"Get out!" said Joe, good-humouredly; "didn't you hear him say that the roof was too high to see with a candle?"

"Oh, of course," cried Gwyn. "Then you'd better come. There must be about room enough in a place like that."

Joe laughed merrily; and then with a serious look,—

"I say, though," he cried, "I really would keep Grip tied up for a bit."

"I sha'n't, not for all the Tom Dinasses between here and Van Diemen's Land. I will keep him with me, though; I don't want my lord to be bitten. Wonder whether that fellow will come soon for his money. We'll shut Grip in the inner office, for we don't want another scene."

Chapter Forty Six
A Dog's Opinion

But Tom Dinass did not go to the office for his promised money, neither was he seen by anyone; and Gwyn began to doubt the truth of the report till it was confirmed by Harry Vores, who stated that his "Missus" saw the man go into a lawyer's office, and that there was the name on the brass plate, "Dix."

This recalled the visit they had had from a man of that name.

"Perhaps he is dealing with mines, and can give people work," thought Gwyn; and then the matter passed out of his mind.

Friday morning came, and directly after breakfast the two young fellows met, Gwyn provided with a basket of provender, his hammer, chisel and some magnesium ribbon, while Joe had brought an extra-powerful oil lanthorn.

"Ready?"

"Yes; I've told father I shall be late," said Joe.

"So have I, and my mother, too. Seen anything of Tom Dinass? No?"

"But—oh, I say!"

"Well, say it," cried Gwyn.

"What about Grip?"

"Quite well, thank you for your kind inquiries, but he says he feels the cold a little in his legs."

"Don't fool," said Joe, testily. "You're not going to leave the dog?"

"Why not?"

"Tom Dinass."

Gwyn whistled.

"Soon put that right," he said. "We'll take him with us. He'll enjoy the run."

There was no doubt about that, for the dog was frantic with delight, and as soon as he was unchained he raced before them to the mouth of the pit, as readily as if he understood where they were going.

Sam Hardock was waiting, and he rubbed his nose on seeing the dog.

"I did advise you, sir, to keep him chained up while there's danger about," he grumbled.

"Won't be any danger down below, Sam," said Gwyn cheerily.

"What? Eh? You mean to take him with us? Oh, I see. But won't he get chopped going down?"

"Not if I carry him."

"Nay, sir," said the man, seriously, "you mustn't venture on that."

"Well, I'm going to take him down," said Gwyn.

"I know," said Joe, eagerly; "send him down in the skep."

"Ay, ye might do that, sir," said Hardock, nodding. "Would he stop, sir?"

"If I tell him," said Gwyn; and, an empty skep being hooked on just then, the engineer grinned as Gwyn went to it and bade the dog jump in.

Grip obeyed on the instant, and then, as his master did not follow, he whined, and made as if to leap out.

"Lie down, sir. Going down. Wait for us at the bottom."

The dog couched, and the engineer asked if he'd stay.

"Oh, yes, he'll stay," said Gwyn. Then, obeying a sudden impulse, he took his basket, and placed it beside the dog at the bottom of the iron skep. "Watch it, Grip!" he cried, and the dog growled. "He wouldn't leave that."

"Till every morsel's devoured," said Joe. Then click went the break, a bell rang, and the skep descended, while the little party stepped one by one on to the man-engine, and began to descend by jumps and steps off, lower and lower, till in due time the bottom was reached, where Grip sat watching the basket just inside the great archway, the skep he had descended in having been placed on wheels, and run off into the depths of the mine, while a full one had taken its place and gone up.

Then the party started off with their candles and the big lamp, first along by the tram line, after Sam Hardock had peered into a big, empty sumph, and then on and on, past where many men were busy chipping, hammering, and tamping the rock to force out masses of ore, while, before they had gone half-a-mile, there was a tremendous volley of echoes, which seemed as if they would never cease, and the party received what almost seemed a blow, so heavy was the concussion.

But neither Gwyn nor Joe started, and the dog, who had gone ahead, merely came trotting back to look at his master, and then bounded off again into the darkness, as if certain that there was a cat somewhere ahead which ought to be hunted out of the mine.

Familiarity had bred contempt; and fully aware that the noise was only the firing of a shot to dislodge some of the ore for shovelling into the iron skeps, they went on without a word.

They must have been a couple of miles from the shaft, every turn of the way being marked with a whitewash arrow, when Hardock stopped to trim his light, and his example was followed by his companions, the result of their halting being that Grip came trotting back out of the darkness to look up inquiringly, and then, satisfied with his examination, he bounded off again to find that imaginary cat. He soon came rushing back, though, on finding that he was not followed; for, after turning to give his companions a meaning nod, Hardock suddenly turned down a narrow opening which joined the gallery they were following at a sharp angle, and then went on, nearly doubling back over the ground they had traversed before. Then came a series of zigzags, and these were so confusing that at the end of a few hundred yards neither Gwyn nor Joe could have told the direction in which they were going.

"Never been here before, gen'lemen?" said Hardock, with a grin.

"No; this is quite fresh," said Gwyn, consulting a pocket compass. "Leads west then."

"Sometimes, sir; but it jiggers about all sorts of ways. Ah, there's a deal of the mine yet that we haven't seen."

"Rises a little, too," said Joe.

"Yes, sir; slopes up just a little—easy grajent, as the big engineers call it."

"But you said it was natural, and not cut out by following a vein," said Gwyn. "There are chisel-marks all along here."

"Hav'n't got to the place I mean yet, sir. Good half-mile on."

"And farther from the shaft?"

"Well, no, sir, because it bears away to the right, and I've found a road round to beyond that big centre place with the bits that support the roof."

"Well, go on then," said Gwyn; "one gets tired of always going along these passages."

"Oughtn't to, sir, with all these signs of branches of tin lode—I don't."

"But one can have too much tin, Sam," said Joe, laughing; and they went steadily on along the narrow passage, which grew more straight, till there was only just room for them to walk in single file.

"Been getting thin here, gen'lemen," said Hardock; "sign the ore was getting to an end. Look, there's where it branched off, and there, and there, going off to nothing like the roots of a tree. Now, just about a hundred yards farther, and you'll see a difference."

But it proved to be quite three hundred, and the way had grown painfully narrow and stiflingly hot; when all at once Grip began to bark loudly, and the noise, instead of sounding smothered and dull, echoed as if he were in a spacious place.

So it proved, for the narrow passage suddenly ceased and the party stepped out into a wide chasm, whose walls and roof were invisible, and the air felt comparatively cool and pleasant.

"There you are, Mr Gwyn, sir," said Hardock, as he stood holding up his light, but vainly, for it showed nothing beyond the halo which it shed. "I call this a bit o' nature, sir. You won't find any marks on the walls here."

"I can't even see the walls," said Joe. "Here, Grip, where are you?"

The dog barked in answer some distance away, and then came scampering back.

"Oh, here's one side, sir," said Hardock, taking a few steps to his left, and once more holding up his light against a rugged mass of granite veined with white quartz, and glistening as if studded with gems.

"How beautiful!" cried Joe.

"Let's throw a light on the subject," said Gwyn, merrily. "Open your lanthorn, Joe;" and as this was done he lit the end of a piece of magnesium ribbon, which burned with a brilliant white light and sent up a cloud of white fumes to rise slowly above their heads.

The light brightened the place for a minute, and in that brief interval the two friends feasted their eyes upon the crystal-hung roof and walls of the lovely grotto, whose sides rose to about forty feet above their heads, and then joined in a correct curve that was nearly as regular as if it had been the work of some human architect. A hundred feet away the roof sank till it was only two or three yards above the irregular floor, and the place narrowed in proportion, while where they stood the walls were some fifty feet apart.

Then the ribbon gave one flash, and was dropped on the floor, to be succeeded by a black darkness, out of which the lanthorns shed what seemed to be three dim sparks.

"What do you think of it, gen'lemen?" said Hardock, from out of the black darkness.

"Grand! Lovely! Beautiful! I never saw anything like it," cried Gwyn.

"Why, it must be the most valuable part of the mine," cried Joe.

Hardock chuckled.

"It's just the part, sir, as is worth nothing except for show," he said. "It's very pretty, but there isn't an ounce o' tin to a ton o' working here, sir, and—"

His words were checked by a faintly-heard muffled roar, which was followed by a puff of moist air and the customary whispering sound of echoes; but before they had died away Grip set up his ears, passed right away into the darkness, and barked with all his might.

"Quiet, sir!" cried Gwyn; but the dog barked the louder.

"Kick him, Ydoll; it's deafening," cried Joe.

"Didn't that shot sound rather rum to you?" said Hardock.

"Oh, I don't know," replied Gwyn, who was slow to take alarm. "Sounded like a shot and the echoes."

"Nay; that's what it didn't sound like," said Hardock, scratching his head. "It was sharper and shorter like, and we didn't ought to hear it like that all this distance away."

"Isn't the roof of the mine fallen in, is it?" said Gwyn, maliciously, as he watched the effect of his words on his companions. "You, Grip, if you don't be quiet, I'll rub your head against the rough wall."

"Nay, this roof'll never fall in, sir," said Hardock, thoughtfully. "More it's pushed the tighter it grows."

"Well, let's get some of the crystals," said Gwyn; "though it does seem a pity to break the walls of such a lovely place. But we must have some. Be quiet, Grip!"

"Let's have some lunch first," said Joe.

"Nay, gen'lemen," said Hardock, whose face looked clay-coloured in the feeble light. "I don't think we'll stop for no crystals, nor no lunch, to-day, for, I don't want to scare you, but I feel sure that there's something very wrong."

"Wrong! What can be wrong?" cried Gwyn, quickly.

"That's more than I can say, sir," replied the man; "but we've just heard something as we didn't ought to hear; and if you've any doubt about it, look at that dog."

"You're not alarmed at the barking of a dog?" cried Gwyn, contemptuously.

"No, no, not a bit; but dogs have a way of knowing things that beats us. He's barking at something he knows is wrong, and it's that which makes me feel scared though I don't know what it is."

Chapter Forty Seven
For Life

"What nonsense!" cried Gwyn, laughing. "Don't you be scared by trifles, Joe. There's nothing wrong, is there, Grip?"

The dog threw up his head, gazed pleadingly at his master, and then made for the farther opening.

"No, no, not that way," cried Joe.

"Yes, sir, we'll try that way please; it works round by the wet drive, and the big pillared hall, as you called it."

"But look here, Sam, are you serious?" said Joe; "or are you making this fuss to frighten us?"

"You never knowed me try to do such a thing as that, sir," said the man, sternly. "P'raps I'm wrong, and I hope I am; but all the same I should be glad for us to get to the foot of the shaft again."

"Why not go to where the men are at work?" suggested Gwyn; "they'd know."

"We shall take them in our way, sir; and we won't lose any time please."

"I should like to light up the place once more before we go."

"No, no, sir. You can do that when you come again."

"Very well," said Gwyn, who did not feel in the least alarmed, but who could see the great drops standing on the mining captain's face. "Lead on, then. Where's Grip?"

The dog was gone.

"Here! Hi! Grip! Grip!" cried Gwyn.

There was a faint bark from a distance, and Gwyn called again, but there was no further response.

"He knows it's wrong, sir," said Hardock, solemnly, "so let's hurry after him."

"Go on, then," said Joe; and Gwyn reluctantly followed them through the grotto, and then along a natural crack in the rock, which was painful for walking, being all on a slope. But this soon came to an end, and they found themselves in another grotto, but with a low-arched roof and wanting in the crystallisations of the first.

"You have been all along here, Sam?" said Gwyn, suddenly.

For answer Hardock took a few steps forward, and held up his lanthorn to display a roughly-brushed white arrow on the wall pointing forward.

"You can always tell where we've been now, sir," said the man. "This bends in and out for nearly a quarter of a mile; now it's caverns, now it's cracks, and then we come again upon old workings which lead off by what I call one of the mine endings. After that we get to the big hall, and that low wet gallery; I know my way right through now."

"But it's all a scare," said Gwyn, banteringly.

"I hope so, sir, but I feel unked like, and as if something's very wrong."

"Think of old Grip playing the sneak," said Joe, as they finally cleared the grotto-like cracks, and came upon flooring better for walking.

"Nay, sir, he's no sneak. He's only gone to see what's the matter."

"Without a light?" cried Gwyn.

"He wants no light, sir. His eyes are not like ours. Would you mind walking a little faster?"

"No; lead on, and we'll keep up. But how long will it take us to get to the foot of the shaft?"

"Two hours, sir."

"So long as that?"

"Every minute of it, sir—if we get there at all," said the man to himself. And now they walked on at a good steady rate, only pausing once to trim their lights, and at last came to a turn familiar to both the lads, for it was the beginning of the passage where they had had the scare from having to pass through water, but at the end farthest from that which they had come by in the early part of the day.

"Won't go through here, Sam?" said Gwyn.

"Much the nighest, sir; but we don't want to be soaked. Would you mind going a little way down here?"

"Not I," said Gwyn; and the man led on, Joe following without a word.

"Don't look like that, Jolly," whispered Gwyn. "I suppose everyone gets scared at some time in a place like this. It's Sam's turn now. Hallo!"

"Can't go any farther, sir," said Hardock, huskily. "The water's right up to here, and farther on it must reach the roof."

Gwyn needed no telling, for the reflection of their lights was glancing from the floor, and he knew perfectly well that no water ought to be there.

A chill ran through him—a sensation such as he would have experienced had he suddenly plunged neck deep in the icy water, and he turned a look full of agony at Joe, who caught at his arm.

"The sea has broken in—the sea has broken in!" he cried; and quick as lightning Gwyn bent down, scooped up some of the black-looking water, and held it to his lips.

It was unmistakably brackish.

"It can't have broke in, my lads—it can't," cried Hardock. "Come on, and let's go round by the pillar place and get to the men as quick as we can. There must be some spring burst out; but they'll set the pumps at work as soon as they know, and soon pull it down again. Come on."

With their hearts beating heavily from excitement, the two lads followed the captain as he hurried back along the gallery to the spot where they had turned down; and then, as fast as they could go, they made for the pillared hall, expecting to find some of the men close by; but when they reached it, there being no sign of water, there was not a soul visible. There was proof, though, that it was not long since there were men there, for the ends of two candles were still burning where they had been stuck against the wall; tools were lying here and there, and a couple of half-filled skeps were standing on the low four-wheeled trucks waiting to be run along the little tramway to the shaft.

No one said so, but each saw for certain that there must have been a sudden alarm, and the men had fled.

"Come on," said Hardock, hoarsely; but his heart was sinking, and Gwyn knew that there was a gradual descent toward the bottom of the shaft. But they walked rapidly on for fully half-an-hour before they came to the first trace of water, and it was startling when they did.

The gallery they were in entered the next—a lower one—at right-angles; and as they reached that end dry-footed, their lights gleamed from the face of running water which was gliding rapidly by in a regular stream of a few inches deep.

It was Joe who stooped quickly down now to scoop up some of the water and taste it, which he did in silence.

"Salt?" cried Gwyn, sharply.

There was no reply, and the lad followed his companion's example and tasted the water.

"Salt, sir?" said Hardock.

"As the sea," said Gwyn, with a groan. "Hah! good dog then. Here, here, here! Grip, Grip, Grip!"

For there had been a faint barking in the distance, but the noise ceased.

"Can we go round any way?" said Gwyn.

"No, sir; we must face it," said Hardock; "and as quick as we can, for it gets lower and lower, and the water sets this way fast, so it must be rising. Ready, sir?"

"Yes."

"Then come on."

Hardock stepped down into the rapid stream, which was ankle-deep, the others followed, and they splashed rapidly along, to hear the barking again directly; and soon after Grip, who must have been swimming, came bounding and splashing along, barking joyously to meet them again, and barking more loudly as he found that his master was making for the way from which he had come.

"Can't help it, old fellow. When it gets too bad for you, I must carry you," muttered Gwyn, as they hurried along; their progress gradually becoming more painful, for the water soon became knee-deep, and the stream harder to stem.

But they toiled on till it was up to their waists, and so swift that it began to threaten to sweep them away; so, after a few minutes' progression in this way, with the water growing yet deeper, Hardock stopped at a corner round which the water came with a rush.

"It's downhill here, gen'lemen, all the way to the shaft, and even if we could face it, the water must be five-foot deep in another ten minutes, and round the next turn it'll be six, and beyond that the passage must be full."

"Then we must swim to the foot of the shaft," said Gwyn, excitedly.

"A shoal of seals couldn't do it, sir," said the man, gruffly. "Come back, sir!" he roared, for, as if to prove his words, the dog made a sudden dash, freed himself from Gwyn's grasp, and plunged forward to swim, but was swept back directly, and would have been borne right away if Gwyn had not snatched at his thick coat as he passed, and held him.

"But we must make for the shaft," cried Joe, passionately.

"We can't sir! It's suicide! We couldn't swim, and just a bit farther on, I tell you, the place must be full to the roof. Why, there must be eight or ten foot o' water in the shaft."

"Then are we lost?" cried Joe.

"A fellow's never lost as long as he can make a fight for it," said Gwyn, sharply. "Now, then, Sam, what's to be done—go back?"

"Yes, sir, fast as we can, and make for the highest part of the mine."

"Where is that?"

"The water will show us," said Hardock. "I pray it may only be a bit of an underground pool burst to flood us; and they'll pump and master it before it does us any harm."

"No, no," groaned Joe; "we've heard it beating overhead before, and the sea has burst in. We're lost—we're lost!"

"Then if the sea has bursted in," cried Hardock, fiercely, "it's that fellow Tom Dinass's doing. He's a spite against us all, and it's to flood and ruin the mine."

"Don't be unreasonable, Sam," began Gwyn, but he stopped short, for, like a flash, came the recollection of their seeing the man go down towards the point at low-water, where they had heard him hammering in the dark. Did that mean anything? Was it a preparation for blowing in the rock over one of the passages that ran beneath the sea?

It seemed to be impossible as he thought it, but there was the fact of the flood rising and driving them onward, the waters pressing behind them as they waded on, but getting shallower very slowly, till, by degrees, they were wading knee-deep and after a time Grip could be set down. But that the waters were rising fast they had ample proof, for whenever they stopped, the stream was rushing by them onward, as if hastening to fill up every gallery in the mine.

"The water will show us the highest part," Hardock had said; and they went on and on deeper and farther into the recesses of the place, but with the swift stream seeming to chase them, refusing to be left behind, but ever writhing about and leaping at their legs as if to drag them down.

Grip splashed along beside or in front, whenever they were in a shallow enough part, and swam when he could not find bottom; but at last he began to show signs of weariness by getting close up to his master, and whining.

"Catch hold of my lanthorn, Joe," cried Gwyn.

"What are you going to do?"

"What I should do for you if you felt that you could go no farther; what you would do for me. We've brought him down here to be safe from Tom Dinass, and thrown him into the danger we wanted to avoid. Here, come on, Grip, old chap."

To the surprise of his companions, Gwyn knelt down in the water, turning his back to the dog and bending as low as he could, when the intelligent beast, perhaps from memories of old games they had had together, swam close up and began to scramble up on his master's shoulders.

Then Gwyn caught at the dog's fore-legs, dragged them over, and rose to his feet, carrying the dog pick-a-pack fashion, Grip settling down quietly enough and straining his muzzle over as far as he could reach.

Hardock said nothing, but tramped on again, taking the lead with one lanthorn, Joe bringing up the rear with the others, having one in each hand, while the light was reflected brightly from the surface of the water.

At first the mining captain seemed to be working with a purpose in view; but, after being compelled to turn back times out of number through finding the water deepening in the different passages he followed, he grew bewildered, and at last came to a standstill knee-deep in a part that was wider than ordinary.

"I think this part will do," he said, looking helplessly from one to the other.

"Not for long, Sam."

"Yes, sir," said the captain, feebly; "the water isn't rising here."

"It must be pouring into the mine like a cataract. Look how it's rushing along here, and I can feel it creeping slowly up my legs."

"Yes, sir, I'm afraid you are right. I've been thinking for some time that we couldn't do any more."

"Whereabouts are we now?"

"I'm not quite sure, sir; but if we go on a bit farther you'll find one of my arrows on the wall."

"Come on, then," cried Gwyn, "you lead again with the light. No, Grip, old chap, I can carry you,"—for the dog had made a bit of a struggle to get down. He subsided, though, directly, nestling his muzzle close to his master's cheek, and they went on, splash, splash, through the water till they reached one of the turnings.

"Don't seem to be any arrow here, sir," said Hardock, holding up his light. "Can't have been washed out, because the water hasn't been high enough."

"But you said you had put an arrow at every turn," cried Gwyn.

"Every turning I come to, sir; but I'm sure now; I was in a bit of a doubt before—I haven't been along here. It's all fresh."

"Turn back then," said Gwyn.

"But the water's running this way, sir, and it must be shallower farther on."

"How do we know that?" cried Gwyn; "this stream may be rushing on to fill deeper places." And as if to prove the truth of his theory, the water ran gurgling, swirling, and eddying about their legs, but evidently rising.

"Yes, sir, how do we know that?" said the man, who was rapidly growing more dazed and helpless. "I don't kinder feel to know what's best to be done with the water coming on like that. No pumping would ever get the better of this, and—and—"

He said no more, but leaned his arm against the side and rested his head upon it.

"Oh, come, that won't do, Sam," cried Gwyn; "we must help one another."

"Yes, sir, of course; but wouldn't one of you two young gents like to take the lead? You, Mr Joe Jollivet—you haven't had a turn, and you've got two lights."

"What's the use of me trying to lead?" said Joe, bitterly, "I feel as helpless as you do—just as if I could sit down and cry like a great girl."

"Needn't do that, Jolly," said Gwyn, bitterly; "there's salt water enough here. I'm sure it's three inches deeper than it was. Hark!"

They stood fast, listening to the strange murmuring noise that came whispering along.

"It's the water running," said Joe, in awestricken tones.

"Yes, it's the water dripping, and running along by the walls. Why, there must be hundreds of streams."

"And you're standing talking like that," cried Joe, angrily. "We know all about the streams. Do something."

Gwyn stood frowning for a few moments.

"You lead on now," he said, "and try again. I'll come close behind you."

"But it gets deeper this way."

"Perhaps only for a short distance, and then it may rise. Go on."

Joe started at once, for he felt, as if he must obey, but before they had gone a hundred yards the water had risen to Gwyn's waist.

"Back again," he said; "it gets deeper and deeper."

"Then it's all over with us, gen'lemen," said Hardock. "Tom Dinass has got his revenge against us, and it's time to begin saying our prayers."

"Time to begin saying our prayers!" cried Gwyn, angrily. "I've been saying mine ever since we knew the worst. It's time we began to work, and try our best to save our lives. Now, Joe, on again the other way, and take the first turning off to the left."

Joe obeyed, and they struggled back amidst the whispering and gurgling sounds which came from out of the darkness, before and behind; while now, to fully prove what was wrong, they noticed the peculiar odour of the sea-water when impregnated with seaweed in a state of decay, and directly after Gwyn had called attention to the fact Joe uttered a cry.

"What is it?" said Gwyn anxiously. "Don't drown the lights."

"Something—an eel, I think—clinging round my leg."

"Eel wouldn't cling round your leg; he'd hold on by his teeth. See what it is."

"Long strands of bladder-wrack," said Joe, after cautiously raising one leg from the water.

"No mistake about the sea bursting in," said Gwyn. "Why, of course, it has done so before. Don't you remember finding sand and sea-shells in some of the passages?"

No one spoke; and finding that the efforts he had, at no little cost to himself, made to divert his companions' attention from their terrible danger were vain, he too remained nearly always silent, listening shudderingly to the wash, wash of the water as they tramped through it, and he thought of the time coming when it would rise higher and higher still.

Gwyn could think no more in that way, for the horror that attacked him at the thought that it meant they must all soon die. Once the idea came to him that he was watching his companions struggling vainly in the black water; but, making a desperate effort, he forced himself to think only of the task they had in hand, and just then he shouted to Joe to turn off to the left, for another opening appeared, and the lad was going past it with his head bent down.

Joe turned off mechanically, his long, lank figure looking strange in the extreme; and as he swung the lanthorns in each hand, grotesque shadows of his tall body were thrown on the wall on either side, and sometimes over the gleaming water which rushed by them, swift in places as a mill-race.

And still the water grew deeper, and no more arrows pointed faintly from the wall. The water was more than waist-deep now, and the chill feeling of despair was growing rapidly upon all. The lads did not speak, though they felt their position keenly enough, but Hardock uttered a groan from time to time, and at last stopped short.

"Don't do that," cried Gwyn, flashing into anger for a moment; but the man's piteous reply disarmed him, and he felt as despairing.

"Must, sir—I must," groaned the man; "I can't do any more. You've been very kind to me, Master Gwyn, and I'd like to shake hands with you first, and say good-bye. There—there's nothing for it but to give up, and let the water carry you away, as it keeps trying to do. We've done all that man can do; there's no hope of getting out of the mine, so let's get out of our misery at once."

Chapter Forty Eight
In Dire Peril

For a few moments, in his misery and despair, Gwyn felt disposed to succumb, and he looked piteously at Joe, who stood drooping and bent, with the bottoms of the lanthorns touching the water. Then the natural spirit that was in him came to the front, and with an angry shout he cried,—

"Here, you, sir, keep those lights up out of the water. Don't want us to be in the dark, do you?"

There is so much influence in one person's vitality, and the way in which an order is given, that Joe started as if he had had an electric current passed through him. He stood as straight up as he could for the roof, and looked sharply at Gwyn, as if for orders.

At the same time the dog began to bark, and struggled to get free.

"Oh, very well," said Gwyn, letting go of the dog's legs; "but you'll soon want to get back."

Down went Grip with a tremendous splash, and disappeared; but he rose again directly, and began to swim away with the stream and was soon out of sight.

"Oh, Joe, Joe, what have I done!" cried Gwyn. "He'll be drowned—he'll be drowned!"

"Ay, sir, and so shall we before an hour's gone by," said Hardock, gloomily.

"I can't help it—I must save him," cried Gwyn; and snatching one of the lanthorns from Joe, he waded off after the swimming dog.

"We can't stop here by ourselves, Sam," cried Joe. "Come along."

Hardock uttered a groan.

"I don't want to die, Master Joe Jollivet—I don't want to die," he said pitifully.

"Well, who does?" cried Joe, angrily. "What's my father going to do without me when he's ill. Come on. They'll be finding the way out, and leaving us here."

"Nay, Master Gwyn wouldn't do that," groaned Hardock. "He'd come back for us."

Gwyn's pursuit of the dog had done one thing; it had started his companions into action, and they, too, waded with the stream pressing them along, till away in the distance they caught sight of the light Gwyn bore, shining like a faint spark in the darkness or reflected in a pale shimmering ray from the hurrying water.

For how long they neither of them knew, they followed on till Gwyn's light became stationary; and just then Hardock raised his, and uttered an exclamation.

"I know where we are now," he cried, as he raised his lanthorn and pointed to one of his white arrows. "It looks different with the place half full of water, but we're close to that dead end that runs up."

Just then they heard the barking of the dog.

"And that's where he has got to," continued Hardock. "How did he come to think of going there?"

"Ahoy—oy—oy—oy!" came halloaing from Gwyn, who had long been aware from their lights that his companions were following him.

They answered, and dragged their weary way along, for the water still deepened, and in his impatience Gwyn came back to meet them.

"Come along quickly," he cried; "the dog has gone into that short gallery which rises up. Did you hear him barking?"

"Yes."

"Just as if he had found a rabbit. He leaped up on the dry part at once, and if we follow there is plenty of room for us as well."

"Beyond the water?" panted Joe.

"Yes. At the far end."

Trembling with eagerness, they splashed through the now familiar way, conscious of the fact that a current of air was setting in the same direction—a foul hot wind, evidently caused by the water filling up the lower portions of the mine, and driving out the air; but no one mentioned it then.

The entrance of the place they sought was reached, and they were waist-deep, the water sweeping and swirling by with such force that, as Gwyn entered, lanthorn in hand, and Joe was about to follow, a little wave like an imitation of the bore which rushes up some rivers, came sweeping along and nearly took him off his feet, while Hardock, with a cry to his companions to look out, clung to the corner.

Gwyn turned in time to see Joe tottering, and caught at his arm, giving him a sharp snatch which dragged him in through the low archway where the water, though deep, was eddying round like a whirlpool. Then together they extended their hands to Hardock and he was dragged in.

"Runs along there now like a mill-race," panted the man. "How did you manage, Mr Gwyn?"

"It was only going steadily when I followed Grip, and he swam in easy enough."

"Must be coming in faster," groaned Hardock. "Oh, my lads, my lads, say your prayers now, and put in a word for me; for I haven't been the man I ought to have been, and I know it now we're shut up in this gashly place."

"Don't, don't talk like that," cried Gwyn, wildly.

"I must, my lad, for the water's rising faster, and in a few minutes we shall be drowned."

"Then come on with the stream and let's find a higher place," cried Joe.

"Nay, we aren't got strength enough to go on. Better stay where we are."

"Hi! Grip! Grip! Grip!" cried Gwyn, holding up the lanthorn and wading farther in, but there was no answering bark.

"Come along, Sam," said Joe, hoarsely, as he opened his lanthorn door to let the water he had got in, drain out. "Here, look, it's shallower where he is."

"Ay, it do rise, you see," groaned Hardock, who was now completely unmanned.

"Come on!" shouted Gwyn; "it isn't up to my knees here."

They followed till, toward the dead end where the old miners had ceased working in the far back past, the lode had narrowed and run up into a flattened crevice, up which Gwyn began to clamber.

"Follow me," he said; "I'm quite clear of the water. It's a natural crack. There has been no picking here, and it comes up at a steep slope."

He climbed on, the others following him; and he called to the dog again, but there was still no reply.

"Are you clear of the water?" he cried.

"Yes, sir, four foot above it," said Hardock, who came last, "but it's rising fast."

"I say," cried Gwyn, wildly, "is there a way out here?"

"Nay, sir, this is only a blind lead. What is it up where you are?"

"Like a flattened-out hole with the rock all covered with tiny crystals. There must be a way up to the surface here; don't you feel how the wind comes by us?"

"Yes; my light flickers, but it burns dull," said Joe.

"Ay, and it will come sharper yet," said Hardock; "the water's driving it all before it. Don't you feel how hot it is?"

"Yes."

"Maybe it'll suffocate us before the water comes."

"Grip! Grip! Grip!" shouted Gwyn; and then, after waiting, he made his companions' hearts beat by crying back to them loudly, "I don't care, there is a way out here."

"Can't be, sir."

"But Grip has gone through."

"Nay, sir, he's wedged himself up, and he's dead, as we shall soon be."

"Oh, Joe, Joe!" roared Gwyn, passionately; "kick out behind at that miserable, croaking old woman. There is a way out, for I can feel the hot air rushing up by me."

"Ah!" groaned Hardock, "it's very well for you young gents up there; but I'm at the bottom, and the water's creeping up after me. To think after all these years o' mining I should live to be drowned in a crack like this!"

Just then a loud rustling and scrambling noise was heard.

"What is it, Ydoll? What are you doing?"

"There's a big stone here, wedged across the slope, or I could get higher. It's loose, and I think I can—hah!"

The lad uttered an exultant shout, for with a loud rattle the flat block gave way, and came rattling and sliding down.

"Got it!" cried Gwyn. "I'm passing it under me. Come close, Joe, and catch hold, as it reaches my feet."

Joe climbed a little higher, by forcing his knees against the wall of the crack facing him, and, reaching up, he got hold of the block and lowered it, till, fearing that if he let go, it might injure Hardock, he bade him come higher and pass it beneath him.

"Nay, nay, let me be," groaned Hardock; "it's all over now. I'm spent."

"Let it fall on him to rouse him up," shouted Gwyn.—"You, Sam, lay hold of that stone."

The man roused himself, and, climbing higher over the ragged, sharp, prickly crystals, reached up and took hold of the stone, passed it under him, and it fell away down for a few feet, and then there was a sullen splash.

The light showed Gwyn plainly enough that they were in a spot where a vein of some mineral, probably soapstone, had in the course of ages dissolved away; and, convinced that the dog had found his way to some higher cavern, and in the hope that he might find room enough to force his way after, he scrambled and climbed upward, foot by foot, pausing every now and then to shout back to his companions to follow.

There was plenty of room to right and left; the difficulty was to find the widest parts of the crack, whose sides were exactly alike, as if the bed-rock had once split apart, and pressure, if applied, would have made them join together exactly again. And this engendered the gruesome thought that if that happened now they would be crushed out flat.

There was plenty of air, too, for it rushed by now in a strong current which made the flame of the candle in the lanthorn he pushed on before him flutter and threaten to go out. For the air was terribly impure, as shown by the dim blue flame of the candles, and so enervating that the perspiration streamed from the lad's face, and a strange, dull, sleepy feeling came over him, which he tried desperately to keep off.

Roughly speaking, the crack ascended at an angle of about fifty degrees, turning and zigzagging after the fashion of a flash of lightning, the greatest difficulty being to pass the angles.

But Gwyn toiled on, finding that the great thing he dreaded—the closing-in of the sides—did not occur, but trembling in the narrowest parts on account of one who was to follow.

"Joe will easily manage it," he said to himself; "but Sam will stick."

"Time enough to think of that," he muttered, "if he does."

"Can you get higher?" panted Joe, after they had been creeping slowly along for some time.

"Yes, yes; but there's an awkward turn just here. All right, it's wider on my left. Hurrah! I've got into quite a big part. Come on!"

Joe climbed on, pushing his lanthorn before him, till it was suddenly taken and drawn up, when, looking above him with a start, he saw his friend's face looking down upon him, surrounded by a pale, bluish glow of light.

"Want a hand?" cried Gwyn.

"No; I can do it," was the reply, and Joe climbed beyond an angle to find himself in a sloping, flattened cave, whose roof was about four feet above his head; how far it extended the darkness beyond the lanthorn concealed.

"Come on, Sam," cried Gwyn, as he looked down the slope he had ascended expecting to see the man's face just below; but it was not visible, and, saving the hissing of the hot wind and the strange gurgling of rushing water, there was not a sound.

"He's dead!" cried Joe, wildly.

"No, no; don't say that," whispered Gwyn. "It's too horrible just when we are going to escape;" and, without pausing, he lowered himself over the angle of the rock and began to descend.

"Hold the light over," he said. "Ah, mind, or you'll have it out."

For the candle flickered in the steady draught which came rushing up from below, and it had to be drawn partly back for shelter.

"Sam!" cried Gwyn, as he descended; but there was no reply, and the dread grew within the lad's breast as he went on down into the darkness.

"I shall be obliged to come back for the light," he shouted. "I can see nothing down here. How far is he back?"

"I don't know," said Joe, despairingly. "I thought he was close behind me. Shall I come down with the lanthorn?"

"Yes, you must, part of the way—to help me. No, I can just touch his lanthorn with my foot—here he is!"

"All right?" faltered Joe.

"I think so," replied Gwyn, slowly. "Here, Sam Hardock, what's the matter?—why don't you come on?"

"It's of no good," said the man, feebly; "I'm done, I tell you. Why can't you let me die in peace?"

"Because you've got to help us out of this place?"

"I? Help you?"

"Yes; it's your duty. You've no right to lie like that, giving up everything."

"I'm so weak and sleepy," protested the man.

"So was I, but I fought it all down. Now then, climb up to where he is."

"I—I can't, Mr Gwyn; and, besides, it's too narrow for me."

"How do you know till you try? Come: up with you at once."

"Must I, Mr Gwyn, sir?"

"Yes, of course; so get up and try."

Sam Hardock groaned, and began to creep slowly up the steep slope, Gwyn leading the way; but at the end of a minute the man subsided.

"It's of no use, sir; I can't do it. I haven't the strength of a rat."

"Keep on; it will come," cried Gwyn. "Keep on, sir, and try. You must get to the top, where Joe Jollivet is."

"No, no; let me die in quiet."

"Very well; when I have got you into a good dry place. You can't die in peace with the cold black water creeping over you."

"N–no," said Hardock, with a shiver.

"Come on, then, at once," cried Gwyn; and, unable to resist the imperious way in which he was ordered, the poor fellow began to struggle up the narrow rift, while Gwyn, keeping his fears to himself, trembled lest the place should prove too strait.

Twice over Hardock came to a stand; but at a word from Gwyn he made fresh efforts, the way in which the lad showed him the road encouraging him somewhat; till at last, panting and exhausted, he dragged himself beyond the last angle, and rolled over upon the stony slope where Joe had been holding his lanthorn over the dark passage, and looking down.

"We can go no farther till he's rested," whispered Gwyn.

"No; but look how the water's rising. How long will it be before it reaches up to here?"

Gwyn shook his head, and listened to the murmur of the rising flood, which sounded soft and distant; but the rush of wind grew louder, sweeping up the cavity with the loud whistling sound of a tempest.

Gwyn rose to his knees, trimmed his light, and said less breathlessly now,—

"Let Sam rest a bit, while we try and find how Grip went."

And he held up the light and shaded his eyes.

There was no need of a painted white arrow to point the way, for the whistling wind could be felt now by extending a hand from where they lay in shelter; and as soon as Gwyn began to creep on all-fours towards the upper portion of the sloping cavity in which they lay, the fierce current of air pressed against him as the water had when he was wading a short time before.

"Better keep the lanthorn back in shelter," said Gwyn, hastily; "it makes mine gutter down terribly."

He handed Joe the ring, and once more went on to find the wide opening they had reached rapidly contract till once more it resembled the jagged passage through which they had forced themselves.

The slope was greater, though, and the way soon became a chimney-like climb, changing directions again and again, while in the darkness the wind whistled and shrieked by him furiously, coming with so much force that it felt as if it was impelling him forward.

And still he went on climbing along the tunnel-like place till further progress was checked by something in front; and with the wind now tearing by him with a roar, he felt above and below the obstacle, finding room to pass his arm beyond it readily; but further progress was impossible, the passage being completely choked by the block of stone which must have slid down from above.

Chapter Forty Nine
Sam Hardock at his Worst

Gwyn tugged and strained at the block, hoping to dislodge it as he had the former one; but his efforts were vain, and at last, with his fingers sore and the perspiration streaming down his face, he backed down the steep chimney-like place, satisfied that Grip must have made his way through the narrow aperture beneath one corner of the block, where the wind rushed up, but perfectly convinced that without the aid of tools or gunpowder no human being could force a way, while the very idea of gunpowder suggested the explosion causing the tumbling down of the rock around to bury them alive.

"Well," said Joe, looking up at him anxiously, with his face showing clearly by the open door of his lanthorn, "can we get farther?"

Gwyn felt as if he could not reply, and remained silent.

"You might as well tell me the worst."

"I'm going to try again," said Gwyn, hoarsely, and he glanced at Hardock, who was lying prone on the rock with his face buried in his hands. "The way's blocked up."

"Then we shall have to lie here till the water comes gurgling up to fill this place and drown us, if we are not smothered before."

"We can't be smothered in a place where there is so much air."

"I don't know," said Joe, thoughtfully—his feeling of despair seeming to have deadened the agony he had felt; "I've been thinking it out while you were grovelling up there like a rat, and I think that the air will soon be all driven out of the mine by the water. Ugh! hark at it now. How it comes bubbling and racing up there! If you put your head over the edge of the rock there, it's fit to blow you away, and it smells horribly. But can't you get any farther up?"

"No, not a foot. Go up and try yourself."

"No," said Joe, slowly. "A bit ago I felt as if I could do anything to get out of this horrible place; but now I'm fagged, like Sam Hardock there, and don't seem to mind much about it, except when I think of father."

"Don't talk like that," cried Gwyn, passionately, "I can't bear it. Here, we must do something; it's so cowardly to lie down and die without trying to get out. You go up there, and perhaps you will do better than I did."

"No; you tried, and you're cleverer than I am."

"No, I'm not. You try. You shall try," cried Gwyn, with energy. "Go up at once. Stop; let's put up a fresh candle."

"It's of no use; you can't—I've been trying."

"Joe! Don't say there are no more candles."

"Wasn't going to. There's one, but the wick's soaked and it won't burn."

Gwyn snatched at the candle, examined the blackened end and sodden wick, and then turned it upside down, holding the bottom end close to the flame of his own light and letting the grease drip away till fresh wick was exposed and gradually began to burn.

"I should never have thought of doing that," said Joe, calmly, as he lay on his chest resting his chin upon his hands.

"There," cried Gwyn, sticking up the fresh candle in the tin sconce, and waiting till the fat around it had congealed. "Now you go on up, and see what you can do. Keep the door side of the lanthorn away from the wind."

"Must I go?" said Joe, dolefully.

"Yes, if you want to see the poor Major again."

"Ah!" sighed Joe, and taking the lanthorn, he crawled up to where Gwyn had been, while the latter searched eagerly round to try and find out some other opening. But, saving that by which they had come, and up which the whistling, roaring and gurgling increased in intensity, and sounded as if some writhing mass of subterranean creatures were fighting their way through the dark passage to escape from the flood, there was not the smallest crack, and he turned again to where Joe was passing out of sight, his boot soles alone visible as he slowly crawled up the narrow chimney-like place.

Then they disappeared, and Gwyn turned to where Hardock was lying on his face.

"Sam," he said.

There was no reply.

"Sam!" he cried, angrily now; and the man slowly raised his face and gazed at him reproachfully.

"Might let me die in peace," he groaned.

"You rouse up, and try and help us," said Gwyn, firmly; and his will being the stronger, the man began to raise himself slowly into a sitting position, shuddering as he listened to the furious hurricane of sounds which came up the narrow rift.

"It's only a noise, Sam," said Gwyn. "I say, there has never been any mining done up here, has there?"

"Never, sir. It's all natural rock. Look at the crystals."

"That's what I thought. But look up there at Joe."

"Eh? Where's Mr Joe Jollivet?"

"Clambering up that hole where Grip must have gone. He must have got up to the surface."

Hardock shook his head.

"Why not?" continued Gwyn, eagerly. "The wind rushes up there."

"Ay, but wind will go where even a mouse couldn't."

"But if Grip hadn't got up there, he'd have come back."

"If he could, sir—if he could. But don't, don't ask me questions; I'm all mazed like, and can't think or do anything. I only want to go to sleep, sir, out of it all, never to have any more of this horror and trouble."

"Look here, Sam," continued Gwyn; "this noise of the wind coming up means the water filling up the passages and driving it out, doesn't it?"

"I s'pose so, sir."

"How long will it be before the mine is quite full of water?"

"Who knows, sir? Tends on how big the hole is. Maybe hours, for it's a vasty place—miles of workings."

"Then the water won't come up to us till the passages are all full."

"No, sir, and maybe not come to us at all. We may be too high."

"Too high? Of course. If we're above sea-level now, it won't reach us."

"No, sir. You see the mouth of the mine's quite two hundred feet above sea-level, the workings are all below."

"Then we may escape yet?"

"Escape, sir?" said Hardock, despairingly. "How?"

"Grip has gone up to grass."

"Ay, perhaps he has escaped," said Hardock, dismally.

"And if he has, do you think he will not bring us help? Why, it may come any time."

"Yes, to the hole he got out of; and it'll take five years to dig down through the solid rock to get us out. Nay, Master Gwyn, you may give it up. We're as good as dead."

A faint sound, half groan, half cry, arrested them; and Gwyn hurried to the crack up which Joe Jollivet had crawled.

"What is it? Can you get by?"

"No, no," came back faintly, the words being half drowned by the noise of the wind; "stuck fast."

"Oh, why did he grow so long and awkward!" muttered Gwyn. "Here, Joe, turn round a bit and try and come back on your side."

"Been trying hard, and I can't come back."

Gwyn's heart sank, and he hesitated for a few moments, till the piteous word "Help!" reached his ears, when he crept into the hole, leaving his lanthorn burning outside, sheltered from the current of air which rushed to the outlet, and began to crawl up as fast as he could.

"Help!" came again.

"Coming. You must turn."

"Can't, I tell you. Oh, Ydoll, old fellow, it's all over now I—ah!"

Then there was a wild cry that petrified Gwyn, just as he was nearing the place where Joe had managed to wedge himself, for it might have meant anything.

Then came relief, for Joe cried exultantly—

"My arm wedged round the block of stone; I've got it out."

It was Gwyn's turn to cry "Ah!" now, in the relief he felt; and for a few minutes he lay listening to the peculiar rustling noise beyond him, unable to stir. But he was brought to himself by a kick on the crown of his head, and began to back away from his companion's feet as fast as he could, getting out at last to find Sam Hardock kneeling by the hole, lanthorn in hand, looking utterly despondent.

"It's no good, my lad," he said, with a groan. "What's the use o' punishing yourself in this way? You ought to know when you're beat."

"That's what Englishmen never know, Sam," cried Gwyn.

"Ay, so they say, sir—so they say; but we are beat now."

The appearance of Joe's boots put an end to their conversation; and a few minutes after he turned his face to them, looking ghastly in the feeble light of the lanthorns.

"Thought I was going to die caught fast in there," he said, with a sob, "Oh, Ydoll, it was horrible. You can't think how bad."

"Lie down for a bit and rest," said Gwyn, gently, for the poor fellow was quite hysterical from what he had gone through; and without a word he obeyed, lying perfectly still save when a shudder shook him from head to foot, and he clung fast to Gwyn's hand.

"Do you think you could do any good by trying?" said Gwyn at last.

"Me, sir?" said Sam. "No; I'm too big. I should get stuck fast."

"No, there's room enough. He got himself fixed by wedging his arm in beyond the stone."

"Yes, that was it," sighed Joe; and, to the surprise of both, Hardock picked up his lanthorn, crawled to the hole, thrust it in and followed, while the two lads lay listening to the rustling sounds he made, half drowned by the shrieking and whistling of the wind.

In about a quarter-of-an-hour he backed out, drawing his light after him.

"It's of no use, my lads," he said; "we may shake hands now, for we've done all that we can do. I've been trying hard at that stone, but it's wedged in fast. A shot o' powder might drive it out, but our hands aren't powder nor dinnymite neither, and we may give it up."

No one spoke, and they lay there utterly exhausted in mind and body, hour after hour, while their clothes began slowly to dry upon their bodies. The rush of wind and the gurgle of water went on as if it were boiling violently; and something like sleep overtook them, for they did not move.

But from time to time Gwyn bent over one or the other of the lanthorns to see to the candles, his one great dread being now lest they should sink into a deep stupor, and come to, finding that they were in the dark.

Then suddenly, after lying down for some time trying to imagine that it was all some terrible dream, there was a quick, short bark; and unable to bear this, the lad uttered a wild cry, and then, from the terrible tension being taken so suddenly from off his nerves, he burst into a hysterical fit of laughter.

The next minute Grip was licking at his face, following it up by the same endearment bestowed upon the other two, and then bursting into a prolonged fit of barking.

Chapter Fifty
News from Grass

"Ydoll! Ydoll! Look! look!" cried Joe, suddenly. "Here, Grip! Grip! Quick!"

But Gwyn had seen and caught at the dog's collar as soon as Joe had shouted to him; and as rapidly as his trembling fingers would allow, he untied the string which bound a white packet to the ring in the dog's collar.

It was a note written in pencil, the words large, and easy to see; but they seemed to sail round before the lad's eyes, and minutes had elapsed before he could read in his father's bold hand:—

> "Try and keep a good heart. Grip has shown us the way, and, please God, we'll reach you before many hours have passed. Tie a handkerchief to the dog's collar if you get this, and are all well. Send him back at once.
>
> "Arthur Pendarve."

A strange sobbing sound escaped from Gwyn's lips as with trembling hands he tied his pocket-handkerchief tightly to the dog's collar.

"Now, Grip!" he cried in a husky voice which did not sound like his own; and the dog, who was standing panting, with his tongue out and curled up at the tip, uttered an eager bark. "Home! home!" cried Gwyn; and the dog made for the hole, dashed in, and disappeared, while his master crept away into the darkness of the lowest part of the long, sloping grotto-like place, and half-an-hour must have passed before he joined the others and lay down close to the hole where Grip had disappeared.

They had no idea of how the time passed, and they could not speak, for their hearts were too full. Words did not come till they heard a fresh barking, and the dog came scuffling out of the opening into the light, this time with the Colonel's flask tied to his collar, and stood panting while it was untied.

It was one of the large flat leather-covered bottles with a silver screw top and silver cup, which slipped on the bottom; and now, for the first time awaking to the fact that he was in a fainting condition, Gwyn slipped off the cup, unscrewed the top, and poured out some of the contents of the bottle, handing the vessel to Hardock, who shook his head.

"Nay, sir," he said, "I'll wait till we get out; I'm a tot'ler."

Gwyn handed the silver cup to Joe, who tasted it.

"Eggs and milk," he cried, and drank the contents with avidity before returning the cup.

"Now, Sam," said Gwyn, refilling it.

"Ay, I don't mind that, sir," said Hardock; "and I was thinking I was a bit too particklar when it was sent to save our lives. Hah! That's good," he added, as he drained the last drop. "Sorry I can't wash it out for you, sir. Shall I go down to the water?"

"No, no, I don't mind drinking after you," said Gwyn, as he tremblingly poured out his portion, which was less than the others had taken; and he, too, drank the most grateful draught he had ever had, while the dog, who had couched, placed his head on the lad's knee and looked up at him with all a dog's reverence and affection for his master.

But there was no note this time.

The flask was re-fastened to the dog's collar, and he was sent back; and then the prisoners lay listening to the rushing and gurgling of the air and water, wondering how long it would take to reach them, for Hardock had been down to find that it had ascended the cavity for some distance; but he expressed his belief that it would be hours before it would hurt them, and the consequence was that, heartened by the prospect of escape, utterly exhausted mentally and bodily as they were, Nature came to their aid, and they all dropped off into a deep sleep.

Gwyn was the first to awaken many hours later, to find all in darkness, and fight alone through the strange feeling of confusion in which he was. But once more Grip came to his help; for no sooner had his master begun to move than he burst out barking loudly.

This woke the others, equally confused and startled at being in the darkness, while the noise of the wind roaring through the cavity sounded appalling.

Gwyn's first effort to light a match was a failure, but the second, within the shelter of a lanthorn, succeeded, and a fresh candle was finally lit.

By this they found that Grip was the bearer of another note, and in addition a packet, which upon being opened was found to contain a card and a pencil.

The note was very brief, stating tersely that efforts were being made to enlarge the way through which the dog had come up, and asking for information regarding their state.

This was furnished as well as the circumstances would allow, Joe holding the light, while, after placing the card on the smoothest place he could find, Gwyn wrote the answer—the principal point he emphasised being that they were safe so far; but the water was rising, and they had nearly come to the end of their candles.

But even as he wrote there was a cheering sound heard through the whistling of the wind—a sharp, clear clink as of hammer and chisel upon stone.

"Hark! do you hear?" cried Joe, wildly; "they are coming down to us. Oh work, work hard, before the water rises."

He shouted this in a wildly frantic way, and then watched eagerly while Gwyn tied the card in a handkerchief and secured it to the dog's collar, Grip going off directly, as if he quite understood the business now.

This done, Joe and Hardock lay down close to the orifice and listened to the clinking of the hammers, trying the while to imagine what kind of passage existed beyond the wedge-like block of stone, and calculating how long it would be before they were rescued. But that was all imagination, too, for there was nothing to base their calculations upon.

Meanwhile Gwyn was more matter-of-fact; for he took the lanthorn and descended to where the water had risen, and there, clinging with one hand, he held the light down, to gaze with a feeling of awe at the bubbling surface, which was in a violent state of agitation, looking as if it were boiling. Every now and then it was heaved up and then fell back with a splash.

Gwyn's object in descending the sharp slope had been to make a mark upon the rock with his knife just at the level of the water, and then try and scratch other marks at about a foot apart, so as to descend again and see how much higher the water had risen.

But this seemed to be impossible, for the level was always changing, the water running up several feet at times and then descending, playing up and down evidently as the pressure of the confined air increased or sank.

Still he made some marks, and then returned to the others to join them in listening.

But this proved weary work, for it was only now and then that they could hear the sound of the hammer, for the current of air seemed to bear it away; while, when by chance the sounds did reach their ears they were most tantalising, at one time seeming very near, and at others so faint that they felt that the work going on must be very distant.

The dog came back with food and lights and stayed with them, now trotting to the opening to bark at the sounds; and at times standing at the edge of the lower cavity to bark fiercely at those from below, his ears and the thick wolf frill about his neck being blown about by the fierce current of air.

And so the time went on, first one and then the other descending to find that the water was steadily rising, and after each examination there was a thrill of dread as the looker-on asked himself, Would they win the race?

How long was it? Was it night, now, or day?

Questions, these, which they could not answer, and at last, with their miserable state of despondency increasing, they lay half-stupefied, listening for the help which, as the hours wore slowly by, seemed as if it would never come.

The end was unexpected when it did arrive, after what, in its long-drawn agony, seemed like a week. Gwyn had sent a message by the dog imploring for news, for he said the water was very close to them now, as it was lapping the top of the cavity, and every now and then brimming over and slowly filling the bottom of the sloping cavern.

All at once, heard plainly above the rush of the air and apparently close at hand, there was the loud striking of hammers upon stone.

Gwyn thrust his head into the opening at once, and shouted, his heart bounding as a hollow-sounding cheer came back from just the other side of the wedge.

"Who is it?" cried Gwyn, with the despondency which had chilled him taking flight.

"Vores," came back. Then—"Look here, sir! I can't break through this stone. I've no room to move and strike a blow. How far can you get away from it?"

"About sixty feet," said Gwyn, after a few moments' thought.

"Any place where you can shelter from flying stones?"

"Oh, yes, several."

"Then I'm going back for a cartridge, and I shall put it under the stone, light a slow fuse and get away. It must be blasted."

"But you'll blow the roof down and stop the way."

"No fear of that, sir. If I do, it will only be in pieces that we can get rid of this end, you that. It must be done, there's no other chance."

"Is there plenty of room out your way?"

"Sometimes. Here and there it's a close fit to get through. I've been nearly fast more than once. Now, then, I'm going."

"Must you go?" said Gwyn, mournfully.

"Yes, but I'll soon be back. Keep a good heart, and we'll have you out now."

"Is my father there?"

"Yes, sir, and the Major, and your mother, too."

Gwyn's emotion choked his utterance for a time. Then he spoke, but no answer came, and the feeling of loneliness and despair that came over him was horrible.

He backed out and repeated the conversation, Joe giving a faint cheer, and Hardock shaking his head.

"He may bury us alive," he said, "but the smoke and damp can't hurt us, for this wind will sweep it all out at once. How long will he be?"

It seemed quite an hour before Gwyn, who had crept right up the hole till he could touch the stone, heard any sound, and then it came all at once, when he was beginning to lose all hope again.

The sound was the tap of a hammer upon stone, so near that he felt the jar.

"Mr Gwyn, sir," came from close by.

"Yes, here."

"I've got the cartridge, and I'm going to wedge it under the stone, but it's going to be a hard job to light the match in this strong wind. Now, you go back, and when you're all safe I'll do my work and get safe, too, for it will be like a great cannon going off at both ends at once. How long will it take you?"

"Two minutes," said Gwyn.

"I'll count two hundred, and then begin."

Gwyn shuffled back, gave his news, and the trio of prisoners crept behind angles of the cavern, Gwyn taking the light; and then they waited what seemed to be an hour, with the conclusion growing that Vores had been unable to light the fuse, and had gone back.

"Sam!" shouted Gwyn at last.

"Ay, ay, sir."

"You both stay where you are; I'm going to crawl up to the mouth of the hole, and speak to Vores."

"Nay, stay where you are," cried Hardock. "It may be an hour before the charge is fired. We don't know what trouble he has to get it to—"

A deafening roar broke Hardock's speech in two; and to Gwyn it seemed as if he had received a violent blow on both ears at once. Then in a dull, distant way he heard pieces of stone rattling, and there was perfect silence; the wind had ceased to roar and whistle, and Gwyn began to struggle, for he felt as if a hand had suddenly clutched his throat, and he knew he was suffocating.

The next moment there was a rush and roar again; the air that had been compressed and driven back rebounded, as it were, rushing through the open cavity, and Gwyn felt that he could breathe again.

"Where are you?" cried Hardock; and now Gwyn realised that the explosion had put out the light.

"Here. Where's Joe Jollivet?"

"I'm here," panted the lad. "I couldn't breathe for a bit. Think the block's blown away?"

"I'm going to feel," replied Gwyn. "Here!" he cried, excitedly, "the floor's covered with pieces of broken stone; but I can't find my way. Yes, all right; I can feel the way in."

"Mind you don't get wedged in with the bits, my lad," cried Hardock, excitedly. "Here, let me go first."

"No," said Gwyn, "I—"

His next words were not heard, for his head and shoulders were in the cavity and his voice was swept on before him ere he could say, as he intended, "I shall soon be back."

But there was no risk of getting himself wedged, for the explosion had swept everything before it; and he crept on and on, till his heart gave a bound, for he realised that he must have passed the spot where the stone had wedged up the orifice, and the way to life and light was open.

"Ahoy!" he shouted with all his might; and "Ahoy!" came from a distance, for the wind, which was whistling by him, drove the answer back. But in another minute, as he extended his hand to feel his way along, he touched something warm in the darkness, and his hand was seized.

That warm grasp, which meant so much to the lad, acted upon him like the discharging rod of the electrician upon a Leyden jar; in an instant his energy seemed to have left him, and he lay prone in the narrow way, only half-conscious of being very slowly dragged over rough stone for some time before the dizzy, helpless sensation passed off, and he struggled slightly.

"Let go!" he cried. "I must go back and tell them."

"No, my lad, I'll do that," said a familiar voice. "There's room to pass here. Think you can go on crawling up now?"

"Yes—yes, I'm all right. Did I faint?"

"I suppose so, sir. Wait a moment." There was a moment's pause, and then Gwyn heard the words bellowed out, "All clear! Got to them! Coming now."

There was a murmur at a distance, and then Vores spoke again,—

"I'm coming by you now. Are the others strong enough to crawl?"

"Yes," said Gwyn, faintly, for his heart was beating strangely now just when he felt that he ought to be at his strongest and best.

"You, there, Ydoll?" came loudly.

"Yes; all right," cried Gwyn. "Where's Sam Hardock?"

"Crawling up after me," came more loudly.

"Then I must go back," said Vores. "P'raps I'd better lead, Mr Gwyn."

"Yes, yes, go on, and we'll follow," said Gwyn, more faintly; and he felt the man pass him again, there being just room.

"Must go very slowly," said Vores, "because there's no room to turn for another fifty yards or so. Going backward takes time. Now, then, come on, all on you."

Once more Gwyn's dizzy feeling came back, but he struggled on, conscious that his rescuer's face was close to his—so close that at times their hands touched. Then, after what seemed to be a long nightmare journey, the man's words sounded clearer on his ears.

"It's wider here. Goes zigzagging along with one or two close nips, and then we're out to the crack in the cliff."

Gwyn did not reply. He felt that if he spoke his words would be wild and incoherent, and that all his strength was required to crawl along this terrible crevice in the rock. He was conscious of a hand touching his foot from time to time, and of hearing voices, and of passing over loose, small pieces of shattered rock which might have resulted from the explosion.

At last, after what seemed to be a terrible distance, a voice said, "Out of the way, dog," and directly after a cold wet nose touched his brow, and there was a snuffing sound at his ear, followed by a joyous barking. Then gradually all grew more dense and dark in his brain, and the next thing he remembered was being touched by hands, and feeling the contraction of a rope about his chest followed by a burst of cheering which seemed to take place far away down in the mine; for the roaring and whistling of the wind had ceased, so that he could hear distinctly that hurrahing; and then he heard nothing, for, strong in spirit while the danger lasted, that energy was all used now, and of what took place Gwyn Pendarve knew no more.

Chapter Fifty One
In the Light

"Yes, what is it? Who's there?"

"Oh, Gwyn, my boy, my boy!" came piteously; and two soft arms raised him from his pillow to hold him to a throbbing breast, while passionate lips pressed warm kisses on his face.

"Mother! You! What's the matter? Ah, I remember. You there, father? Where's Joe? Where's poor old Sam Hardock?"

"Joe Jollivet's in the next room, sleeping soundly; Sam Hardock's at Harry Vores' cottage getting right fast."

"And Tom Dinass? Where is he?" cried Gwyn.

"Dinass? Great heavens! Is he somewhere in the mine?"

"No," said Gwyn, frowning. "I only want to know where he is."

"Never mind about him," said the Colonel.

Gwyn nodded his head and became very thoughtful.

"There, you had better lie in bed to-day, and the effects of your terrible experience will pass off. We have suffered agonies since the alarm was given."

"Did the lads all escape?"

"Every man," said the Colonel; "but some of the last up were nearly drowned, for the water had risen to their necks at the foot of the shaft when they reached the man-engine."

"Grip came and told you where we were?" said Gwyn, after a pause.

"Yes, and led us to the opening up which he had come."

"Where was it, father?"

"In the face of the cliff—a mile away."

"What, overlooking the sea?"